A Painted Ship

A Thomas Ford Mystery

Other novels by John Rhodes

Nutcracker (2004)
Hank's Idea (2005)
Desert Wind (2006)
Who Killed Callaway? (2007)

A Painted Ship

A Thomas Ford Mystery

BY

JOHN RHODES

iUniverse, Inc.
New York   Bloomington

iUniverse books may be ordered through booksellers or by contacting:

iUniverse
1663 Liberty Drive
Bloomington, IN 47403
www.iuniverse.com
1-800-Authors (1-800-288-4677)

ISBN: 978-1-4401-4717-3 (sc)
ISBN: 978-1-4401-4718-0 (hc)
ISBN: 978-1-4401-4719-7 (ebook)

Printed in the United States of America

iUniverse rev. date: 07/09/2009

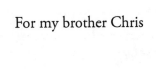

For my brother Chris

Day after day, day after day,
We stuck, nor breath nor motion;
As idle as a painted ship
Upon a painted ocean.

From the *Rime of the Ancient Mariner,* by Samuel Taylor Coleridge

One

Detective Chief Inspector Thomas Ford stared into his wife's eyes, trying to reassure himself that she really was there, that they really were married, and they really were on their honeymoon. It all seemed so implausible—while she was beautiful, vivacious, brilliant, a shining star lighting up an otherwise drab firmament, he was merely pedestrian, plodding, mundane, mediocre, a dim planet visible only indirectly in her reflected radiance.

To make the whole matter even more unlikely, she had married him in the teeth of her family's fervent opposition, including several false heart attacks simulated by her mother; she had chosen him in preference to a duke; and she had stepped down from the upper crust of patrician society to take his plebeian hand.

They were sitting outside the Duke of Cornwall, an inn beside the harbor of the Cornish fishing village of Trethgarret Haven, in the far west of England, where the English Channel meets the Atlantic Ocean. The sun shone almost as brightly as she did. Fishing boats stirred at their creaking moorings alongside the wharf. The sea sparkled and murmured, and the breeze was pungent with the tang of salt water and fresh fish. Seagulls cackled and wheeled overhead. Somewhere out in the shallows a bell buoy clanged dolorously.

Fishermen bent over their tackle as they worked on their salt-streaked boats. A creaking derrick cranked a vast dripping net from the hold of the nearest boat and over the dock. From the net a silver cataract of flashing, flapping fish poured forth, the harvest of last night's labors in the English Channel. A diminutive steam railway locomotive snorted fussily as it waited to haul away the morning's catch.

But all of this made no greater impression on Ford than a damp and dreary day beneath leaden skies in Manchester, for the brilliant scene faded into insignificance in comparison to the vision of his wife—yes, his *wife!*—sitting across from him at the rickety cast-iron table, with the breeze playing with her boyish bob cut and the sun bringing a fresh pink color to her cheeks, and bread and cheese and cider set before her.

A local worthy they had nicknamed the "Ancient Mariner" sat dozing in the sun beyond her. Ford imagined himself many years in the future, hoary with age, also dozing in the sun, dreaming of this perfect honeymoon. He examined his new wife's features intently so that her face, at this idyllic moment, would be imprinted indelibly on his memory forever.

"You're staring again, Thomas," she said. Her smiles always seemed to originate deep within her brown eyes before spreading in enchanting stages through a delightful crinkling of her nose to the merest quiver in the corners of her mouth—the left corner slightly before the right—before bursting forth upon her lips. If her smile grew into a full-fledged grin—as on this occasion—she would lean slightly forward as if inviting the viewer to join in the fun.

"Darling Victoria," he told her earnestly, taking her hand and entwining his fingers with hers, "I can't quite convince myself all this isn't an extravagantly glorious dream."

"Oh, this is very real, I promise you," she said, squeezing his hand. "Just to prove it, after lunch we'll …"

Ford had to wait to find out what she planned, however, for at that moment there were cries of alarm from the jetty, and people were running to see what was causing the commotion. Ford and Victoria would have remained wrapped in their private cocoon, but the shouting intruded.

"Fetch the doctor!" and "Good God, it's Lord Pengriffon!" and, finally, "Someone fetch the police!"

Ford found himself rising to his feet in automatic response, and he and Victoria crossed the street and joined the crowd. The body of a man with a ruined mottled blue-green-white face and hideously empty eye sockets lay half-hidden in the silver mound of fish and seaweed and crabs and random flotsam. Victoria shuddered, and Ford, feeling immensely husbandly, turned her away and shielded her eyes from the scene with his manly shoulder.

"The crabs got him," one of the fishermen said phlegmatically.

"Can't have been down there more than a day at most," said another, making an expert judgment of the crabs' progress.

"'E were in the Duke last night as usual, saw him meself," offered a third.

The fishermen were all immensely tough, Ford thought, looking around the group, as tough as the battered yet infinitely resilient fishing boats they took into the stormy English Channel.

Their features were pickled to mahogany by salt winds and lashing rain squalls and the burning sun, and their eyes were surrounded by webs of tiny lines etched by constantly staring toward endless maritime horizons. They stood foursquare, with their feet apart as if braced against the heaving of a deck in rough weather. Their hands were powerful and calloused from constant drudgery and hung half-clenched by their sides as if ready to seize a rope. They exuded a sort of stoic tranquility born from living in harmony with the sea, a force infinitely more powerful than themselves, and yet a force that permitted them—on its terms—to work upon its waters.

Now the sea had claimed a life, and they stood in silent contemplation. It occurred to Ford that perhaps they were remembering other ruined faces, faces of crewmates and friends, fathers and sons and brothers, whom the waters had also taken in tribute.

"Now then, now then, what's all this commotion?" sounded a voice of officialdom, and a burly policeman pushed his way through the crowd. "Strewth, is that his lordship?"

The crowd filled in the details.

"He was at the inn last night, Alfie, four sheets to the wind."

"Drunk?"

"Not 'alf—couldn't 'ardly walk. Must've come over 'ere for a Jimmie Riddle and fallen in, poor old bastard."

"Naw, he never fell in here—we picked him up in the trawl net. We was out by the Little Dogs last night; it's ten fathoms deep there if it's an inch."

"'Ow did he get out there? That's five miles or more."

"The tide's not right if he fell in here."

"No wind to speak of—flat as a pancake."

"Not washed overboard, then, not in a calm."

"In the trawl net, you said? What was he doing on the seabed, sixty feet down?"

"How'm I supposed to know?"

"What's that round his leg?"

"Blow me down, that's a rope!"

"And, see here, a bloody great lump of concrete tied to it!"

"Well, then, 'e must have gone out in 'is launch and done 'imself in."

"Never—that's 'is launch, over there, moored where she always be. 'Sides, Lord Pengriffon weren't the type for no suicide; not a care in the world, not his lordship."

"'Specially if he'd been knocking back a pint of scrumpy or two."

"An' gettin' a regular bit o' you-know-what from you-know-who."

"Well, someone tied that rope round his bleedin' leg."

"Cor blimey, then 'e must have been murdered, mustn't 'e, poor old bugger!"

"Murdered?" the policeman demanded. "What do you mean, *murdered*?"

"Haven't you been paying attention, Alfie?" one of the fishermen asked him, and the crowd chuckled. Clearly the policeman did not have a reputation for being quick on the uptake.

"Well now," the constable said, removing his helmet to scratch his head as if this act would bring his thoughts to order. "Murdered? Done in? Well, I never! What am I supposed to do about murder? I'd best telephone to Penzance and tell the inspector."

"You want us to get 'im out of here, Alfie?" one of the fishermen asked.

"Well, yes, I suppose. He's a bit of a fright, not meaning offense to the dead, of course, and women and youngsters'll see him. You blokes better hose him off, and we'll move him up to the church and make him decent, like." More scratching suggested another thought. "And someone better tell Lady Pengriffon, I suppose. Well, I never! There's not been a murder in these parts for nigh on twenty years, not since the old queen died."

He looked forlornly round the faces in the crowd, clearly hoping for help or guidance, and Ford spoke reluctantly.

"Excuse me, Constable, but I suggest you examine everything in detail before he's touched. There may be evidence."

"What sort of evidence?" the constable asked, continuing to grapple with a situation far beyond his experience.

"I have no idea, but you'd best go through everything in the net and photograph it as you go."

"Are you from Scotland Yard, sir?" another of the fishermen asked with a smile, and the crowd chuckled at the joke.

"Well, yes, I am, actually," Ford admitted humbly and unwillingly. Lord Pengriffon, it seemed, was about to disrupt his honeymoon. "If there's anything I can do to assist you, Constable, until your inspector takes over."

"And I'll tell Lady Pengriffon, if you like, Constable," Victoria said, avoiding another look at the corpse. "Her sister and I were at school together, and we've kept in touch."

"You would, madam? You would, sir?" The policeman's brow cleared—help had appeared as if by magic. "I'd be very grateful."

"I'd better speak to your inspector first," Ford said. "I don't want to invade his turf without him asking me."

"Of course, sir. Got it! Immediately! The police station's next to the post office at the bottom of the High Street; just across the street and round the corner."

"Perhaps some of you chaps would take turns to see that no one touches anything," Ford said to the fishermen. "And perhaps someone would fetch a doctor—that would be very helpful, although he shouldn't disturb the body until it's been photographed. Is there anyone in the village who can take decent photographs? And we need to know if anyone saw the deceased after he left the pub last night. Could some of you ask about?"

He turned to the policeman. "I suggest we telephone Penzance right away, Constable. I assume these fish will smell no better after two or three hours in the sun. Can we put a tarpaulin over everything until we can search it?"

"Inspector, telephone," the constable said, as if committing Ford's instructions to memory, "guard his lordship's remains, doctor, photographs, inquiries, tarpaulin; got it, sir."

Ford looked about him. The sun still shone, the seagulls still cried and wheeled above, the oblivious Ancient Mariner still slept on, the sea still sparkled—but he feared the magical spell of their honeymoon had been broken. He had far, far more important things to think about and do than to shuffle about on the outskirts of a murder investigation. He looked forlornly at Victoria, and she pulled his head down to whisper in his ear.

"I love you, Thomas, darling, and I always will," she murmured, reading his thoughts. "We'll have lots of time to catch up."

* * *

Clarence Danglars Pengriffon, third Earl of Pengriffon and twelfth Baron Pengriffon of Trethgarret, presented a hideous sight as Ford reluctantly bent over him, inwardly cursing not only the Penzance police inspector for accepting his offer to help and himself for having made it, but also the stench of putrefying fish that enveloped the dock.

The inspector had been delighted to hear that a Scotland Yard detective was on the scene. In fact, it would be an obvious step to request the chief constable of Cornwall to enlist Ford's help officially. That, his tone of voice over the telephone implied, would relieve the inspector of both the responsibility of taking over the case and the inconvenience of driving all the way from Penzance to the crime scene, particularly on a beautiful afternoon.

In the meantime, Victoria had been escorted to a taxi that Ford thought might possibly be the oldest self-propelled motor vehicle in the United Kingdom, if not in Europe, and she had departed on her mission to inform her friend Lady Pengriffon of the disaster. As the taxi had turned into the High Street and disappeared from Ford's view, it had been overtaken by an elderly man on a bicycle.

Ford sighed and returned his attention to the corpse. The crabs had robbed his lordship's face of much of its surface tissue, although enough remained to indicate that his lordship had sported long muttonchop sideburns and a prodigious moustache. Unless the body revealed some obvious wound, like a bullet hole or a stab wound, it would not be possible to tell if Pengriffon had been killed first and then tossed overboard or simply heaved over the side while in a drunken stupor and drowned. That, of course, assumed that the fishermen were right, and that he had, in fact, been murdered.

Three of the fishermen—Jimmie, Eddie, and Bertie, Ford learned—assisted Constable Alfred Crocker, the village policeman, and Ford to sift through the evil-smelling mound of rotting fish in which his lordship lay. The dead fish were tossed into the harbor, to the delight of the seagulls, while Jimmie, whose trawler had dredged Pengriffon from the depths, bemoaned the loss of his catch. Everything else the net had trapped was set to one side for inspection, although Ford doubted the growing pile of sodden rubbish would yield anything of interest.

As they worked, the men told Ford that Lord Pengriffon had been a mild man without an enemy in the world, cheerful, generous and without stuck-up airs or graces. He was well-liked in the village—a most unlikely murder victim, in their opinion. His passions in life were alcohol and painting, and he often combined the two.

"He did seascape paintings—boats in the harbor, and that sort of thing," Eddie said.

"'E 'ad a nice touch with 'is brush, if you ask me," Bertie added. "The sort of thing done with dabs of paint that look like something if you stand back and squint a bit."

"'Pressionism, he called it," Eddie said authoritatively. "They showed some of his paintings in Penzance Museum and even as far away as Lunnon itself."

"And nudes, begging you pardon, Mr. Ford," Bertie said. "He had a fine eye for the female form, if you follow? I saw a couple of naked pictures of …"

"Never mind all that, Bertie, you old wurzel," Eddie said primly. "It's different for an artist, same as a doctor."

"Whatever you say, Eddie," Bertie grinned, and he winked at Ford.

When the body was fully revealed, Ford knelt in the slime and examined it. The crabs had feasted on the exposed flesh, and Ford pulled the tarpaulin over his lordship's ruined head to protect the eyes of passersby. The crabs had also been busy with his fingers, and the knuckles and nails—invaluable indicators of a struggle—were missing. The pockets of his sodden tweed suit revealed an almost empty bottle of whiskey, a jumble of painting supplies—sopping tubes of artist's oil paint, turpentine, brushes, rags, charcoal—five shillings in loose change, and a black leather wallet that Ford set aside to examine later. There were no tears or rents in his clothing to suggest a violent struggle.

A gangling youth engaged in a losing battle against pimples appeared, carrying a variety of battered photographic equipment. Evidently this was the village's photographic expert, and Ford's heart sank.

"Young Frank's a very dab hand with a Brownie camera, sir," Crocker said enthusiastically. "He earns his pocket money taking snaps of holidaymakers in the summer. Develops them himself, he does, with chemicals and such; they come out a treat."

"I see," Ford said, not reassured.

"I'll use a Number 2A Folding Pocket Kodak Brownie, sir," Frank said in a cracking contralto. "I'll use different f-stop exposures to make sure I get it right."

"I'm sure you will," Ford said—at least the lad was trying. "I'd better warn you; he's not a pretty sight."

He drew back the tarpaulin, and the youth quailed, stepped abruptly to the edge of the jetty and lost his luncheon.

"I'll be all right, sir," he croaked eventually. "Sorry about that."

"Take your time," Ford said, as his stomach heaved in sympathy.

The youth squared his shoulders manfully and set to his task.

When young Frank had taken a dozen exposures, with agonizing care and much biting of his lower lip, Ford and Crocker rolled Pengriffon's body over. The ends of his tie—Ford recognized the black and purple stripes of Balliol College, Oxford—stretched down from the back of his neck. On closer examination Ford could see that the tie had been used as a tourniquet and pulled around his neck so tightly that it had not been visible from the front, lost in the folds of seaweed-covered flesh.

"Oh my *Gawd*," Crocker gasped, and hurried to the side of the dock to duplicate young Frank's earlier reactions.

Ford knew it was not possible for Pengriffon to throttle himself in this manner. This was unquestionably a case of murder. He sighed;

the chances of an early return to matrimonial bliss retreated a little
further.

* * *

Ford sat in the diminutive village police station. It had only one
room and shared a common entrance hall with the local post office.
When one entered the main door from the High Street, one could turn
left to buy stamps or postcards, or turn right if one had business with
Constable Crocker.

It transpired that Mrs. Crocker was the postmistress, and the two
branches of His Majesty's Government seemed to have been commingled
into a single public service. Thus, Constable Crocker interrupted his
written report of the discovery of the body to sell stamps to a small boy,
and Mrs. Crocker took down details about a missing dog while he was
thus engaged.

The post office also sold newspapers, picture postcards, cigarettes,
chocolate, and ice cream. It was something of a local gathering place,
as post offices tend to be, and several housewives were engaged in loud
speculation about his lordship's death.

Behind the police counter, next to the cold chest where the ice
cream was kept, and in front of the sturdy door that led to a store
room which served as a temporary holding cell for those denizens of
Trethgarret who transgressed sufficiently to be locked up, stood a small
and rickety card table, and here Ford sat to begin his investigation of
Lord Pengriffon's murder.

He lit a cigarette, willed himself to ignore the housewives' chatter,
and tried to think. He would need to find out the exact location of
the Little Dogs, whatever they were, and obtain expert advice on the
tides and currents. He'd need to make sure there was no possibility
whatsoever that his lordship had sailed out to sea of his own accord and
jumped overboard. He'd need to discover what vessel had carried him
on his final journey. He'd need …

Ford borrowed a sheet of writing paper and began to scribble notes
to himself. If Pengriffon had died from strangulation—as appeared
to be the case—where had he been strangled? Some combination of
the warm weather and irritation was causing Ford's palms to sweat,

and each stroke of his fountain pen was creating its own little marshy puddle. Would there be water in his lungs if he was already dead when he entered the sea? Strangulation and drowning were both forms of suffocation. Could a doctor confirm the actual cause of death beyond reasonable doubt?

And, of course, all of that paled beside the central questions of who had killed him, and why. If …

A large man with a florid complexion entered the post office/police station, and introduced himself to Ford.

"My name's George Thompson," he said, in a manner that implied that Ford should have damned-well known who he was. He drew himself up in self-importance. A silver fob watch chain was stretched tautly across his ample belly, and a line of small silver medallions, hanging from the chain, quivered at the motion. "I'm the mayor of Trethgarret. Of course, Londoners might think it's only a small town, but there's work to be done and someone needs to do it."

"I'm sure there's a lot to be done, Mr. Thompson," Ford said, rising to his feet, his train of thought lost. Did one address a mayor as "your honor" or "your worship"? He couldn't remember. "My name is Thomas Ford. I'm assisting Constable Crocker, at least for the time being, Your, er, you'll need to know."

"Take the sewers, for example," Thompson said, as if he needed to justify his official position. "People take them for granted, never think about them. Then one day there's a heavy rain and the sewers overflow, and then there's hell to pay."

"Dear me," Ford said, shaking his head sympathetically, and Thompson warmed to his theme.

"If it's not the sewers it's the drains, or the potholes, or the railway crossing gates up at the top of the High Street by the railway station. It'll be different, you mark my words, when that Tory idiot Stanley Baldwin gets voted out of office. There'll be a Labor government that puts the needs of the working man ahead of the selfish interests of the …"

"Never mind all that silly nonsense, George Thompson," one of the housewives cut in. She pronounced his name Gee-arge in the slow, soft, gentle local accent. "What we want to know is who did that horrible thing to poor Lord Pengriffon."

Her friends agreed enthusiastically.

"Have you got any clues, Mr. Ford?" the housewife asked. "What have you discovered so far?"

"Well, madam, I haven't really had a chance to …" Ford said.

"How can you solve a murder without any clues?" she demanded. Evidently the lack of clues was entirely Ford's fault.

"It'll look bad for the village," Thompson said, nodding crossly in agreement. "An unsolved murder will hurt the summer holiday trade."

"That's true," said a second woman. "People won't want to come if there's a killer on the loose. Perhaps it was the German sailors."

"There are no German sailors, Mabel," the first woman retorted, answering Ford's half-formed question. "That's just a bunch of baloney, and well you know it."

"Well, then, Clara, perhaps someone's gone crazy, like Jack the Ripper."

"Don't be daft, Mabel," Clara snapped. "Jack the Ripper killed young girls of ill repute, not middle-aged men like Lord Pengriffon."

"It's not daft, Clara," Mabel insisted hotly. "It was nighttime, don't forget; perhaps, in the dark, the murderer thought his lordship was a girl. What do you think, Mr. Ford?"

"Well," Ford began, grasping at the notion of a crazed killer mistaking the rotund and heavily bewhiskered Lord Pengriffon for a young prostitute—perhaps the murderer was extremely shortsighted—and searched for a polite reply. He was saved by Victoria, who entered the room, saw Ford surrounded by housewives, guessed his predicament, and grinned.

"Ah, there you are, darling," she said. "I'm just back from Pengriffon Hall. Such a wonderful old rambling place; I must give you all the details. The taxi driver is such a nice man; he took me by the scenic route along the cliffs." She turned to the gathering. "I'm Mrs. Ford, by the way; I'm delighted to make your acquaintances. We're so enjoying our stay here."

"How did Lady Justicia take the news, poor woman?" Mabel asked.

"Does she know who did it?" Clara added.

"I'm afraid I'll have to speak to my husband first," Victoria said.

"I'm fear it's a police matter. Naturally, she was most upset, but I can't say more—I do hope you're not offended?"

It was clear that Victoria would provide no details, so the ladies passed on to more important matters.

"They say you're on your honeymoon? All alone by yourselves, up at Cliff Cottage?" Mabel asked, invoking a general fit of giggles, and Ford felt himself blushing hotly.

"Indeed we are," Victoria smiled innocently, unperturbed. "We were married on Saturday. I must confess that I'm still getting used to calling myself Mrs. Ford, instead of Miss Canderblank, but I like my new name immensely."

The ladies eyed Ford speculatively, and Ford felt his cheeks blossom from rosy pink to bright scarlet.

"I have to claim him from you, ladies," Victoria continued, taking Ford's arm. "Come, Thomas, let's walk down to the harbor."

She swept him from the room and into the High Street, and Ford shuddered with relief.

"God, V, is there no privacy? I feel like a public spectacle. I can't work in the middle of a shop, for God's sake! I'll have to telephone my boss, and every word will be overheard. How am I supposed to …"

"Now, darling, calm down. We'll find you somewhere private to work, far from the madding crowd. I shall be your gatekeeper and bodyguard, turning away the prurient and prying, and in return you will suppress your petty petulance."

"But …"

"As for those ladies, who can blame them, when they are confronted by the most handsome man in Britain, if not the entire British Empire?"

"Do you really think so?" Ford asked, his thoughts diverted.

"There can be no question of it, my darling, and we'll discuss it later, and at length. In the meantime, let's see if there's a spare room at the inn where you can work undisturbed—our cottage is too far away. Perhaps the inn even has its own telephone."

* * *

In a remarkably short period of time, Victoria had talked Charlie, the proprietor and licensee of the Duke of Cornwall, (*Established 1493*, according to a plaque above the main door to the inn) into reserving his best and largest room, installing in it a large table and chairs, and making the telephone in his office available for Ford's use. Such were her powers of persuasion that the innkeeper—whom she discovered was also the mayor's cousin—had completed the arrangements by bringing them a large pot of tea and a plate of freshly baked biscuits, carrying them up the steep and creaking flight of stairs with his own hands, and offering to be of service, any hour of the day or night. She only had to ask.

Ford stood staring out of the open mullioned window, which overlooked the harbor and the wet patch on the dock where Lord Pengriffon had lain. The tarpaulin now covered the heap of nonpiscine debris that the net had yielded, and Harry stood guard over it. Directly below the window Ford could see the head and shoulders of the Ancient Mariner, still slumbering peacefully in the sunshine.

"Now, V, darling, tell me about Lady Pengriffon, if you would," he said, as Victoria poured tea.

"Yes, of course, darling," she said. "Justicia Pengriffon—Justie, as everyone calls her—was completely shocked, of course. It was quite horrid, having to break the news, as I'm sure you know better than I do. I told the butler to send for the doctor to see if she needs something to calm her down." She paused warily before continuing. "To make matters worse, I'm very sorry to have to report that my mother is staying with her as a houseguest, and she, in her inimitable way, turned a tragedy into a national disaster."

"Oh, *God!*" Ford burst out in horror. "Your mother's *here?*"

"I fear so; moreover, she believes that his lordship's death is evidence of an incipient communist uprising."

Lady Deborah Canderblank, Victoria's mother, filled Ford with fear and loathing. He detested everything about her: her haughty manner, her lashing tongue, her delight in making his life as miserable as possible. She had fought her daughter's desire to marry him with merciless determination. She had attempted, through her contacts in the government, to ruin his career. She had even retained the services of a private detective in a futile attempt to find something she could use to discredit his character.

She had made Victoria—in a confrontation of titanic proportions—

decide between him and her; and when Victoria had unhesitatingly chosen him, her bitterness toward him had deepened into hatred.

And why had she done so? In part, he knew, it was because she considered him to be socially inferior and unworthy of her daughter's patrician hand—a position he admitted to himself that he could understand. But, in large part, Ford believed it was because, in the course of a previous murder investigation, he had uncovered the hidden details of Lady Canderblank's sordid past, and for that she would never forgive him, even though he had scrupulously reburied her secrets and left her reputation untarnished.

"Well, I'll have to see Lady Pengriffon, which means I'll have to see *her*, I suppose," Ford said. "I'd better get it over with. I'll go today, now, so that it won't be hanging over me."

"Poor darling, this is all my fault," Victoria said. "I'll come with you and try to head her off."

"It's not your fault, V; you can't help your mother's attitude toward me."

"Perhaps not, but I can at least attempt to mitigate it."

Ford found himself filled with self-pity.

"We're on our *honeymoon*, for God's sake! I was so happy, and now she'll ruin everything!"

"Only if you let her, darling, and I won't let you let her."

She crossed the room and hugged him.

"Now, repeat after me, Thomas: 'She has no significance in my life'."

"I ..."

"Repeat it!"

He found himself grinning.

"Also, Thomas, repeat: 'She is a mere ant upon a picnic sandwich, disposed of with a flip of the fingers'—or, better yet, a mere horsefly upon a horse's rear quarters, banished by a flick of a tail."

He laughed.

"Very well, V. Whenever I see her I'll think of a horse's hind quarters. I confess that should be quite easy. Now, let me telephone to my boss, and then we'll go and slay the dragon."

They descended to the main floor, where Ford entered the innkeeper's office to face the technical challenge of making a phone call all the way across England to London, and Victoria set off to find transportation.

Detective Superintendent Brownlee of Scotland Yard, Ford's boss, had always believed that the performance of a telephone could be enhanced by shouting into it, and the longer the distance involved, the louder it was prudent to shout.

"*Can you here me, Ford?*" Brownlee's voice bawled, as Ford held the telephone several inches from his ear. "It's two hundred miles from London to Cornwall."

"I can hear you perfectly, sir," Ford replied in normal tones, grinning.

"I received a call for help from a chap named Boxer, the chief constable of Cornwall. I've already sent Sergeant Croft down to help you. He should be there in the morning. Mrs. Croft is with him; they'll stay on for a holiday when the case is over."

Croft was Ford's assistant and right-hand man.

"Thank you, sir. That'll be very useful."

"Anything else you need? Bit of a nuisance on your honeymoon, old chap, of course. I had a similar situation on my own honeymoon, as a matter of fact. Chap got crushed by a falling beer barrel and foul play was suspected, and I got pulled in—not as a suspect, I should clarify."

Brownlee's voice paused, and the telephone emitted a slurping sound. Ford fondly pictured his bearlike boss hunched over the shambles of his overflowing desktop in Scotland Yard, the telephone earpiece gripped in one vast fist and a teacup in the other, with a tobacco pipe burning itself out in an ashtray for want of a third hand to hold it.

"Anyway," Brownlee's voice resumed, "it turned out that the victim had witnessed a crime, and the murderer killed him to keep him quiet. Mrs. Brownlee was most annoyed—not at the solution, I should explain, but at the interruption to our honeymoon. It all ended well enough, however, because the local inspector decided that the barrel had to be kept as evidence but not the contents."

Ford grinned again.

"Look, is there anything else I can do, old chap?" Brownlee asked, and proceeded to answer his own question, as he often did. "I'll see what I can dredge up on Pengriffon in London—no pun intended,

I hasten to add. Telephone me tomorrow to let me know how you're getting on, will you, Ford?"

"Of course, sir," Ford said, and a sharp clicking noise, followed by silence, restored the distance between Cornwall and London to its natural dimensions.

He glanced at the elderly clock ticking on the wall. Less than three hours had passed since Pengriffon had been discovered, but his interrupted honeymoon seemed three years ago. Besides, there were the contents of the net still waiting to be inspected, the doctor's report to be obtained, the body to be examined without clothing; and he still hadn't even opened Lord Pengriffon's wallet, which he could feel damply in his jacket pocket beside his own.

He'd better take a quick look through Pengriffon's papers while he was up at the manor, and remove anything that looked interesting—after all, Lady Pengriffon was an automatic suspect. But the servants and his lordship's other effects could probably wait until tomorrow, when Croft, who was a master of painstaking routine, would be here to help. He wondered if the pimply stripling had managed to take usable photographs. He wondered if Pengriffon had left a will, and, if so, whether there were any beneficiaries to profit from his lordship's untimely death.

Who would inherit the title? Thank God Victoria would be there to deflect his mother-in-law! In the car going up he'd ask Victoria if Lady Pengriffon—*Justie*, had V called her?—was capable of murder. Victoria was an excellent judge of character, except possibly his own, and he prayed God that time would prove her right.

If …

Victoria reappeared, with the mayor in tow, and announced that his worship—ah, so it was "his *worship*"—had generously donated the use of his own fine vehicle, and for the duration of the investigation, no less, because of the pressing need to bring matters to a close as soon as possible, for fear of an adverse effect on the tourist trade and consequent damage to the well-being of the working class. And inversely, as she had pointed out to him, a *solved* murder might bring something of an economic boom, reinforcing the usual tourist traffic with free-spending if ghoulish curiosity-seekers.

A stately and remarkably unsocialist Humber touring car stood throbbing before the entrance to the inn, its quivering canvas top neatly folded back to let in the sunshine. The mayor personally opened the door to assist Victoria into it, offering, like the innkeeper, to be of service, any hour of the day or night; she only had to ask.

She rewarded him with a stunning smile, while Ford cautiously selected what he hoped was an appropriate gear—or, at least, a forward one—and slowly released the clutch. Luck was with him, and they set off briskly, and in the right direction, and his worship was sufficiently moved by the entire episode to wave good-bye.

Two

V ictoria gave him a thumbnail sketch of Lady Justicia Pengriffon as they left the village and began to climb the cliff road. Justie, as she was known to her family and friends, was the older sister of one of Victoria's school friends and was now, Victoria estimated, thirty-fiveish. She was a placid, vague woman who had married an older man—Lord Pengriffon must have been well in his fifties—presumably seeking the security of a mature relationship rather than taking on the risks of a younger man.

"Did you meet Lord Pengriffon, V?" Ford asked, as he botched a gear change and some internal mechanism or other squealed in protest.

"I did, at the wedding. He was jolly and avuncular, as I recall, and something of a bottom patter," she said, and then frowned as Ford gripped his thigh. "Is your leg hurting, darling? Shall I drive?"

Ford's right leg had been injured in the trenches during the war, and shards of shrapnel had buried themselves deeply in his thigh, producing a chronic condition of permanent pain that varied from a deep throbbing ache on good days to sharp and agonizing stabs on bad ones. Victoria had insisted on an operation to solve the problem once and for all; it had been remarkably successful, but certain exercises— like trying to push down on a heavy clutch pedal—rekindled the old furies.

"Well, just a tiny bit," Ford confessed. "It's nothing, I assure you."

"It's probably not healed completely inside, Thomas, and I need you in tip-top physical condition. I'd better take over; besides, I happen to be a much better driver than you are."

"But it's a husband's duty to …" Ford began to protest.

"I am discovering far better ways by which I can judge your masculinity, my darling, and in those you are peerless, I assure you— not, of course, that I have any basis for comparison. Now, please stop being foolish or I will begin to nag you like an old and shriveled crone."

They changed places. Victoria was, he readily conceded, an excellent driver, able to coax the best out of any vehicle. Ford sat back to enjoy the ride, watching the wind whipping through her hair and tugging at the hem of her skirt, which she had hitched up above her knees in a most beguiling manner to keep her legs free as she worked the pedals with the expertise of a racing driver. She laughed with infectious gaiety and held out one hand to be kissed.

The singing wind, the panoramic sweep of the cliffs, the thunder of the engine, and the graceful proportions of his wife's long legs, all seduced Ford into believing that his honeymoon had returned, until they roared into the gravel forecourt of Pengriffon Hall, and Ford's daydream was abruptly shattered by the prospect of an imminent encounter with his mother-in-law.

The house was long and rambling, built of the local granite so that it had a weather-beaten but indestructible quality, hunkered down against the wind—an outcropping of stone rather than a house, it seemed—with eclectic additions like massive boulders contributed at random by various earls past.

A vast and shiny Rolls Royce stood imperiously before the main entrance. Ford noticed the Canderblank coat of arms was painted on the passenger doors, confirming, to Ford's horror, that his mother-in-law was in residence.

"Is this a new motorcar of your mother's?" he asked.

"Oh, yes, I think it is. God knows how she affords it; she must be living beyond her means, as usual."

The entry hall into which they were admitted by a groveling footman contained an extensive collection of model railway locomotives—Lord Pengriffon's grandfather, the first earl, had made his fortune by investing in the Great Western Railway in its early days, Victoria had told him—and was hung with a number of Lord Pengriffon's impressionist works.

Indeed, as they followed the footman through a series of somnolent sitting rooms, Ford formed the impression that the house was a gallery for its former owner's work, with seascape following seascape following seascape, punctuated at random intervals by the fading stare of a former earl or baron peering out from the cracked and yellowing pigments of an ancient formal portrait.

Ford was struck by the vibrant quality of Pengriffon's impressionist works. They shone with sunlight and burst with energy, as if their painter had rejoiced in the endless motion and countless moods of the sea and sky, and in his life beside and beneath them. Ford would have stopped to examine them more closely, but he hurried after the disappearing footman for fear of getting lost.

They reached the doors of the final such room. The footman stopped and knocked, and Ford squared his shoulders. He was here to see Lady Pengriffon, he reminded himself; he could not let Lady Canderblank, Victoria's mother, be more than a minor irritant. The footman announced their arrival and stepped aside, and Ford marched in, as best as his aching leg would permit, resolutely staring past his mother-in-law's forbidding countenance to that of a second lady, who sat white-cheeked and red-eyed by the fireplace.

"Lady Pengriffon," he said. "My name is Ford. Permit me to offer my condolences on the tragic …"

He got no further.

"This is *precisely* the kind of insufferable intrusion I have come to expect of you, Forge," Lady Canderblank erupted in a harsh contralto. She quivered with indignation, and she had the trick of staring down at one, even when she was seated and the object of her derision was standing. "Have you no concept of propriety?"

She turned to Lady Pengriffon. "Justie, my poor dear, you must send him away at once. He certainly isn't the sort of person with whom you would wish to have an acquaintance."

"But …" Lady Pengriffon began.

"Lady Pengriffon," Ford began again, trying to ignore his mother-in-law's overwhelming presence, "I am a police officer, and …"

"That proves my point, I think," Lady Canderblank said, and sat back with a satisfied smile.

"I must ask to speak to you in private, ma'am," Ford continued, as bravely as he could. He summoned up an image of a belligerent and overweight mare, viewed from behind the animal, but it offered scant comfort.

Lady Canderblank addressed herself to Lady Pengriffon, and spoke as if Ford was not present. "Fork, or whatever this man's name is, is a policeman of junior rank. It has been my misfortune to encounter him before. If one must speak to a police person, I always find it best to speak to a senior officer."

"But I thought ..." Lady Pengriffon said uncertainly, and her voice trailed away.

Ford felt a wave of despair. The delightful drive along the cliffs had been a mirage, the prospects of a blissful marriage a mere chimera. The brutal reality, he feared, was that his mother-in-law was now a permanent fixture in his future and that she would always materialize from nowhere to overwhelm each pint of happiness with Victoria with a gallon of her own venom. Her bristling disapproval of his very existence, her perpetual and deliberate mispronunciation of his name, her biting sarcasm, her ...

Victoria walked around Ford and advanced into the room.

"Justie, I'm so sorry to burst in again like this, but Chief Inspector Ford is from Scotland Yard, and it really would be best to speak to him." She turned to Lady Canderblank. "Mother, let's not interrupt a police officer on official business, shall we?"

"I ..."

"Now, Mother," Victoria overrode her, and Ford saw, as he had seen before, that she matched her mother's force of personality, even though Victoria's character was the absolute antithesis of her mother's. "Can you think of a single good reason why a Scotland Yard police inspector should not speak to the widow of the victim of a ... of a tragic accident, in the proper course of his investigations?"

Without waiting for a reply, she turned to Lady Justicia. "She's such a silly old dear," she said with a rueful smile, managing to convert Lady Canderblank from an imperious matron into a querulous elderly lady.

"I'm sure she's trying to protect you, Justie, even though she's foolishly mistaken."

She advanced to Lady Canderblank and made to assist her from her chair, as if her mother were infirm. "Come on, Mother dear, and tell me what Daddy's been up to."

Lady Canderblank could demean Ford before others without a qualm, but even she hesitated to get into an open argument with her daughter; she allowed herself, with ill grace, and to Ford's infinite relief, to be escorted from the room.

* * *

Lady Pengriffon looked up at Ford uncertainly as the door closed. "I'm afraid I'm a bit confused," she said. "V told me you were her husband, but Lady Deborah seemed … oh, I don't know, I suppose it's the shock; I still can't believe he's dead. Sorry, I'm not being very coherent."

"That's perfectly all right, madam," Ford told her. "We were married last weekend. However, as you can see, Lady Canderblank is very much opposed."

"Oh dear, poor you. I know Deborah can be a little difficult at times. Do you suppose he died peacefully?"

She spoke so softly that Ford took a step closer. He wondered if this was habitual or whether it was the product of her shock. Her conversation veered from one point to another, as if each thought had never quite crystallized. Perhaps her mind was as cluttered as her home, he speculated, glancing at the battered chintz sofas, the side tables and mantelpiece piled with ormolu clocks, graceful statuettes, and family photographs framed in silver—all excellent pieces, he noted, but plunked down at random as if the task of arranging them to display their elegance was too much for her.

A large impressionist painting of a steam launch in Trethgarret harbor hung above the mantle. Ford was reminded of the fisherman Bertie's comment about the apparently random daubs of paint that formed a vivid picture when one stood back from the canvas. Lord Pengriffon had been an excellent as well as a prolific artist, Ford saw. The little white ship—perhaps the Pengriffon family launch—floated buoyantly upon the sparkling waters of the harbor; above it the soaring seagulls were buffeted by an almost palpable sea breeze.

He stepped closer, and the light bouncing from the wavelets resolved itself into tiny spots of cadmium white oil paint. The jaunty brass funnel of the launch, shining in the sun, so tall and sturdy at a distance, was no more than a few streaks of yellow. In one regard a close inspection revealed details rather than obscuring them, for the name *Justice IV*, and the name of the launch's port of origin, *Poole*, a large harbor in Dorsetshire, were carefully painted on the stern.

"That was his last work," Lady Justicia murmured. "He hung it just a few days ago."

She blew her nose with determination and rose from her chair to ring the velvet bell cord that hung beside the fireplace, and Ford imagined a bell jangling in some distant servants' hall.

"It's very fine, very fine indeed," he said.

"You and V can have it if you wish," she said, flapping her arm around the crowded room as she returned to her chair. "God knows, I have enough to remember him by."

"Tell me about him," Ford said, and sat down opposite her.

"Oh, he's an easy man—*was* an easy man—I suppose. He loved life, he loved to paint, he was kind and considerate …" Tears welled in her eyes, and Ford gave her a moment to recover. The door opened silently as he waited, and the groveling footman entered bearing a tea tray.

"I'm afraid I have to ask you some difficult questions, Lady Pengriffon," he said at length, when the groveler had departed. "I need to know if he had any worries or financial difficulties, or any enemies, or whether he'd been behaving strangely, as if he had a secret. In short, anything that might help to explain this tragedy."

"You don't—didn't—know my husband, Mr. Ford. He wasn't that sort of man. He lived for the good things and simply ignored the unpleasant. He was, I suppose, almost childlike in that regard, and, like a happy child, it was impossible not to love him. He saw only the good in people. He was absurdly optimistic. Will you take tea?"

"Thank you, I'd love some."

It may have been impossible not to love Lord Pengriffon, Ford thought, but someone—at least one person—had also found it possible to hate him.

He braced himself for unpleasantness. "I hate to ask you this, Lady Pengriffon, but were you happily married? I understand he liked to drink, for example. Did he ever mistreat you?"

"Goodness, no!" she responded immediately, smiling for the first time. "As I said, you didn't know him. He certainly drank a great deal, it's true, but it made him giggly and floppy, and he'd fall asleep in the oddest places. Do you take milk and sugar?"

"A little milk and one lump, please."

"As for our marriage, we rubbed along comfortably enough, probably better than many couples. He had a mistress, but I didn't mind, and he didn't try to hide her from me."

She was completely calm, as if she had just told him that Pengriffon had an old school chum with whom he fished. How would Victoria react to such a situation, he wondered? Not that it would ever happen, of course, but he doubted that calmness would be included in her emotions.

"Can you tell me who she is?" he asked as delicately as he could, rising to take his teacup from the tray.

"Her name is Amy Robsart; she's a nurse at the cottage hospital and lives with a companion a couple of miles along the coast. She was one of his models; he did nudes as well as seascapes, and Clarence loved well-endowed women, if you understand me, and I saw no reason to deny him a harmless pleasure."

"I see," Ford said.

"I thought of it as no more than Clarence scratching an itch," she said, and took a sip of tea. "She's a perfectly pleasant woman. I give her a lift into the village from time to time."

Her demeanor would make a Trappist monk look agitated, he thought. She seemed to have loved Lord Pengriffon as one loves an elderly and companionable dog. One fondly tolerates the animal's eccentricities, and when it dies, one mourns its passing. There is a void in one's existence, but life continues, and the void will soon be filled by the clamor of one's daily round.

"I see," Ford said again, wondering what it would take to stir her passions. "May I ask about the state of your finances? Any issues? Any business problems?"

"Oh, I'm afraid I'm rather vague about all that, Mr. Ford, and Clarence wasn't much better informed," she said, shaking her head. "All the money, or most of it, is tied up in the family trust. When we need money, we simply write a check."

Ford thought of the parlous state of his own finances, and his feverish, oft-repeated calculations on whether he could afford to marry Victoria—calculations invariably ending in gloom and despondency—and tried to imagine a life in which one just wrote checks whenever one wanted to, and the money was somehow, magically, always there.

"Who administers the trust?"

"There's a firm in London—Pollock, Pollock and someone, if I recall correctly—which sends us statements once a quarter. Clarence used to toss them in his desk; I don't know if he even opened them."

"Is there any other source of income, or other assets?"

She found another, even deeper level of placidity.

"Well, there's the estate, of course, and this house, and the tin mines. They all involve money, I suppose. The farms are managed by our tenant farmers, and the mines by a mine manager, and the butler and the housekeeper look after the house. One gains the impression the farms and the mines pay for themselves, with enough left over for the upkeep of the house and the charities we support, although the price of tin is falling, I believe."

She waved an uncertain hand.

"There's a man in Trethgarret who keeps our accounts; you'd better ask him—Joseph Crutchfield, who has an office in the High Street. Oh, and recently Clarence's paintings have begun to sell rather well. That's how we could afford to buy the launch. There's a gallery in London that hangs his pictures, and Clarence is—was—one of the owners. The launch is new, the fourth we've owned, and Clarence always names them after me."

"I see," Ford said again, confused by her description of their finances—hopefully the accountant would be more coherent. "Er, and your husband had no enemies, locally or in London?"

"None, I'm sure of it. The mayor didn't like him, I know, but he certainly was not an enemy."

"Mr. Thompson? Was that because of what I understand Mr. Thompson's politics to be?"

She smiled again.

"Oh, no, it was nothing like that. No, it's because my husband loved practical jokes, particularly when the butt was someone with an inflated sense of self-importance. My husband was an expert at *trompe-l'œil* as well as impressionism. Are you familiar with that term, Mr. Ford?"

"*Trompe-l'œil?* Isn't it a trick or deceit of the eye, a realistic painting that makes you think there's something there that isn't?"

"Exactly. For example, there is no mantelpiece above the fireplace. Clarence painted it on the wall. It's a completely flat mural, I assure you."

He stared at the mantelpiece—it looked utterly real.

"Good lord!" Ford said. "I could have sworn—and I stood right in front of it!"

"He loved to watch people trying to lean against it or place their teacups on it. Your mother-in-law tried to do so yesterday and dropped her cup. She did not, I should say, appreciate the joke."

He stood to examine it. Even at close quarters, where he could see it was a flat, two-dimensional painting, his mind was sure he could reach out and pick up one of the photographs that seemed to litter the apparent surface.

"Good lord!" he said again, marveling at his lordship's skill. "And so, the mayor also dropped his cup?"

"Oh, no; it was far more ambitious than that. Clarence painted a life-sized picture of the harbor, as seen from the front door of the Duke of Cornwall. Clarence waited until Mr. Thompson parked his motorcar—of which he is inordinately proud—in the right spot and went inside for a drink. My husband then erected the painting in front of Mr. Thompson's vehicle. When Mr. Thompson emerged, he thought his car had been stolen and driven away, and he reported the theft at the police station in considerable agitation."

She smiled at the memory.

"He became a laughing-stock; it took him a long time to live it down."

Ford found himself chuckling.

"The mayor's not well liked, I'm afraid," she added, "although I suppose someone must concern themselves with the sewers."

Clearly Thompson's refrain of self-justification was a universal one.

"Clarence laughed so much I thought he'd do himself an injury."

Ford was reminded of his earlier analogy about a well-loved family dog. Lady Pengriffon was speaking of her husband as a fond memory, even though it was a scant four hours since she had been informed of his violent death. The loss was deep but not overwhelming. It was as if a rock had been tossed into her still waters, but the ripples were already spreading and dissipating across her tranquil surface. He was not sure if he found her stoicism admirable.

"I think I've intruded on you long enough, Lady Justicia," he said, rising to his feet. A twinge reminded him of his earlier encounter with Mr. Thompson's clutch pedal. "My condolences once more. With your permission, I'd like to take a look at his lordship's study before I leave, and temporarily remove any papers that may seem relevant—I'll give you a list. And I'll need to speak to the trustees, and Miss Robsart, and so on. I hope you understand? Oh, and I'll need a photograph of your husband—let's see, can I borrow this one on the piano? Is it a good likeness? I'll return it as soon as possible, I promise."

He did not need her permission in any of these matters, but ever since he first became a policeman he had always felt compelled to ask.

"Of course, Mr. Ford, please do as you think best," she said, and looked up at him. "You know, you're not even remotely as your new mother-in-law described."

"I sincerely hope not," Ford said. "And now I'll leave you in peace, Lady Pengriffon."

She nodded gracefully and poured herself another cup of tea.

* * *

A man's study is a true reflection of his character, Ford thought, as he looked around Lord Pengriffon's inner sanctum. The thought generated an inner shudder at the utter sterility of his own grim bachelor's flat off Sloane Street in London, soon to be abandoned, thank God, in favor of Victoria's exuberantly eclectic apartment near Hyde Park.

What would someone conclude about Pengriffon? Artwork and artist's equipment of every shape and size dominated the room. Every inch of wall space was crammed with his own work or reproductions of the works of others.

Pengriffon must have drawn insight and inspiration from the great masters. This Botticelli, for example, must have provided guidance for a rendition of an unrobed female figure of extravagant proportions, whom, from Lady Pengriffon's description of her figure, Ford took to be Miss Robsart. Sketches and copies of work by some of the more prominent French impressionists—Ford recognized the iconic *Impression, soleil levant* by Monet, for example—and the work of the earlier English painter Joseph Turner, seemed to be reflected in a series of studies of sunrises and sunsets over Trethgarret harbor. Another rendition of Miss Robsart—if she was indeed Pengriffon's model—hung beside an image of a young lady with disassembled limbs and one eye. Leaning closer, Ford saw it was signed by Picasso, and wondered why the art world praised the notorious Spaniard so highly.

A framed photograph of Isambard Kingdom Brunel, the famous engineer and founder of the Great Western Railway, was given a place of prominence, as if Lord Pengriffon had wished to pay tribute to the source of his wealth.

Beyond his work as an artist, Ford thought, one would find ample evidence of his lordship's fondness for alcohol—bottles and glasses stood ready on every surface—and his sense of humor, which Ford discovered when he sat down at Pengriffon's massive rolltop desk. On its surface lay an untidy scattering of papers and a pen. Ford reached to clear them to one side, only to discover they were painted images, another example of Pengriffon's whimsical and skillful *trompes-l'œil*.

The desk's many drawers revealed a man with little patience for paperwork. He had not so much failed to respond to correspondence as to totally ignore it, for many of the letters had been stuffed in unopened. Lady Justicia had been right—an entire drawer was devoted to mostly unopened envelopes inscribed with the name Pollock, Pollock & Poole, of Lincoln's Inn Fields in London. Ford opened the most recent he could find and whistled at the size of the Pengriffon trust holdings. No wonder Lady Pengriffon had never bothered about money!

There were other letters, also mostly unopened, from an art gallery named the L'Arte Moderne, situated in Brick Street, which Ford thought he remembered as running behind Piccadilly near Hyde Park Corner in London. He opened a letter and discovered that the gallery was hanging Pengriffon's works on consignment. If someone bought one of his pieces, the gallery would pay him. Ford whistled again to see that Pengriffon's work was fetching fifty pounds or more.

The rest of the desk's contents identified friends and relatives, who shared a common complaint about his lack of communication; the arcane workings of the House of Lords, which Pengriffon attended only rarely; and the draconian proceedings of the omnipresent, omnivorous, and ominous Inland Revenue Service, whose existence Pengriffon seemed to have chosen to ignore.

An album contained a jumble of newspaper clippings and photographs. There was a grainy school photograph from his lordship's days at Eton and the announcements of Lord and Lady Pengriffon's engagement and subsequent marriage in the *Times*. Deeper into the album Ford found an unlikely image of Pengriffon in military garb, possibly taken during the Boer War, and a formal portrait of the Pengriffons in the full regalia of an earl and countess, complete with coronets, doubtless dating from the king's coronation in 1911. His lordship looked as if he was fidgeting, while Lady Pengriffon—my God, she must have been a young bride—looked as if she was carved from alabaster.

The collection allowed Ford to sketch the bare bones of his lordship's curriculum vitae but gave him no sense of the man, and he set it aside.

The only active correspondence that Ford could find was with various French artists and galleries, with whom he maintained a lively interaction in semiliterate French. He smiled at Pengriffon's description of a famous artist's latest work, *plus ça change, plus c'est la même ancien merde*—the more it changes, the more it's the same old crap.

Ford was on the brink of losing interest in Pengriffon's desk when a thought struck him, and he ran his hands across every surface of the desk and its drawers. Pengriffon had loved deceptions of the eye ...

ah, sure enough, the bottom right-hand drawer was shallower than it should have been. Ford bent over and probed delicately with his fingertips until a hidden catch released itself with a tiny clicking sound. The drawer had a false bottom, and Ford removed it, revealing several folders.

Some were reworkings of the few trust accounts that Pengriffon had bothered to open. The typed pages from the law firm of Pollock, Pollock & Poole were covered with columns of figures and calculations written in what Ford recognized to be Lord Pengriffon's hand. Not only had he paid close attention to his accounts, he had also reviewed them in minute detail. Why? It was out of character from Lady Pengriffon's description, and yet he had no doubt she had told him the truth. And why had Pengriffon hidden the results?

Another folder contained the business accounts of the L'Arte Moderne gallery, including listings of painting sold. These were also heavily annotated.

Ford set aside the folders to be studied in detail. Perhaps he'd send them up to London to be reviewed by Scotland Yard's financial experts.

A final folder contained not business papers but a sheaf of delicate charcoal drawings of Lady Pengriffon, drawn, Ford guessed, at various times throughout their fifteen-year marriage. Ford was struck by their almost voyeuristic feel—clearly the subject had not been aware of his attention. In addition, unlike his usual work, they were drawn in the school of realism, and, Ford saw with sudden insight, with intense emotion. She was presented as a delicate flower, like a fine porcelain figurine—perfect, and yet easily shattered.

Pengriffon had loved his wife deeply, Ford saw, but he had hidden the strength of his feelings. Was it because she was so much younger, and he feared to make a fool of himself? No, the Pengriffon that Ford was building in his mind would not have cared a fig about appearing ridiculous. Rather, Ford guessed, his lordship had feared to disturb her limpid surface, to roil her serenity with his passion, for fear he might destroy her inner essence. Perhaps that was why he had sought out other, more robust, companionship.

He sat for a moment with his hands on the desk, fingering Pengriffon's *trompe-l'oeil*. He had been impossible not to like, Lady

Justicia had said, and the fishermen at the wharf had said the same. But to pull a tie so tightly about his neck—that hadn't taken mere dislike, it had taken malice and even hatred.

Ford collected up the folders and found an empty envelope large enough to hold them. He replaced the false drawer bottom without the contents. He stood, glanced carefully around the room, and felt that he should good-bye, as if he had just met his lordship and was now leaving his presence. Ford thought they could have been friends, even though his lordship was now dead, and smiled grimly at his own absurdity.

He was struck by a sense of contradiction. The cluttered room looked chaotic, but also—Ford searched for a word—pragmatic, as if everything had a purpose. The books in the overflowing bookcases looked well-read, like old and faithful friends; the jumble of odd electrical equipment on a side table, which Ford took to be several disemboweled wireless receivers, looked as if some new mechanism under construction would arise phoenixlike from the debris of the old; the canvases piled at seeming random against the walls were, on closer examination, carefully signed and dated, and organized in chronological order, as if Pengriffon had wanted to observe his artist progress.

Ford decided neither to tell Lady Pengriffon about the secret desk compartment he had found nor to tell her that he was bearing away its contents. He hesitated a moment longer, trying to absorb the essence of Pengriffon from the room. Why had so fair a life ended in so foul a manner? What had he done to deserve his fate?—not just to be strangled, but taken out and anchored to the ocean floor, there to be consumed by the creatures of the deep.

* * *

Ford found his mother-in-law berating Victoria in one of the many rooms that lay between himself and freedom.

"You insisted on marrying a minor functionary in an obscure appendage of the Home Office." Lady Canderblank's raised voice carried through several adjacent rooms.

"Mother," Victoria shot back, "the Criminal Investigation Department of Scotland Yard is not an obscure appendage, nor is a chief inspector a minor functionary. Scotland Yard, in fact, is universally acknowledged to be the premier law enforcement organization in the world, and well you know it."

Lady Canderblank glanced at Ford as he approached but did not stem the tide of her invective.

"Don't bandy words with me, young lady. I know nothing of the sort! I do know, however, that it is not a fit place for gentlemen of good character. Indeed, one wonders if one can be a detector of criminality in others without having more than something of the criminal mind oneself."

Ford grimaced inwardly. He'd often privately wondered the very same thing.

"Mother, that's *preposterous!*" Victoria snapped back.

Lady Canderblank must have decided to take another tack.

"Victoria, I appeal to you for your own good, as your mother. Will you come belatedly to your senses? It was the height of foolishness to strike out at me by deliberately marrying beneath yourself. You rejected the Duke of Bigsby solely because you knew I favored the match, and you threw yourself at this, this *person,* solely because you knew I find him contemptible."

"That's absurd! I ..."

Lady Canderblank overrode Victoria and turned to Ford. "And, I must add, it was the height of malice, Freud, for you to permit her to do so. A gentleman would never knowingly condemn a lady to a life of misery."

It was as if she'd reared back and struck at him like a cobra, and Ford recoiled. He had hesitated for a year before asking Victoria to marry him, for precisely the reasons Lady Canderblank had just stated. Would she actually be happy, he had wondered, living on a policeman's salary? After the first ardor faded, as inevitably it would, would she settle for the cramped and humdrum existence that was all he could offer her?

"Ford, you were born to exemplify mediocrity," his old school headmaster had once told him. "You perform this duty admirably." The words had stuck with him through the years, and he had even invented the private Latin motto *exemplum mediocris,* to define his existence.

But all of that was before Victoria had burst into his life with the explosive force of a howitzer shell, insisting he was the most extraordinary man in England, extravagantly gifted in far too many ways to enumerate, and possessed of an overpowering animal magnetism.

Now Victoria was standing toe-to-toe with her mother.

"I married Thomas because I love him," Victoria responded vehemently, her chin jutting forward and her eyes flashing. "Your opinion is the exact, the precise, polar opposite of mine."

Lady Canderblank bore on as if Victoria hadn't answered, still staring at Ford. "I trust you have not been despicable enough, wanton enough, *intemperate* enough to consummate this disastrous marriage?"

"I'm delighted to say we have," Victoria answered triumphantly for them both.

"Then all is lost," Lady Canderblank groaned in a tone of sudden despair, as if this final burden was too great a cross to bear, and slumped down onto a chaise. She held her hand to her forehead with the palm turned outwards, in a theatrical gesture of desolation.

"The last bastion of decency has been breached, and the honor of the House of Canderblank has been indelibly besmirched."

She transferred her hand to her heart. "I must go and lie down; I fear the onset of palpitations."

She saw that Victoria was unmoved by this prospect, stood, and strode from the room with remarkable vigor for a woman experiencing an incipient heart attack, and they heard her disappearing voice yelling robustly for a servant.

Three

"It's still only five o'clock," Ford said to Victoria, as they roared along the coast road away from Pengriffon Hall. He raised his voice above the wind and gave her a summary of his interview with Justicia Pengriffon and his discoveries in his lordship's study. Neither of them mentioned Lady Canderblank.

"I wonder where she lives—the pulchritudinous Amy Robsart, that is to say," Victoria said. "It must be around here somewhere. Shall we find out, my adorable Thomas, and try to see her? Could she be a pulchritudinous suspect?"

"I have no idea, V," Ford said. "Still, I suppose we may as well see her while we're here."

They stopped to ask a farm laborer on a horse and cart, pungent—the horse, the cart, and the laborer—with the odor of horse manure, and he directed them toward a narrow, winding lane, which led at length to a cottage half overgrown with a riot of climbing wisteria.

Their knock upon the cottage door was answered by a young lady who might have been attractive to horse lovers. Her nose was long and prominent, and her dark eyes were large and wide set; her straight hair tumbled manelike down her back. Her generally equine appearance was reinforced by the jodhpurs she was wearing, which made her look disproportionately large above and spindly below. She stared at them with an expression that combined fear and hostility.

"Miss Robsart?" Ford asked with some uncertainty—surely Lord Pengriffon's renditions of his model had not taken such bold liberties with the truth?

"No, I'm Josephine Langley," the young lady replied. "I share the cottage with her. Amy isn't at home."

She seemed to be torn between wanting to close the door in their faces and finding out why they had come.

"My name is Ford. I'm a police officer," Ford said quickly, for fear she'd retreat. "I'm investigating …"

"You've found Amy?" Miss Langley burst out.

"No, to the contrary, I was hoping to find her here."

The look of fear strengthened in Miss Langley's face, and she seemed close to tears.

"Well, she's missing," she said. "She didn't come home last night, and she hasn't shown up since. I was just about to bicycle down to the village and make a report to Constable Crocker."

Ford felt the cold draft of an ugly premonition.

"May we come in for a moment? This is my wife, Victoria."

Even at this moment he spared a moment to feel the surge of pride that simple statement brought him. Miss Langley stood indecisively, glancing back and forth between them, and Ford squeezed by her before she could refuse him.

The room they entered was shabby but comfortably furnished; a room lived in by occupants not overwhelmingly concerned with tidiness. A portrait of Amy Robsart in Pengriffon's style hung above the fireplace, and Ford noticed a second, more intimate, portrayal through an open bedroom door. Both paintings had an urgent, unfinished look about them, as if Pengriffon could scarcely wait to finish his current work before starting on the next.

"He paints her three or four times in a single afternoon," Miss Langley said in a voice taut with inner tensions, as if she had read his thoughts.

"Lord Pengriffon, you mean, Miss Langley?" Ford asked.

"Yes, of course," she said. "Why have you come? Have you heard something about Amy?"

"No, I'm afraid I haven't. I came to interview Miss Robsart in connection with Lord Pengriffon's death."

"His *what?*" she shrieked. "He's *dead?*"

"Didn't you know, Miss Langley?"

"No, of course not. How should I know? I've been waiting for Amy and worrying all day." A sob escaped her.

"Perhaps you'd better sit down," Victoria intervened, and led her to an armchair. Victoria's head came only to Miss Langley's shoulder, and Ford had the vivid image of a young lady leading a horse by the bridle.

"It must be a shock," Victoria said gently. "I'll see if I can find your tea things, if I may?"

"There's brandy in the cupboard by the kitchen sink," Miss Langley gasped, sinking into the chair; her long limbs made it seem too small. "I think I'm going to faint." She turned back to Ford. "What do you mean, he's *dead?*"

"I'm afraid his body was recovered from the sea a few hours ago," Ford said as gently as he could. "He drowned."

"Amy didn't do it," Miss Langley said immediately. "She'd never do a thing like that, in spite of everything."

Now, here is a curious thing, Ford thought. She had assumed that Lord Pengriffon had been murdered, whereas the normal reaction would be to assume a boating accident. In addition, Amy Robsart apparently had a motive, the "everything" to which Miss Langley had referred, and was, therefore, at least in Miss Langley's eyes, a suspect.

Ford saw Victoria, standing behind Miss Langley, open her mouth to form a question. He saw her catch herself and stay silent. No gesture could have endeared her more to Ford—she had swallowed her own instinctive question in deference to him.

Ford had considered Amy Robsart a suspect only in the vague sense that everyone in close contact with a murdered person—a wife or a mistress, for example—is an automatic suspect until eliminated from the list.

"Are you sure, Miss Langley—in spite of everything?" he asked, as if he knew a great deal more than he did. He usually refused to indulge in such subterfuges, but something about Miss Langley struck him as discordant—or perhaps he was just giving way to his exasperation over his disrupted honeymoon.

"Look, lovers quarrel all the time, but it doesn't come to murder," Miss Langley shrugged. "Married men make promises, but in the end it was obvious he wouldn't leave his wife. He was a cheat and a liar, just like all men, only interested in one thing, and one thing only."

"I see," Ford said, imagining the whole squalid affair, feeling a little sad that Lord Pengriffon had been a lesser man than he had thought him. "You're sure Miss Robsart wouldn't carry out her threats?"

"Look, it's one thing to say you'll kill someone, and another thing to kill them, another thing entirely."

"Did she say that?" Ford asked.

Miss Langley paused, as if realizing that she was incriminating her friend.

"She, well, she might have done, I suppose, perhaps, in a manner of speaking," she mumbled, and then added, with more conviction, "but she'd never actually do it."

"That's very possible, Miss Langley, and yet the basic facts are that he is dead and that she has disappeared."

She stared at him speechlessly, her brown eyes vast and troubled, and dissolved into a sobbing fit. Victoria offered her brandy, but Miss Langley pushed her arm away, and thereafter ceased to be entirely coherent. Ford gathered that Amy and Pengriffon had been together at the cottage on the previous afternoon. It had been "the usual"—giggles and laughter sounding through Amy's bedroom door, succeeded by the harsher wails of an argument—after which Pengriffon had set off on foot across the fields to take the shortcut to the village. Amy had emerged disheveled from her bedroom, announced that she was going to kill him, mounted her bicycle, and set off in pursuit.

She had not returned.

*   *   *

By this time Miss Langley had become completely distraught. Victoria tried to comfort her, and Ford took the opportunity to glance quickly into the other rooms. One, which he took to be Amy Robsart's, was hung with numerous examples of Pengriffon's impressions of her at her most pulchritudinous.

The second bedroom, presumably Miss Langley's, was bare—almost barren—in comparison, as if its occupant slept in it but did not occupy it; the room reminded him of his own Spartan quarters in Chelsea.

Much of the comfortable country kitchen and the diminutive bathroom was hung with female garments in various stages of laundry.

There was no telephone in the cottage, and therefore there was no way for Ford to summon help; in the end they bundled her into the backseat of the Humber, her face buried in Ford's large white handkerchief, and rumbled back to town. They stopped at the post office/police station, where Ford transferred her to Crocker's safekeeping, and informed him of Amy Robsart's disappearance.

"I know you haven't any resources, Constable, but you've got to organize a search," Ford told him.

"How can I organize a search and take care of Miss Langley at the same time, sir?" Crocker asked; it was clearly a quandary rather than a complaint.

"Ask your wife to take charge of Miss Langley and send one of your neighbors to fetch the doctor. Miss Langley probably needs a sedative, and she'll have to make a formal statement in the morning."

"Right sir—the missus, a neighbor, the doctor, a sedative, a statement in the morning—got it."

"Next, go to the inn and ask for help. Get a group of volunteers to cover every house in the village—one person per street, for example—asking if anyone's seen Amy Robsart since late yesterday afternoon. She was last seen on her bicycle riding toward Trethgarret."

"The inn, volunteers, house-to-house, Miss Robsart's whereabouts since last afternoon—got it, sir."

"Next, has young Frank produced his photographs yet?"

"I don't know, sir. I'll check on my way to the inn. He lives right across the street."

"Good, as quickly as he can, please. Next, when does the next train leave for London? I have a package of papers I need to send to Scotland Yard."

Crocker chuckled at Ford's metropolitan presumption. "Lord bless you, sir, there's only one passenger train to and from Penzance each morning. The only way to do it this evening is to have a driver take them to Penzance, to catch the overnight mail train. It leaves at ten o'clock."

"Then, while you're in the inn, see if anyone is prepared to make the journey."

"I'll go, Thomas," Victoria volunteered. "It's probably the fastest way."

"Yes, Miss," Crocker said, "but who will drive you?"

"I'll drive myself, of course!"

"You can *drive*, Miss?"

This revelation of feminine liberation and accomplishment caused Crocker to remove his helmet and scratch his head in amazement.

"Whatever is the world coming to?" he asked at large. He spoke not as a man who demeaned women, but simply as a man who could not comprehend that a woman's role could extend so far beyond its traditional domestic boundaries.

"Thanks, V," Ford intervened, lest Victoria make a comment. "Next, Constable, is that pile of flotsam and jetsam still on the dock?"

"It is, sir."

"Good. When you leave the inn, join me there and we'll go through it while it's still light."

"Got it, sir."

"Finally, Crocker, please ask your wife that when the doctor comes to attend Miss Langley, she should ask him to find me on the quay to report on his examination of Lord Pengriffon's body."

"Got it, sir, I think—Miss Langley, the missus, a neighbor, the doctor, a sedative, a statement in the morning, the inn, volunteers, house-to-house, Miss Robsart's whereabouts since last afternoon, young Frank's photographs, the papers for London, Mrs. Ford, the night train to London from Penzance, the rubbish on the dockside, the doctor again, his report to you on the quay about Lord Pengriffon—got it!"

"Exactly so, Crocker," Ford said, thinking of all the other stones—such as Lord Pengriffon's wallet, still damply in his breast pocket, for example—as yet unturned.

* * *

The pile of rusting scrap and refuse on the dockside, trawled up in Jimmie's net from the seabed along with Lord Pengriffon's body, contained nothing relevant to Ford's investigation, as far as he could tell. He was struck by how much discarded debris automobiles could generate. If a time ever came when every family in England and France owned a motorcar, he conjectured, the entire English Channel would become filled with broken bits and pieces; islands of junk would rise above the waves, and eccentrics would claim them as sovereign territories and declare themselves to be princes.

This piece of metal, he thought, hefting a piece of rusting pipe in his hand, might have come from a ship's guardrail, and could have been used as a club; but Lord Pengriffon's body had shown no signs of a violent attack, beyond the tie twisted tightly around his neck—unless the doctor had found evidence to the contrary.

"There's nothing here that I can see, Crocker," he said, shaking his head. "You can get someone to dispose of it, if you would."

"Got it, sir," Crocker said, removing his helmet to scratch his head.

"Did you speak to Frank about the photographs, by the way?"

"Done it; he said he'd be ready for you in half an hour, sir."

Ford imagined Crocker's brain to be a box of filing cards, each with an action written on it. The phrase "got it" caused a new card to be added, and "done it" caused the relevant card to be deleted from the box and tossed away. Perhaps his habitual head scratching triggered the mechanism.

Without any physical evidence near or on the body, Ford would have nothing to identify the murderer. He'd be entirely dependent on motive. Not only would he not know where Lord Pengriffon was murdered, he might not even know how. If the doctor ...

A tall man strode up and introduced himself to Ford as the village doctor, as if summoned by Ford's train of thought. Dr. Anderson struck Ford as a man of contradictions—hurried and yet precise, thoughtful and yet in constant motion. He seemed to be about Ford's own age, and perhaps, like Ford, climbing into the middle rungs of his profession. He was obviously competent and also familiar with drowning, as one would expect a seaside doctor to be.

Dr. Anderson also proved to be an impatient man. "I've only a moment, Chief Inspector, so I'll get straight to the point," he said. "We'll have to do an autopsy in the morning to prove it, but I'll bet my pension he was strangled before he entered the water. There's severe bruising beneath that tie, and the dead don't bruise."

He had the trick of punching his fist into the palm of his other hand to drive home his observations.

"The tie was tight enough, Doctor?" Ford asked. "I couldn't be sure."

"The larynx—the so-called 'Adam's apple'—was crushed," the doctor said with finality. "I doubt there's much water in the lungs, even though he was submerged; his throat was so constricted very little would have seeped through."

"Was …" Ford began, but Dr. Anderson cut him off, as if unused to interruptions.

"He was my patient. He was somewhat overweight, and he drank to excess, but he was very healthy for a man of his age. His heart and lungs were as sound as a bell, and he had an excellent constitution. I am fully confident an autopsy will confirm my findings."

"Was there any evidence of an attack, other than the tie?"

"None; it was strangulation, pure and simple. He'd probably been drinking and would've offered little resistance. And now, if you will excuse me, I have a couple of house calls to make, and we're short-staffed at the hospital."

"Thank you, Doctor," Ford called to his retreating back. "One more thing before you go, if I may? How much strength was applied to the tie?"

"A considerable amount, I'd say," Anderson said over his shoulder. "His assailant was a strong man. And now …"

"Definitely a man?"

The doctor paused and turned back briefly.

"Almost certainly, or an exceptionally strong woman, I suppose. It occurred to me it might be someone used to working with ropes—one of the local fishermen or sailors, for example, although I doubt it was anyone from here—Pengriffon was too well liked. And now I really must …"

"A final question, Doctor, if I may. What is Miss Langley's condition?"

"Oh, she's emotionally overwrought, that's all, nothing a sleeping draft won't cure. She'll be fine in the morning. She's as strong as an ox—all the nurses are, as a matter of fact—they're constantly lifting heavy patients. This sort of thing is most unusual in her, I have to say. I know her well because I see her at the hospital every day."

"Thank you," Ford said. "I'm sorry to keep you from your duties."

"That's perfectly all right," Anderson said, looking at his wristwatch. Ford assumed he was finished, but the doctor continued. "Look, Pengriffon was a very decent man. He was a most generous donor to our cottage hospital. He'll be missed. Anything I can do to assist you in your investigation—you have only to ask. And now, I must insist …"

Dr. Anderson turned on his heel and marched away, and Ford wondered if he was ever touched by moments of uncertainty or self-doubt. Probably not, Ford thought, and therefore perhaps the trajectory of his career would prove to be far higher than Ford's own.

Ford sighed and glanced around the harbor. Six hours ago he would have marveled at its beauty as the sun moved lower in the western sky, flooding the scene with golden, orange light. He'd seen a similar canvas on the wall of his lordship's study, *Trethgarret at Dusk, II,* and wondered how Pengriffon could make his flat daubs of pigment *glow.*

The harbor was approximately square. Ford stood at the base of the square, where the seagoing fishing boats were moored. To his right lay the railway dock, where fish were packed in ice in reeking warehouses and loaded directly onto railway trucks, to be transported to the markets of great cities. To his left, forming the third side of the square, a jumble of whitewashed houses and cottages came right down to the water's edge, some with their own little docks with boats tied up, so that the inhabitants could step directly from their back parlors into their craft.

At the far end of this row stood an ancient church, standing upon a rocky promontory looking out to the English Channel—St. Christopher-Upon-The-Waters, Ford had learned. The forth side of the harbor, directly across from where Ford stood, was formed by a massive seawall, with a stubby lighthouse at the end. The entrance to the harbor lay between the church and the lighthouse.

The houses of Trethgarret rose up the hillsides surrounding the harbor, scattered like a child's building blocks wherever the ground was flat enough to support them. It was a sight of extraordinary beauty: the harbor filled with fishing boats and pleasure craft; the storm proof masses of the church and lighthouse, crouched down against the winds; the hodgepodge houses on the hillsides—no wonder Pengriffon had painted it again and again.

Now, however, Ford saw the scene as a catalog of tasks undone. He'd better take a look at Pengriffon's launch before the sun set. Perhaps his lordship had hidden some vital clue in a secret compartment. And his lordship himself lay in St. Christopher's. Ford should examine him, although he doubted he'd spot anything the doctor had not already told him.

And he still had to find out if anyone had seen Pengriffon after he left the inn last night. He glanced in that direction; a few holidaymakers stood outside the bar with pints of cider in their hands, carefree and laughing, while the Ancient Mariner dozed unheeding in their midst.

Ford groaned and lit a cigarette. There was the wallet, he thought, and the papers he'd pulled from Pengriffon's desk. Victoria must be halfway to Penzance by now, her hair rioting in the wind and her bare legs catching the evening sun. He'd pulled one set of accounts from each folder to study himself, and he'd need to do that later this evening, trying to decipher Pengriffon's scrawling calculations instead of gazing into Victoria's eyes across a candlelit dinner table. Phrases such as "it's not fair!" and "why me?" and "paradise lost" chased themselves across his mind.

There was something not quite right, something jarring, about Josephine Langley. She'd been in shock and incoherent, but, even so, her emotions did not seem to fit together. She was the first, and so far the only, person to criticize his lordship. Her reaction to her friend's disappearance had seemed somehow off-key, disproportionate, a little larger than life. Or was it that she was simply a large and ill-proportioned woman?

Ford shook his head at his lack of charity and tossed his cigarette into the harbor, where it hissed to death in protest.

"Is there a dinghy we can use to row out to the launch?" he asked Crocker, and received the customary "Got it" in reply.

* * *

Lord Pengriffon's steam launch was fifty feet in length, Ford estimated. The hull and deckhouse were dazzling white, and a jaunty brass funnel rose at a rakish angle. They scrambled aboard, and Ford saw that *Justicia IV* consisted of three sections—if sections were a nautical term.

Ford's knowledge of boats was limited to punts upon the River Cam in Cambridge, narrow flat-bottomed boats propelled by long poles wielded by elegant and frequently intoxicated young students, and to troopships ferrying inelegant but also intoxicated recruits to the killing fields of the Western Front. A private pleasure craft, such as the *Justicia*, belonged to a world of wealth and privilege far beyond his means.

The stern was given over to a large deck, where the Pengriffons and their guests could enjoy the sun and wind, and do a spot of fishing or swimming, if the spirit so moved them. It had a white canvas awning in case of rain or if the sun grew too strong.

A low deckhouse, with a little glass roof like a hothouse, stood amidships. It was no higher than Ford's waist, and, peering in, he see could the shining brass and steel mechanisms of a steam engine. The brass funnel rose from the engine house and high above his head.

A taller wheelhouse stood forward of the funnel. A short, steep flight of steps led up to the bridge and another led down to the accommodations.

Ford eased his way down to the low cabin, which contained a miniscule galley, bunks along each side, and a table in the center—at least that was what Ford thought it contained, since almost every surface was covered by painting equipment, and canvases were stacked against the walls—bulkheads, Ford reminded himself. An oil lamp hung low from the ceiling, and no adult could move about without constantly clunking his head, as Ford discovered. The only light was admitted by a folding hatchway that gave onto the front—bow—deck of the launch. The cabin was alive with the sound of the harbor wavelets against the hull, and the atmosphere was dank and stuffy.

One bunk was reasonably clear and covered with unmade bedding.

"He often slept aboard, sir" Crocker volunteered. "If he was too drunk to drive home, he'd doss down here for the night."

A narrow slatted door revealed a tiny lavatory and sink—a "head," in nautical terms, Ford remembered—and a second revealed a closet filled by a jumble of his lordship's clothing, foul weather gear, and an assortment of rubber boots. Ford reached to open a third door, only to discover it was another of his lordship's *trompes l'oeil*.

He stood back and tried unsuccessfully to imagine a murderous struggle. The cabin was untidy, certainly, but nothing had been wrecked. Ford doubted that two grown men could fight without causing widespread destruction—at least, not without knocking the lamp off its hook. If Pengriffon had been murdered here, he must have been asleep on the bunk. His killer would have crept in, eased Pengriffon's tie about his neck, and then tightened it with a sharp heave. That would have been it. The killer would have dragged him up the steep stairs to the deck, and then …

"Can one man handle this boat, Crocker?" Ford asked.

"It's better with two, sir, what with keeping an eye on the boiler to keep the steam pressure up, but one can do it at a pinch. His lordship had the coal firebox replaced by fuel oil, so you don't have to keep stoking every fifteen minutes. Coal makes everything filthy, and the smuts from the funnel soiled the ladies' dresses."

Ford bent to examine the bunk, pulling off the bedclothes and shaking them out, but no clues fell out. Tomorrow, when Croft arrived from London, he'd have to remove everything and search the cabin with a magnifying glass—the entire launch, for that matter.

They returned to the deck—each man clunking his head against the oil lamp in comic sequence, as if they were Keystone Cops in an American moving picture show—and Ford drew in deep drafts of fresh air. The launch was the most likely murder scene, he decided. Pengriffon would have come here to sleep off the effects of an evening's worth of cider. The killer would have followed him in the darkness, strangled him, fired up the engine, and chuffed out to sea. He'd have improvised an anchor—yes, Ford found several blocks of concrete in the anchor locker, as well as the traditional metal kind—and heaved his lordship over the stern.

Without a body there would have been no murder. People would assume he'd run off with the missing Amy Robsart. A local folktale would have grown up to explain the disappearance—they'd decamped to the attic studios and raucous cafes of Paris, like as not, a hive of modern artists and lechery, where pulchritude, real or painted, were equally highly regarded.

In due course, after the legally required waiting period of seven years, his lordship would have been declared officially dead. But instead, within a matter of hours, Jimmie's net had dredged Pengriffon's body from its resting place deep beneath the waves. And Amy Robsart ...

"Have you ever seen Amy Robsart aboard this launch, Crocker? Did they meet here when his lordship didn't return home?"

"What, sir?" Crocker asked, as if confused by the question.

"I've heard that she was his model and more. Did they come here, do you know?"

"Well, sir," Crocker mumbled, as if embarrassed to acknowledge infidelity in so God-fearing a place as Trethgarret. "Well, yes, I believe I did see them, sir. Well, yes, quite often, I'd say. Well ... But it's a civil offense, sir, and there was nothing I could do about it, and his lordship was always very decent to me, sir."

He lapsed into silence and looked about awkwardly.

"Of course it wasn't your fault, Constable, and not in your purview, unless they caused a public spectacle. But does Amy know how to drive—steer, pilot, whatever the correct expression is—the launch?"

"Can she take the helm, do you mean, sir, and manage the engine? Well, I don't rightly know, but she must have watched his lordship often enough."

And there it was, Ford thought. Amy and Pengriffon had argued in the afternoon, as Josephine Langley had testified. Pengriffon had left, and she'd pursued him. She'd gone out to the launch and waited for him. Perhaps she'd given him a final ultimatum—divorce Justicia Pengriffon and marry me, or else. He'd refused, or offered an excuse, and fallen into a drunken stupor. Enraged by his rejection, she'd throttled him. The doctor had stressed the strength needed to tighten the tie, but Amy would have been consumed by fury, and Ford knew well that murderers in the height of passion could accomplish astonishing feats of strength.

Or, come to think of it, Amy might have used a tourniquet—she was a nurse, and she'd know exactly how and where to apply pressure, and she'd know the precise results of a crushed Adam's apple.

Having killed Pengriffon, she'd proceed to cover up the crime.

According to Crocker's statement, it was likely Amy could handle the *Justicia* alone, even at night— Ford wondered if she was struck by the irony of murdering her lover in a boat named for her rival—and she had taken the launch out to sea and disposed of the body.

Ford lowered himself down into the engine compartment and examined the brass fittings and levers to see if there was anything that she might not have been able to do. To the contrary, he found a neatly typed notice: *To start the engine, first open the oil input spigot painted red,* and so on, and Ford, who was hopelessly unmechanical, was confident that even he could do it.

He clambered out and went forward to the bridge, with Crocker at his heels. In addition to the pilot's wheel, there were gauges for the water and oil tank levels and steam pressure, and two large brass levers, one marked *Ahead, Neutral* and *Astern*, and the other marked in gradations from *Idle* to *Full Steam*. Again, Ford was convinced even he could handle the *Justicia*. A final lever, beside the side panels of the wheelhouse, was marked with arrows pointing *Up* and *Down*. Ford stopped his hand as he reached toward it—this time his lordship's *trompe l'œil* had not fooled him.

He took a last look around, but the light was fading too fast for any further investigation, and Crocker rowed them back to the fishing dock. The bell buoy clanged solemnly in the dusk, and Gray's *Elegy* sprang into Ford's mind—"*the curfew tolls the knell of passing day*"— perhaps it was tolling for Lord Pengriffon.

Amy Robsart was a credible suspect, Ford thought, lighting another—yet another—cigarette. With Pengriffon's body anchored sixty feet below the surface of the sea, there'd be nothing left to hold her in Trethgarret, and doubtless she'd left immediately. A little patient detective work would turn up witnesses. She'd probably hitched a ride to Penzance and taken the first train to London. Someone would have seen her and remembered her—after all, she was notably pulchritudinous.

She was probably known in the London artistic community, or to the hospitals; he and Croft, with all the resources of Scotland Yard behind them, would track her down within a day or two. All they'd need to do would be to find physical evidence of her recent presence on the boat—her fingerprints on the engine controls, for example—and she'd be forced to confess.

The case would be solved and his honeymoon would recommence, paradise regained. "Got it," he murmured.

Four

It seemed almost a formality to collect the photographs from young Frank. Crocker rowed Ford back to the dockside, and Ford scrambled up awkwardly, explaining he'd see Frank and then meet Crocker at the inn, where, hopefully, someone had seen Pengriffon and Amy Robsart late on the previous evening.

Frank lived almost exactly across the High Street from the post office/police station. The door was answered by his mother, a lady as broad as she was tall, who yelled "*Frank!*" before Ford could introduce himself, and jerked her thumb over her shoulder in the direction of the stairs.

Frank's room was obviously his childhood bedroom, as the narrow bed against the wall testified, but it had been taken over almost entirely by photographic equipment and supplies. Ford was reminded of Pengriffon's rooms, consumed by his art. The thick curtains were drawn against the setting sun and the room was minimally lit by a red bulb hanging from the ceiling. Frank used his handkerchief to unscrew it and substitute a stronger normal light, and Ford blinked in the sudden brightness.

"One day I'll get another light fixture," Frank said. "Or, better yet, a real darkroom. Mom's always going on about the smell of chemicals."

He hesitantly offered Ford a sheaf of black and white photographs, as if anticipating criticism. Ford drew in his breath in surprise. The images were sharp, with excellent depth of focus. Every detail was clearly visible. Ford knew professional police photographers with elaborate equipment who could not do as well. But there was more;

young Frank had not only captured factual images of Pengriffon's death but had also conveyed its pathos, its tragedy, its brutality—the abrupt ending of a man who loved life cut down before his time.

Ford studied the photographs of the tie with particular attention. Could a woman have drawn it so tight? Was there evidence Amy had inserted a lever to tighten the tourniquet—perhaps here, at the knot? Yes, it was possible, although he'd have to look at the actual tie to confirm his suspicions.

He raised his eyes from the photographs.

"These are excellent, Frank," he said. "Very fine craftsmanship, if I may say so."

Frank's cheeks grew pink beneath the pimples.

"Do you really think so?" he asked. "I wasn't sure they'd be good enough."

"If you want a career as a photographer, I'm certain you'll do very well."

Frank's eyes gleamed.

"Well, Lord Pengriffon was always very kind and encouraging." He paused, and then his plans began to tumble from his lips. "I want to go up to London and freelance for magazines and newspapers, sir, as soon as I'm eighteen. It pays nothing, so I'll have to have another job, like a night clerk in a factory or a waiter in a hotel. Then, if I do well, a paper will take me on as a stringer—social events, marriages, fashions, and such. Then, finally, if I do well enough, they'll employ me full time and assign me to news stories."

"I've no doubt you'll succeed, Frank," Ford said. "A long and successful career awaits you in Fleet Street."

"Oh, no, sir!" Frank's aspirations evidently stretched beyond the home of the British press. "America's the place; that's where all the best work is being done. I'll save every penny and work my passage to New York. Then—oh, I don't know, the *Saturday Illustrated Post,* or *Life* magazine, or there's a new one called *Time.*"

"I wish you every success, wherever you go," Ford said, meaning every word.

"England's dead, sir, to be honest," Frank said with a dismissive wave of one hand. "The best photographers are in America and the best cameras are made in Germany and Sweden; there's nothing here."

Ford glanced round the bursting but, as he now realized, precisely ordered room—a cramped and youthful version of Pengriffon's study.

"May I see some samples of other things you've done?"

"Oh, well, I'm just learning, sir," Frank said with a modest shake of his head, but clearly pleased by Ford's interest. He pulled out a large folder. "I throw all my recent work in here and sort it out later."

Ford riffled through the pile, admiring the beautifully captured gaiety of holidaymakers, giggling in the sunshine on the dock; the breathtaking sweep of the cliffs on a stormy day, with whitely foaming spray flung high from the crashing rollers at their feet, and lowering clouds frowning down above their heads; the solemnly rendered dignity of a seated couple celebrating their fiftieth wedding anniversary; and ...

"Good God!" Ford exclaimed.

"Oh, gosh, sir, I'm terribly sorry—I hope you're not ..."

Ford stared unblinkingly at an image of Victoria, seated at the table in front of the inn, photographed from behind his own shoulder, her eyes on his unseen face and her hands gripping his. In spite of her many fervent declarations, in spite of her obvious happiness in his company, and in spite of the passions so joyously released in the first few days of their marriage, he had never quite been able to convince himself that she loved him; but now he saw in her expression that she really did. Frank's lens had penetrated mere flesh and bone and exposed the essence beneath, just as Pengriffon's charcoal strokes had revealed Lady Pengriffon.

Frank was babbling something about unwarranted intrusion, but Ford cut him off.

"Could I have this, please, Frank?" he asked, knowing it would grace his desk forever—joy captured, bottled, and preserved.

"Of course, sir," Frank replied in relief, as if he had expected Ford to bite his head off. He leaned over to stare at the image critically, a serious professional rather than a pimply youth.

"I used a new camera that his lordship gave me as a birthday present. I was thirty feet behind you, but I got the depth of field just right, even if I say so myself," he said. "I'm glad it worked; she's the most beautiful woman I've ever seen."

"Me too," Ford murmured, and then collected himself. "Well, anyway ..."

Not all of Frank's work came out perfectly, Ford saw, as he glanced through the rest of the portfolio. Some images were so dark they were indecipherable, some were fuzzy, and some were merely faint.

"Well, I'm still learning, sir," Frank said. "You have to take chances, try experimenting, and learn from your mistakes; that's what his lordship always says—said. Gosh, it's hard to realize he's dead!"

"I'm sure it is, Frank. Well, thank you again for this remarkable photograph and for your work on Lord Pengriffon's remains as well. I'll arrange for the police to pay for your time, and, let's see, is a pound a fair price for this photograph of my wife?"

"A quid? Of course not, sir, that's far too much. Two bob or half-a-crown, I suppose, if you really want to pay."

"A pound it is, Frank," Ford said, reaching for his wallet. "It's worth every penny to me."

* * *

Ford's cheerful mood carried with him to the inn. He'd never solved a case so quickly, although his innate caution warned him not to jump to conclusions, particularly neat conclusions. But still, there were clearly the makings of a case against Amy Robsart, a strong case, and he indulged his imagination to the extent of visualizing the prosecution's closing argument at Amy Robsart's trial.

"We do not need to *guess*," he imagined a bewigged and gowned barrister addressing a jury. He would have ponderous tones and an invincible manner, and he'd whip his pince-nez spectacles from the end of his nose and stab them toward the jury to emphasize his points.

"We *know*, gentlemen of the jury, that Lord Pengriffon and the accused had an adulterous, one might say a *brazenly* adulterous, relationship." Stab. "We can but *shudder* at her moral character." Stab in the direction of Amy Robsart, white-faced in the dock, with tear-stained cheeks and her pulchritude lost beneath a shapeless prison smock. "We *know* that Lord Pengriffon and the accused quarreled bitterly. We *know* from Miss Langley's eyewitness testimony that the accused threatened to kill him." Stab, stab. "We *know* that she pursued him to Trethgarret that fateful night …"

Ford chuckled at his own conceit, but if there was a witness who had seen her about the docks, or, better still, on the *Justicia*, which he could see on the placid waters of the harbor, gleaming in the last rays of the setting sun, then his imaginary trial scene might take a step toward reality.

He entered the Duke of Cornwall's crowded public bar. The long, low room was abuzz with anticipation and speculation. Even the Ancient Mariner had roused himself to totter to the bar, where he announced that the place hadn't seen such excitement since the railway station welcomed its first train in 1851—a mere seventy-two years ago, Ford realized with a jolt. Holy Moses, just how ancient *was* the Ancient Mariner?

Crocker's "got it—done it" methods of police work had produced several witnesses, who were lined up by the fireplace lubricating their voices with cider. The room hushed at Ford's appearance. Crocker put on his helmet as if to indicate the start of official business, took center stage, cleared his throat dramatically, and called the first witness.

"Davey Garret! Come forward and tell the Chief Inspector what you know."

"The truth, the whole truth, and nothing but the truth," George Thompson added, pushing himself officiously to the front of the crowd, obviously unwilling to let Crocker have all the limelight. "And no elaboration, if you please."

Davey Garret, evidently nervous at all the attention, took a step forward and removed his cap, which he twirled nervously in his fingers.

"Well, sir, I saw his lordship when he left 'ere last night. He left the same time as I did."

"And then what happened?" Crocker asked.

"Well, he said good night, and then … and then …"

"Come on, man," Thompson demanded. "What did he do, exactly?"

"Well, if you must know, he crossed the road to the harbor and took a piss."

This produced a round of chuckles and giggles.

"Now watch your tongue, Davey, there's ladies present," Thompson thundered.

"Well, Gee-arge, you said to say exactly what he did," Davey said. "But I never said to ..."

"Never mind all that," Crocker interjected. "Go on, Davey. Then what happened?"

"He started off toward his dinghy, sir, to row out to the *Justicia*."

"Are you sure?"

"We all keep an eye on his lordship when he's had a belly-full, in case he stumbles and goes into the harbor. You know that, Alfie."

Ford cleared his voice to speak, but Crocker didn't hear him, and Ford remained silent, letting Crocker have his moment. It was almost as if he was witnessing Amy Robsart's trial, just as he had imagined.

"Did you see him row out?" Crocker asked Davey.

"I saw him climb down into the dinghy, and ship the oars well enough, and row a stroke or two without catching a crab, and I decided he was safe. You know how his lordship is—was, I should say—you can tell if he's too far gone, or when he's still got 'is wits about 'im, and so I went home." He turned to Thompson. "You must have seen 'im yourself, Gee-arge, you was walking that way."

"No such thing, Davey. I was home in bed by nine o'clock," Thompson said. "Now, do you have anything else to tell us? No? Very well; you can be excused."

Davey had recovered from his earlier embarrassment sufficiently to say, "Thank you, Gee-arge," with heavy sarcasm, and retreated to the fireplace, where the remainder of his pint of cider disappeared down his throat in seconds.

"Now, then, we'll hear from you next, Clara and Mabel," Crocker said, and two women, whom Ford recognized from the post office, stepped forward.

"We were walking home and saw her," Clara said, clearly excited at the attention of the crowd and drama of the moment.

"Amy Robsart, that is," Mabel added. "She was down by the docks where the railway siding finishes."

"It's on our way home," Clara said. "We go together for company in case there're German sailors about."

"There are no German sailors," Mabel answered as if she'd said it a thousand times, and Ford made a note to find out just who these sailors might be, if they existed.

"It's where his lordship usually parks his car and keeps his dinghy, right across from the *Justicia*," Clara said.

"When he hasn't rowed over to the inn, that is," Mabel clarified.

Ford mentally kicked himself. Why had it not occurred to him to check on the whereabouts of Pengriffon's car? Was it up at the Hall or down at the docks? Josephine Langley had said that ...

"She was leaning on her bicycle by his car and smoking, waiting, like."

"Did you speak to her?" George Thompson demanded.

"No, of course not, Gee-arge, we just said 'good night'; we knew well enough what she was doing there," Clara retorted, and knowing smiles circulated the room like leaves stirring in a breeze—his lordship's assignations with Amy were obviously a matter of common knowledge.

"I see," Ford said in as neutral a tone as possible. "Did his lordship row over and pick her up?"

"Not that we saw, not last night," Mabel said. "But I expect so; it's what he often did."

"Did you see anyone else?" Ford asked.

"Clara thought she did, but I didn't," Mabel said.

"I thought I saw one of the German sailors, a-lurking in the shadows," Clara said.

"There *aren't* any German sailors, and well you know it," Thompson and Crocker said as one.

"How do *you* know?" Clara shot back.

"That's enough of that," Thompson said, "You ladies can ..."

But Ford was compelled to intervene. "If Lord Pengriffon didn't take Miss Robsart to his launch, was there some other way she could get there?"

"Oh, yes," the irrepressible Thompson answered for the room. "Dinghies are a bit like common property in Trethgarret; you can borrow them providing you return them all shipshape and Bristol fashion."

The room nodded in collective agreement, and Ford remembered a similar protocol with bicycles when he was an undergraduate at Cambridge.

"Everyone's honest about these parts," Thompson added, not wishing to let an opportunity to extol Trethgarret's civic virtues pass untaken. "No crime here, none."

"Except for his lordship's murder," the Ancient Mariner growled from his perch on his barstool, and the room smiled.

"Now, that's enough, Jeb," Thompson said. He glanced at Ford and raised his eyebrows as if to suggest senile dementia. "Step back, ladies, and let's see who else can make a contribution."

"Has anyone seen her since?" Ford asked. Thompson opened his mouth, perhaps to tell Ford not to interfere with the proceedings, and then closed it again, evidently thinking the better of it.

No one spoke.

"Well?" Thompson asked the room at large, seeing a new opening. "Has anyone seen her since?"

It seemed no one had.

"Well, Mr. Ford, that seems to be that," Thompson said, having taken over Crocker's role completely.

"I have to thank you all," Ford said. "You've been very helpful."

"So what do you think, sir?" Clara asked, speaking for the crowd. "Did she do it? Did Amy do him in?"

"Well," Ford began, trying to think of a way of avoiding the question without seeming officious or like an idiot.

"You know better than that, Clara," Thompson intervened once more, drawing himself up. "You can't interfere in an official investigation. Mr. Ford will inform the proper authorities in due course." It was clear to Ford that he included himself in that category.

"She never did, not her," the Ancient Mariner growled from the bar. "It's not in her character."

"Never mind old Jeb, sir," Crocker said, and removed his helmet to indicate the official proceedings were over. "Perhaps you'd like to try the local brew, sir, now we're off duty?"

Ford accepted his offer and lit a cigarette. Victoria should be back from Penzance at any moment, he thought, glancing at his watch. Perhaps they could stay here at the inn rather than returning to the cottage they'd rented along the cliffs. He suppressed a yawn; the last eight hours had taken its toll.

"The Chief Inspector knew it was her all right, Mr. Crutchfield," he overheard Crocker saying further along the bar, above the hubbub of gossip and speculation. Crocker was speaking to a tall, thin man, who, unlike the rest of the village, was consuming whiskey; this must be the bookkeeper Lady Justicia had mentioned. "He deduced it on the *Justicia*."

Victoria would soon be here, Ford thought, and he wanted to give his attention entirely to her, but there was still his lordship's wallet, and the papers he had hidden, and …

"No, he's too cagey to say it in so many words," Crocker's voice intervened in his train of thought. "He's a deep one—cautious, like."

Ford took a sip of cider and watched idly as the Ancient Mariner climbed down from his perch and prepared to walk home. As the old man tottered past Ford, an action that took some time, he said again, "It's not in her character; you mark my words." He glanced at Ford, gripped his arm in friendly greeting—or perhaps for momentary support—smiled at some inner joke, and moved slowly on.

Ford stared after him; the old man's china blue eyes were remarkably clear and penetrating, and Ford's mind jumped to the classic *Rime of the Ancient Mariner*, by Samuel Taylor Coleridge.

> He holds him with his skinny hand …
> He holds him with his glittering eye …
> He cannot choose but hear
> And thus spake on that ancient man
> The bright-eyed Mariner.

* * *

"And so, everyone's concluded it was Amy Robsart," Ford finished telling Victoria, "except for the Ancient Mariner."

"And what do *you* think, Thomas?"

Charlie's wife had improvised a late supper for them, and Victoria sat across from him in the inn's deserted dining room as they eat cold sliced ham, tart pickled onions, and tiny, cold, boiled potatoes, all washed down with an inevitable glass of scrumpy.

"At this point Amy Robsart's the obvious suspect, but we're only nine hours into the case. It may all look very different tomorrow, although, I'm bound to say, people have been convicted and hanged on less evidence. If it went into court, it would turn on Josephine Langley's testimony, because she establishes Amy's motive. She explains *why* Amy Robsart was waiting on the dock."

Victoria glanced round the shadowy room.

"This is the first time I've really felt married, Thomas," she said. "Until now we could have stolen away for an illicit affair. But now, here we are, having a plate of cold ham and discussing your day at the office like an old married couple. Perhaps I should darn a pair of your socks after supper."

"How does it feel?"

"Darning socks or being your wife?" She laughed and reached across the table to squeeze his hand, looking exactly like Frank's photograph of her. "Heavenly, so far. However, apart from the obvious, which, I trust, needs no further clarification, the only wifely thing I've done so far is to drive madly across the highways and byways of western Cornwall in pursuit of the night train to London. I addressed the envelope to Superintendent Brownlee, incidentally."

"Excellent, my good wife."

"Thank you, oh lord and master. I gave the envelope to the guard on the train—his name is Stan and his wife is expecting their fourth any day now—and made him promise to give it to a railway policeman as soon as they get to the station in London in the morning, with instructions to take it to Scotland Yard immediately."

"Excellent again!"

She hefted a large pewter tankard of cider with her pinkie finger stuck out, as if she were sipping tea in a stylish restaurant, and grinned.

"One must remain elegant at all times," she told him as he laughed. "Refinement is all; we had pinkie-pointing classes at my finishing school in Switzerland. It's all part of proper etiquette, and I happen to be an excellent pinkie pointer."

"I've never seen a pinkie so properly pointed, I must admit."

"Thank you—it's the only A I ever got, I'm afraid; my efforts at deportment and comportment earned only a sad assortment of B minuses and C plusses. On less important matters, I also saw the stationmaster and made him find the ticket collector who was on duty this morning—we tracked him down in a rather jolly pub named the Pirate's Lair—and he, Harry, the ticket collector, said he hadn't seen the pulchritudinous Amy Robsart, and he was sure he'd have remembered her, based on my description."

"That's wonderful, V!" Ford said, genuinely impressed. "I didn't think of asking you to do that. You'd make an admirable detective."

"Undoubtedly, Thomas, but I think I'll make a much better detective's wife; I'll certainly try to be. Apart from my aforesaid conversations, I drove with, I should say, verve punctuated by élan. My double-clutching was particularly impressive; you should have been there to see it."

"I'm sorry to have missed it."

"I'll give you a detailed demonstration on the first available occasion, I promise, Thomas."

"I can't wait."

"You can, you will, and you must; you still have work to do—his lordship's wallet and the rest of the papers. We'll do them together before we go to sleep."

"I suppose so," Ford groaned.

He'd never leave work undone before he was married, for work occupied time otherwise spent in despondency. He'd sit alone in his grim flat in Chelsea late in the evening, a stack of case files before him at the kitchen table, drinking endless cups of tea and smoking endless cigarettes until his tasks were done, his conscience clear, and he could fall safely into bed exhausted, knowing that sleep would soon make him oblivious to his loneliness.

But that was then, and this is now. Now he was not alone, and there were infinitely preferable ways to occupy the end of the day.

* * *

"What's the fastest you've ever solved a murder, Thomas, darling?" Victoria asked Ford's ear, between nibbles. "Your ear tastes of salt, incidentally. I rather like it."

The innkeeper had been pleased to let them stay for the night, and Ford had experienced a giddy moment as he boldly and guiltlessly entered a hotel room with Victoria.

"Oh, a couple of weeks, I suppose," he mumbled as he returned the complement. "Of course, most cases drag on forever and many go unsolved."

"Well, I'd like you to solve this one in a couple of days, if you would, or three at the most; I feeling very neglected."

"I still have nothing more than a working hypothesis," Ford protested. "Besides, how can I concentrate when you're doing that?"

She leaned back in his arms. "Look, I'll be your Watson, darling. The sooner we get your work finished, the sooner we can go to bed. Summarize the case as you would to Superintendent Brownlee. What have you learned so far?"

Ford groaned theatrically, disengaged from her arms reluctantly, and lit a cigarette.

"How would you start your analysis?" she insisted. "What's the first thing you'd do?"

He struggled to focus his mind on police procedure.

"I'd lay out the basic facts without interpretation, I suppose. One tries to set the scene *prior* to the crime, so that one isn't deceived into post hoc rationalization."

"Good. Begin, if you please."

"But ..."

"Later, Thomas. The night is still young. Now, let's sit at the table and forget what we'd rather be doing. Begin, if you please, my angelic salt-tasting Sherlock."

Ford groaned again, diverted his eyes from Victoria to a pattern of cracks in the ceiling plaster, and tried to concentrate on the case.

"First, what do we know about Lord Pengriffon? He was middle aged. He was wealthy. He was an avid painter. He liked to drink. His marriage was distant but not broken, I should say; they gave each other distance but were still amiable companions, and he drew her as if he loved her."

"So far, so good, Holmes."

"His money, or most of it, is tied up in a trust, so there's no basis for thinking his murderer had a financial motive. His heirs—whoever they are—have nothing to gain that they won't get anyway, and he and Lady Pengriffon had all the money they needed; enough to buy that steam launch, for example. Unless those hidden papers reveal something strange, we'll have to assume this was a crime of passion—of hatred or revenge or something of that sort. Or perhaps, as sometimes happens, the murder was the consequence of some other crime."

"Indubitably, my dear Holmes."

"He had no known enemies," Ford continued, warming to the task. "To the contrary, he was well liked; only Josephine Langley has said anything against him. He stayed close to home, according to Crocker, except for going up to London once a month to visit the gallery that handles his paintings—someone will have to go and take a look at it, I suppose. Apart from that he was here, painting and spending the evenings drinking at the inn. He used his launch as an auxiliary studio, and slept there if he'd had too much to drink."

"He often painted Amy Robsart in the nude," Victoria offered. "At least, she was in the nude, and his state of dress is undetermined. His paintings were passionate panoramas of pulchritudinosity, one might say."

"One might."

"He was having an affair with her, but with his wife's knowledge and tacit approval," Victoria continued. "We know from the equine Miss Langley that she—Amy, that is to say, for fear of confusing you, my angelic Holmes—was pressing his lordship to divorce his wife, and he was refusing, thus setting up a premise for murder most foul. But I fear I'm straying from the ante hoc to the post hoc, and you will regard me with derision; indeed, you may even snort."

"Never, my divine Watson," Ford said. "Derisive snorting is not within the spectrum of authenticated Holmesian expressions. But, to return to the case, almost all murders arise from money, or passion, or in pursuit of another crime. We have no financial motive so far; we know of no other crime, and we do have a motive based on passion. Therefore, we can safely declare Amy Robsart to be Suspect Number One. In addition, she's missing. She didn't leave by train, as you skillfully deduced, and Crocker tells me there is no omnibus service, so she may have left by motorcar, and Pengriffon had no further use for his."

He clicked his fingers in annoyance and stood.

"I stupidly failed to see if his car is by the dock, where Crocker says he usually kept it when he was here in town, or up at Pengriffon Hall. If it's in neither place, we can reasonably suppose she took it. I'd better go and look immediately."

"And I shall accompany you, Holmes, to admire your detective skills and capabilities. Then we can return to the equally important task of ear nibbling."

* * *

Pengriffon's car was not at the dock. She drove him up to Pengriffon Hall in the Humber, with several flawless examples of double-clutching as they went, and they looked round the stable yard and the carriage house in the darkness, but Pengriffon's car was nowhere to be seen. They left again quietly, for fear of disturbing Lady Pengriffon, or, far worse, Victoria's mother.

Victoria pulled off the road above the cliffs. The moon played hide-and-seek behind vaporous clouds, the breeze was warm and soft, and the surf roared far below them.

"If we weren't an old married couple, Thomas, and tired of each other, we might stop in a place like this, and you might seek to inflame my passions."

"And would you yield?"

"I'm certain of it; I'm discovering I'm highly inflammable."

"Are inflammatory initiatives permitted Holmesian activities?"

"Not only permitted, but encouraged."

Back at the inn, Ford steeled himself to concentrate on his duty, to tuck away his emotions and return to the prosaic and unwelcome task of finding his lordship's murderer. He sighed heavily and sat down at the table to examine Lord Pengriffon's wallet.

It contained a few pound notes, still slightly damp from their exposure to the sea.

"That means he wasn't robbed, V. It's another indication that the murderer wanted his death rather than his money."

"I agree, all-wise Sherlock," she said, sitting down across from him.

"What's this?" Ford asked, holding up a piece of folded writing paper. "The ink has run, but it looks to me like a list of painting supplies he needed."

"Let's see. Yes, it's for various shades of oil paints and a large bottle of artist's turpen-smudge."

"What's this one?" Ford asked. "A bill for fuel oil for the *Justicia* ... another bill, this time from a local wine merchant, I think ... this is illegible, unless you can make it out ..."

"A library card, I think, in the name of Lord Clarence Dribble-Splotch." She looked at the small pile of soggy paper. "Is that all, Thomas? How disappointing!"

"It's the humdrum wallet of a man leading a simple life."

"Ho hum. With nothing to hide?"

"An excellent question, my delectable Watson," Ford said. "He hid those accounts in a secret drawer; he loved *trompes l'œil*; let's take a look."

She took the wallet and turned it over, and then began to probe the pockets and flaps with her fingers.

"Now, if *I* were a secret government agent—and of course I can't tell you if I am—my wallet would have a hidden pocket between the back cover and the inside leather lining."

"I see," Ford smiled.

"Indeed," she said, continuing to probe. "I'd probably have to pull a little flap thing, that would be hidden under the main pocket."

"I'm sure you would."

"It would probably be rather like this one."

She pulled something Ford could not see, and a hidden seam opened.

"Good lord, V, you've actually found something!" Ford exclaimed. "You really have!"

She laughed in triumph.

"I must admit I've managed to exceed my own expectations, which is extremely hard to do. Let's see if there's anything inside."

The hidden pocket contained nothing but a torn scrap of paper, on which his lordship had inscribed:

WB IHS 372435

"What does it mean?" she asked, handing it to him. "Is it a cipher, a secret message?"

"I don't know, V. You're the espionage agent."

"But you're Sherlock Holmes. You should be saying, 'Elementary, my dear Watson,' and explaining it."

"He wrote notes to himself," Ford pondered aloud. "Shopping lists, errands to run. Perhaps he had a poor memory. We'll have to ask Lady Pengriffon if he did; or, indeed, if this code means anything to her. I assume it's something he wanted to remember and couldn't be certain that he would."

"WB could be someone's initials," Victoria said. "It could stand for William Brown or Wilhelmina Bogbottom, for example. IHS could be a place, like Ilfracombe High School. Or the whole thing could be an anagram for 'WIBSH.' Or, if you turn it upside down, 'WBIHS' almost turns into 'SHIBM.'"

"Of course, darling!" Ford exclaimed. "I should have thought of that! In the morning I'll telephone Brownlee and ask him to put out an alert for the notorious Mr. Shibm."

"I think that would be wise. The Shibm Kid is best known for robbing stagecoaches, so you should ask Crocker to organize a posse."

"Got it. Alternatively, I could ask Brownlee to give the cipher to the Scotland Yard staff cryptographers."

"How very banal, Holmes!" Victoria groaned. "What do you suppose the numbers 372435 stand for?"

"I have no idea, V. It's not a telephone number."

"Hmm … perhaps, judging by his paintings, it could be Miss Robsart's pulchritudinous measurements—37, 24, 35. I'm bound to say I can't compete."

"What are …" Ford started, and stopped. He was far too shy, and far too new to marriage, to ask such a question.

She grinned.

"We'll have to borrow a measuring tape so that you can make an accurate determination for yourself, darling."

Ford stood, but the piles of unsearched evidence lay scattered on the table between them.

Victoria grimaced. "I hate to ask, but should we look through these account folders, or can we make a fresh start in the morning?"

"I suppose we'd better take a quick look, damn it!" Ford groaned.

"Do you think the papers are important?" she asked.

"They were to Lord Pengriffon."

"Touché, Holmes," she said, and opened the first folder. "Let's see … this is a statement from the trustees, reporting …"

She broke off and whistled. "Wow! I knew they were rich, but the Pengriffon Trust is *filthy* rich, if I might use so coarse a term."

She pushed the document across to him.

"Look, oodles of shares of Great Western Railway stock; oodles more shares in something called G. Binswanger and Company—whatever that is, it seems to be worth a *ton* of money—yet more oodles in South African gold mining … and another page full of odds and ends …"

"G. *Binswanger*?—surely you jest, Watson?"

"No, look, it's right here, Holmes," she said, pointing at the account. "Perhaps it's the name of one of Clara's German sailors, whoever they're supposed to be."

Ford tried unsuccessfully to smile, yawn, and groan at the same time

"Let's get this over with, Watson. You look at the art gallery accounts in this folder, and I'll look at these. See if you can tell what Pengriffon was trying to do with all these scribbled calculations and annotations."

"I would normally grovel to obey, but on this occasion I'll flit downstairs and see if I can persuade my friend Charlie, our worthy host, to give us a pot of coffee."

"But it's past ten o'clock, V. Surely …"

"Did he not say 'at any time'? Besides, Mrs. Charlie may lend me an inch tape."

* * *

Ford discovered an immediate and overpowering urge for coffee, and Victoria departed. He lit another cigarette—he always smoked too much on cases, but he told himself it helped him think—and applied himself to the trustee accounts. His lordship's calculations seemed to bear little relationship to the neatly typed report from Pollock, Pollock & Poole. His lordship had written, for example:

```
5,000
    2.45
    2.5
   20
   100
  122.5

6,000
    2.75
    3
   25
   24
  120
  147
  122.5
   23.5  !!!!!!
```

It had obviously taken hours of laborious effort to produce dozens of these figures, with numerous crossings out and corrections, but why had he done so? Was he calculating alternative investments to discuss with Pollock, Pollock & Poole? Was he questioning their calculations? Ford took a sample investment and calculated the interest due; his own figures matched the trustees' exactly and were lower than Pengriffon's.

He set down the report in frustration, hoping that Pengriffon's work would be self-evident to Scotland Yard's financial experts, and took up the art gallery documents. These proved to be monthly profit and loss statements, which Pengriffon had amended by adding several sales of his own paintings, as if he had wished to make the commercial value of his work seem greater than it was. Thus, for example, he had added the sale of *Nude in Bath IV*, 1922 (AR), for the sum of twenty-three pounds and ten shillings.

Ford struggled once again to find a reason why his lordship would make these amendments, and in secret. Was this some delusional fantasy of success? If so, was the easy-going, well-liked Pengriffon of entirely sound mind?

Victoria returned with a pot of coffee, milk, sugar, and biscuits.

She poured him a cup and stood leaning over his shoulder to see the accounts.

"Any progress, O mighty Holmes?"

"I fear not. I'm not an accountant or a stockbroker, nor yet a trustee or art gallery proprietor. I've learned the hard way to leave expert analysis to the experts, although they may drag this out for days, and I do not wish this investigation to drag out. Besides, I can't concentrate with you leaning over me like that."

"Do you wish me to move?"

"No."

"Let's see," she said, leaning even farther forward. "'*Nude in Bath IV*, 1922 (AR) £23/10/—'. This, my dear Holmes, refers to a painting depicting either the fourth rendition of a nude in a bath or a nude in a public bathing establishment, in cubicle number four, sold for the sum of twenty three pounds and ten shillings—the painting, one assumes, rather than the naked woman."

"Perhaps I may snort in derision after all."

"AR undoubtedly refers to the pulchritudinous Amy Robsart."

"Agreed."

"I must say, Thomas, in all seriousness, that he used the same numbers over and over. He took numbers from the gallery and calculated them on the PP&P accounts, or vice versa."

"What? Let me see. By Jove—you're right, V! £23/10/ is 23.5 pounds! How clever of you to notice that, and how extraordinary. What the *hell* was he doing?"

He closed his eyes and ran his fingers through his hair in a futile attempt to understand his lordship's work—or, indeed, his lordship. Lady Pengriffon said he was uninterested in money, and yet he had labored over these accounts. Everyone liked him, from the fishermen on the wharf to Dr. Anderson, and yet he had treated Amy Robsart shabbily. His art suggested he painted to express beauty, or, in the case of his *trompes l'œil*, for fun, and yet he apparently craved commercial success and invented imaginary sales to bolster his ego.

His study and his boat were those of a man Ford felt he would have liked, a man exulting in his talents and squeezing every ounce of fun and life out of every day. Yet here was evidence of a crabbed soul, a rich man chafing over pennies, and he seemed to have been an exploiter of young women, dangling promises without fulfilling them.

"I thought I was going to like him, V, but now I'm not so sure." Ford waved his hand vaguely at the papers scattered across the desk. "Recalculated accounts, fraudulent sales of paintings, making Amy Robsart's life so much of a misery she couldn't stand it any more."

"Yes, I see what you mean," she said. "On the other hand, I *did* know him, and he was a good man, I promise you."

"I hope so, V. I always hate it when the victim deserves to die."

She yawned, and Ford found himself yawning too.

"Have you finally done enough to call it a night, Holmes? Is your conscience clear?"

"I have, and it is."

"In that case, Holmes, you can revert to being my adored Thomas," she said, yawning again. "I'm sorry. All this sleuthing and driving and double-clutching, and one thing and another, has exhausted me."

Ford hesitated and then asked, "You didn't happen to run into Mrs. Charlie by any chance, did you, V?"

"As a matter of fact, I did," she replied.

Five

The Ancient Mariner must be an early riser, Ford thought, for he was already in his customary seat outside the inn when Ford emerged to sniff the morning air.

"Good morning," Ford said, and almost added, "thou bright-eyed ancient man."

"That it is," the mariner replied, with a nod of his head.

Ford stretched, lit his first cigarette of the day, and glanced round the sparkling harbor. Several of the fishing boats were absent, he noted, and reminded himself to ask someone why commercial fishing seemed to be a nocturnal activity. Did fish get sleepy or fail to see the net in dark waters?

Farther out in the placid surface of the harbor the *Justicia* floated at her buoy, her white hull gleaming and her brass funnel flashing in the morning sun. It would be wonderful to own a boat like that, he thought idly. He and Victoria could wander up and down the coast, sunning themselves indolently each day and anchoring in a different harbor each night. He would buy a peaked cap with an anchor embroidered on it, just like the Ancient Mariner's, and puff a yellowed corncob pipe, and he'd sit in the wheelhouse and yell obscure nautical commands to Victoria, such as "avast" and "hard-a-lee," whatever they meant, and Victoria, delightfully decked out in a negligible swimming costume, would scurry to obey.

All he would have to do to make the dream come true was to resign his job as a policeman and go and do whatever it was one did in a stock brokerage or a merchant bank in the narrow, crooked streets of the City of London, and thereby become rich enough to afford a steam launch like *Justicia*.

In the world of financial and professional reality, however, he had a murder case to solve. He shook his head to clear it of delusions of grandeur and sat down at one of the tables to finish his cigarette.

He'd start his morning with a telephone call to Brownlee, to see if anyone at Scotland Yard could decipher Pengriffon's secret code, and to make sure the two sets of accounts sent up by train had been delivered. He'd also ask Brownlee to send someone to the offices of the trustees, Pollock, Pollock & Poole, and to the L'Arte Moderne gallery.

Ford hesitated. What exactly would Brownlee's men be looking for? They'd have to probe for a reason that his lordship had spent hours—in secret—scribbling calculations and penning exasperated question marks. They'd have to contrast his image of Pengriffon—dynamic, jovial, and yet secretive—with whatever impression the lawyers and art gallery managers gave. But anyone Brownlee sent would have no sense of Pengriffon as a man, and a deeply depressing thought struck Ford. Perhaps he'd have to go up to London himself, thereby shattering any remaining hope that his honeymoon had not been irreversibly ruined.

After telephoning Brownlee, it would be time to meet Sergeant Croft at the railway station, who had been traveling all night toward Trethgarret. After bringing him up to date, what should he give Croft as his highest priority? Should he search Pengriffon's study in more detail, or the *Justicia?* Or should he focus on finding Amy Robsart, or his lordship's car, if they were not together?

Ford had a list of new questions for Lady Pengriffon, but visiting Pengriffon Hall probably meant another confrontation with Lady Canderblank, and Ford blanched at the prospect. And it wouldn't hurt to talk to Josephine Langley for a second time, since she was pivotal to establishing Amy Robsart's motive—assuming, of course, that a good night's sleep had calmed her down. Perhaps he'd better check with the harried Dr. Anderson before talking to her. Then he had to obtain a nautical chart and get the fishermen to explain exactly what were the Little Dogs, and the prevailing currents and tides. Was any one particular spot of sea floor preferable to any other as a burial place?

Were the trustees also the solicitors, and would they have a copy of Pengriffon's will? Who would inherit the title? Then there was Mr. Crutchfield, who kept Lord Pengriffon's local accounts for his farms and the tin mines. He still hadn't had time to examine Pengriffon's body. Had he missed some vital clue on his person or in his clothes? Then there was …

"It's a puzzlement, right enough," the Ancient Mariner chuckled, and Ford jumped.

"Oh, sorry," Ford said. "I was miles away."

"That you were," the old man replied. The Ancient Mariner had the trick of certainty, Ford noticed, and found himself, bizarrely, envying him. Ford looked at him more closely; the old man might be physically frail, Ford decided, but he still seemed to have all his mental faculties.

"I should have introduced myself," Ford said. "My name is Thomas Ford, from Scotland Yard."

"I be Jebediah Ham," the mariner replied. "I've seen thee about with Mrs. Ford, these past few days."

He chuckled again, and his chuckle managed to communicate his approval of Victoria.

He'd been in the background of Frank's photograph of her, Ford recalled. He was a fixture, a part of the frontage of the inn, like the bright window boxes crowded with red geraniums and trailing ivy, and the whitewashed walls and black window shutters, and one's eye registered his presence but did not remark upon it—an old curmudgeon dozing in the sun, with just enough energy to totter into the bar for a pint of scrumpy every now and then.

He spoke with the soft, slow, buzzing murmur of the Cornish dialect, an accent so gentle it was almost like the contented purring of a cat. "Ize zeen thee a-boot with Mizziz Foo-ard." It was an accent that outsiders often made fun of, foolishly imagining that Cornishmen were a little slow on the uptake and a trifle soft in the head.

"Mr. Ham, you said last night that Amy Robsart did not kill Lord Pengriffon, that she doesn't have it in her. Do you know her well?"

"I know her well enough to know her character." He paused, gathering his breath for a longer statement. "Every few weeks some kindly soul decides I'm dying, and takes me up to the cottage hospital. She's the one to care for me. She's as gentle as a kitten."

"Did you see her the night his lordship died?"

"I did."

"What was she doing?"

"She rode her bicycle along the dock and around to the jetty near his lordship's launch." A boney finger extended itself toward the railway wharf. "There she went."

"Are you sure it was her?"

"I am."

"It was dark, Mr. Ham, and the dock is unlit at night. It could have been another woman." He was too polite to suggest the Ancient Mariner's eyesight might be failing.

The Ancient Mariner chuckled.

"Not with those fine long legs and not with those grand bosoms. No man would mistake her."

Ford found that he was chuckling, too.

"I see."

It was absolutely contrary to all his principles to discuss an ongoing case with a bystander, but, for some completely illogical reason, the Ancient Mariner did not seem to count. He was a fixture, part of the landscape, like the lighthouse above the harbor wall and the perpetually fussing railway locomotive.

"I have yet to find anyone who benefits from his death, Mr. Ham, and I have no physical evidence. We don't even know for sure where the crime was committed."

"The net brought up his lordship. Perhaps there's more to be found."

It was almost like having a conversation with Brownlee, Ford thought.

"I'd ask myself what else might be down there, if I was thee, which I'm not," the old man said.

"You mean …"

"Divers, that's who's needed."

The Ancient Mariner's train of thought was completely logical, Ford thought. Many a murder had been solved because of evidence found with the body—but surely not in sixty feet of water?

"Can divers operate in those depths, Mr. Ham?"

"Those depths, and twice as deep; there's navy divers at Plymouth, Mr. Ford."

"Well, Mr. Ham, you've been very helpful," Ford said, stubbing out his cigarette and rising. "I'll think about what you said."

"That thee will, Mr. Ford."

Ford glanced across the harbor, to the *Justicia* and the railway dock beyond it, where the ladies had seen Amy Robsart, his lordship's car, and—if Clara was to be believed—a loitering German sailor. A thought struck him, and he turned back to the Ancient Mariner.

"Did you happen to see his lordship's car that night, Mr. Ham? It's missing."

"That I did; it came past here nigh to midnight."

"Was his lordship driving it?"

"He was not," the Ancient Mariner replied with absolute certainty.

"Did you see who was?"

"'Twas a man; no one I recognized. I'd know him if I saw him."

His lordship left the inn about nine, and Amy Robsart was waiting by the dock ... say it took an hour for a final argument and for her to kill him ... the fishermen had said it was five miles to the Little Dogs; an hour there and an hour back, perhaps? ... three hours in all, and then her getaway in his lordship's car. Yes, the timeframe worked.

"It couldn't have been Amy Robsart, could it, Mr. Ham?"

"Only if she'd turned into a man, Mr. Ford, and that would be a rare pity."

The Ancient Mariner adjusted his position, raised his deeply bronzed face to the morning sun, and closed his eyes.

* * *

Ford strolled along to the police station and found Crocker and George Thompson emerging from it.

"Good morning, gentlemen," Ford said, glancing round the harbor. "It's such a marvelous view. I envy you seeing this every morning."

"It'll be a better view when that launch is gone," Thompson muttered. "I hope Lady Pengriffon sells her."

"You mean the *Justicia* might detract from the holiday trade, because she was Pengriffon's launch?" Ford asked, remembering Thompson's comments about the local economy.

"No, I mean it's a capitalist eyesore, an aristocrat's toy, an example of conspicuous consumption that's offensive to the working men of England."

Ford wondered if the *Justicia* was offensive to the working men who had earned their living building the launch, but he did not express that thought.

"Well, George," Crocker said, "don't go forgetting his lordship took all the miners out for a day of fishing, with sandwiches and scrumpy and all sorts, and a ten bob note for the biggest fish. It was Harry ..."

"I've never been aboard her, never will," Thompson interrupted, as if this proved his case. "There's principle at stake; just wait for the next general election for parliament, and then we'll see."

"Anything new this morning, Crocker?" Ford asked, if only to lighten the mood.

"Not since last night, no, sir," Crocker replied.

"Jebediah Ham says he saw someone driving his lordship's car past the Duke at about midnight. I'll need to ask you to check if anyone else saw it."

"Got it, sir," Crocker said. "If it came past the Duke from the dock, it was likely headed past here and up the High Street. I'll go door to door."

"It must have been Amy Robsart, making her getaway," Thompson said.

"Mr. Ham says the driver was a man."

"The man's an old fool. He's lost touch with reality," Thompson snorted. "He makes up stories; it's sad, really, because he really believes them."

"He sees remarkably well for his ..." Crocker began in the Ancient Mariner's defense, but Thompson overrode him.

"For example, he's convinced he fought in the battle of Balaclava in the Crimean War—you know, the Valley of Death and the Thin Red Line, and all that. But, of course, he was never in the army."

"I see," said Ford. "Does he claim to have been in the army?"

"No. That's what makes it so pathetic. He was in the Royal Marines, or so he says."

"Mr. Crutchfield walks his dog every evening at about that time," Crocker said. "I'll ask him if ..."

"You're wasting your time there, too," Thompson interrupted again. "That man's word isn't worth the breath it takes for him to say it."

"Is that the Mr. Crutchfield who keeps the Pengriffon estate's books?" Ford asked.

"Chartered accountant—licensed busybody, if you ask me," Thompson growled. He made a show of examining his fob watch. "Well, you may have time to waste, but I do not. There's work to be done, for those with eyes to see it."

He strode off in the direction of the harbor, with a tiny jingle of fob medallions, and Crocker shook his head mournfully.

"I'm not sure we can rely on what Mr. Thompson says about Mr. Crutchfield, I'm afraid, sir, nor vice versa."

"Why not, Crocker?"

"Well, they're not exactly on speaking terms, I'm afraid, sir."

"Why not?"

"Well, it began over the church Christmas tree, sir, and it's been going on ever since—it's got to be five years or more, by now. They're both church wardens, and how the vicar can manage with two wardens at daggers drawn is a miracle."

Ford recalled from his childhood that the affairs of a parish church were managed by a group of churchgoers known as the church council, which was led by two officials, called church wardens. One, the vicar's warden, was appointed by the vicar and represented his interests; the other, the people's warden, was elected by the congregation and represented the parishioners.

"There was a dispute over a Christmas tree. Mr. Crutchfield wanted a tree inside the church, lit by candles on Christmas Eve, same as always, like, but Mr. Thompson wanted a much larger tree outside the church, all lit up by electrical lighting in the branches, same as they do in big towns. He said it would be good for Trethgarret and help to put us on the map."

"The council sort of divided into rival parties, if you know what I mean, just like the House of Commons. The vicar tried to smooth it over by saying we'd have two trees, one inside and one out."

"That didn't solve the problem?"

"I'm afraid not, sir. George Thompson made a big palaver out of his tree, and half the town turned out on Christmas Eve to see the lights turned on. George even got a newspaper person to come, so there'd be a story about it in the Penzance newspaper."

Crocker scratched his head as if to stir his memory.

"Anyway, to cut a long story short, Mr. Thompson went to turn the lights on and there was a big bang, and the electrical fuse box caught on fire, and the power went off in the houses all round the church, even as far as halfway up the High Street. His lordship was there, and he said something funny about George creating an electrifying event, and everyone laughed at George."

Crocker chuckled at the memory.

"It took days for the county to mend the damage, and no one had electricity for cooking their dinners on Christmas Day. Then George came into the Duke and accused Mr. Crutchfield of sabotaging the church fuse box, and Mr. Crutchfield denied it and said George was too big for his boots, which is true, although someone's got to worry about the sewers and such, when all's said and done, and they haven't spoken since."

And thus trivial disputes harden into bitter feuds, Ford thought, like the Montagues and the Capulets in *Romeo and Juliet*.

"Then, of course, there's the elections," Crocker said, warming to his theme.

"The elections, Crocker?"

"Well, George Thompson is a member of the Labor Party—socialism and trades unions and all that, and the rights of the common man, if you know what I mean, sir—and Mr. Crutchfield's the secretary of the local Conservatives. George says there'll be a Labor government for the first time, with that chap Ramsey McDonald as prime minister." He gazed out over the harbor and shook his head. "I never saw the point of it, myself, sir, politics, to tell you the truth, all the back-and-forth and arguing and whatnot. Life's what it is, and you just get on with it."

Ford, who considered all politicians to be knaves and vagabonds, could not have agreed more, but discussing politics with Crocker did not contribute to the task of nailing down the case against Amy Robsart, and thus being able to give his undivided attention to Victoria.

"Well, let's see if we can find someone else who saw his lordship's car on Sunday night, Crocker."

"Got it, sir."

* * *

Ford returned to the Duke, where he began the laborious process of seeking a telephone connection all the way across southern England to London. Could he rely on the Ancient Mariner's testimony? Every sentence that issued from his mouth was declarative, Ford thought. In response to, "Good morning," for example, the old man had responded, "That it is."

Unfortunately, while Ford believed the old man believed he had seen Amy Robsart on the night of the murder, Ford was not certain he really had. Could one trust the eyesight of a man in his eighties, or however old he was, with a pint or two of scrumpy in his belly? Would his testimony stand up in court against the rapier thrusts of an experienced barrister? He shuddered as he imagined the scene.

"If I understand you correctly, Mr. Ham," Ford imagined his cross-examining lawyer saying, "it was dark, and you claim you recognized the young lady not from her facial features, as one might expect, but from the size and shape of—I apologize to the court, M'lord, but my point is apposite—her *bosoms?*"

"That I did."

"Are we to conclude that you were more familiar with those particular ... er ... *attributes*, if I may put it that way, than with her face, Mr. Ham, particularly at night?"

"No, I was not."

"Then, Mr. Ham, we will have to leave it to the jury to assess the verisimilitude of your, one must say, *unusual* contention."

Still, if the Ancient Mariner was to be believed, his evidence was crucial, for Josephine Langley had provided a motive, and now the old man had put her at the scene of the crime at the critical time, in support of the housewives, Clara and Mabel. A lawyer for Amy Robsart's defense might be able to persuade the jury to dismiss the testimony of one witness to her presence, but not three. If Croft found her fingerprints on the launch controls, then ...

On the other hand, who had been driving his lordship's motorcar? Had it simply been stolen, or had the Ancient Mariner's eyes deceived him, and he'd mistaken the shadowed features of the driver as it passed by?

Ford's train of thought was interrupted by a series of sharp clicking sounds from the telephone, followed by a cockney voice saying, "You're through, sir," followed by Brownlee's voice bellowing, "*Is that you, Ford?*"

"Good morning, sir," Ford said, removing the earpiece several inches away.

"*Pengriffon was well regarded*," Brownlee yelled at his customary volume, without preliminaries. "I've never heard of anyone so well-liked. And his reputation as an artist was growing. Came up to London every few weeks, did a round of the galleries and exhibitions—and most of the pubs in central London, I gather—stayed at the Combined Services Club, saw a few friends, and went home again."

A brief silence followed. Brownlee must be pausing for tea to ease the strain he was putting on his vocal chords.

"I've given the accounts you sent us to the Bank of England chaps that help us out in fraud cases; we'll see what they have to say."

"Thank you, sir, and I could use some help on another puzzle." Ford described Victoria's discovery of the *WB IHS 372435* cipher, and Brownlee undertook to present it to the code breakers whose services Scotland Yard retained.

"Now, sir, I have a possible suspect," Ford continued. "I have a motive and proximity to the probable crime scene."

Brownlee was silent as Ford summarized the potential case against Amy Robsart, and Ford pictured him sitting with his eyes closed as he listened, as he always did when concentrating.

"Well, Ford, old chap, it's circumstantial, but it's a good start. We'll send out a general enquiry and track her down. There's a good chance she'll confess. These sorts of crimes of passion often turn out that way, as you know, and we won't have to prove it to a jury. I'll take care of it from this end; besides, if she fled the scene, she's more likely to be here than there."

"Thank you, sir."

"What about the trustees and the gallery? Want me to follow up on that?"

Ford hesitated. "On balance," he said finally, "I'd better come up to London and do it myself; I don't know what I'm looking for ..."

"Aren't you on your honeymoon, old chap?"

"I've decided to get this over as fast as possible, sir."

"Ah, yes, honeymoonus interruptus—I remember it all too well. In any case, you'll have to come up to interview Amy Robsart, when we find her."

"True, sir. I'll plan to come up on the night train, and there's plenty for Croft to do here while I'm gone."

"Very well, Ford. I'll see you tomorrow. Give my regards to your wife—if she's still speaking to you." A loud chuckle issued from the telephone, followed by silence.

* * *

"I *am* still speaking to you, darling," Victoria said, entering the office in time to hear Brownlee's fortissimo closing remarks. "I am, however, somewhat perturbed to hear that you are forsaking me after a mere three days and three nights."

"Darling, the sooner I can close this case the sooner ..."

"I understand completely, Thomas," she interrupted him. "I'm sure all men leave their wives in pursuit of a more pulchritudinous alternative after three whole days. My allure has faded. Familiarity has bred contempt. I am being abandoned, cast aside, spurned, rejected and discarded, with no more thought than a worn-out pair of socks. I have been weighed in the pulchritude scales and found wanting—only by a mere inch, as you determined last night, but I accept that an inch is pulchritudinarily significant. I must accept my fate as best I can; I shall therefore retire to a nunnery and contemplate a chaste eternity."

"But ..."

"Before I get me to a nunnery, however, I shall make one final attempt, one last stand, to rekindle the fires that once burned so brightly. I will call it Operation Phoenix, incidentally, and it will consist of nine phases. I'll give you an overview as we walk to the railway station to meet the Crofts."

She led him from the inn, and they turned toward the High Street.

"Phase One of Operation Phoenix will also be known by the code name Ignition," she continued, and took his arm with both hands, a sort of sideways hug, a gesture of public affection that Ford found delightful. "It requires the skills of an expert gymnast, but, fortunately, I am a virtuoso. Imagine yourself, if you will, to be a vaulting horse, and I ..."

Dr. Anderson hurried toward them along High Street.

"Good morning, Doctor," Victoria said, breaking off her description.

Ford was sure that the doctor would have rushed past them without breaking stride, had it not been for her irresistible smile.

"Oh, Mrs. Ford, Chief Inspector, good morning," he said as he paused, consulting his wristwatch. "I didn't see you. Please don't think me rude, but I have no time—no time at all. It's chaos up at the cottage hospital with two nurses missing. My wife's filling in, as best she can, and I'll sleep there tonight, but even so ..."

"How many nurses are there?" Victoria asked.

"There're five." He broke into a rapid-fire explanation of their working hours. "They work twelve-hour shifts. One works from midnight to noon, the second from noon to midnight, and the other two alternate between six in the morning and six in the evening, so there are always two on duty. Then the fifth nurse takes odd shifts, so they can take a longer break and rotate their shifts on a two-weekly basis. But Josephine Langley couldn't work for her six o'clock night shift last night, and Amy Robsart is again missing for her six o'clock day shift, so everything's at sixes and sevens, if you follow me."

"I see," Victoria said, looking somewhat dazed. "It must be difficult to manage when you're so short-staffed."

"That's not the worst of it," Anderson continued, perhaps relieved to have a sympathetic audience for his troubles. "Mrs. Granger needs to have her appendix out today—not tomorrow, but *today*. If she doesn't, I fear peritonitis might set in, and that's often fatal. But Mildred, my wife, isn't a trained operating room nurse, and I really don't want to put Mrs. Granger in a jolting ambulance all the way to Penzance—her appendix might burst at any moment."

Ford saw that Victoria was thinking the same thought as his own.

"Look, Doctor," she said, "I haven't nursed since the war, but if you're in a crisis ..."

"Would you *really?*" Anderson asked immediately, like a drowning man clutching for a rope.

"I'll be very rusty, but I worked in a field emergency hospital behind the front lines in France."

"*Thank you*, Mrs. Ford," Anderson said, his expression clearing from worry to urgency. "That would be *incredibly* helpful. Look, my car's parked just over there. We'll ride up to the hospital together. We'll leave at once—there's not a moment to lose."

Ford thought that the doctor would have seized Victoria and carried her to the car, had she not turned in that direction.

"Good-bye, darling. I still love you," she called over her shoulder. Ford, suddenly feeling very lonely, continued up the hill to the railway station. As he walked, he wondered what she would do once he had positioned himself as if he were a vaulting horse.

* * *

An antique tank engine, resplendent in brass fittings and green livery, and drawing two elderly railway carriages, chuffed ponderously into view and clanked to a stately halt at Trethgarret railway station. It emitted a loud hiss of excess steam as if sighing in relief. Ford watched as a smattering of passengers alighted, and he spotted Sergeant and Mrs. Croft emerging from the last carriage. He hurried toward them.

Sergeant Croft was his solid professional foundation, his anchor, his rock of Gibraltar—always patient, always pleasant, always thoughtful. Now he was taking off his hat to run his fingers through his closely cropped, iron-gray hair, and looking eagerly about him, his chin slightly uplifted to sniff the salt sea breeze. With Brownlee as his boss, and Croft as his assistant, Ford considered himself to be a truly fortunate man.

Mrs. Ford was her husband's complement, just as tenacious and competent in her own way, and without a single ounce of meanness in her entire buxom frame. She had found a wide-brimmed straw hat, encircled by a garland of silk rosebuds, to celebrate the occasion.

"I'm delighted to see you both," Ford beamed as he approached.

"Well, sir, you shouldn't be," Mrs. Croft answered, with a pretty smile that the passing years had not eroded. "Not on your honeymoon, at any rate. And how is the new Mrs. Ford?"

"We were both on our way to meet you when the local doctor

scooped her up to help out at the hospital," Ford said. "They have a staffing crisis and Victoria volunteered."

He shook Croft's powerful hand. "Welcome to Trethgarret, Croft—to both of you. Here, let me help you with those suitcases."

"Nonsense, sir," Croft said, and picked up all four of them as if they were as light as feathers.

"We booked a room for you at the inn. We're staying there as well, until this mess gets sorted out; our cottage is a bit remote."

"Look, if there's a shortage at the hospital, perhaps I can help out too," Mrs. Croft said. "Many hands make light work. Perhaps I can do a little cooking."

Ford considered Betty Croft to be absolutely, beyond question, the finest cook in all England.

"If you cook, all the patients will put on twenty pounds and refuse to go home, Mrs. Croft," he said.

"Oh no, sir, don't be silly! I'll just do something light and healthy. I'm sure they have fresh fish in a village like this. Dover sole sautéed in butter and lemon juice, for example, with some chives and parsley and perhaps some finely chopped shallots to give it more flavor, and lightly steamed asparagus to give the poor dears their roughage, with a cold cucumber consommé to start—that's very healthy—and then something tasty to finish, like a custard tart, or a raspberry jelly. And then I should do something more substantial for dinner to build up their strength—a nice rack of lamb, or a beef Wellington, or something like that, with a lobster bisque to start. I'll just do simple things like that, sir."

"Then I fear I may fall sick and have to go into the hospital myself," Ford grinned.

"Not on your honeymoon, sir; you've got better things to do," she said with a smile. "Now, I'll ask inside the station for directions to the hospital. You two go ahead and get started with your investigations, and Mrs. Ford and I'll find you later. Go on, now, off with you!"

She bustled through the station door. Croft shook his head at her departing back.

"She'll never change, sir," he said with a bemused smile. "And thank God she won't."

Croft, under pressure, handed Ford the lightest suitcase, and they walked down the High Street to the harbor and the Duke of Cornwall.

Croft stood for a moment, drinking in the scene. Then they entered the inn, and Ford introduced him to Charlie, who relieved them of their burdens. Ford asked for coffee and sandwiches and they went back outside to sit in the sun.

"Mr. Ham—this is Mr. Croft, my partner in crime," he called over to the Ancient Mariner, still seated at his habitual table, and the old man raised his glass in solemn greeting.

"Well, Croft, we almost have a case," he said. "Let me give you a summary while we eat. Cheers, incidentally, and welcome to Trethgarret!"

"Thank you sir, although what Betty said is right—it's not fair to have your holiday upset like this." He lifted his cup. "Cheers!"

"Wait until you taste the local brew, Sergeant. It's something else, I assure you!" He lit a cigarette. "Now, let me tell you what I've done so far."

Ford talked for fifteen minutes while Croft listened intently, writing notes in his battered leather notebook. There was something infinitely comfortable in Croft's presence, Ford thought. The world became more ... more manageable; the case ceased to be a random collection of facts and conjecture, and transformed itself into a logical process, a purposeful journey toward an orderly conclusion.

"Don't forget to eat, sir," Croft said when Ford had finished. "So, if I follow you, our hypothesis is that Amy Robsart killed Lord Pengriffon in a fit of rage, because he wouldn't leave Lady Pengriffon. Two nights ago she followed him onboard his launch—that's the one, sir, I assume, anchored, or, I should say, *moored* over there—and strangled him with his own tie. He was drunk, so he wouldn't have put up much of a fight. Then she took him out to sea and dropped him over the side."

"Exacthly, Croth," Ford mumbled, his mouth full of ham and cheese sandwich.

"Well, now, let's see, sir," Croft said, checking his notes methodically. "We have motive, jealous rage, per Miss Langley, with whom she shares a cottage. We have means, the tie she could have used to strangle him. We have opportunity, per Mr. Ham and the ladies who saw her by the dock on Monday night waiting for him."

He paused to drain his coffee.

"So, what we need, sir, is physical evidence she was on the launch and took it out to sea." He glanced out toward the harbor entrance, defined on one side by the lighthouse and on the other by the church. "Perhaps there was another witness, although it was dark, who saw the boat leaving the harbor."

"Good point, Croft; we'll get Crocker, the local constable, to ask around for someone out on the harbor mole at that time—or even the lighthouse keeper."

"If she was acting out of anger, sir, on the spur of the moment, she probably didn't take a lot of precautions. Her fingerprints may be on the wheel and the engine controls, or even on the hatch covers. They'd need to be fresh ones, because we can assume she'd been on the launch before. I brought the fingerprint equipment. I hope I won't make a hash of it. We can get her prints off something at her cottage and match them to something on the launch, and we've got a case."

"Exactly, Croft. More coffee?"

Croft gazed out at the beauty of the harbor while Ford went inside to refill their cups. He returned, offered Croft a cigarette, and lit another one himself.

"Very well, then, Croft; I'd like you to go over the launch, the *Justicia*, and see what you can see. The most likely murder scene is the cabin—don't bang your head, incidentally—and we need to know who drove it, er, *took her helm*, last. I'll introduce you to Crocker, the local copper, and he'll take you out there."

"Right, sir."

"Crocker's a good chap, but he's never been involved in anything like this."

"Nor had I, sir, before I met you."

"True," Ford said with a smile, remembering Croft as a village policeman, deep in the heart of the bucolic Cotswold Hills, where a crime wave consisted of the theft of more than one chicken in a month.

"In the meantime, I'll go back to Pengriffon Hall and see if Lady Justicia can explain his lordship's hidden calculations and the weird cipher I told you about. I also need to find out more about who inherits the trust and the title. Theoretically, that person also has a motive."

"They have no children, sir?"

"No direct heirs, I understand. I'll also stop at the cottage on the way back to fetch something with Amy Robsart's fingerprints, and get a more complete statement from Miss Langley."

"Right, sir," Croft agreed, and leaned back, his face tilted to the sun. "What a spot! Superintendent Brownlee said we could stay on for a holiday when this is over. Do you think Amy Robsart really did it?"

"Well, Croft, I'm leaning in that direction, although it's early days yet. It would have worked very well if the trawler hadn't caught his body so quickly. He would have simply disappeared. She went back to London, or wherever she came from, and no one would have been the wiser. Oh, we have to find his car, incidentally. It's missing, and one assumes she took it to get away."

"But you're not convinced, sir?"

"The key to this case seems to be that the body was buried at sea. The murderer didn't want anyone to know what had happened to Lord Pengriffon. With no body there'd have been no crime."

"She wouldn't even have needed an alibi, sir."

"Very true, Croft. But I'll be a lot happier when we find her, and she confesses."

Six

Ford glanced about warily as he followed the footman through the hallways of Pengriffon Hall, for fear his mother-in-law would suddenly leap from behind a pillar with a battle cry of, "Aha, Forté, I demand you leave this establishment *immediately!*"

He found that he was tiptoeing like a child playing hide-and-seek, fervently wishing that the footman's shoes did not make such sharp rapping sounds on the marble floors. Alfred, Lord Tennyson rose unbidden in his mind:

> ... and all to left and right
> The bare black cliff clanged round him, as he based
> His feet on juts of slippery crag that rang
> Sharp-smitten with the dint of arméd heels

"Detective Chief Inspector Ford," the footman announced, and Ford was abruptly transported from the dying moments of King Arthur Pendragon to Lady Pengriffon's sitting room.

"Do come in and sit down," she said. "Perhaps you'd like a cup of tea? And please feel free to smoke, if you wish."

Ford looked round the room carefully, but—to his infinite relief—Lady Canderblank was nowhere to be seen.

"Thank you, Lady Justicia," he said, "That's very kind of you. How are you feeling today?"

"Well, the shock's worn off a little, I suppose, and now I feel I'm suspended in a sort of vacuum. I keep waiting for him to come through the door."

"That's what my mother used to say, when my father died."

It struck Ford that both he and Lady Pengriffon were completely different people without Lady Canderblank's malevolent presence.

"How long did that last, may I ask?" Lady Pengriffon asked as she poured tea.

"Oh, I think it took a year or so for her to get used to it. He was killed on the Western Front, and I think the end of the war was difficult for her, because he didn't come home with everyone else."

He remembered when he and his father had set off to war together. His mother had kissed them both at the garden gate and made them promise to come back safely, as Ford supposed all mothers do. She had been waiting at the gate years later when he returned, on crutches, and alone.

"She remarried recently, as a matter of fact, Lady Pengriffon. She was a widow for—let me see—six years. Now she says she cherishes her memories and enjoys her new life."

"She sounds like a very sensible woman, if I may say so. Sugar, Mr. Ford? One lump or two?"

"One, thank you," Ford said, rising to take the cup. "I have to say, Lady Justicia, that the worst part of my job is bothering people when they shouldn't be bothered."

"Oh, I quite understand; please ask away. I'd rather be talked to than cosseted. I've noticed that my visitors all whisper to me; it's really very silly, and I can't hear what they're saying. Anyway, what would you like to know?"

"Thank you. Well, to begin, who is Lord Pengriffon's heir?"

"Clarence's sister's boy, James, is the heir to the title," she said. "He's lived in Australia for quite some time, since before the war. He has a sheep station—I believe that's the correct term. Lady Canderblank has been kind enough to go into Trethgarret to send him a telegram."

Ah, Ford thought, that explains the calm.

"And so the proceeds of the trust will pass to him?"

"Oh, yes, I'm sure of it."

"Lady Justicia, when I was looking through your husband's study yesterday, I found these accounts. As you can see, he'd done a lot of calculations on them."

Ford handed her the financial statements covered with Pengriffon's computations, and she held them at arm's length to bring them into focus.

"Goodness!" she said. "I have no idea why he ... this isn't like him ..."

Ford watched her closely and was convinced her surprise was genuine.

"As I told you yesterday, Mr. Ford, he took no interest in financial matters. I can't think why ..." Her voice faded away uncertainly.

"He mentioned no problems with the accounts, or any other financial matters?"

"No, the trust is like a machine that produces a nice check every quarter, and the gallery is doing well and his paintings are selling for ridiculous amounts of money. There are no financial problems with the estate, I'm sure."

She shook her head, perhaps at the complexities of financial matters, or perhaps at her own good fortune.

"The tin mines are in decline, but so are everybody's, and I think they still break even, as I believe businessmen say, so he was thinking of closing them before things got any worse, and finding other employment for the men. Something to do with radios, I believe. He was very keen on radio communications, and he worked on them in the war. He'd gone so far as to interview a manager, a young man named Carter, or Carpenter, or something of the sort. He was going to make his mind up this week. Mr. Thompson was very much put out, I'm afraid."

"Well, we'll keep looking into these accounts, Lady Justicia. In any case, it may have nothing to do with his death."

"Quite so," she said, turning the pages over as if Pengriffon had written an explanation on their backs. "I wonder if, perhaps, it was all part of a complicated practical joke. No, no, that's as silly as it sounds."

"I had the very same thought, Lady Justicia, but I can't make sense of it." He paused to take a sip of tea, and asked, as gently as he could, "How will you live now, if I may ask?"

"Oh, Clarence's will leaves me well provided for, I assure you," she said. "I'll get money from the estate and the mines as long as I live. Mr. Crutchfield can doubtless tell you exactly how much I have, to the nearest ha'penny. I think I'll probably build a little house on the cliffs;

it's silly to rattle around here in this mansion, and, besides, it belongs to James now, and he's welcome to it."

Ford remained convinced she was speaking the truth.

"There's one other puzzle, if I may?" he said, and showed her the scrap of paper from his wallet."

She was just as perplexed with the cipher as with the accounts.

"I can't think of anyone we know whose initials are WB, or IHS, I'm afraid."

Tears filled her eyes, and she dabbed them with a lace handkerchief. "I'm afraid I didn't know him as well as I should ... I feel so guilty ... perhaps we were too distant ..."

"On the contrary, Lady Justicia, if I may say so," Ford said, and gave her the sheaf of Pengriffon's charcoal drawings of her. "I also found these hidden away. I was struck by the overwhelming sense of love they communicate."

She examined them carefully, and Ford was again convinced she'd never seen them. He glanced away as more tears appeared, and he waited until he heard the sound of her blowing her nose.

"That's really very kind of you Mr. Ford," she said finally. "You know, you're really not at all like the man Lady Deborah describes; you are, in fact, precisely the kind of man I'd expect Victoria to fall in love with, and for extremely good reason."

"Lady Canderblank is doing what she thinks is best for her daughter," Ford said, astonished to be defending his mother-in-law.

"Perhaps, but even so ... well, she's being very helpful to me, with all the arrangements, but I *wish* she wasn't here."

They sat in companionable silence as they contemplated Lady Canderblank's character. Finally Ford roused himself.

"There's one more unpleasantness, I'm afraid. To get directly to the point, there's evidence—not proof, but still evidence—that Amy Robsart caused your husband's death."

"Amy? That's ridiculous; she wouldn't hurt a fly. Why ever do people think that?"

"We've been told she was very angry with him," Ford said. "She wanted him to leave you. She was seen on the dock at the right time. Now she's disappeared—run away, one assumes—and your husband's motorcar is missing."

"Clarence's new toy, the Bentley? Such an odd motorcar, I think, but Clarence was convinced that Bentley will one day be as famous a marque as Rolls Royce."

"We think Amy may have stolen it to make her getaway."

"That's all nonsense," Lady Pengriffon said firmly. "Amy always speaks fondly of him. It may seem strange that I like my husband's mistress, but I do. She's a free spirit, I grant you; self-indulgent, if you will. She lives for the day, but she's the most generous person you could wish to meet."

She shook her head in disbelief. "She'd never have wanted to marry Clarence; she doesn't care a fig about money or social position; and she told me, and I believe her, that she could never marry an older man. 'I want a husband, not a patient,' I remember her saying. I'm certain she wouldn't have harmed him—she wouldn't hurt a fly."

Ford stood and almost placed his cup and saucer on the nonexistent mantle.

"I won't mention the mantle to James," she smiled. "It'll give Clarence a chuckle from the grave."

Ford looked up at the painting of the *Justicia* he had admired the day before.

"Oh, yes," she said, following his glance. "I meant what I said yesterday—I've decided to give you and Victoria that painting. It's one of his best, I think, as well as his last."

"But we couldn't possibly ..."

"Consider it a wedding gift," she said. "It's such a happy picture, and it will remind you of your honeymoon. I'll have it sent down to you, and that's the end of it."

"That's very ..."

"Tush, Mr. Ford, enough! Clarence would agree with me, I know." She glanced at a clock. "Now, I'm enjoying our conversation, but Lady Canderblank may return at any moment."

* * *

Ford drove back to Trethgarret slowly, wincing as he grated the gears and wishing he'd learned how to double-clutch—or even precisely what double-clutching was. He had no idea how long appendix operations took, but he was sure that Victoria would be waiting for him at the Duke of Cornwall. He'd bet the Crofts would find a way to disappear, so that he and Victoria could be alone for dinner and an early night. No, damn it, he'd promised to go to London. Of all the ...

Double damn! He'd driven past the entrance to the lane that led to the cottage shared by Amy Robsart and Josephine Langley. Thank God Victoria wasn't there to witness the horrendous hash he was making of turning the car round on the narrow road.

Perhaps his concentration was slipping. It was remarkably easy to lose track of the present and slip into a pleasant reverie. Perhaps he should resign, as he had imagined, and become a fisherman, and Victoria and he could mend tackle together; or he could become a village policeman, like Crocker, and she could be the postmistress. Anything would do, as long as they were constantly together.

He navigated the narrow lane without further disaster, and tapped on the front door of the cottage, determined not to spend more than five minutes. Josephine Langley answered immediately, almost as if she'd been waiting by the door.

"Oh, it's you," she said in a disappointed voice, and, judging by her fading smile, Ford was certain she was expecting someone else.

She stared past his shoulder to the Humber.

"Is George Thompson with you?" she asked in confusion.

"No, Miss Langley. Why do you ask?" He followed her glance. "Oh, I see; he's lent us his car so that we can get about. I hope you're feeling better. Can you spare me a few minutes?" Ford asked, and removed his hat.

"I can't spare more than that," she said, and stood aside ungraciously.

"Thank you, Miss Langley, that's very kind of you," he said with elaborate courtesy. "I'll be as brief as possible. I'd like to look over Miss Robsart's room, if you don't mind, and then I have a few more questions, I'm afraid."

"Be my guest," she shrugged. She glanced out through the window, and Ford was more convinced than ever that she was expecting another visitor.

Amy Robsart's room resembled a jumble sale for women's clothing. Many of the surfaces were heaped with clothes, and the floor was a thicket of shoes of every conceivable shape, purpose, and description. The walls were overly crammed with examples of his lordship's work, in which her unquestionable pulchritude was the dominant recurring theme.

Oddly enough, her bed was perfectly clear and pristine, and, to Ford's amusement, the bedding was tucked in with immaculate hospital corners. A dressing table stood in front of the window, littered with the apparatus of the cosmetic arts, just as the dressing table at their honeymoon cottage was heaped with what Victoria insisted was the bare minimum necessary for rudimentary survival.

Ford found a small powder compact amid the piles, picked it up with his fingernails, wrapped it in his handkerchief, and dropped it into his pocket. He glanced through the dressing table drawers, but found nothing but routine domestic correspondence. Some of the envelopes were addressed to her in South Kensington, in London; judging by the dates on the postmarks she must have lived there before coming to Trethgarret. There was no statement of confession to the murder of Lord Pengriffon.

A small bookcase stood in one corner. The books were mostly medical textbooks, and when he riffled through their pages he saw that she had read and annotated every one of them. There was also a smattering of art books, as if she had been encouraged to study the subject by Lord Pengriffon—and, indeed, he found a couple with *ex libris C Pengriffon* written inside their covers.

On top of the bookcase were two photographs. One was a family group; an older couple, whom he took to be her parents, was surrounded by young men and women, all of whom bore a family resemblance. Ford picked out one face as Amy's, based on Pengriffon's paintings of her. Someone must have made a joke just as the photograph was taken, for they were all laughing uproariously.

A second picture showed a group of nurses standing in a muddy field before a large canvas tent, and Ford guessed it had been taken during the war. The same laughing face was also in this photograph.

He paused. The picture was not exactly square in its frame. He turned it over and removed the backing. Behind the wartime photograph was another of Lord Pengriffon, seated at his easel by the harbor. His head was turned back over his shoulder toward the camera, and he was smiling, as if the photographer had surprised him. The photograph had been taken by an expert, Ford judged, and wondered if it was the work of young Frank. The half-completed canvas looked very like the painting hanging over the faux mantle in Pengriffon Hall, with the launch moored in the harbor. Such was Frank's skill that the name *Justicia IV, Poole*, was clearly legible on the stern—Pengriffon and his canvas, ten feet away, and the *Justicia*, a hundred feet away, were both in focus.

On the back of the photograph Pengriffon had inscribed: *To the future Doctor Robsart, your devoted friend and admirer, CP.* Ford started to replace the hidden photograph in its frame, and then decided—he was not sure why—to take it with him.

He stood back and glanced around the room, trying to get a sense of her. Youthful, energetic, a dedicated nurse who evidently had aspirations to become a doctor; too busy with life to bother tidying her room, and yet too professional not to make her bed with millemetric precision; openly displaying nude pictures of herself painted by Pengriffon, and yet hiding away a photograph of her lover.

He shook his head. Surely this was not the room of a woman planning a murder; this was the room of a woman enjoying life to its fullest, just as Lady Pengriffon had described, and with ambitious plans for her future. Ford wondered how many women had become doctors—indeed, if there were any woman doctors at all.

Would he be comfortable being examined by a woman, regardless of how professionally detached she might be? Still, women over the age of thirty had now been given the right to vote, and there was talk of lowering the age limit. Victoria was more than competent to become a doctor, but how would he feel if she had male patients?

He smothered that line of thought and returned to the living room, where Miss Langley was pacing nervously and smoking a cigarette with jerky, staccato movements. She was not inhaling, Ford noted. She was smoking to relieve an inner tension, and not out of ingrained habit, he decided.

"I have just a couple of points of clarification, Miss Langley, if I may," he said. "Then I'll be on my way."

"Yes?" she asked in a tone just short of rudeness. Her large eyes stared at him, and Ford was again reminded of a horse. Victoria's vibrant eyes were full of expression, windows into her soul, whereas Miss Langley's were curiously opaque, as if Miss Langley had shuttered her thoughts or, perhaps, she had few thoughts to express.

"First, you are certain that Miss Robsart said she wanted to kill Lord Pengriffon, and she said it on the afternoon before he was killed?"

"Yes."

"Do you recall her exact words? Did she say, 'I wish he was dead,' for example?"

Her forehead wrinkled in concentration.

"She said, 'I'll strangle the lying old bastard.' Those were her exact words. Then she got on her bicycle and rode after him."

"And this followed an argument between them, Miss Langley?"

She glanced toward Amy Robsart's bedroom.

"These walls are very thin," she said. Her harsh tone belied her empty eyes. "I heard them copulating. I heard them arguing about getting married. I saw him come out with a smug smile on his face and leave. I saw her come out with her clothes pulled on any-old-how. I heard her say, 'I'll strangle the lying old bastard,' and I saw her follow him. Is that clear enough, Mr. Ford?"

"Very clear, Miss Langley. Thank you."

She had spoken with absolute finality, and there was nothing else for Ford to say. He picked up his hat and said good-bye, and her relief was palpable.

* * *

Ford drove off, wondering for whom she was waiting, and half expecting to see a motor car coming in the opposite direction.

He reached the end of the lane without passing another vehicle and turned toward Trethgarret. Perhaps he would try an experimental double-clutch on the way back along the cliff road, when there was no one to observe him. A loud grating noise emanated from the gearbox, as that mechanism literally gnashed its teeth, and the car, stuck in neutral, coasted to a halt. Not even the full force of Ford's frantic obscenities was sufficient to propel it forward.

He looked into the glove compartment in hope of finding a mechanical instruction manual, but there was nothing there but a sheaf of papers containing a handwritten draft of a political pamphlet entitled *An Unjust Society*, by George Thompson.

A pony and trap approached him from the direction of Trethgarret, and Ford's misery deepened when he saw George Thompson was driving it. Ford, feeling like a guilty schoolboy caught red-handed in commission of a crime, stuffed the papers into his pocket, leapt from the Humber, leant against the car in what he hoped was a languid attitude, lit a cigarette, and stared out to sea. To add to his confusion, he realized it was the very spot where Victoria had parked the car the night before.

Thompson brought the trap to a halt and jumped down to join him.

"Oh, good afternoon, Mr. Thompson," Ford said, feigning surprise. "I didn't see you coming."

"Enjoying the view, Mr. Ford?"

"Yes, I envy you the opportunity to see this every day, sir." Something compelled him to pretend he wasn't lollygagging—in spite of the fact that he was, indeed, trying to give that impression. "I was just trying to sort through a few facts in the case."

"Well, it'll be over as soon as you catch the Robsart woman," Thompson said with finality. "Open and shut case, it should be."

"Well …"

"You can be frank with me, Chief Inspector. You've got your sergeant checking the launch for evidence, you've got witnesses that saw her on the dock that night, and you've got her friend admitting that the Robsart woman wanted to strangle him."

Ford made a mental note to tell Crocker, in the firmest possible manner, not to discuss the case with anyone—for where else would Thompson have acquired this neatly summarized information?

"Well …" Ford said again, remembering guiltily that he himself had confided in the Ancient Mariner, of all people, that very morning.

"She's brazen—brazen!" Thompson huffed, setting his fob medallions jingling. "She even laughed at the Labor Party—said socialism was nothing more than class envy! That's not right! The haves have whatever they want, whenever they want it. What's wrong with an honest, hardworking bloke like me getting a slice of the pie?"

"I'm very grateful for the Humber, incidentally," Ford said, anxious to change the subject, only to realize that now he had given himself another cause for embarrassment, since he was driving—mis-driving—the stately Humber, while Thompson was reduced to a humble pony trap.

"It's no more than my duty as an elected public official," Thomson said grandly. "I'm a mere servant of the people; if a trap is good enough for the working classes, it's good enough for me. Besides, with the case all but closed, I'll get my motorcar back tomorrow or the next day."

He glanced proudly at the Humber, frowned, and bent to examine the right front mudguard. His finger probed a slight discoloration that Ford had not noticed. When he straightened, setting his row of medallions dancing, he was beaming.

"It's just a speck of mud," he said. "I thought it might have been scratched. One must maintain a certain standard, in my position." He walked to the driver's door and peered in at the controls, and Ford experienced a moment of panic lest he decide to take the car for a test drive.

Eventually he turned away from his prize possession and returned to the theme of Amy Robsart's manifest guilt.

"It'll do Trethgarret no harm to be rid of that public hussy, Chief Inspector. How she ever expected to get away with it is beyond me; no body, no murder, I suppose. I assume you'll charge her *in absentia*, I believe the term is, in her absence, even if you never find her?"

Ford tried to formulate an inconclusive reply, but Thompson saved him the need to equivocate; he drew himself up into his most magisterial pose and said, "I'll write an official letter of commendation for your swift conduct and conclusion of the case, Chief Inspector, and send it to the chief constable of Cornwall."

"I'm not sure …" Ford began.

"It's the least I can do," Thompson cut him off, chuckling at his own *noblesse oblige*. "Besides, there'll be a Labor government sooner than you might think, and it won't do you any harm to have a friend in the House of Commons."

He seemed to take his political advancement for granted, and he saved Ford the need to find a reply by turning toward the pony trap.

"And now I must get up to Pengriffon Hall. Life goes on; there's a new shaft starting at the mine and repairs to the harbor walls, and—

oh, I won't bother you with everything on my plate. Good day to you, Chief Inspector."

He hurried back to the trap, transferred his bulk to its protesting springs, and clicked the pony into reluctant motion.

Ford turned his attention to the Humber, hoping that the gearbox had magically righted itself, and wishing that he was as certain of the case against Amy Robsart as Thompson was. Still, there could be no question that motive, means, and opportunity, the three golden principles of detection, pointed in her direction, and the notion of closing off the case and returning to his honeymoon was infinitely more attractive than trying to dot every "i" and cross every last "t." Good Lord, there really was a blemish on the immaculate mudguard—no, it was just the imprint of Thompson's probing index finger. He bent to wipe it away with his handkerchief but paused indecisively and then left it in place.

He climbed into the driver's seat and waited until Thompson was halfway up the hill, where the lane to the cottage turned off the cliff road, and then started the engine. He depressed the clutch and tentatively wiggled the gear lever. The car grumbled but did not protest, and Ford, with bated breath, pushed the lever more firmly in the direction he was almost certain was first gear. He was rewarded with a satisfying *clunk*, and the car inched forward as he let out the clutch. He glanced back, wondering if Thompson had paused to observe his driving skills, but the trap had disappeared.

Victoria should be back at the inn by now. He had to leave for Penzance in time to catch the night train, but they would at least have a few hours together; perhaps the secret of the vaulting horse would be unveiled. Perhaps there'd be a message from Brownlee saying Amy Robsart had been found and had confessed, and there'd be no need to journey up to London.

He imagined her in the dock, and Josephine Langley in the witness seat testifying as she had done to him. As Thompson had said, Amy Robsart had told Josephine Langley she'd strangle Pengriffon, and within hours he was duly strangled. No juror could have a reasonable doubt. If Croft had found her prints on the *Justicia*, Amy Robsart would hang.

* * *

Ford arrived at the Duke and took the stairs two steps at a time, but their room was empty; Victoria had not returned. Ford would have devoted the next few minutes to the extraordinary fact that his enthusiasm for seeing her had outweighed his innate caution at overstressing his leg in bounding up the stairs, had not a large package wrapped in brown paper been standing against the foot of the bed.

He removed the wrapping and discovered it was the painting Lady Pengriffon had insisted on giving them. He propped it up on the mantelpiece—having assured himself that there really was a mantelpiece—and stood back to admire his lordship's work. It really was remarkable, he thought, glancing back and forth from the painting to the view of the harbor through the window. It was—he searched for the right words—a celebration of life. But was it also a murder scene? Had his lordship, through some ghastly coincidence, chosen the scene of his own demise as his last subject?

He pulled the hidden photograph from his pocket and stuck it in the corner of the frame; he was convinced that young Frank had captured Pengriffon painting this very picture.

The church, both through the window in reality and as depicted by his lordship, reminded Ford that he had one more duty to perform. He scribbled a note to Victoria, *Back in half an hour,* and started toward the door. He paused, turned back, and smiled as he added, *I miss you passionately, love and kisses.* At the doorway it occurred to him that this was not only their bedroom, but also the office that he and Croft were now sharing. The odds that Croft would think that the note was intended for him were long, but even so ... He grinned, crumpled up the note, and substituted a more prosaic and businesslike, *Back at six o'clock; Croft, please take fingerprint from front right Humber mudguard,* and hurried downstairs before he could change his mind again.

Ford followed Front Street to where St. Christopher-Upon-The-Waters stood on a granite outcrop at the harbor mouth. He walked—in spite of misgivings about his leg—because it seemed an appropriate tribute to Trethgarret's beauty and, besides, he wasn't entirely certain he'd be able to turn the motorcar around in the narrow street without making a hash of it.

The church dated from Norman times, and had a massive, enduring quality to it, as if it were an ancient bulldog lying on the shore and staring endlessly out to sea. It reminded him of the same qualities he had observed in Pengriffon Hall. Having withstood howling gales and lashing rainstorms for nine hundred years, St. Christopher's would doubtless survive the next nine hundred.

A clergyman emerged from the church porch as Ford was approaching. Ford produced his card, and the clergyman introduced himself as the vicar, the Reverend Theobald Asquith. He was so colorless, so self-effacing, that he seemed to be a shadow rather than a man, and Ford felt that he was shaking hands with a wraith.

"Oh yes, of course, I'm sorry," he said when Ford asked to see Pengriffon. "Oh dear, he's in the apse, I'm afraid."

The apse stood at the eastern end of the church; it was semicircular with an elegantly vaulted ceiling, and its walls were filled by stained-glass windows, through one of which the afternoon sun was streaming. Ford judged it had been added at a later stage, for the arches were pointed in the Early English style, rather than the rounded Norman arches of the rest of the building.

His lordship's coffin stood in the center of the apse, supported by sawhorses and covered by a heavy purple altar cloth, while the heavy coffin lid leaned against one wall. The apse also served, Ford saw, as a mausoleum for Pengriffons past. There was a splendid stone coffin for a Sir Henry Pengriffon, with a life-sized effigy of Sir Henry in the carved accoutrements of a crusader lying on the lid; an elaborate sarcophagus for Edward Lord Pengriffon and Anne, His Beloved Wife, dressed in the ruffles of Elizabethan England; a haughty, Byronesque marble head of General Lord George Pengriffon from the Napoleonic Wars; and numerous other lesser memorials and plaques upon the walls and floor.

Ford wondered what it would be like to live with the relics and memorials of countless generations of one's forebears. Had it served as a constant, grim reminder of his lordship's mortality, or had it been a source of comfort, to know that one would rest with one's ancestors in the kaleidoscopic rainbows thrown by the windows, lulled by the endless murmuring of the breakers?

And where would Ford be buried? Before Saturday, before he was married, he would have said he didn't care—that his dead body would simply be a piece of old rubbish that could be dumped anywhere or donated to a hospital so that novice doctors could carve it up and explore his innards. But now, suddenly, he imagined a shaded plot on a hillside overlooking the sea, where he and Victoria would lie together forever.

The vicar cleared his throat, which Ford guessed was probably the most vicious expression of annoyance of which Asquith was capable, and Ford returned to the present.

He lifted a corner of the cloth covering his lordship's open coffin and gazed down at the latest addition to the distinguished catalog of former Pengriffons in residence. The local undertaker had made an energetic but unsuccessful effort to disguise his lordship's injuries, and Ford kicked himself for not examining the body sooner. Large, roughly sewn incisions in the neck and upper torso indicated where and how Dr. Anderson had verified the cause of death.

"One wants to help, of course," the vicar said, "but one wishes that Trethgarret had a mortuary. The cottage hospital is far too small, I'm afraid, and the undertaker's workshop seemed inadequate."

"Quite so, sir," Ford said, berating himself for failing to tell Crocker that the body was *not* to be touched, except by Dr. Anderson. Any physical clues had been literally washed away. Crocker was an idiot! First he'd obviously said far too much to Thompson, now he'd let the body be disturbed—he should have known better.

No, Ford stopped himself, Crocker was not an idiot, but simply a man out of his depth trying to do the right thing, and the fault was entirely Ford's for not having given him appropriate instructions.

"The funeral is on Saturday, Vicar, I believe?" Ford asked.

"That is what Lady Canderblank told me."

"Lady Canderblank?"

"She told me she is in charge, and that I should not disturb poor Lady Justicia under any circumstances. There is to be a memorial service in the church, so that the townspeople can pay their respects, and then a private burial here in the apse. She's making all the arrangements."

He made a fluttering gesture with his hands. "I went to the Hall to offer my services, but Lady Canderblank informed me that she herself was providing Lady Justicia with spiritual guidance. One is somewhat at a loss. The Lord moves in mysterious ways his wonders to perform. He has certainly appointed a redoubtable handmaiden on this occasion."

Ford had envisaged his mother-in-law in many ways, but never as the Lord's chosen handmaiden.

"I see," he managed, and moved on. "Someone removed his lordship's clothes—Dr. Anderson, I assume, when he confirmed the cause of death. Do you know what happened to them?"

"Dr. Anderson put them in a parcel to be given to you, Chief Inspector, but Lady Canderblank came and took them away this afternoon."

Ford would have sworn if he had not been in church.

"I told her what Dr. Anderson had said, but Lady Canderblank said they were private property, and you had no right to them."

"I see," Ford said, struggling to contain his anger.

"I saw no harm in it," the vicar added, fluttering a defensive hand. "George Thompson told me you already had all the evidence you needed."

"He did, Vicar?"

"Oh, yes; he said the case is closed and you are issuing a warrant for the arrest of Amy Robsart. It's so sad to see a young woman fall prey to the temptations of the flesh."

The urge to swear on sacred ground was almost overpowering.

"I see," Ford managed once more.

Seven

Ford halted in front of the post office/police station. Part of his mind was intent on speaking firmly to Crocker, but the dominant part knew he could never vent his ire on a subordinate, any more than he could kick a dog simply because he was in a bad mood. Thompson's grating *noblesse oblige*; Lady Canderblank's willful removal of potential evidence; the flabby, circumstantial nature of the case; the wreckage of his honeymoon, and the thought of a night without Victoria. None of this was poor Crocker's fault.

He glanced at his watch and saw he still had a few minutes to spare before six o'clock. He had gone to the church to examine evidence, only to find no evidence to examine. Still, Lady Pengriffon had mentioned that the accountant Joseph Crutchfield had an office in the High Street; Ford might as well occupy the time usefully, rather than waste it in irritation.

The firm of Jos. Crutchfield & Son, Chartered Accountants, occupied a whitewashed building halfway up the High Street. Unlike its neighbors it lacked cheerful window boxes bursting with geraniums, as if accounting was too serious a matter for such frivolity. Ford rapped on the brass doorknocker and obeyed the highly polished sign that read *Please Enter.*

The room was divided by an old-fashioned mahogany railing into a waiting area and a business area. The walls of the waiting area were devoted to prints of racehorses in stiff, unlikely postures, dating from the time before photography when the details of a galloping horse's gait were uncertain; while on those on the business side stood rows of leather-bound accounting books. A portrait of a severe man, dressed in the fashion of Queen Victoria's era, stared down from a place of honor above the fireplace.

An elderly man bearing a resemblance to the portrait sat at a desk in the inner sanctum, using a brassbound adding machine at breakneck speed. The keys made a distinctive clicking sound, and the lever, used to calculate a total, made a satisfying clank. Ford noted that the accountant's eyes were on a column of numbers in a ledger before him, and he was operating the machine without looking at the keys.

Ford stood waiting, hoping his expression transmitted admiration for the accounting profession in general and awe at Crutchfield's legerdemain in particular. Ford had never used the services of a financial accountant, for, as he ruefully told himself, to need an accountant one needed finances to be accounted for. Ford's fortune, even though he was a frugal man, would have taken Crutchfield's machine no more than thirty seconds to weigh, measure, and find risible.

Crutchfield glanced up and saw Ford, and completed his calculations while staring at him, with a virtuoso *click-click-click-clank*.

He stood, and advanced to the railing.

"Joseph Crutchfield at your service," he said, flexing his fingers lest Ford had failed to be impressed by his operation of the adding machine. "And of what assistance can I be to you today, Chief Inspector?"

Evidently he recognized Ford—perhaps everyone in Trethgarret knew who he was, Ford realized, after the meeting at the Duke the previous evening. Crutchfield was tall, spindly, and balding, with a large head set atop a skeletal frame. His gauntness was emphasized by his prominent ears and nose. He was, of course, the man that Ford had seen talking to Crocker the night before at the Duke's bar.

"Welcome to my humble establishment," he added with a cringing half-bow, and Uriah Heep, the obsequious character in Charles Dickens's *David Copperfield*, leapt into Ford's mind.

"As you may know, Mr. ... Mr. Crutchfield, I'm investigating the death of Lord Pengriffon." Ford had barely avoided calling him Mr. Heep.

"Ah, yes, his lordship, poor man, cut down in his prime, alas; *such* a tragedy for poor Lady Justicia, to be sure," Mr. Crutchfield said, now wringing his hands together as if washing them, and managing, despite his words, to look remarkably cheerful.

"Indeed, sir, a tragedy," Ford said. "I understand you keep the books of all the Pengriffon's local business affairs—everything, in fact, apart from the family trust?"

"I have that duty, indeed, that *honor*, just as my father did before me." His eyes moved to a long row of leather-bound account books which stood on their own shelf, supported at each end by brass bookends fashioned in the shape of lions. Each book had a year inscribed in gold on the spine, and Ford saw that the first book was dated 1883.

"Obviously, in a case of murder, one must look into the victim's finances. I have spoken to Lady Justicia, and she understands the necessity. Can you summarize the accounts, sir?"

"I would be glad to, Chief Inspector," Crutchfield said, with more hand-wringing. He opened the railing gate and invited Ford to a seat at his desk with a wordless gesture.

"Well, now, Chief Inspector, let me see, the accounts of the Pengriffon estates, in *summary*," he said, taking his own seat behind the desk. "In 1883, when my father first started …"

"No, no, sir," Ford interrupted. "I meant to ask you about the *current* state of affairs—whether the Pengriffons receive a good enough income to cover their expenses, whether they have debts, whether someone owes them a lot of money; that sort of thing."

"Ah, I see, Chief Inspector—how silly of me." Crutchfield said, with an unlikely childish giggle. "A summary of the *current* accounts?"

"Exactly, sir."

"Well, let me see, let me see. There are two principal sources of *income*, the tenant farms and the mines." He held up two fingers, perhaps fearing that Ford was not adept at mathematics. "In *summary*, his lordship provides them with working capital, and, in return, receives a share of the profits, if any. It is an unusual and generous arrangement, if I may say so. The farmers and the mine manager give me their journals each month, and I calculate the amounts due. I trust I make myself clear, Chief Inspector?"

"Very clear, thank you."

"I'm gratified to hear it," Crutchfield said, bowing his head. "The major source of *expense* is Pengriffon Hall; the butler and the head housekeeper provide me with their accounts, and I provide them with petty cash and settle with the local suppliers."

"And is there enough income to cover these expenses?"

"Oh, indeed there is, Chief Inspector, indeed there is."

"Does anyone owe the Pengriffons a significant sum, Mr. Crutchfield?"

"We all do, Chief Inspector, we all do," Crutchfield said, with yet more hand-wringing. "I, for example, owe them a debt of gratitude for the many kindnesses they have extended to me and my family."

Uriah Heep could not have been more unctuous, Ford thought.

"No doubt, Mr. Crutchfield," he said, smothering the warning signs of recurrent irritation. "Does anyone owe the Pengriffons a sum of *money* that is past due?"

"Well, let me see, Chief Inspector. Farm prices have fallen since the war, of course, and there are good years and bad. But there's nothing unusual in the present balances of the tenant farmers, I would say; nothing that cannot be repaid after the harvest." He paused and glanced slyly at Ford. "Nothing, one might say, of a *murderous* scale."

He looked at Ford with an expectant smile, and Ford's sense of irritation rose a notch.

"I see," he said without inflexion. "What about the mines, Mr. Crutchfield?"

"The mines, however, are almost worked out," Crutchfield said, evidently disappointed that Ford had taken no notice of his comment. "Tin is mined less expensively in the colonies these days—in Tasmania, for example. Mines are failing all over Cornwall, alas, and ours manage to eke out only a minimal profit."

Ford, who had grown up in an agricultural village, knew well that farmers experience years of profitability and periods of loss, feast or famine, as his father used to say, but he knew nothing of mines and nothing about the economics of tin.

"The Pengriffon mines are just about breaking even?"

"Alas, I fear they are, Chief Inspector. His lordship has mentioned he might have to close them. The price of tin has dropped precipitously since the war, and he didn't want to start pouring money into a losing venture. The Old Morehead Hole, as we call it, has been in production for more than two thousand years, since before the Romans conquered England; the end of an era—such a pity."

Ford has seen the mine, perched improbably on a cliff above the sea, during a long and blissful walk with Victoria, in the far ago days of his honeymoon. They had initially mistaken it for a castle guarding the coastline, but what they had taken for a tall turret—occupied either by a fearsome witch or a damsel in distress, Victoria had not decided—was, in reality, merely a large chimney.

"*Sic transit gloria mundis,* as they say," Crutchfield declaimed in solemn tones, but Ford gained the impression that there was nothing that cheered him more than the misery of others.

The front door opened to admit a female counterpart to Crutchfield, laden with two shopping bags.

"Ah, this is my sister, Gertrude," Crutchfield told Ford, pointing a finger in her direction lest Ford fail to grasp his meaning, and Ford rose politely.

"Good evening, madam," he said. "I am a police officer."

"This is Chief Inspector Ford, Gertrude," Crutchfield added. "He's …"

"Did you catch her yet?" Gertrude demanded. "Did you get that Robsart woman?"

She advanced as if to join them.

"Let's not bother the Chief Inspector, Gertie," Crutchfield intervened. "Here, let me help you with those bags."

He seized her shopping bags and propelled her through a doorway leading to the rear, leaving Ford alone and with the distinct impression that Crutchfield regarded his office as his sole domain.

* * *

Ford glanced at his watch and saw it was almost six o'clock; perhaps Victoria would be back from the hospital by now. He was torn between a desire to flee and the obligation to complete the interview in full.

Crutchfield returned while Ford was debating with himself and seemed to find it necessary to explain his sister.

"Neither of us ever entered into holy matrimony, Chief Inspector.

Gertie keeps house for the two of us." He paused. "I hope you didn't find her question too intrusive into police matters? Just harmless tittle-tattle, I sure you; women, as you know, are prone to …"

"Of course not," Ford said, controlling his impatience. "I've been asked that very question several times today. Now, sir, if we can return to the point you were making when we broke off. Is there any hope of rescuing the mine?"

It was the first hint of a financial cloud on his lordship's sunny horizon. Could it somehow be a cause for murder?

Crutchfield looked at Ford obliquely. "Mr. Thompson, the manager of the Old Morehead Hole, wants to open a new shaft at the thousand-foot level and cut a new tunnel under the sea, but that will mean new hoists and new pumps, and a new crushing factory for the ore, and his lordship isn't—dear me, *wasn't*—sure if he'd ever get his money back."

"Is that George Thompson, the mayor?" It had not occurred to Ford that Thompson had other duties and occupations. Lady Pengriffon had mentioned that Thompson was most put out by his lordship's plans to shelve the tin mine in favor of a new business, but Ford had failed to see the significance until this moment.

"It is indeed, Chief Inspector. Despite, if I may say so, Mr. Thompson's protestations, his civic duties are not onerous and, in any case, his public stipend is minute. His *job* is at the mine. Let me see, I have his proposal somewhere here."

He reached into a drawer in his desk and pulled out a manila folder, again without looking at what he was doing. Ford wondered if this was a pattern in his life and hoped for his sake he did not shave in this manner.

The folder contained a typed document entitled *Proposed Expansion of the Old Morehead Mine*. It contained a list of proposed capital improvements, calculations of the amount of ore to be extracted from the new tunnels, and a *pro forma* income statement, which listed anticipated revenues and expenses, including labor costs.

"Mr. Thompson receives a salary of £500 per year?" Ford asked in surprise. Perhaps he should resign from the police force and manage a failing tin mine!

"He does, and he has the use of a company motorcar; indeed, it is the very conveyance you have been using."

"I see. You think his lordship was disinclined to take this proposal on?"

"As you can see, Chief Inspector, Mr. Thompson is asking for a great deal of capital. The expanded mine would only be profitable if the price of tin increases, and his lordship was reluctant to take that risk. If, for example, the price of tin remained at its present depressed level, then ..."

His hand flew over the adding machine keys. *Click-click-click-clank. Click-click-click-clank.*

"Ah, yes, the venture would bear a capital loss of ten thousand pounds over the next ten years. His lordship is—*was*—far from poor, Chief Inspector, far from poor, but he wasn't *made* of money, if you will permit me to use that somewhat vulgar expression. Besides, most of his fortune is tied up in the family trust, so he'd have had to borrow personally to meet Mr. Thompson's request."

"I see," Ford said again. "What would happen if the mine closed, Mr. Crutchfield?

"I believe his lordship intended to start a new business venture that would employ the laborers."

"Would Mr. Thompson have managed it?"

Crutchfield paused and stared over Ford's shoulder.

"Who can tell what his lordship intended?" he answered, ducking a direct answer, and Ford reminded himself that there was bad blood between Thompson and Crutchfield.

"What kind of new business was he contemplating, do you know?"

Crutchfield smirked.

"He was considering starting a business to manufacture radio wave receivers. He had acquired some expertise in that area during the war, while serving in the Royal Engineers. Be that as it may, his lordship subscribed to the curious notion that wireless communications could be received in ordinary homes, so that people could *hear* music without a gramophone, and *listen* to the news without buying a newspaper! He had gone so far as to reach an agreement-in-principle with the General Electric Company to pursue this, this, um, adventure."

This was a side of Lord Pengriffon that Ford had not seen before.

"Was he a shrewd businessman, Mr. Crutchfield?"

"Ah, now, Chief Inspector, *far* be it from me to comment on my clients—upon a client as *illustrious* as the Earl of Pengriffon," Crutchfield said, at his most Heepish.

"Come, come, Mr. Crutchfield, is anyone better qualified?" Ford asked just as Heepishly, hoping that flattery would encourage Crutchfield, and he was rewarded by a fresh bout of hand-wringing.

"Well, Chief Inspector, I suppose I could go so far as to say that his lordship was no fool. He ignored business almost all the time, but he focused his attention when necessary, you can be sure, and he had an instinct for an opportunity."

Ford thought of Pengriffon poring over the hidden accounts in his study, and he nodded encouragingly, hoping Crutchfield would expand.

Crutchfield lowered his voice, as if they were not the only people in the room.

"His lordship had more than enough income from the trust, and so he ran his local business affairs to the benefit of the town. If the mine closed, he would have started something else to employ the men. A good portion of the excess income from the trust goes to support the cottage hospital." Crutchfield paused and again looked at Ford obliquely, as if testing him. "His lordship believed in the gospel according to St. Mark, chapter 10, verse 25."

Ford wracked his brains. His father had been a priest in the Church of England, and he had been steeped in the New Testament since earliest childhood, but what the devil—an inappropriate phrase in the circumstances, he reflected—was in the twentieth verse of the tenth chapter of Mark's gospel?

Ford had not opened a Bible in years. He had turned away from God in the wartime trenches—no God worthy of Ford's reverence could conceivably have permitted such brutally inhuman carnage on so grand a scale—and he had not been to church since, except for obligatory births, marriages, and funerals. Something about generosity? The Good Samaritan, perhaps? Or—oh yes, of course—"It is easier for a camel to go through the eye of a needle, than for a rich man to enter into the kingdom of God."

"He wanted to die a camel, Mr. Crutchfield?

"Ah, very apposite, Chief Inspector!" Crutchfield beamed, as if

Ford had just passed a test in a Sunday school Bible class and deserved a reward. "Would you care for a cup of tea?"

"I fear I've intruded on you too long, sir." Ford needed to get away and ponder what, if anything, he had learned that might have a bearing on Pengriffon's murder. Besides, this interview was taking far longer than he had expected, and Victoria was probably waiting for him.

"My time is entirely at your disposal," Crutchfield said, and disappeared into a back room, leaving Ford to speculate on whether Crutchfield would pour tea without looking at what he was doing. He would never know, however, for Crutchfield returned with two cups already poured.

"Thank you, sir," he said. "What will happen now? Will Lady Justicia go ahead with the mine closure or wait for his lordship's heir to make the decision?"

Crutchfield took a prim sip of tea before replying. "Her ladyship is not, if one may say so, a particularly decisive person; nor is she experienced in business matters."

"I'm sure she will consult you, Mr. Crutchfield," Ford prompted him.

"Well," Crutchfield said, with his most prolonged hand-wringing yet, "I would naturally wish to follow his lordship's wishes to see that the men found gainful occupation and could continue to support their families."

He gave Ford another sidelong glance before continuing. "However, alas, the notion that we might all have radio receivers in our houses is a little too *farfetched* for me to be able to recommend that particular course of action."

This judgment was delivered with a sound remarkably like a derisive snort.

"Perhaps so, sir," Ford said without inflection. "Would you advise Lady Justicia that Mr. Thompson should manage a new venture, whatever it might be?"

"Well now, let me see, Chief Inspector; if I thought it was within his area of competence, perhaps ..."

Crutchfield's voice petered out, and the sidelong Heepish glance returned. Something in Crutchfield's manner made Ford decide to press the point.

"I'm afraid I don't know Mr. Thompson well enough to judge his competence as a business manager, Mr. Crutchfield."

"How true, Chief Inspector—but, unfortunately, I do. In addition, I have reason to believe his lordship had already decided that matter, by securing the services of a young man named Carpenter, who would be transferred from General Electric if the venture went forward. As for Mr. Thompson ..."

Crutchfield allowed his voice to peter out once more, as if to imply that Thompson's career was already fading into the past, and the accountant's expression took on the general appearance of a partially disguised smirk. Ford was again seized with the urgent need to escape. This time he made a show of consulting his wristwatch.

"I have to consult with Sergeant Croft, I'm afraid, Mr. Crutchfield. You've been of enormous help."

He rose before Crutchfield could offer him more tea and turned to leave. Crutchfield followed him to the door with a fresh bout of Heepish offers of assistance. Ford stepped into the High Street, thanked the accountant one more time, and headed down the hill. The fresh sea breeze blew away Crutchfield's cloying sycophancy, and the prospect of Victoria's company drove him on.

Glancing back, he could see Crutchfield wringing his hands on his doorstep.

* * *

But when Ford returned to the Duke of Cornwall he discovered that Victoria and Mrs. Croft were still at the hospital watching over Mrs. Granger, thus condemning Ford and Croft to an evening devoid of feminine companionship.

They ate a supper of cold ham—which appeared to be the Duke's standard fare—sitting in the bar near the fireplace watching the locals; Ford wondered if his lordship's murderer was among the crowd, covertly watching them.

Ford bought Croft his first pint of scrumpy and watched Croft's expression change from caution to appreciation as the amber liquid ran smoothly across his tongue.

"Not bad," Croft said. "Not bad at all."

"It packs a surprising punch, I should warn you," Ford said. "Now, how did you get on today?"

Croft had extracted a number of promising fingerprints from the engine compartment of the *Justicia*, which appeared, as best they could tell, to match fingerprints on Amy Robsart's powder compact. The sooner the prints were in the hands of Scotland Yard's forensic experts, the better. The evidence was now carefully wrapped in tissue paper and tucked inside Ford's overnight bag, together with the sample of Thompson's print from the Humber—taken, Ford had to admit, for no better reason than Thompson's pomposity.

"If the prints from the engine do match Amy Robsart's, Croft, we can put her on the boat and at the controls for a trip to the Little Dogs," Ford said.

"It's a funny thing, sir," Croft said, "but there's no prints on the steering wheel, or whatever it's called. It's as if she wiped it down and forgot the engine controls."

"It was dark in the engine compartment, and she must have been feeling her way. Besides, murderers make mistakes, thank God— otherwise we'd never catch them. These prints, plus Miss Langley's testimony—assuming she's believable—could well be enough put a rope around Amy Robsart's neck."

"Is she believable, sir—Miss Langley, I mean?"

"She's very sure, but that isn't the same thing, of course," Ford said. "There's something about her that doesn't quite add up, if you know what I mean—something about her eyes."

"Shifty, sir?"

"No, something else ... obstinacy, perhaps. Why don't you go see her tomorrow and form your own opinion?"

"Very well, sir," Croft said, drawing out his notebook. "Let's see, I've also got his lordship's study tomorrow, the house-to-houses for someone who saw his lordship's car, or Amy Robsart, or anyone down by the docks. What else, sir?"

"I interviewed Crutchfield, the accountant that keeps the local books for the Pengriffons. There was nothing there to suggest a financial motive—no disputes, no bad debts, nothing of that sort. The only point of interest, which I doubt is relevant, is that the tin mines are losing money and may have to be closed."

"Lost jobs, sir?" Croft pondered, draining his glass. "Disgruntled workers? Scarcely a motive for murder, I'd have thought, but it might bear looking into."

"I agree, Croft, although Pengriffon was evidently a generous employer. According to Crutchfield he'd have started another business just to employ the men." Ford set down his knife and fork, pushed back his chair, and eased his aching leg over the other. "Meanwhile, it looks like we're stuck on a crime of passion, although it fails Cicero's test."

"Cicero, sir? The Roman chap?" Croft asked.

"Exactly. In criminal trials without strong evidence he had a test he called *cui bono*? or 'who benefits?' in English. If you lack sufficient clues, look at who benefits from the crime. But we haven't found a single person, including Amy Robsart, who actually benefits from Lord Pengriffon's death. Even the heir would have received the trust eventually."

"That's true."

"Anyway, Croft, it's early days yet. This case will take some time, I'm afraid, even though I sincerely wish it wouldn't. Let me get you another pint."

"It slips down very easily, doesn't it, sir? I'd better not have more than that, not if I have to drive you to Penzance. Let me make a note of that Latin phrase before I forget it, sir; *cui bono?*, meaning 'who benefits?' That sums up our job very neatly."

George Thompson emerged from the crowd to interrupt them. He drew up a chair and sat down uninvited, as if he were part of the investigating team.

"Has Amy Robsart been caught yet?" he asked.

"No, not yet," Ford replied, keeping the annoyance from his voice.

"Well, she did it; everyone knows that."

Ford noticed Croft's expression, and guessed he was muttering "*cui bono?*" to himself—of what benefit to Amy Robsart was his lordship's death?

"Perhaps it was one of the German sailors," Ford said with a smile, trying to divert the conversation.

"German sailors?" Croft asked.

Thompson took it upon himself to answer.

"There's an old wives' tale that a German U-boat was wrecked off the coast near here, during the war, and some of the sailors survived and made it safely to shore." He snorted derisively. "A lot of stuff and nonsense, in my view. The sailors are supposed to have gone into hiding and then committed all sorts of crimes—robberies and such like, and even piracy. Even now, after all these years, every time some passing tramp steals eggs from a chicken coop, half the town swears it's the Germans."

Thompson waved his hands to dismiss the absurdity of the myth.

"In the meantime, we've harbored a woman without a scrap of decency," he pressed on. "Amy Robsart is a disgrace to the community—shameless, as everyone knows. And she even distributed pamphlets for the Conservative Party! Mind you, given the moral values of the Tory Party, it's quite appropriate."

Ford noticed that the bar had stopped to listen. He saw Crutchfield in the crowd; his prominent ears seemed to be trained in Ford's direction, like hearing trumpets. This was like solving case in a fishbowl, he thought—although, to be fair, it's their fishbowl, their town, their victim, and very probably their perpetrator.

Thompson thumped the table for emphasis. "It was Amy Robsart, beyond a doubt—you mark my words."

"That may be, Mr. Thompson," Croft said, rescuing Ford from the need to state a position. "However, we have to follow procedures before we can reach firm conclusions."

Thompson puffed himself up to make a declaration, but Croft beat him to the punch. "I must say, however, that everyone is being very helpful and patient. We're very grateful, sir."

This was greeted by a murmur of support, and Thompson had lost his opportunity to advance the case against Amy Robsart. The crowd returned to its own conversations, and Ford heard Clara's voice above the hubbub; "It was so too the Germans."

Ford was called to Charlie's office for a telephone call from Brownlee. A woman answering to Amy Robsart's ample description had been seen in South Kensington, close to the address that Ford had found at the cottage; she would probably be apprehended in the next few hours.

There were, therefore, a number of compelling reasons for Ford to travel up to London, and no legitimate excuses for him to stay. He scribbled a note to Victoria—sealed in an envelope, this time—and Croft drove him in the Humber to Penzance, where he caught the night train by a whisker. He was secretly annoyed to discover on the journey that Croft, like Victoria, was an expert at double-clutching.

* * *

As the train drew out of Penzance, Ford climbed into the bunk in his sleeping compartment and attempted unsuccessfully to find a comfortable position on the rocklike mattress. He always slept soundly on trains, lulled by the monotonous clickerty-clack of the wheels, but on this occasion sleep did not overcome him.

He composed himself for the third or fourth time and turned his thoughts to Victoria, but this served only to amplify her absence. Very well, he thought, I'll think about the case until I nod off. He dragged himself into a sitting position, turned on the tiny bedside light, and pulled out his notebook and pen.

"Pengriffon," he wrote. "Wealthy / bon vivant / in good health / no known enemies / married, no children / mistress / painter of impressionist works and *trompes l'œil*."

He paused, and then wrote:

"Inconsistencies:
Impressionist works—'dabs of paint'—versus painstaking exactitude of *trompes l'œil*
Happily married yet had mistress
Careful, idyllic charcoals of wife versus pulchritudal extravaganzas of mistress
Careless about money (had so much) yet did detailed calculations and hid them."

He stared at his notes without enthusiasm. Was there something in Pengriffon's manifest contradictions to explain his death? And what about the cipher he'd hidden, *WB IHS 372535,* what did that suggest? He shook his head and tried again:

"Suspects:
Lady P Not as calm as seems? Secretly enraged over Robsart? Strong enough to do deed?
A Robsart   Where is she and where is the Bentley?

Odds and ends:
Thompson's pamphlet—must read
Closing of Old Morehead Hole—unlikely, but theoretically possible motive?
Is Miss Langley a bit too weird? Too overemotional?
Cui bono?"

He sighed and tossed the notebook aside. He knew next to nothing, and the less he knew, the longer his honeymoon would be suspended. He took up Thompson's sheaf of papers, which he had hurriedly stuffed into his jacket pocket and then forgotten, but recoiled from the notion of studying the doubtlessly manifold injustices of *An Unjust Society* at so late an hour, put it down again, and turned out the light.

Crutchfield was sooo obsequious. Perhaps the rhythmic *click-click-click-clank* of his adding machine could lull one to sleep. Thompson was sooo pompous—the obsequious in opposition to the pompous, to the detriment of parish business. God damn it! Had the Great Western Railway Company conducted a competition for the most uncomfortable mattress ever made, and awarded its contract to the winner? He'd slept more comfortably on bare boards in the trenches!

If only the murderer had waited another couple of weeks, he'd have avoided this mess ... in a just society, policemen would not have to investigate murders on their honeymoons ... if only he and Victoria hadn't been sitting there, on the spot, at the very moment when the body was discovered ... if only he had one really solid clue ... if only Amy Robsart would confess ... if only Lady Canderblank would have a real heart attack instead of a pretended one ... if only Victoria were here ...

Eight

"**D**amn, damn, and double damn!" Ford snarled at his face in the tiny shaving mirror. "Triple damn with brass knobs and laurel wreathes!"

The night train from Penzance lurched across a set of points somewhere in the western suburbs of London, and Ford grabbed at the side of the sleeping bunk to save himself from stumbling. It would be a miracle if he managed to complete shaving without slashing some vital artery or removing an ear. Either disaster would be a denouement consistent with the past eight hours.

The mattress had won the battle between it and Ford's body—indeed it had been a rout. He had tossed and turned from Penzance to Plymouth, stared gloomily out of the window at the darkened countryside from Plymouth to Exeter, catnapped as far as Taunton, stepped out into the corridor for a smoke as they reached Swindon, tried unsuccessfully to will himself to sleep from Swindon to Reading, and managed to slump into a semiconscious stupor of exhausted self-pity from Reading to the outskirts of London.

Now, of course, he was so tired he couldn't keep awake. The face in the tiny, cracked mirror was bleary-eyed, and his clothes looked disheveled. The train grumbled into Paddington Station in central London, and Ford stepped down onto the platform, smelling the unique, faintly acidic odor of London's perpetually smoky air. Surely the modern world could invent a fuel better than coal.

The sleeping carriage attendant was far too cheerful for the hour, and the ticket collector's voice was far too loud. The man behind the counter of the station cafeteria was a virtuoso whistler; his rendition of the wartime song "Pack Up Your Troubles in Your Old Kit Bag and Smile, Smile, Smile," complete with operatic flourishes, bounced ruthlessly off the tiled walls. Ford groaned, and gloomily accepted the fact that his plate really did hold the eggs and bacon he had ordered, despite their dubious taste and appearance.

It was all so damned *unfair*. He should be lying luxuriously in bed with Victoria. He should be listening to her gentle breathing as she slept and feeling the soft touch of her hair across his shoulder. He should be in Trethgarret on his honeymoon, goddamn it, instead of in the station buffet at Paddington.

It was still only six in the morning. He had time to go to his flat and bathe before going to the Yard, but that would only reemphasize his abrupt and cruel return to bachelorhood.

Why did he have to bother with the dreary routine of closing the case? Amy Robsart was probably sitting in a detention cell by now— she might have confessed already. If not, the fingerprints and Josephine Langley's emphatic testimony would seal the case, even if she denied it. The trust accounts and the cipher were irrelevancies, products of Lord Pengriffon's eccentricities; it would be a waste of time to see the art gallery and the alliterative Pollock, Pollock & Poole.

And yet ... something was amiss. Something did not add up. Something, some discordant note, had been scurrying round the edges of his subconscious mind all night, playing catch-me-if you-can. It was ... it was ... what the *hell* was it?

Ford permitted himself one final self-pitying groan, and went to find a taxicab that would take him to his flat. He did not smile, smile, smile.

* * *

Ford arrived at Scotland Yard two hours later. A bath, a fresh set of clothes, and several strong cups of tea had improved his exhausted self-pity to a sulky background haze.

"The Yard," or New Scotland Yard, to be precise, stood on the Westminster Embankment overlooking the Thames, a stone's throw from Big Ben and the Houses of Parliament. Ford always thought of it as a preposterous building—a stone and brick Victorian gothic extravaganza, with absurd rounded turrets at each corner and ridiculously high gables encrusted with bizarre architectural flourishes. It seemed to Ford that the architect had focused his entire attention on the exterior, and, as a result, the interior was illogical, labyrinthine, and filled with nonsense—Ford's own office, for example, measured fifteen feet on a side but had a twenty-foot-high ceiling.

Ford climbed a grandiose marble staircase which led—out of the public's eye—to the maze of shabby offices that housed the Criminal Investigation Division. He chuckled dutifully at the ribald newlywed comments of two of his colleagues conversing in a corridor, and entered Brownlee's office.

Superintendent Brownlee always reminded Ford of a St. Bernard dog, except that the analogy was too cramped to encompass the essential Brownlee; he was large both in body and in spirit, and everything about him seemed small in comparison. His owlish reading glasses perched precariously on his nose; his teacup all but disappeared in his fist; his chair emitted squeaks of protest every time he rearranged himself.

"Ah, Ford, my dear fellow," Brownlee rumbled in his habitual greeting. "You've arrived just in time for tea."

He raised his head to the ceiling, just as a St. Bernard might lift its chin to bay at the moon, and bawled "*Caruthers—two teas.*"

"While you've been enjoying the comforts of modern long-distance travel at its finest, Ford, courtesy of the Great Western Railway Company, other, lesser mortals have been laboring. The examiners of the Bank of England have been poring over those accounts, the code breakers of Special Branch have been studying your cipher, and a team of eagle-eyed detectives has been watching Miss Robsart's former residence."

Constable Caruthers arrived with tea. He opened his mouth to welcome Ford back from his honeymoon but wisely retreated with the greeting unsaid.

"Unfortunately, these labors, although Herculean, have yielded nothing," Brownlee continued without apparent concern. "The Bank of England can find no irregularities in the typed accounts, the codes remain unbroken, and Miss Robsart remains at large. The score stands at Criminals 3, CID 0. You may choose to visit the carnage and see for yourself."

"Well, sir, it's not even halftime yet," Ford said, following Brownlee's soccer score allusion. "There's still plenty of time."

"In one sense that's true, Ford, but not in another. I had the pleasure of attending your wedding last Saturday, and you will recall the solemn words, *Those whom God hath joined, let no man put asunder.* Yet you and the newly minted Mrs. Ford are asunder, and I consider my duty to rejoin you at the earliest possible moment."

"I appreciate that, sir, but unless we get something definitive …"

"I've put Harry West in charge of the odds and ends here, Ford. I'd be glad to have him take over the case, if you'd like?"

Ford shook his head. "That's very tempting, sir, believe me, but I know it would just keep nagging away at me."

"Well, I'll keep the offer open, old chap, dangling before you in case you have a weak moment. In the meantime, let's see if there's any fresh news. *Caruthers!*"

The constable appeared.

"Ask Inspector West to step in, Caruthers, if you please."

"Three teas, sir?"

"Need you ask?"

Caruthers returned shortly with three cups of tea balanced expertly in one hand, followed by Inspector West. Most police work is tedious and boring—requiring a fatalistic, plodding patience and a literal turn of mind, rather than a sharp intellect and a keen insight—and therefore Ford privately considered West perfectly suited to the job.

"Ah, West, do sit down," Brownlee said. "Anything new on Lady Dudley?"

"Lady Dudley, sir?" West asked in puzzlement, as he sat down next to Ford and drew out a notebook.

Ford saw the allusion but sat back to watch Brownlee explain it.

"When Elizabeth became Queen of England in 1559, her favorite and putative lover was a certain Lord Robert Dudley, later the Earl of Leicester. It was possible they might have married but for one detail—he was already married. Shortly thereafter, Dudley's wife fell to her death down a flight of stairs, thus freeing Dudley to marry Elizabeth, if she would have him."

"Yes, sir?" West asked.

"Lady Dudley's name was Amy Robsart, a woman remembered in history for her death rather than her life. As it transpired, Elizabeth and Dudley never married, but Amy Robsart's death was never satisfactorily explained."

"I see, sir," West said stolidly, and Ford saw him make a note, Amy Robsart = Lady Dudley. "Do you want me to use the name 'Lady Dudley' in my reports, sir?"

"Have we found her?" Brownlee asked, moving on.

"Not yet, sir."

"Well, let's hope we do," Brownlee said. "In the meantime, get these fingerprints matched, if you would, West. They belong to Miss Robsart, and they may match these prints Croft took from Pengriffon's pinnace."

"Pinnace, sir?" West asked.

"It's the correct nautical term for a small seagoing vessel, West, or so I believe," Brownlee told him. "When we checked to see if Pengriffon was the lawful owner of the *Justicia*, that is the expression the shipyard used. Pengriffon purchased it about six weeks ago."

West added pinnace = launch to his notes, picked up the fingerprints, and left.

Brownlee eyed Ford severely.

"Inspector West is uniquely qualified to assist you on this case," he said.

"I don't doubt it, sir," Ford said, returning Brownlee's stare.

"To the best of my knowledge, he is the only member of the CID whom one can instruct to search South Kensington for an exceptionally well-endowed, attractive young woman, and ask her for her name, address, and telephone number, who would receive the order just as if one had requested him to seek out elderly and evil-smelling vagabonds."

"I see, sir," Ford grinned. "I'm sure he's not short of volunteers."

"There's a rumor that the commissioner feels he spends too much time behind his desk, and has offered to help out."

* * *

ord found the firm of Pollock, Pollock & Poole in the august
surroundings of Lincoln's Inn Fields in the Temple district of
London, where lawyers and their minions cluster as thickly as pigeons
in Trafalgar Square. Impressively gowned and bewigged figures strode
to and from the Courts of Chancery, the seat of English civil law, and
lesser mortals scattered in their paths.

Pollock, Pollock & Poole, Ford discovered, shared a fine Georgian
town house with two other firms. He climbed an elegant flight of stairs
to the upper floors, passed a door leading to Cornstalk, Abercrombie &
Cornstalk, and entered the outer office of Pollock, Pollock & Poole.

The room was lined with bookcases filled with fat, leather-bound
legal volumes, punctuated by portraits of lawyers past. The air had a
dusty smell, as if it had been held captive in this room for fifty years,
and Ford would not have been surprised to see one of the characters
from Charles Dickens's *Bleak House* step forth from the shadows.

A young lady—clearly not from Dickens's era—sat before her
typewriter at a desk in the center of the room, staring with total
concentration at the polish of her fingernails.

"Good morning," Ford said.

She spared him a flickering glance, saw that he was male and under
fifty, and gave him her full attention.

"Good morning," she responded. She removed her glasses and
replaced them. Evidently she was torn between her wish to look her
best and her wish to be able to see him clearly. "Can I help you?"

"My name is Ford; I'm a police officer," he said, and saw the
reflexive narrowing of her eyes that everyone makes when a policeman
announces his presence. Ford knew it was impossible to prevent a list
of one's petty misdemeanors rising unbidden before one's inner eye—a
shilling coin found in the street and surreptitiously pocketed, a model
soldier taken from a toy shop at the age of four, a "Do Not Walk On
The Grass" sign ignored.

"I'm here with regard to the Pengriffon trust," he said.

"Oh, yes, Mr. Ford. That poor man!" she said, perhaps relieved that
he was not here to arrest her for her inner list, and titillated by being
involved—however peripherally—in a murder investigation. "I saw it

in the *Evening Standard* on the bus home to Clapham Common last night. Murdered! Who'd have thought it? You'll be wanting to see our Mr. Jeremy Poole; he'll be in shortly. Would you like a cup of tea while you wait?"

She glanced up at him coyly, her eyes bright and promising behind her glasses. Such glances had always made him uncomfortable, with an overpowering urge to turn and run; but now, in the new security of his marriage, he returned her gaze.

"I expect Mr. Poole keeps you very busy," he said.

She glanced about to make sure there were no eavesdroppers and took him into her confidence.

"Well, Sir David Pollock's just a figurehead at PP&P these days, and young Mr. Charles Pollock's not too bright, between you and me and the gatepost. Not the brightest candle in the chandelier, if you know what I mean, so most of the work falls on poor Mr. Poole's shoulders. I don't think it's fair that he's the junior partner, with a simpleton like Mr. Charles over him."

"Dear me, I suppose not," Ford murmured.

"Still, Mr. Poole's trying to bring in his own clients, building up business, like, through entertaining and such, so Sir David will see where the future of PP&P lies, and it's not with Mr. Charles, even if his name is Pollock."

"Let's hope Mr. Poole succeeds," Ford said. He perched awkwardly on the corner of her desk to encourage the flow, feeling ridiculous.

She noted the gesture. "My name's Pattie, by the way, Patricia Edwards."

"I'm pleased to meet you, Miss Edwards," Ford said as gallantly as he could, feeling even more ludicrous and thanking God that Victoria could not see him.

"Mind you," she said, discretion tossed completely to the winds, "how Mr. Poole affords it all is beyond me. He even bought a yacht to take clients out, and they're not cheap, not by a long chalk. Sir David should've paid for it, in my opinion, but the old coot's too mean."

"Oh dear," Ford said.

"In the end, Jeremy—that's Mr. Poole's name, such a *lovely* name, I've always thought, not that I call him that to his face, of course—returned it to the boat makers. He said he didn't like it because his guests complained about the coal dust from the engine and the smoke, but between you and me, I think it was the money."

"Dear me," Ford said, grasping for sympathetic platitudes.

She settled comfortably to the task of gossiping. "And Mrs. Poole, Jeannie Clark as was, isn't any help to Mr. Poole's career, in my opinion, for all her stuck-up airs and graces. She's not as polished as I am, to be frank; it don't come to her natural-like. She was just the bookkeeper here until he got her in the family way, and she threatened to go to Sir David if he didn't do the decent thing. He's one for the ladies—Mr. Poole, that is—always was and still is, married or not, if you know what I mean. I have to say, in strict confidence, that his lordship was just the same, if not more so. He offered to paint me, and we all know what *that* means."

This must have triggered a thought, for her speculative glance returned. "Fancy a drink after work? I get off at five-thirty, just when the pubs open. I could meet you in the ..."

But Ford would never know her trysting ground of choice, for the outer door swung open and a tall man with heavily oiled black hair swept into the room.

Ford stood up, feeling almost as if he had been caught *in flagrante delicto*.

"Good morning, Mr. Poole," Miss Edwards said, changing upon the instant into a demure office assistant. "This is Mr. Ford, a police officer, come about Lord Pengriffon's murder."

Ford could detect no reaction to her announcement.

"I see," Poole said, and turned his attention to the secretary. "Fetch some tea, if you would, Miss Edwards, and bring me the Framlington files. Oh, and telephone Sir Robert Carstairs's office, and see if he can come in tomorrow."

Having dealt with more important matters, he turned finally to Ford.

"You're from the Cornish police? What's your name, again?" he asked.

"Detective Chief Inspector Ford, CID, sir," Ford said, and handed him his card.

"Why is the Yard involved?" Poole asked, examining the card

carefully, as if he suspected it might be a forgery, and deciding reluctantly that it wasn't. "Come, come, Inspector—you have no jurisdiction."

Ford could not tell if he was speaking from lawyerly caution or from a habitual arrogance that required him to find fault in everyone he met. Ford feared the latter.

Ford groaned inwardly. He found he had taken an immediate dislike to Poole, and he knew he'd therefore feel compelled to treat him with elaborate courtesy, and to fall over backwards to accommodate him, for fear of thinking himself prejudiced.

But there was something about the man that grated on Ford's nerves. Poole's oiled hair, smarmed down like a shiny skullcap so that it covered much of his forehead, his tailored business suit, and his stiffly starched shirt and collar, were somehow *too* elegant and *too* fashionable, as if they had been purchased to prove that Poole could afford them, rather than as a consequence of taste. Miss Edwards had described him as a lady's man, which would suggest he was hot-blooded, but he struck Ford as cool and calculating.

"We are assisting the county police, sir," Ford explained. "You may wish to telephone them, or Scotland Yard, in order to confirm my authority."

"No, I'll take you at your word," Poole said, in a manner that caused Ford to wait in case he added, "for the time being."

Poole made a show of examining the grandfather clock that stood against the wall and then demanded "Well, what is it?" as if Ford was an annoying schoolboy interrupting his busy schedule.

"I understand this firm is the trustee for the Pengriffon Trust, sir?" Ford asked him.

"We are, but I cannot divulge the details, as well you know."

Ford knew nothing of the sort—a trust is a contractual arrangement not protected by lawyer-client confidentiality—but he had no wish to argue.

"Perhaps you could give me some indication on how it is set up, sir: the authorities, the beneficiaries, and so on? I need to find out if the assets of the trust could somehow provide a motive for murder."

"That would not be possible," Poole said. "The information you seek is confidential."

"It would be very helpful to know if ..."

Poole overrode him.

"We can't have our files ransacked by every Tom, Dick, and Harry who walks through the doors claiming to be from Scotland Yard, nor can we permit private family matters to find their way thereby into the hands of the tabloid press."

Ford's first reaction was to wonder whether Mr. Poole was a relative of Lady Canderblank. No, he decided, for her invective arose from the fierce fires of her titanic temper whereas Poole appeared as cold as ice. He noticed that Miss Edwards's head was swinging back and forth between them as if she were a spectator at a tennis match, and now she was waiting to see if Ford could return Poole's volley.

"Very well, sir, thank you for your time," he said, in a tone devoid of emotion.

"You're *leaving?*" Miss Edwards burst out, unable to believe that Ford had surrendered and the confrontation was ending on such a pathetic note. Ford was reminded of a new poem that Victoria had read to him, written by a young American at Oxford and as yet unpublished, which ended, "not with a bang but a whimper."

"For the time being, Miss Edwards," he said to her, as if Poole were not in the room. "I'll have to obtain a search warrant for these premises. I hadn't realized it would be necessary. In the meantime, a uniformed policeman will be posted outside the door to ensure that no materials are removed from this office."

Miss Edwards tried unsuccessfully to suppress a grin—Ford had returned Poole's volley with even more force than Poole had delivered it. Her head turned immediately toward Poole, now left stranded on her imaginary baseline as the ball was whizzed by beyond his reach.

"That won't be necessary, Inspector," Poole said after a short silence, and Ford wondered if Miss Edwards would leap to her feet with a cry of "game, set, and match!"

Poole again made a show of examining the grandfather clock.

"Very well; I can spare you fifteen minutes. You'd better come into my office."

He turned to Miss Edwards.

"I believe I asked for tea some minutes ago, Miss Edwards, and yet I have no tea."

If Ford had thought him cold before, he was now arctic. Having failed to browbeat Ford, Poole had evidently decided to vent his spleen on his helpless secretary. She jumped up to obey.

"Nor do I see the Framlington files, Miss Edwards. Nor have I heard you telephoning Sir Robert's office."

He turned abruptly on his heel, and Ford followed humbly in his wake.

* * *

Ford followed Poole past the doors to two fine offices with views overlooking the verdant lawns of Lincoln's Inn Fields—with Sir David's and Mr. Charles Pollock's names engraved above their doors in gold leaf—and around a corner to the back of the building, where, beyond a dusty filing room, Poole's own narrow office had a view of a blank brick wall and a variety of Victorian rainspouts.

"I will resist providing you with the original documents, Inspector," he said, even before he sat down behind his desk. "I will, however, give you a description of the pertinent stipulations provided that you give me your word they will remain confidential."

He sat down without offering Ford the visitor's chair, and Ford remained standing, wondering if he could maintain his outward calm in the face of Poole's continuing rudeness. He suddenly imagined Victoria telling him not to allow himself to be upset by a man with an appalling hairstyle, and he grinned to himself.

"I can give you no such assurance, I'm afraid, sir," he said. "The details of the trust may become central to a prosecution. I will assure you, however, that the trust will not be mentioned unless it is germane."

"Very well, I'll have to take your word on that," Poole said, as if he were magnanimously conceding the point against his better judgment. *"Corpus delecti,"* he added, evidently hoping that Ford would be forced to ask what the Latin phrase for "relevant evidence" meant.

"Quite so, sir," Ford said, and Poole looked disappointed.

Miss Edwards hurried in with a tea tray balanced precariously in one hand and a large file labeled "Framlington" in the other. Ford took the tray from her before she could drop it and placed it carefully on the desk.

"I've telephoned Sir Robert's office, Mr. Poole," she said. "The appointment has been arranged."

Poole searched for something to criticize.

"I only need one cup. The Inspector will not be staying."

He leaned back smugly, evidently cheered by this fresh insult, and launched into a description of the Pengriffon trust.

"The first earl established the trust in the year 1860 and provided strict guidelines as to how it should be invested. The trustees have little discretion in that regard; it's as if the founder is still managing the money from his grave. The trust provides his heirs with a quarterly stipend."

"Who inherits on Pengriffon's death, sir?

"Lord Pengriffon's nephew, his late sister's son, is now the fourth earl. He is in Australia and may not yet be aware of his lordship's demise. I shall of course, be writing to him, since he is now entitled to the quarterly stipend."

"I see. What are his circumstances, do you know?"

"He is a sheep farmer, of all things, I believe. He has property in a place called Cootamundra, which I understand is in New South Wales."

Poole glanced at Ford crookedly, and his sneer returned.

"*Cootamundra*, one understands, is in the vicinity of *Wagga Wagga* and *Gundagai*," he smirked.

Ford wondered if Poole also mocked the residents of Chipping Sodbury, near Bristol, or the villagers of Over Wallop, Middle Wallop, and Nether Wallop in Hampshire.

"I see," he said without reaction, and Poole was forced to continue.

"The trust is a self-contained machine, Inspector, if you can grasp that simple analogy. There is nothing that can be done to modify it. The only beneficiary is the new earl, who would inherit anyway—unless one imagines some bizarre story under which he has traveled secretly from Australia and killed his uncle, in order to gain a few years of income."

"I see," Ford said yet again.

"You can therefore ignore the trust," Poole said. "That is why I was unwilling to divulge its contents—it cannot possibly be relevant."

He poured himself a cup of tea and smacked his lips to indicate pleasure. Ford, buoyed by Victoria's imagined comment about his hairstyle, launched onto a new tack.

"You saw much of the Pengriffons, sir?"

"I have never met them. I have never visited Trethgarret. Sir David, the senior partner, prefers to represent the firm to the family."

Poole tried but failed to keep resentment out of his voice. Clearly here was a bone of contention, just as Miss Edwards had implied.

"That seems a trifle, er, odd," Ford said, hoping to draw him out.

Poole, however, would not be drawn. "I repeat, Chief Inspector, I have not met the Pengriffons," he said. "Nor have I visited Trethgarret, nor Pengriffon Hall, nor its environs, nor their fine oil-fired fifty-two-foot launch in the harbor. I am happy to report, in fact, that I have never set foot in Cornwall, and, God willing, I never will. I am not a devotee of rural life, nor of those who live it. Do I make myself sufficiently clear?"

He lifted his fingers to his brow in a curiously tentative manner, and Ford realized that his improbable hairstyle had been designed to cover a large bandage on his forehead. Such a blow must have caused a prodigious headache, and the thought cheered Ford immensely.

"Very clear, sir. But you managed the day-to-day details of the trust, sir?"

"Such as they are."

"If Lady Pengriffon is not a beneficiary, how will she manage, do you know?"

Poole shrugged.

"The local estate is directly in the earl's hands, rather than in the trust. Presumably he made arrangements, but I really wouldn't know."

"Thank you, sir. One final question, if I may. Did Lord Pengriffon ever write to you about the accounts, or ask Sir David, to your knowledge?"

"Never," Poole said, and his tone hardened. "One understands he was something of a country bumpkin, more familiar with the workings of a cider barrel than with the mechanisms of a trust. He was, one gathers, and not to point too fine a point on it, a drunken Cornish idiot."

"I see," Ford said for the last time and made his departure.

Nine

Ford crossed the cobbled street to the spacious lawns of Lincoln's Inn Fields. He found a spot beneath a tree from which he could observe the front entrance of PP&P and lit a cigarette.

He reran the interview with Poole in his head. He had no reason to suppose that Poole was lying about the trust, in which case the only financial beneficiary in Pengriffon's murder would be the new earl. Ford would ask Brownlee to send a cable to the New South Wales police to start inquiries in Cootamundra. If James Pengriffon was well established and respected, and had not left Australia in the recent past, he could be ruled out as a suspect, and Ford would be back to Amy Robsart, and that would bring him back to Josephine Langley's testimony.

No one had left PP&P, he noted, stubbing out his cigarette against the tree trunk. He supposed he'd half hoped that Poole would rush out of the building and commit a criminal offense, so that Ford could arrest him and see if his arrogance sustained itself in the grim confines of a holding cell beneath Scotland Yard.

What a honeymoon! He was stuck with a missing suspect, and Victoria was stuck in a cottage hospital until Dr. Anderson could replace his missing nurse. At least Amy had been working day shifts, and Victoria would be released from her duties at six o'clock. But that didn't matter, because he was stuck in London, and she was two hundred miles away, almost as if she was a figment of his imagination.

"I'm an idiot" Ford burst out, much to the alarm of a passing nanny with a baby carriage. "A complete, *blithering* idiot!"

He began to walk as rapidly as he could toward Fleet Street, causing the nanny to adopt a protective, crouching posture before the carriage and to brandish her umbrella defensively, as if she feared Ford would attack her and snatch the baby.

"Excuse me, madam," Ford said, raising his hat. "I hope I did not startle you."

"I'll fetch a policeman," she said querulously, looking about for help.

"I *am* a policeman, madam," Ford replied. "Good day to you."

He plowed on, leaving her speechless, wondering if his leg could stand the strain of running. Better not risk it. He cut through an alley and into Chancery Lane, which leads down to Fleet Street, and there, thank God, was a passing taxi.

"Scotland Yard, as quick as you can," he told the cabbie, and clambered into the back.

"Are you sure, guv?" the cabbie asked, in a tone that suggested that Ford was an overgrown schoolboy having a joke at his expense.

"Quite sure," Ford said, and leaned back on the worn brown leather seat cushions so that he could berate himself at leisure.

Josephine Langley had described the afternoon before the night when Pengriffon was murdered. Pengriffon had painted Amy and then taken her into her bedroom. Later, Josephine had heard their voices raised in argument. His lordship had left, and Amy had emerged from the bedroom and said, "I'll strangle him!" and set off in pursuit.

In the circumstances, it was a completely believable account—*except that Amy Robsart hadn't been there.* She'd been at the hospital completing her day shift. She worked reciprocal shifts with Josephine Langley, as he recalled Dr. Anderson had explained; indeed, they could seldom have been in the cottage at the same time. The entire story, and therefore the entire basis for Amy's motive for murdering Pengriffon, was a fabrication.

"This is Scotland Yard, guv," the cabbie announced, as if he doubted Ford would recognize it.

"Are you *sure*, cabbie?" Ford grinned and gave him a ridiculously generous tip.

* * *

"Point taken, old chap," Brownlee said, after Ford had burst into his office without ceremony and explained the inconsistency in Josephine Langley's statement. "And therefore other points arise in consequence. For example, point, if Amy Robsart didn't do it, because she had no apparent motive, where is she, and why did she run away? Point, if Amy Robsart didn't do it, who did? Point, why is Josephine Langley lying?"

"*Ah!*" Ford exclaimed, as the sneaky thought that had evaded him all night suddenly stepped into plain view.

"Are you in pain, old chap?" Brownlee asked with mock alarm. "Have you managed to stab yourself in some unusual manner? *Caruthers!* Tea for the Chief Inspector before it's too late."

"Sorry, sir," Ford grinned. "But there was something rattling around inside my skull all night, and I couldn't quite put my finger on it until now. When I saw Josephine Langley for the first time, she was so distraught over Amy Robsart's disappearance that she needed medical attention. But the second time I saw her, yesterday afternoon, she didn't even ask if we'd found her."

"Ah," Brownlee said, and leaned back in his chair. "I hear the unmistakable glugging sounds of a thickening plot. Incidentally, Ford, it's quite difficult to put one's finger inside one's skull, so don't feel badly. So, let me see; point, does she know where Amy Robsart is and forgot to pretend that she didn't?"

Caruthers arrived with tea. Brownlee composed a wireless message to the New South Wales police in Sydney, Australia, to be transmitted courtesy of the Royal Navy.

"Science never ceases to amaze me," he said as he handed the message to Caruthers. "I'm sure the day will come when we can speak to them by telephone." He sat back. "Now, tell me a story, Ford."

It was his habitual way of asking Ford to summarize the facts in the case.

"Lord Pengriffon was an amiable man, sir," Ford began, sinking into a chair and easing his throbbing leg over the other. "He was a hedonist, I think; he lived for wine, women, and painting. I'm no art expert, God knows, but his paintings are cheerful and full of life, a celebration of beauty, if I'm not being too fanciful, and I can't help thinking they reflect his character."

"I've heard it said that a man's art reveals his soul," Brownlee mused. "If it's true, may God have mercy on Wagner's soul—or Igor Stravinsky's, for that matter."

Ford smiled. He'd known Brownlee for several years on a close day-to-day basis, and his boss still had the capacity to surprise and amuse him.

Brownlee, meanwhile, had adopted his customary listening position, with his eyes closed and his hands folded before him on the desk, as if in prayer, and Ford continued.

"Pengriffon got on well with his wife, in spite of having a mistress, and I think he loved Lady Justicia. He was popular and seemed to have no enemies—at least, no enemies that we've been able to discover so far. Now that we know Miss Langley was lying about Amy Robsart's outburst, we have no motive based on hatred, or any other emotion for that matter. Pengriffon had all the money he needed, and, as far as we know, he had no debts. The money—or most of it, anyway—is tied up in a trust, so there's probably no financial motive. We'll see what the Australian police say about his heir, but it seems unlikely he's involved."

"I concur," Brownlee murmured.

"The physical evidence of his death reveals nothing useful. He was murdered by strangulation with his own tie, with the knot behind his neck. He was drunk; it's possible he collapsed facedown into his bunk on his launch, and the murderer strangled him from behind. He was taken out to sea, presumably in the launch, and thrown overboard with a concrete block tied about his ankle. But that's all supposition; we don't even know where he was murdered."

Ford adjusted his leg and lit a cigarette while Brownlee remained sphinxlike.

"Therefore, sir, at this point we are reduced to inconsistencies and false notes. We have no explanation for Pengriffon's scribbles on the accounts or the cipher we found in his wallet. We have no explanation for Miss Langley's false statements, and we have no explanation for Miss Robsart's disappearance. We also assume that the murderer wished to conceal the crime, because he or she went to the trouble of burying the body at sea."

"*Véritable*," Brownlee murmured. He had spent some time in a collaborative transfer to 36 Quai des Orfèvres, which was roughly the French equivalent of Scotland Yard, and would sometimes trot out an odd French phrase or two. "In addition, old chap, we have no idea whether these facts have any relationship with each other." He opened his eyes. "Any ideas?"

Ford hesitated. "Perhaps we should ask the navy to lend us a diver to take a look at the spot where Pengriffon was found. It's probably a waste of time, but we don't have much to go on now that the case against Amy Robsart appears to have fallen apart. One of the locals suggested it, and it's not a bad idea. What do you think, sir?"

Brownlee took up his tobacco pipe and began to disassemble it.

"This thing requires more maintenance than a motorcar. A search of the burial area is a long shot—or perhaps I should say a deep shot—but not ridiculously so. I'll get the bureaucratic wheels in motion, and see if they can up-anchor and steam over to Trethgarret this very afternoon, or whatever it is the navy does to propel itself from one place to another. Anything else?"

"No other facts, sir; just the loose ends."

"Hmm …" Brownlee muttered. "I am struck by a *non sequitor*, if you can grasp my meaning, Ford. If the murder had remained undiscovered, as the murderer apparently intended, all the existing financial arrangements would have remained in place for at least seven years, until he could be declared legally dead." He paused to rap the bowl of the pipe smartly against the ashtray. "I must say, it's remarkable how disgusting the inside of a pipe can become—it's enough to put one off smoking. God alone knows what one's lungs must look like. In the meantime, Lady Pengriffon would have received the trust payments as if nothing had happened. Can you think of a crime in which someone was murdered for a benefit seven years into the future?"

"No, sir, I can't."

"Exactly. Perhaps Lady Pengriffon was not as happily married as we thought, or as placid as I understand she seems. Great Scott, it's remarkable how easily these wretched things can snap! Now I shall be forced to smoke the pipe my mother-in-law gave me for Christmas.

It's carved in the shape of a devil, and it summarizes our relationship perfectly."

"I dread to think what my mother-in-law would give me," Ford said.

"*Chaqu'un a sa belle-mère, mon brave,*" Brownlee grunted. "I'm bound to say, incidentally, that only a race as contrarian as the French would call a mother-in-law a 'beautiful mother.' I wonder if she's expecting a child."

"Your mother-in-law, sir?" Ford asked, nonplussed. "Mine?"

"Miss Robsart, old chap. If she is, the plot might thicken in a broad variety of ways."

Ford felt as if he had been struck by lightning for the third time in as many hours. "Good God, sir, I hadn't considered that!"

"Well, you're newly married," Brownlee grinned. "Perhaps you're still getting used to the, er, biological consequences of the, er, process."

"I'm an *idiot!*" Ford said, as he tried to see all the consequences at once. "The sooner we find her, the better, sir."

"Well, old chap, we have half the Yard searching for her, and I'm sure that every other police force in England would be glad to join in. In the meantime, I suggest you return to Trethgarret posthaste and get to the bottom of this Langley business, with the additional benefit that you and Victoria will thereby be de-sundered. The art gallery and the Bank of England can wait."

Ford scarcely heard him. How could he have missed such an obvious possibility? If Amy Robsart was pregnant, and Pengriffon had refused to take care of her, perhaps Josephine Langley had been telling the truth after all. Well, not the literal truth, but still the basis for a strong motive. Amy Robsart's medical ambitions would have been ruined, her chances of a successful marriage to someone else greatly reduced, despite her pulchritudinous appeal. The tie about Pengriffon's neck had been tightened in fury ...

Or, if the childless Lady Justicia somehow knew Amy Robsart had conceived, perhaps Lady Justicia had feared that Pengriffon really did intend to throw her over and marry Amy Robsart in the nick of time, thereby securing a legal heir and the pulchritudinous opportunity to engender many more, while Lady Pengriffon would lose her status in society and her financial comfort. The tie about Pengriffon's neck had

been tightened in fury, and hell hath no fury like a woman scorned
...

If he hadn't been so wrapped up in his honeymoon, he'd have grasped the obvious immediately. How stupid could he be?

"Well, sir, I'll just keep plodding along, I suppose. I've still got time to visit Pengriffon's gallery before the train leaves, and to look in on the Bank of England chaps—oh, and I've a pamphlet I'd like Dr. Waggoner, the psychiatrist, to take a look at."

He paused, and felt compelled at ask, "Look, sir, to be frank, are you sure you still want me on the case, after missing something so obvious? If you think I'm not ..."

"*Trainassez vous, mon vieux,*" Brownlee said, his eyes on his pipe. "Plod on, old chap." He pushed the broken pieces together hopefully, as if they might miraculously repair themselves, but the age of miracles, it seemed, was past.

* * *

The L'Arte Moderne gallery occupied a narrow, whitewashed structure in Brick Street, a cobbled street that hid behind the imposing buildings lining Piccadilly near Hyde Park Corner. The gallery's front window was given over to a large painting of a municipal gasworks on a rainy day, rendered in shades of gray and replete with angular pipes. A small card gave its title, *The Futility of Modern Life*, and Ford read that one could take this picture home and contemplate futility at one's leisure for a mere £100.

Ford entered and was greeted by a young man with floppy blond hair, which he cleared from his face with periodic tosses of his head. He was dressed in a corduroy suit and brown suede shoes, and a loosely tied polka-dot ascot sprawled from the open collar of his blue shirt. Why is it, Ford wondered, that "artistic" people go to such enormous lengths to dress in clothes that don't match each other?

"Good afternoon," the young man greeted Ford. "Are you interested in industrial art? I saw you looking at *Futility* in the window. It's representative of an important new trend—the industrial landscape as an allegory for the modern human condition."

"I'm afraid not, sir," Ford said. "I am a police officer, and I'm interested in Lord Pengriffon's work."

He handed his card to the blond gallery manager, who glanced at it, evidently disappointed that Ford was not a customer.

"Ah, yes, I read about his death in the newspapers, of course." The young man did not seem particularly upset by Pengriffon's death. "My name's Carrington, by the way; I'm the manager of this establishment."

Ford looked round the gallery walls and spotted two of Pengriffon's works in a far corner, squeezed between paintings of a sewage plant and an abandoned iron foundry.

"Those two back there are his lordship's work, Mr. Carrington?"

"Yes, Inspector; we also have a number of his works in the storage room."

"May I see them?"

Carrington led the way into a rear room, which was stacked with canvasses and crated works of sculpture. Ford guessed there were at least thirty of Pengriffon's canvases piled against the walls.

"How well do the Pengriffon works sell, Mr. Carrington?"

"Well, now and again. They're nice pieces, in their way—one might even say vivid—but they lack a sense of *gravitas*."

"*Gravitas*, Mr. Carrington?"

Carrington tossed his head and launched into an assessment of modern art. "The chaps who are defining modern art have moved far beyond Monet and Degas. Now it's the cubists like Picasso and Braque, and the surrealists like Max Ernst. Artists have come to understand that the world is not simple, and what we see is not what is. Indeed, I think that Picasso may one day be viewed as the most important painter of this century, although few would agree, of course."

He looked over at Pengriffon's work and shook his head. "Lord Pengriffon, on the other hand, was far too cheerful, far too hopeful, far too—shall one say too *bourgeois*?—to be important. A work of art shouldn't charm one's eye or give one pleasure. It should kick one in the stomach."

"I see, sir," Ford said. "So his work is not in demand?"

"Well, I should say not among serious collectors, Inspector; although I must admit his nudes exude a certain *joie de vivre*—one might even say *extravagance*—that appeals to a certain type of client." His tone left it clear that this was not a refined class of customer.

"He was, I believe, an investor in the gallery, sir?"

"Yes, he provided our funding and he paid for the lease," Carrington said, tossing his head once more. "I suppose if one cannot produce fine art, one can at least support those who can."

"Will the funding continue, Mr. Carrington?"

"Good God—I hadn't thought of that!" Carrington exclaimed, and brushed away his forelock in agitation as fear for his livelihood replaced condescension. "This could threaten the gallery. The art world requires capital. I'd better go and see the widow; it would be very unfair to cut us off without a penny. Has she mentioned the gallery?"

"I don't think she's addressed any business issues, sir, as far as I'm aware. But I will need to see the gallery's financial books and records."

"The books? Well, Lord Pengriffon did most of that himself; I just told him what I'd spent, and he wrote me a check each month. All I've got is my daily cash ledger—expenses, receipts for works sold, that sort of thing."

"I'll have to borrow that, sir, I'm afraid," Ford said. "I'll return it as soon as possible. How did you handle Lord Pengriffon's own work?"

"His work was on consignment. If we sold a piece he'd get three-quarters of the price, and the gallery would keep the rest, although, as I said, sales were fairly infrequent."

Ford recalled Pengriffon's secret scribbles.

"Do you recall selling a painting entitled *Nude in Bath IV*, Mr. Carrington?"

"Not offhand, but I can check." Carrington took out an account book and riffled through the pages. "Let's see … *Nude Reclining II … Nude Kneeling … Nude En Plein Air …* that's 'Nude in the Open Air,' in French. No, I'm afraid not."

"Well, thank you for looking," Ford said. "I'll return this as soon as possible." He took the account book, saddened by this concrete example of Pengriffon's self-delusion.

A fresh thought struck him. "I've heard it said that an artist's death raises the value of his work. Perhaps you could put some of these pieces on display? I think it might please Lady Pengriffon if you had some sort of exhibition in memoriam."

"Good lord, Inspector—that's an excellent idea!" Ford could almost see the cogs turning in Carrington's head beneath the flaxen locks. "I'm sure all the publicity could be put to good use. I'll put all this industrial art in the back; it isn't selling worth a damn. Perhaps I could even get the *Times* or the *Telegraph* to write a piece about the gallery and play up Pengriffon as a serious English name. This could be worth a small fortune!"

Here, at last, was someone who could benefit financially from Lord Pengriffon's death, Ford supposed, but he could not, for the life of him, attribute murderous intentions to Carrington.

"I'll put the seascapes on display for the general public, and arrange a private viewing of the nudes. I could raise the prices, and ..." Carrington checked himself. "Not, of course, that I'm pleased by his death, Inspector—he was a very decent man."

"So I understand, sir."

* * *

The Bank of England, known informally to Londoners as the 'Old Lady of Threadneedle Street' was one of Ford's favorite buildings in London—a large, pillared building in the classical style, but situated on a street too narrow for the passerby to be able to see it in perspective, and overshadowed by the more impressive London Stock Exchange; the overall effect was somehow pleasingly self-effacing.

A Bank of England guard—at least Ford thought he was a guard—dressed in a red uniform and wearing a top hat, led Ford silently through hushed, dim corridors. Occasionally they passed elegantly dressed bankers, who glided like wraiths in the surrounding gloom. Ford noticed a faint, somewhat musky odor, and wondered if it was the smell of money.

Eventually he was ushered into a room containing a table, three chairs, and two bankers. At first he took them to be middle-aged, but, as the conversation continued, he realized that they were young men in their twenties—the Bank of England must have an institutional bias that discouraged youth, and they had managed, like chameleons, to conform. They looked remarkably alike and were wearing identical suits and ties. Ford found it convenient to think of them as Tweedledum and Tweedledee, the enantiomorphic brothers encountered by Alice in Lewis Carroll's *Through The Looking Glass.*

The accounts Ford had taken from Pengriffon's secret drawer were neatly piled before them on the table.

"We appear to have a set of trust accounts that are in order, Chief Inspector," Tweedledum said, when the obligatory cup of tea had been served. "There are no *irregularities.*"

"Therefore the problem, if any, lies not in the *calculation* of interest and dividends, but in the *implied* capital," Tweedledee said.

"Implied capital?" Ford asked.

"The interest and dividend paid out by the trust can only be questioned if one questions the amount of *capital* involved—the number of shares in a particular company held by the trust," Tweedledum said.

"That is the *implication* of Lord Pengriffon's calculations," Tweedledee finished.

"Is it possible to check the accuracy of the numbers?"

"Interest and dividends are public information, of course, published in any newspaper," Tweedledum said.

"The *number* of shares *upon* which said dividends and interest were paid, on the other hand, would be known only to the trustees and the companies," Tweedledee contributed.

"Can *those* be checked?" Ford asked, finding—ridiculously—that he was falling into the idioms of their speech.

"They are not *public* information, Chief Inspector," Tweedledum replied. "However, in a *murder* investigation …"

"Cooperation with a police investigation would be *implied,*" Tweedledee completed his colleague's sentence.

"Quite so," Tweedledum said, and they both sat back.

So, there was nothing wrong with the statements at face value. If Pengriffon had doubted them, he had doubted the accuracy of the number of shares recorded. Or so, Ford thought with an inner smile, his scribbled calculations would *imply.*

"Would it be possible for you to be so kind as to telephone the companies involved?" Ford asked with elaborate courtesy.

"It might be simpler to ask the *custodian,* the bank in whose vaults all the physical securities owned by the trust are held," Tweedledum suggested. "In this case, I see it is Coutts and Company."

"In that manner, a *single* communication with Coutts would obtain *all* the underlying information," Tweedledee explained.

"Or one could, of course, telephone the *trustees*," Tweedledum said. "However, the situation implies …"

"That might not be *prudent*," Tweedledee finished.

"Quite so," Ford said. "Let me see if I understand your point. If the trustees were reporting smaller holdings than the trust actually owned—or held, perhaps I should say—then they would pay a smaller total in dividends."

"Exactly so!" the twins responded in unison.

"In which case, the missing dividend payments would be, er …"

"Missing!" they crowed.

He thanked them and left. As he trudged out through the musky halls he recalled that he had imagined, only yesterday, that he would resign from the police force and become a banker, in order to become sufficiently rich to enjoy a life of indolence in Victoria's constant company. Now he knew that he could never, ever, be a banker—at least by *implication,* he muttered to himself.

Ten

Ford's cheerful mood as he returned to Trethgarret was in sharp contrast to his grim frame of mind during his journey up to London the night before. This time he was traveling toward Victoria, rather than away from her.

He had telephoned her from Scotland Yard before leaving for the railway station. She and Mrs. Croft were still helping out at the hospital, Victoria had informed him, until Dr. Anderson could find other replacements for Amy Robsart and Josephine Langley. The hospital was experiencing a sudden inrush of patients—many claiming they had the symptoms of malnutrition—as news of Mrs. Croft's culinary magic spread rapidly through the community.

Sergeant Croft had conducted a detailed search of Pengriffon's study and had found yet another hidden drawer, containing—wait, she had written down Croft's words exactly, just a moment, she had had it in her hand not ten minutes ago, where the *hell* was it, ah yes, silly her, what was it doing there, of all places?—financial information about the estate indicating Lord Pengriffon had definitely decided to close the tin mines, which were managed by Mr. Thompson, the mayor, interestingly enough—well, perhaps it wasn't *that* interesting, come to think of it, and perhaps Ford knew that already. There was also a sheaf of correspondence between his lordship and the General Electric Company, with proposals for a new business venture, which seemed to be in their advanced stages.

Croft had summarized the information and then bundled the files up and sent them off to London to Brownlee, for the financial experts to review.

The operation on Mrs. Granger had been a success despite Victoria's tendency to confuse scapulas with forceps after all that time, and Dr. Anderson was hopeful for Mrs. Granger's full recovery. The other nurses thought Amy Robsart was far too nice to commit a murder, incidentally, and her absence—assuming it was permanent—would be a loss to the hospital. But, on the other hand, Josephine Langley was decidedly weird, and the hospital would be much better off if she never came back. It was their concerted opinion that Miss Langley had a crush on Lord Pengriffon and was jealous of Amy Robsart's pulchritudinous advantages, although the hospital almoner held the contrarian position that Miss Langley's ambitions were centered on none other than George Thompson—could you believe it?

Croft had also been contacted by the Royal Navy in Plymouth, and a naval diving tug was now anchored in Trefgarret harbor, captained by a handsome and dashing young lieutenant named Julian Graham, who just happened to be Victoria's aunt's nephew through the Shropshire branch of the Canderblanks; although, in comparison to Ford, she hastened to add, Victoria considered him to be downright ugly, since he, Ford, was unquestionably the most attractive, not to mention alluring, man in Europe—well, it could be mentioned, since it was self-evidently true.

There was also a diver named Chief Petty Officer Starkey who was pink, hairless, spherical, and monosyllabic, and she could now see the back of his rosy skull through the window, where he was sitting in the evening sunshine with the Ancient Mariner drinking a companionable glass of scrumpy.

And Croft, who was currently taking a stroll around the harbor with Mrs. Croft, had also tried unsuccessfully to see Miss Langley, who had not been at home on the two occasions he had called at her cottage. Clara had started a rumor that she'd been abducted by German sailors, or possibly a reemergent octogenarian Jack the Ripper.

Croft, incidentally, was a very clever man. He had found out that his lordship had filled the petroleum tank of his Bentley on the day before his death, and, therefore, Croft had been able to calculate how far it could have been driven by whomever, or was it whoever, had stolen it. He had then contacted the police in all the major cities within range, even as far away as Bristol, with an emphasis on those with major railway connections.

Oh, and Constable Crocker, such a nice man, had said that Mr. Crutchfield had seen his lordship's car driving up the High Street late at night, followed shortly by—guess what—the mayor's Humber. In the meantime, Crocker had been trudging the steep streets of Trethgarret, going door to door to see if anyone had seen Amy Robsart, or the *Justicia*, on the night of the murder. Mrs. Crocker, who knew the names and addresses of everyone in the village—naturally, since she was the postmistress—had compiled a list of inhabitants, and was dispatching poor Crocker hither and yon so that no potential witness would be forgotten.

In the meantime, and to move to more important matters, Victoria was feeling abandoned and cast off, and it was only because she felt she couldn't let Dr. Anderson down that she had not already applied for admittance to a nunnery, or whatever one did, although she might not pass the entrance exams, she supposed, due to her newly discovered but enthusiastically embraced devotion to matrimony in all its aspects, to which a vow of chastity would be hard to reconcile. It was therefore urgently necessary for Ford to return as soon as possible, and to try as hard as possible to solve the murder on the train—not that she expected there to be a murder on the train, of course, but she was sure he knew what she meant.

Following this telephone call Ford caught the night train to Penzance with a minute to spare and found the restaurant carriage, where he slowly chewed his way through what had once been a cheese sandwich, washed down with a whiskey and soda. He found himself grinning, despite the Great Western Railway's version of a Late Evening Supper, for he never ceased to be amazed by Victoria's ability to transform his mood from its customary pessimism into radiant happiness.

Life was changed in the blink of an eye, he thought grandiloquently, from a long, drab, gray suburban avenue eventually leading to a forgotten headstone in an overgrown country churchyard, into an exhilarating adventure, a journey full of unanticipated joys and unexpected delights.

Suddenly he was exhausted, and his brain refused to catalog and analyze the consequences of Amy Robsart's possible pregnancy. It would have to wait to the morning. He made his way back to his sleeping compartment through the lurching corridors, yawning prodigiously.

Unlike the journey up to London he slept deeply, and the sleeping carriage attendant had to shake him as the train pulled into Penzance. A railway station at six o'clock in the morning might not generally be considered a romantic spot, but Victoria, smelling sweetly of lavender and tasting of peppermint, was waiting on the platform, and the rest of the world ceased to exist.

"Now, Thomas, we must hurry," she said at last. "I would rather stay here and kiss you until lunchtime, but you and Croft have to try to see the equine Miss Langley. Dr. Anderson is sufficiently encouraged by Mrs. Granger's progress that he has permitted me time off this morning to see you. I will, therefore, drive you to your appointments and give you sultry and seductive looks at frequent intervals. Lieutenant Graham would prefer to go diving this afternoon—something to do with riptides, I understand. I'll pop in and sit with Mrs. Granger while you're gadding about on the ocean wave."

She led him to the waiting Humber and very soon they were purring out of Penzance with the rising sun to their backs.

* * *

Victoria turned the Humber into the narrow entrance of the lane leading down to the cottage shared by Amy Robsart and Josephine Langley. Croft and Crocker were wedged into the back seat. Crocker seemed on edge, and Ford guessed he was somewhat intimidated by such close contact with two Scotland Yard officers and the drama of investigating a capital crime.

"I must admit I don't like Miss Langley, Thomas," Victoria announced, as she adroitly avoided a pothole. "Not only has she deceived you, she's also caused me to forgo the pleasure of your company, and that is entirely unforgivable."

"I'm afraid I agree with you, Miss Canderblank—I mean, Mrs. Ford," Croft volunteered from the backseat. "Bless my soul! Some habits are hard to break."

"If you and Mrs. Croft would address me as V, as I have repeatedly requested you to do, or Victoria, or even, God forbid, Vickie, the problem would be solved."

"Oh, no, that wouldn't be right," Croft said.

"Will you address my firstborn as Master Ford or as Tommie?"

"Well, I don't rightly know," Croft chuckled, and Ford gulped at the sudden realization that he might, at some point, become a father with a son or a daughter. He imagined a daughter with Victoria's features and disposition, a miracle in miniature, who would climb on his lap and throw her arms tightly around his neck, demanding, "Tell me a story, Daddy!"

"There's the cottage," Victoria announced, and Ford was wrenched back from his domestic idyll to the prospect of an imminent and unpleasant interview. "You know, even though I don't like her, I feel sorry for her, for some bizarre reason. Why would she lie about her friend Amy Robsart?"

"Perhaps we'll find out shortly," Ford said.

"I'll wait in the car, Thomas, while you and Mr. Croft and Constable Crocker perform your constabulary duties."

"Got it," Crocker said.

Josephine Langley opened the door, saw Ford and Croft, and began to close it again.

"Miss Langley, it's important that we speak with you," Ford said.

"I've told you all I know, and I'm tired of telling you," she said, and her voice hardened to a snarl. "Now, *leave me alone!*"

She reached to slam the door, but Croft had stepped forward and placed a large boot against the jamb.

"I'm afraid we're well within our rights, miss," he said. "Best not to make a fuss, I always think."

Her face struggled between resistance and resignation. In the end she shrugged, retreated to a large armchair, and threw her long frame into it. Ford noticed a bottle of brandy and a glass on a small side table by the chair. She followed his glance and adopted an expression that reminded Ford of a rebellious adolescent.

Crocker closed the front door and stood before it, while Croft pulled out his notebook and fountain pen. She stared at each of them, and Ford was struck with a shaft of sympathy; three large men had invaded her sitting room, and her only support was a bottle of brandy.

"Well, what do you want?" she demanded, and Ford hardened his heart.

"Miss Langley, you are a material witness in a murder case," he began. "You have sworn that Amy Robsart threatened to kill Lord Pengriffon, that they quarreled, and that she set off in pursuit of him."

"I told you what I know. What's wrong with that?"

"What's wrong with it, Miss Langley, is that it isn't true."

"Prove it!" she said.

Ford sighed internally. It was his experience in similar situations that innocent people tend to respond with a fervent, "It *is* true; I swear to God!" or some such expression; whereas the guilty usually respond with a defiant, "Prove it!"

"Very well," he said. "You described a session in your cottage during which Lord Pengriffon painted Miss Robsart, then made love to her, then quarreled with her, and then left the cottage with Miss Robsart in pursuit."

"So?"

"You stated that all this took place on the afternoon before Lord Pengriffon died."

"Yes, so?" she demanded again.

"Your statement would lead us to conclude that Miss Robsart followed Lord Pengriffon, killed him, buried his body at sea, and then fled from Trethgarret."

"So?"

"But she wasn't here, Miss Langley."

She stopped, as if the express train of her testimony had run off the track and into a mountain.

"What do you mean? Of course she was here," she said finally, narrowing her eyes as if trying to calculate the direction of Ford's questions. "You can't prove she wasn't."

"She was on duty at the cottage hospital at the time, Miss Langley, and there are doubtless many witnesses to support that fact. Your shift times are the opposite of hers, and therefore you see her here at home only infrequently. She currently works from six in the morning until six at night. You start at six and work until the following morning."

"Well ..." she began, but could find no obvious answer. She reached a tense hand toward the brandy bottle, and then she withdrew it.

"Miss Langley, I urge you to change your testimony before you have to swear to it in open court and expose yourself to a charge of perjury. I suggest you tell us what you know about this whole affair, without invention."

She paused, and Ford watched as she tried to mend the tatters of her statement.

"Well … perhaps I was mistaken as to the time; it must have been the last time I saw them together. But it still happened, word for word, just as I said."

"Miss Langley, you have made and signed a false statement to a police officer—that's a criminal offense for which you could be sentenced to a prison term. However, if you now make an honest and complete statement of what you really know, we can disregard your previous account."

"There's nothing wrong with my previous account."

"Very well, Miss Langley," Ford said with a sigh. "I regret that I will have to ask Constable Crocker to take you into custody on a charge of obstruction of justice."

"Got it, sir," Crocker said from the doorway.

"I must also warn you formally, Miss Langley," Ford continued. "You are not obliged to say anything, but anything you do say may be taken down and used in evidence against you."

She looked up at him with a mixture of defiance and fear, while Ford silently berated himself. He'd backed her into a corner, and he knew not one damned thing more than he did when they entered the cottage.

She couldn't conceivably be lying to protect Amy, since her evidence was designed to put Amy in the worst possible light. It was far more likely that she was lying to protect herself, but he had not even an inkling of what her motive might be. If she was lying to protect someone else, then who, and for what reason? All he had managed to do was to expose her lie without discovering the truth.

Croft stirred, his pen poised above his notebook.

"Look, Miss, you're being a bit silly, if I may say so. If you're lying to protect someone, it will just be all the worse for you as well when we get to the bottom of this mess. If you're not protecting someone else, then we'll have to think that you're directly involved in his lordship's murder."

Her hand crept out toward the brandy bottle, and this time she poured herself a drink. The men watched as she gulped it down. Her hands gripped the glass so tightly that her knuckles were white.

"It's best to get it off your chest, I always say," Croft said, his voice little more than a whisper. "Face up to it, take the consequences, and then get on with the rest of your life. Leastways, that's what works for me."

She stared at Croft as if trying to take his measure, and Croft stared stolidly back.

"Amy hated him," she said in a low, fierce voice. "She wanted to marry him, and he wouldn't. He was just using her."

Croft's intervention had not worked, Ford thought; she was still lying.

"Did you know that Lady Pengriffon is aware of their relationship and tolerated it?" he asked. "Did you know that she and Miss Robsart are on pleasant terms? Did you know she told Lady Pengriffon she would never marry an older man?"

"So what? That's just her ladyship's word against mine. Amy was never bothered by age—she'd go with anyone in trousers."

Ford glanced at Croft, who shrugged his shoulders microscopically, as if to tell Ford that Josephine Langley was one of those witnesses who just keep lying, no matter what. So, he thought, until they could find Amy Robsart there was nothing more to be done. Unless … Perhaps he should try a different line of questioning.

"Miss Langley, when I first came to interview you, two days ago, you were distraught over Miss Robsart's disappearance—so distraught, in fact, that you needed medical attention. Since then you have not once asked if we have found her, or how our search is progressing. Why is that?"

"Why is what?"

"In addition, you always refer to her in the past tense, as if she were dead."

"What do you mean?"

"You know exactly what I mean."

She stared at him in defiant silence.

"Do you know where she is, Miss Langley? Do you know what has become of her?"

She shook her head obstinately and said nothing, and Ford was left wondering if she was simply refusing to answer his questions, or whether she didn't know the answers.

"My husband is a fair man, Miss Langley," Victoria said from the doorway, and everyone started with surprise. "Look, this isn't very professional, I know, and he'll shoot me as soon as we leave here, which I doubtless deserve, but you *must* trust him. He'll lean over backwards to see your side of things. Whatever you've done, or whatever you know, you *must* tell him."

Ford was too astonished to do more than gape. Josephine Langley was staring at Victoria with narrowed eyes.

"That's easy for you to say, you with your good looks and your nice figure and your posh husband and on your honeymoon and all," she shot back at Victoria, and Ford had the distinct impression that he, Croft, and Crocker, had all dropped out of her consciousness.

"Were you jealous of Amy?" Victoria asked, and Miss Langley reacted as if she had been pierced by an arrow.

"He came here to paint her, but she wasn't here," she burst out, as if a dam holding back her inner furies had finally broken. "I asked him to paint me instead, but he didn't want to. I told him I was worth painting, and he should take a look, but he wouldn't; he made some excuse and left, all poshlike, and oh, sooo polite." She broke into parody. "Oh, Miss Langley, that's an extraordinarily generous offer, to be sure, but I really mustn't intrude upon you further."

Ford stole a glance at Crocker, who was beet red with embarrassment at this outpouring of raw emotion. Croft was poker-faced, and Victoria looked as if she'd burst into tears at any moment. God alone knew how he himself must be looking.

Josephine Langley's eyes burned with bitterness and self-loathing. "He rogered everything in skirts within twenty miles, but I wasn't good enough for him. I even said we could do it in the dark so he could pretend I was Amy. But he left anyway. I hated him, and I hated her, with their giggles and their rogering here, there, and everywhere. Now he's dead and she's gone, and good riddance to both of them."

"Did you go out to the *Justicia* that night?" Ford asked, willing himself to press on. "Did you see them there?"

"He came that afternoon, on his way to the pub, looking for her, and he left again without giving me a second thought, like I said. I just couldn't face the hospital, so I walked around, and later I saw him in the Duke. So I went out to his boat, and I got into his bunk. I thought he'd come in drunk, and roger me anyway."

Ford thought he heard Crocker groan. Words still tumbled from Josephine Langley's lips.

"I heard him climb on board, but he didn't come down. So I went up on deck and there they were, as naked as jaybirds; he was bare-assed rogering Amy in the open air. He had nothing on but his tie. They saw me and giggled. I wanted to die, I was so ashamed. I hated him, I hated her, and I hated myself. So ... so I climbed down into the dinghy and came home."

"*What*, Miss Langley?" Ford could scarcely believe she had ended so lurid a confession—true or invented—with so lame a conclusion. "You left them? Just like that?"

"I left them to it—what else was I to do? The next day I guessed they quarreled and she'd killed him, by accident perhaps, and dumped him at sea and run off. I've been terrified she'll come back and kill me."

A fresh spasm shook her. Victoria crossed the room to comfort her, and Ford, feeling hideously embarrassed, crept from the room, with Croft and Crocker at his heels.

* * *

Ford and Croft, still shaken by the interview with Josephine Langley, sat down outside the Duke to enjoy the morning sunshine. Crocker excused himself, saying that he felt he needed to go home and have a good wash under the pump in his backyard.

"Let's not start with Josephine Langley, Croft," Ford said with a shudder. "I think we need a little time to pass before we try to digest her testimony."

"I couldn't agree more, sir," Croft said. "That was ... well, it was awful, to my way of thinking."

"Let's start with Justicia Pengriffon instead," Ford said. "She appears to be a passive person, but that doesn't mean she is incapable of strong emotions. She dismissed her husband's infidelity as no more than him scratching an itch, but his scandalous behavior with Amy Robsart must have had *some* effect on her, surely?"

Croft nodded.

"Perhaps she's like a sleeping volcano, sir—dormant, I think the word is, for long periods and then exploding without warning, like that one in Italy, Mount Vesuvius. If she thought Pengriffon might throw her over, particularly if she thought that Amy Robsart might be carrying his child, who knows what she might have done."

"That's true; I agree," Ford said, trying to envision Lady Pengriffon in the grip of uncontrollable rage. "But the murderer was a powerful person, and Lady Justicia doesn't strike me as the violent type."

"You never know, though, do you, sir?" Croft said "She's too calm, to my way of thinking. 'Hell hath no fury like a woman scorned,' as they say."

"On the other hand, Croft, if Amy Robsart really is carrying his lordship's child, she's just as likely a suspect as Lady Justicia. If he was refusing to marry her, Amy Robsart would be ruined."

"So a pregnancy makes them both suspects. It works both ways, doesn't it?" Croft pondered aloud. "They'd both have powerful motives, for opposite reasons."

Ford went inside to fetch coffee. A pint of scrumpy might take the sharp edge off Josephine Langley's astonishing statement, but unfortunately it was too early in the day for such an indulgence. He carried the coffee out to the table overlooking the harbor, where Croft was waiting for him, his face lifted blissfully to the sun. Ford could swear that he could see Croft's nose twitching to the tang of the salt air, and his ears to the cries of the gulls. He sat down reluctantly, unwilling to disturb Croft's moment of reverie, knowing it was his antidote to the ugliness of Josephine Langley's wretched catharsis.

"It's a damned shame to waste such a beautiful day on work, Croft," he said. "Cheers."

"Cheers, sir. God bless," Croft said, lifting his cup in Ford's direction. "I must admit I was miles away. I've always been a freshwater fisherman, but it might be interesting to toss a line into the harbor and see what happens."

Ford loathed fishing and everything to do with it—the wretched business of skewering writhing worms, the inevitable snarling of the line into a Gordian knot, the predictable decomposition of the reel mechanism into tiny, incompatible pieces of metal with a propensity to fall into the water, the endless waiting for a nibble, the frustration of mishandling a bite, the gruesome process of removing a hook from a gasping fish sufficiently hapless to permit itself to be caught in spite of one's blunders—but he also knew Croft loathed golf, Ford's sporting obsession, and Croft, a true gentleman, always feigned interest nevertheless.

"What would you catch, do you think, Croft? Plaice? Cod? Mackerel?"

"I really don't know, sir; perhaps I'll ask those chaps when I get a moment," Croft said, jerking his thumb toward the fishermen on the dock.

"There's fish aplenty," the Ancient Mariner volunteered from his table. "There's garfish, pollock, mullet, gurnard, whiting, bream, dogfish, skate, monkfish; there's whatever you want."

"What's the best bait, Mr. Ham?" Croft asked.

"That depends on where and when; fish be particular. I'll show you, if you like."

"That would be very good of you," Croft said. "There's nothing I like better than a spot of fishing."

"Well, let's solve this case in the next half hour, Croft," Ford smiled. "Then you can spend the next week fishing. In fact, the navy might permit you to try when we're out on their diving vessel this afternoon."

"And you can get back to your honeymoon, sir," Croft said. He turned his back to the harbor, and Ford knew it was to prevent his thoughts from straying from the case.

"Duty afore pleasure," the Ancient Mariner nodded. "It's always best." He closed his eyes.

"You know," Croft pondered, lowering his voice so that they would not be overheard, "I still can't tell if Josephine Langley's telling the truth, or not, sir. She could just be a pretty good actress, and making it all up to embarrass us and make us feel sorry for her. All that talk of … well, you know what I mean, and the way that she said it, as if she hated herself. I didn't know where to put myself, to tell you the truth." He shook his head. "Thank God Mrs. Ford was there, if I may say so, sir; there to get it out of her in the first place, and there to calm her down afterwards."

"I know one thing, Croft, Ford said. "I'm not going to believe a word Miss Josephine Langley says without corroborating evidence."

"Very true, sir."

"Speaking of corroborating evidence, we have housework to do, Croft. We still have to finish the house-to-house check of the buildings facing the harbor, in case anyone saw the *Justicia* leaving the harbor— or any other boat, for that matter."

"I'll do that, sir, while you're out with the navy," Croft volunteered. "And we'd better look for Miss Langley's fingerprints on the *Justicia*, now she's admitted—claimed—she was onboard. And …"

A shadow fell across Croft's face. Ford turned and, squinting up into the sun, he saw his mother-in-law, her baleful face rimmed by a parasol.

"I understand you have been threatening the distinguished partnership of Pollock, Pollock & Poole," she began, and Ford had no doubt that the occupants of the bar inside the Duke, and the fishermen mending their tackle across the way on the jetty, could hear every word—and possibly even the gossipers loitering in the distance at the corner of High Street. "Sir David Pollock is a dear friend of mine, and I will not tolerate your unseemly assaults on his profession. As soon as I return to London I will speak to the Lord Chancellor in the strongest terms."

Ford and Croft stood, as politeness demanded. His attempt to say, "Good morning, Lady Canderblank," was drowned out by her next salvo.

"Sir David telephoned me this morning to inform me that you had attempted to breach the walls of confidentiality which must necessarily and properly surround his trusteeships, and reduced his office to an uproar."

Ford knew that saying, "I did no such thing," would not stem her tide.

"Your repeated attacks on the pillars of society in general, and the aristocracy in particular, lead me to wonder if you are a Bolshevik, and this is all part of some nefarious communist plot. One wonders, in fact, if you are an *agent provocateur* in the employ of that dreadful little Russian Bolshevik—Comrade Lemon, I believe his name is—intent on overthrowing the established order."

Ford had often wondered if the best way of dealing with her was to remain silent, thinking of more pleasant things, such as Lady Canderblank falling into Lenin's hands, until eventually she ran out of ammunition; however, as he now realized, it was quite possible she would never run out of ammunition.

"Are we all to be dragged from our beds and shot by the mob, like the poor czar and his family?" she demanded, her falsetto reaching toward an operatic climax. "Are worthy gentlemen such as Sir David to be impugned with imp—"

She stopped suddenly, and Ford suppressed a giggle. He was certain she had been about to say "impugned with impunity," but had caught herself just in time. He knew that happy thought would sustain him through the remainder of her tirade.

"I'm so glad to see you, Lady Canderblank," Croft intervened unexpectedly, just as she was gathering her breath to continue.

"You are?" she asked in surprise.

"Yes, madam. I was about to come and see you, while the Chief Inspector makes his telephone call to Superintendent Brownlee."

"You were?"

"Yes, madam. We were hoping, what with all your connections in the best society, if you could help us with the question of whether his lordship had any enemies. It would save us from bothering Lady Pengriffon, and, to be entirely honest, you're much more a leader of society than she is."

"Well ..." she said, while Ford marveled at Croft's ingenuity.

"You're late for the telephone appointment, sir, and you know the superintendent doesn't like to be kept waiting," Croft said to Ford, and turned back to Lady Canderblank. "Would you like to sit here in the sunshine, madam, if it's not too strong? Perhaps you'd care for a cup of tea or coffee? Let me go inside and order one while you settle yourself, my lady."

Croft dusted off a chair with his handkerchief and assisted her into it, and then he almost dragged Ford into the Duke.

"Croft, that was marvelous!" Ford burst out as soon as they were out of her earshot.

"Well," Croft grinned, "I thought you'd probably have to telephone him anyway, sir."

"True, but I am forever in your debt, Croft."

Ford found that Charlie's office was empty, and he went through the tedious business of placing the telephone call.

"Ah, Ford, I was about to telephone to you," Brownlee bellowed as soon as the connection had been established. "The examiners at the Bank of England started with Lord Pengriffon's calculations and worked backwards. It seems he was under the impression that the trust had more shares than the trustees were reporting—that's what he was calculating."

Tweedledum and Tweedledee had been true to their promise, and pursued their *implication*.

"*Can you hear me, Ford?*" the telephone erupted.

"Yes, sir, extremely well," Ford answered. He had known artillery officers who had been deafened during the war by constant exposure to the thunder of their field guns, and he wondered if daily telephone conversations with Brownlee might have the same effect. "If I understood them correctly, sir, he—Pengriffon—thought the trust had twenty thousand shares of something, whereas the trustees reported he only had eighteen, for example."

"Exactly, old chap. Therefore he was receiving dividends from eighteen thousand shares, when he thought he should have been paid for twenty."

"Perhaps there's some innocent explanation, sir. Perhaps, for example, the trustees sold some shares, and Lord Pengriffon was too uninterested to pay attention at the time."

"Apparently not, Ford. Let's consider the case of the shares of the firm named G. Binswanger and Company, for example. I have some notes on that in front of me."

The telephone emitted blissful silence while Ford imagined Brownlee positioning his reading spectacles at precisely the right angle on his nose.

"Yes, here it is," Brownlee resumed, shattering the calm. "The trust records report that the trust holds ninety thousand of those shares. However, the chaps at the Bank of England checked with the custodian bank, and their records indicate that the trust holds one hundred thousand, as Pengriffon's notes indicate. They also checked with the company, just to be absolutely certain, and one hundred thousand is the correct number."

"Are they sure—the Binswanger people, I mean?"

"Very sure. It's by far the largest individual holding in the company. Each quarter they pay the dividends on the full amount to the trust, but Pengriffon receives only ninety percent. Pengriffon must have concluded—and, on the evidence to date, the Bank of England concurs, if you follow me—that the trustees were deliberately embezzling his money."

"*What?*"

"There's no need to shout, Ford," Brownlee yelled back.

"Sorry, sir," Ford grinned. "But human error is far more prevalent than fraud, sir. It could be an innocent mistake, copied from report to report to report."

"That's what I thought, old chap, but the Bank of England blokes say the amounts are far too significant for a mistake to have been overlooked."

"But an obscure company named Binswanger ..."

"It was called Binswanger when the old earl set up the trust, and the trustees still report it as such, but it changed its name in 1886, old chap. It's now known as General Electric."

"Oh," Ford said. The probability that the trustees could have overlooked so many shares in such a large company was remote, to say the least.

"We'll obviously have to go back to the trustees, Ford, tomorrow at the latest, and get to the bottom of this. Do you want West to do it, or do you want to come back to London again?"

Ford most emphatically did *not* want to go back again. His lurid imaginings for the evening did *not* include another sleepless night alone in another railway carriage.

"I'll come up tonight by the sleeper train, sir," he heard himself say.

Eleven

Ford returned outside to tell Croft of this latest turn in events, but he and Lady Canderblank had disappeared.

"He drove her off to Pengriffon Hall," the Ancient Mariner volunteered from his habitual table.

"Oh, thank you, Mr. Ham," Ford said, his mind preoccupied with Brownlee's news. Poole had the day-to-day responsibility for the trust accounts, he thought, but surely someone would have noticed the discrepancies—the typist, Miss Edwards, for example—unless, of course, someone else was doctoring the statements or more than one person was involved in the conspiracy to defraud the trust.

However, the whole idea of embezzlement seemed absurdly far-fetched. Someone had simply made a clerical error, and it had perpetuated itself. The balance of the funds, which should have been paid to Pengriffon, was doubtless piling up in the trust. A simple comparison of the trustees' own books, in comparison to the statements sent to Pengriffon, would resolve the matter entirely.

In the meantime, he had to turn his attention to Josephine Langley's bizarre and thoroughly unpleasant statement. No wonder Crocker had felt he had to go home and wash himself after witnessing so ... so obscene a testimony. Hell hath no fury like a woman scorned, as Croft had said; she had set her cap at his lordship and been rejected, and she had been tortured by his scarcely hidden affair with Amy Robsart.

She must have reached her breaking point. She had gone out to the launch and done the deed. Ford recalled how tightly the tie had been pulled round Pengriffon's neck—that was an act of primordial fury, not an act arising from the kind of cool calculation that would inspire the conduct of a sustained financial fraud. The notion that she had seen them *in extremis*, as it were, and simply rowed away, as she had claimed this morning, was ludicrous.

It was almost certain that she would confess. If not, Amy Robsart, when and if they found her, would testify against her. Ford experienced a sinking feeling in his stomach. If Josephine Langley had strangled Pengriffon in fury, would Amy Robsart have escaped unscathed? Perhaps she'd jumped into the harbor to escape Josephine Langley while Langley was throttling Pengriffon, and had swum to the shore. She'd have been scantily dressed or perhaps even naked. She couldn't ride her bicycle in that condition; she'd have taken the Bentley and driven away. Now she was in hiding, fearing Josephine Langley's wrath.

But that made no sense at all. She'd have gone straight to Crocker to raise the alarm, clothed or unclothed. Besides, the Ancient Mariner had said he'd seen a man driving his lordship's Bentley away from the docks, and he would certainly not have failed to note her unclad moonlit pulchritude, a latter-day nocturnal Godiva.

Croft had already planned to search the launch again, this time for evidence of Josephine Langley's presence. If he found it, and if she pleaded guilty, a competent barrister would be able to convince a court that "the balance of her mind was disturbed," as temporary insanity was legally described, and she'd escape the hangman's noose. She'd be remanded to an institution for the criminally insane, and remain there "during His Majesty's pleasure," as the court would phrase it, until she was judged to pose no further threat to society, or until she died.

It *had* to be the Langley woman, Ford thought, and now he doubted that Amy Robsart had survived the encounter. It was a far more likely explanation for his lordship's murder than some convoluted fraud, even if there really was a fraud. If Pengriffon had become convinced he was being defrauded, he'd have confronted Sir David Pollock and gone to the police, and he had done neither. He hadn't even mentioned the possibility to Lady Pengriffon. Any irregularities in the trust arising from financial mismanagement might cause PP&P considerable embarrassment, but that would certainly not have precipitated his murder.

On the other hand, Ford thought in exasperation, the entire

encounter on the launch could have been the product of Josephine Langley's overheated imagination. Without physical evidence to place her on the *Justicia* …

"It's too good a day for a long face, Mr. Ford," the Ancient Mariner broke into his thoughts. "Particularly since Mr. Croft has carried off the gorgon."

"Yes it is, Mr. Ham," Ford laughed. The Ancient Mariner's description of his mother-in-law was perfect—the mythological female monster with vicious fangs and deadly snakes instead of hair, and with the power to turn men to stone with one glare of her dreadful eyes— Lady Deborah Cander-gorgon!

"Unfortunately, until I can solve his lordship's death, my face will get longer and longer."

"That's no way to spend a honeymoon."

"Very true, Mr. Ham." Ford sat down. "However, while I have motives and suspects aplenty, I haven't a single scrap of hard evidence."

"Well, t'wasn't Amy Robsart, like everyone thinks," the old man said, with a knowing nod. "There's not a mean bone in her body, as I told thee afore."

Ford wondered again exactly how ancient the Ancient Mariner was, but could find no polite way of asking. Instead, he surprised himself by asking, "What about Miss Langley, Mr. Ham?"

"There be mean bones aplenty in that particular body," the Ancient Mariner said—once again, Ford noted, speaking with absolute certainty. "Mean bones, and a troubled soul."

Mean bones and a troubled soul, Ford echoed silently. If her fingerprints were on the launch controls, then they'd have her—except, of course, he'd had precisely the same thought about Amy Robsart less than twenty-four hours ago. He stared out at the *Justicia*, serenely at anchor, and he wished the launch could speak.

"They say you're going a-diving, Mr. Ford," the Ancient Mariner said.

"Er, yes, Mr. Ham," Ford said, redirecting his attention to the gray bulk of the naval diving vessel. A dinghy rowed by two sailors was approaching the dock. "I decided to take up your suggestion."

"Well, the tide's turning; best be on your way, Mr. Ford. Time and tide, as they say, wait for no man."

The Ancient Mariner closed his eyes, and Ford crossed the dock to wait for the sailors.

* * *

The English Channel had seemed completely calm from inside the harbor, but as soon the naval diving sloop HMS *Noah* left the protection of the harbor mole Ford discovered that appearances could be deceptive. What Lieutenant Graham described as a "slight swell" felt, to Ford, like heavy seas. The crew seemed oblivious to the heaving of the deck, going about its duties with casual surefootedness, and Ford clung grimly to a stanchion hoping he would not completely disgrace himself.

The *Noah* was broad and stumpy and had a no-nonsense air, as if it were an overgrown version of the tugboats that hauled lighters up and down the Thames outside his windows at Scotland Yard. The deep-throated engines beneath Ford's feet growled and grumbled, and *Noah* shouldered its way through the swell like a heavyset man in a crowded pub, as enduring as the church and lighthouse receding behind them.

"Diesel engines," Graham told him, pointing downwards to the deck. "They're the latest thing; steam will be a memory in twenty years, I shouldn't wonder."

They turned southwest along the coast, and Ford tried to ignore his stomach and focus on the beauty of the cliffs, with tiny, hidden, sandy coves at their bases. He would have to take Victoria for a swim from one of these secluded beaches, guarded by jagged pillars of ancient rock like granite sentinels. Afterwards he would build a fire from driftwood, and they would share a romantic picnic. Then, perhaps, with the warmth of the sun on their skin, and the roar of the surf in their ears, as alone as if they were on an uninhabited desert island, or like Adam and Eve in the Garden of Eden, they might cast their fig leaves aside …

"The Little Dogs," Graham said in his ear, causing Ford to all but topple over the side in his surprise.

"Ah," Ford gulped, in a sudden panic lest Graham could read his mind.

Graham was pointing at two tiny, rocky islands, barely discernable above the waves, their presence announced by flying spumes of spray. "According to the fishermen, they snared Pengriffon's body just about here."

A few brief orders brought the *Noah* into the wind; a massive anchor chain roared through a hawsehole in the eyes of the sloop, and the motion of the deck changed from a roll into a pitch as the *Noah*, now held stationary by her anchor like a reluctant bullock on a leading rope, met the swell head on.

The crew assembled an array of complex diving equipment with practiced ease. Ford recognized none of the equipment, except for a big brass diving helmet with a thick glass faceplate and an electric light, like a motorcar headlight, above it. He stooped to examine it and lifted it cautiously with both hands, only to discover that it weighed at least sixty pounds.

The diver, a chief petty officer named Carney, emerged from a companionway. He was bald, short, plump, and pink, just as Victoria had described him, and was dressed in long woolen underwear, so that he seemed to be an overgrown baby. The illusion was strengthened when he dusted himself with talcum powder. The diving crew gathered round him and helped him into an oversized suit made of rubber and canvas, with permanently attached gloves and feet, and a large brass collar. He stepped into heavy metal boots; the crew hung a belt loaded with lead weights around his waist and attached a variety of wires and tubes to his suit.

One of the crew gave Carney a lighted cigarette, and he took a long, luxurious draught. He stared up into the sky as if he felt he might never see it again. Then he reached down and scooped up the helmet in one hand, as if it weighed nothing, placed it over his head so that it rested on the brass collar, and the crew screwed it into place.

One of the wires was attached to a derrick, and he was hauled up by his shoulders and dangled over the sea, and then he was lowered slowly to where he could stand on a ladder attached to the side. One of the crew placed a pair of earphones over his ears and spoke into a horn-shaped mouthpiece, and Ford realized that the diver must be connected by a telephone cable.

"Diver ready, Captain," the telephonist said to Graham.

"Commence diving," Graham said, and the telephonist relayed the order.

The diver let go of the ladder and he sank into the opaque gray-green water. His brass helmet was visible for less than a second before the sea swallowed him up; only the wires and air tube attested to his existence. Ford felt a sense of anticlimax; he had slipped beneath the waves not with a splash or even a whimper.

The pawl on the derrick capstan clanked steadily as the sailors let out the wire, a foot or so at a time, and an air pump whooshed and squeaked with monotonous regularity. Ford pictured the diver dangling in the green gloom, descending slowly into emerald darkness.

The deck trembled slightly as the engines idled; waves slapped against the sides; the breeze rattled the rigging and blew acrid fumes from the funnel into Ford's nostrils; and the omnipresent seagulls screamed. Ford leaned over the side and willed his eyes to pierce the impenetrable water, but to no effect.

"There's nothing to do but wait," Graham said. "Five minutes to get down, five minutes to get his bearings, and then he'll start to search. His speed will be determined by the nature of the seafloor, the strength of the current, and how far he can see. The correct action in these circumstances, as recommended by the Admiralty Diving Manual, Section Five, is to, and I quote, *(a) adopt a mental attitude of patience and (b) have a cup of tea.*"

Ford grinned, and a young sailor handed him a mug containing the strongest, sweetest tea that Ford had ever tasted. Brownlee would have loved it, Ford thought.

The sailor with the earphones stirred.

"'E's on the bottom, sir; mud and sand mixed, flat, five knot sou'west current, ten foot visibility," he reported.

Ford busied himself with the task of lighting a cigarette against the breeze, and he tried to be patient. He'd look like an idiot if the diver found nothing, he thought. Even if he found nothing, he realized, that didn't mean there was nothing to be found; there might be some vital clue buried in the mud beneath the diver's armored feet, or just beyond the limited range of his searchlight. Perhaps the ship was anchored in the wrong spot. Perhaps ...

"Finished Quadrant One, sir," the telephonist reported. Graham had organized the search into four square quadrants, each a hundred yards on a side, with the anchor marking the center point where the squares met. Carney would be walking—wading—up and down each square, as if he were mowing a lawn. The diver had searched the first quadrant without result. Ford glanced at his watch; that had taken about half an hour.

He watched as the sailors exchanged their duties. Monotony led to carelessness, Graham explained, and almost all diving accidents are caused by human error. By changing jobs every few minutes the men were less likely to become bored.

The breeze picked up. Ford turned up his collar and tried to think about the case. What the *hell* had Pengriffon been up to? Think about it logically, he told himself. His notes indicated that he'd questioned PP&P's accounting, which meant that he'd questioned Poole's accounting. Poole, he recalled from his conversations with Miss Edwards, had married PP&P's bookkeeper, which meant, at least speculatively, that Poole and his wife could have been cooking the books.

But since their marriage Miss Edwards had been preparing the accounts, and she just didn't seem the type to engage in systematic fraud. The Pollocks had not noticed any discrepancies, although, according to Miss Edwards, they were not particularly able—Pollock senior was just a figurehead, and Pollock junior was not the brightest lightbulb in the family chandelier. But even so, one never knew when some outsider—a chartered accountant, for example—might not review the books.

Perhaps there were two sets of books—an honest set kept by Miss Edwards and reviewed by the Pollocks and outside auditors, and a second set concocted by the Pooles. The official set would report all the assets and all the earnings, while the second set would have reported lesser amounts, and it was this second set had been sent to Pengriffon. In that case ...

* * *

"Captain!" the telephonist called, and Ford jumped. "The CPO reports a body in Quadrant Two."

"What do you want him to do, Chief Inspector?" Graham asked Ford.

"What condition is the body in?" Ford asked, resisting the automatic response of, "Is he sure?" Carney did not appear to be a man who made mistakes.

The telephonist relayed Ford's question and then blanched.

"'Alf eaten by crabs, sir. It's, it was, a woman."

The telephonist listened again.

"She's anchored down by her leg, floating, like."

There was not the slightest doubt in Ford's mind that they had found Amy Robsart, or what remained of her. There had been two murders on Tuesday night, and Amy Robsart's death, like his lordship's, was supposed to be undiscovered. They had been buried together, and Jimmie's trawl net had scooped up Pengriffon's body but missed hers.

"Please ask Mr. Carney to search the surrounding area, particularly in the direction of the current," Ford said. "Then ask him if he can bring the body to the surface."

"Aye aye," said the telephonist.

Josephine Langley had discovered them together. She claimed she'd seen them and left, but was that likely, given her overheated state of mind? His lordship was half drunk and presumably thoroughly distracted, if that part of Josephine Langley's account was true. She could have grabbed his tie and, in the grip of a jealous fury, disabled him with one vicious yank, crushing his larynx. He would have been immobilized immediately, and he might well have collapsed on top of Amy Robsart, who would have been pinned down beneath his weight, at least few a few seconds, and perhaps immobilized by shock, and Josephine Langley could have …

"There's bits of debris scattered, the CPO thinks from an old wreck," the telephonist reported. "'E wants a net sent down and 'e'll put some of it in." The crew scurried to attach a large netting bag to a rope, with a couple of lead weights for ballast, and sent it down to the ocean floor.

"'E's tying a rope to the rope round her foot, sir, if you follow?" the telephonist said. "That way she won't get pulled apart in case her leg comes off when we haul her up."

Ford managed not to shudder.

The telephonist listened again. "Mr. Starkey's sending up a marker buoy, sir. 'E thinks 'e's fifty yards abeam to leeward."

Ford looked around wildly but could see nothing but waves, until he noticed that Graham and the rest of the crew were all staring in the opposite direction.

"Buoy-ho starrad, abaft the mizzen," a sailor announced incomprehensibly, and Graham pointed so that Ford could see it; a small orange flag atop a diminutive buoy was playing hide-and-seek amid the wave tops.

"Stand by to maneuver," Graham said.

It took five minutes to reposition the *Noah*. Ford realized that it was no minor feat to move a two-hundred-ton ship sideways, in spite of the current and the wind and the slapping of the waves, and all the while keeping the wires and tubes attached to the diver and the chain tethering them to the anchor, clear of the hull and the churning propellers, and yet the crew accomplished the maneuver with no more effort than Victoria executing a flawless double-clutch.

"Ready on the net; ready on the rope, sir," the telephonist announced eventually.

"Very well," Graham said. "Bring the diver up to five fathoms, if you please. Easy as you go."

"Aye, aye, sir."

Graham turned to Ford. "We'll bring Carney up to thirty feet, and leave him there for half an hour to decompress. If we bring him straight up, there's a risk of the bends—gas bubbles forming in his blood vessels, which is very painful and sometimes fatal."

"I see," Ford said, with a stab of guilt that he had placed the diver's health at risk.

"Don't worry, Chief Inspector; it's completely routine. We'll bring up the rest when he's back on board. The living take priority over the dead."

Ford fretted for forty-five minutes, until CPO Carney was safely back on board, his helmet had been removed, and a cigarette inserted between his lips. He was blue and shaking with cold, Ford saw with another guilty pang. Graham gave him a shot of rum, and a sailor handed him a mug of tea.

"She's no a pretty sight, sir," Carney said to Ford, in a broad Lancashire accent. "Belt around her neck like she was strangled with it, and half her flesh is gone. She's wearing a skirt; that's how I know she's a woman. The crabs have been at her for days."

"Weighed down at her ankle, you reported, Mr. Carney?"

"Aye, with a rope and a lump of concrete." He paused to inhale on his cigarette. "There's other wreckage down there, but nowt to do with her, I'd say. There must have been plenty of ships to founder in these waters over the years."

The crew hauled up the net, now containing an assortment of odd-looking bits and pieces, and dumped it unceremoniously on the deck, where it lay unregarded.

Amy Robsart followed. She rose slowly from the water feet first, secured by a fresh rope around her ankles; her skirt indecorously above her thighs—what had once been her thighs. Her upper torso and her head were concealed beneath her dripping inverted jacket, and her long hair trailed seawater.

A crab disengaged itself from her clothing and returned to the sea with a splash, and Ford barely restrained the urge to vomit. The crew pulled her inboard and lowered her to the deck with surprising gentleness, while managing to avoid looking at her.

Ford knelt on one knee and pulled down her skirt. One glance at where her face and hands had been was enough to tell him that she would have to be identified by her dental work. A thin leather belt was pulled tightly around her neck, in a manner similar to the tie around his lordship's neck. The buckle was in the design of the Red Cross, as nurses often wear, and Ford noted she had no belt around her waist.

She had a large masculine wrist watch on the exposed bones of her right wrist; her pockets were empty. He hesitated over searching beneath her clothes and decided against it. He was not certain whether he was protecting Amy Robsart's privacy from the sidelong glances of the sailors, or whether it was an excuse to delay discovering the full limits of the crabs' foraging activities.

He lifted one shoulder and hip to see her back, but there was nothing to be seen. The belt had not been pulled quite as tightly as Pengriffon's tie, he noted as he tested it cautiously. It was as if the murderer had sought to associate them in death, rather than to kill them in an identical manner; or perhaps Pengriffon had been murdered in passion, and she had been murdered in cold blood. Dr. Anderson would doubtless examine the bruising beneath the belt and render his opinion; in the meantime, it was impossible to tell whether she had sustained any other injuries.

Her skull seemed somehow misshapen. Had the salt water bloated her head? Or had the crabs ... He turned away. The ghastly wreckage of Amy's once rampant beauty, the lurching of the deck ... He bent over, willing his stomach to be still.

"May I have a tarpaulin, please?" he managed to ask, and remained kneeling beside her until she was decently covered.

He stood, and he noticed relief in the crew's eyes. Who knew what hardships and dangers they endured without complaint in the harsh life of the sea?—and yet they could not stomach the sight of a decomposing corpse.

The net contained the same kind of haphazard rubbish that Alfie's net had contained; random flotsam and jetsam lost from passing ships over the decades. One stick-like object, encrusted with barnacles, seemed vaguely familiar; Ford picked it up and turned it over, and saw it was—had been—a rifle.

He showed it to Graham.

"Is this a Mauser 98, do you think?" he asked. It had been the standard equipment of the German infantry in the war, and God alone knew had many Mauser bullets had been fired in his direction across no-man's-land on the Western Front.

"It looks like one, but it seems too short."

Carney bent over it.

"Mauser Karabiner 98 assault carbine," he said. "Seen them before; they were issued to German naval and U-Boat crews for use by raiding parties."

"U-boats? There's a local legend that a German U-boat sank somewhere in these waters."

"Do you want me to go back down?" Carney asked.

"Oh, no, thank you, Mr. Carney. I'm sure it has nothing to do with the case, but this will delight the village gossips."

"Who knows what's down there?" Graham asked. "Phoenician galleys from the old tin trade, from before the life of Christ ... Spanish galleons from the Great Armada, sunk by Sir Francis Drake ... a smuggler or a privateer or a pirate ship or two, I'll be bound. These waters have been a busy thoroughfare for two thousand years and more. Why not a U-boat?"

He turned to the crew. "Well done, chaps. Let's get this tackle squared away, if you please; chop, chop! I want a large marker buoy secured in this spot, in case this gentleman needs us to return." He looked up at the bridge above their heads. "Coxswain, please take bearings off those to headlands and the Little Dogs and mark the chart. Now, Mr. Carney, I suggest you get below and change into warm clothes."

The crew scattered to its appointed duties, and Ford lit another cigarette and tried to stay out of the way. In due course the *Noah* ponderously turned its raked stern to the breeze and chugged back toward Trethgarret, and Ford was left alone to contemplate the pathetic bundle that was all that remained to Amy Robsart. Yesterday I was ready to conclude that she was a murderess, he thought, and now she's a victim.

They passed the bell buoy, and Ford did not need to ask for whom it tolled.

* * *

Young Frank, festooned with photographic equipment, emerged from his front door just as Ford was passing on his way back to the Duke.

"It's a bit late for photography, isn't it, Frank?" Ford asked, pausing to chat, torn between politeness and his desire to see Victoria. "The light's fading."

"Well, Mr. Ford, I often walk around the harbor and see if I can capture the evening light—long shadows, that sort of thing. I'm even trying time exposures at night, now that I've saved up for this tripod."

He adjusted a large mahogany and brass contraption suspended from his neck by canvas straps. The last time Ford had seen something similar was in the trenches holding a periscope, through which he could stare across the hell of no-man's-land and sometimes glimpse the glitter of a German periscope lens staring back.

"At night? Good lord, I can't take a decent snapshot in broad daylight. Do you get anything in darkness?"

"Well, no, not usually; I'm afraid it's hit and miss," Frank admitted. "It helps if the moon's out, of course."

A thought struck Ford.

"You didn't take any photographs on the night Lord Pengriffon died, did you, by any chance?"

"Well, I tried, but nothing came out." As Ford had noticed before, his enthusiasm for his craft overcame his natural reticence. "There a new kind of German camera called a Leica; his lordship gave me one—I couldn't possibly afford it. It's ten times better than anything else, although you're not supposed to say anything good about Germany, not these days."

"What did you take on that night—do you remember?"

"I tried to take Amy Robsart on the railway dock. She was leaning on her bike and thinking, and her face seemed open, somehow, as if you could see her thoughts."

"What time was this?"

"Oh, nine-ish, I suppose."

"Where you in the shadows?"

"I ... I'm not a Peeping Tom, sir," Frank said.

"I'm not suggesting you are, Frank. It's just that you may be the last person to see her alive, apart from her murderer. Tell me exactly where you were and what you did."

"Oh my God—I never thought of that!" Frank spluttered. "Well, I stood back inside the railway shed on the dock. I thought if the camera's in darkness, and the subject's in moonlight, the contrast might be enhanced—less ambient light on the lens. I don't know—I was just playing around, to tell you the truth."

"Did you keep the negatives?"

"Of course, sir, I always keep everything, even if it's a bust."

"May I see?"

Ford followed Frank up the narrow staircase, with his tripod clattering against the banister posts and his unseen mother's voice rising in stentorian protest at the noise. Frank sorted out a developed roll of almost clear negatives and a number of black positives.

"Would you mind lending these to me?" Ford asked. "I'll give it to the Scotland Yard photography labs, and see what they can do. They've got all sorts of equipment."

"God, sir, I'd love to see that. Taking pictures is only half of photography; the other half is in the darkroom."

"Would you like to go? Would your mother let you?"

Ford suffered through fifteen minutes of complaints about encouraging Frank in his foolish fantasies of escaping his inevitable subterranean fate as a tin miner, like his father and his grandfathers before him, in pursuit of a la-di-da job of doubtful morality as a photographer.

When she finally paused for breath, Ford quickly told her that Frank's expenses would be paid, and he would receive a fee for his time. He named a figure that caused her eyes to widen, and her tirade against the foolishness of a photographic career was replaced by a long string of instructions about his best suit, a clean shirt, shiny shoes, and other sartorial details necessary to make a good impression at Scotland Yard. In fact, he'd better have a bath *immediately*, even though the boiler was out and the water was cold. In the meantime, she'd run next door to see if the barber was still open.

Ford left Frank to his packing and walked down to the Duke to buy himself and Croft a quick pint of scrumpy before dinner time.

* * *

Ford stepped out of the Duke to clear his head of the buzz of conversation and the blue-gray pall of tobacco fumes and the sweet, lingering odors of scrumpy, and stepped into a different world. There was a whisper of a breeze, too slight to ruffle the calm waters of the harbor. The moon, huge and gibbous, stared down, and Ford could see every vessel that lay at anchor. He was reminded of the poet Tennyson's words, *And on a sudden, lo! the level lake / And the long glories of the winter moon.*

Lord Pengriffon had stood where he stood. He had crossed the road to relieve himself, and then bumbled his befuddled way down into a dinghy. He had rowed slowly across the placid waters to the *Justicia*, perhaps conjuring up a painting that would capture the sharp, overwhelming, brooding, silent essence of the long glories of the summer moon, and then clambered aboard.

And then what? Was Amy Robsart waiting for him in an amorous mood, or was she filled with murderous fury? Or did he encounter Josephine Langley, unhinged by unrequited passion? Or, if someone else was waiting for him, then who the *hell* was is? And, regardless of whomever it was, where and how did Amy Robsart meet her fate?

The door of the Duke swung open behind him, emitting a brief burst of chatter and fumes; Ford turned and saw it was Clara Davis and her friend Mabel Norris.

"Good evening, ladies," he said.

"Getting a breath of fresh air, Mr. Ford?" Clara asked. "Solved the murder?"

"I wish I had," Ford smiled. "I was just trying to picture the night his lordship died. You saw his lordship's motorcar, over there by the railway sheds?"

"Oh, yes," Mabel said. "Where he usually left it."

"And there was another one, back in the shadows," Clara added.

"Another motorcar, Mrs. Davis?" Ford asked. "Can you describe it? Did you recognize the make?" If there was a second vehicle, it could well have been the killer's.

"Well, *I* never saw no other motorcar in the shadows," Mabel said. "On the other hand, *I* hadn't been drinking enough Guinness to give myself double vision, like some I could mention."

"I did, honest," Clara wailed. "It wasn't the Guinness making me squiffy. Big and black, like … like George Thompson's."

"You saw George Thompson's Humber, Mrs. Davis?"

"Well, I'm not saying it was his for sure," she faltered. "Not for certain, like, not cross my heart and hope to die."

"Well, I'm glad to hear it," Mabel said. "I fear for your immortal soul sometimes, Clara, what with your fibs."

"I'm not fibbing, I just don't know the maker—I can't be more honest than that, can I? Besides, I'd worry about my own soul, if I was you, Mabel Norris, what with that plumber always coming round and …"

"*The plumber?* How *dare* you, Clara Davis! Just because our kitchen sink keeps backing up and …"

"Er, excuse me, ladies, if I may," Ford broke in before more lurid details could emerge. "I wanted to be sure of something you said about the night his lordship died. You said you thought you saw a German sailor, Mrs. Davis, on your way home?"

"Are you making fun of me?" she demanded.

"No, I assure you," Ford said. "It could be very important."

"Well, I really did," Clara said, pointing across the harbor to where the railway dock lay bathed in moonlight.

"Well, *I* didn't," Mable said, equally as firmly.

"I believe it was a clear moonlit night, just like tonight, and I think you said you saw someone lurking in the shadows."

"I saw him out of the corner of my eye, you know how it is," Clara confirmed, and her friend rewarded her with a derisive snort.

"Could it have been a woman?"

"Definitely a man; too tall to be a woman, and wearing trousers, besides."

Josephine Langley was unusually tall for a woman, Ford thought, and wore jodhpurs. If the "German sailor" was really her, it would place her in the vicinity.

"Well, more and more women are wearing trousers in public these days, Mrs. Davis."

"That's not right, in my opinion," Mabel intervened. "Fashions have been shameless since the war, if you ask me. That Amy Robsart was a prime example—her skirts were almost up to her knees, and as for her neckline, if you could call it that, leaving nothing to the imagination, for all the world to ...."

"Well, she was artistic," Clara said, in half-hearted defense.

"Private parts are called 'private parts' for good reason," Mabel said with puritanical severity, perhaps to offset Clara's comments about the plumber.

"Knees aren't private, not in that way," Clara shot back.

"Knees lead you know where, Clara, begging Mr. Ford's pardon."

"A tall woman wearing trousers would look ..." Ford attempted to intervene.

"Just as brazen," Mabel overrode him.

Ford abandoned his attempt to turn the probably imaginary German sailor into a tall English nurse.

"Can you describe the man in the shadows, Mrs. Davis?" he asked.

"Well, tall, definitely tall, and foreign-looking, and skulking about."

"Foreign-looking in what way?"

Clara squeezed her eyes tightly closed.

"Long dark hair, sort of shiny, and wearing London clothes, Mr. Ford."

All the locals referred to anyone who hadn't been born in Cornwall as "foreigners," Ford realized; he was a foreigner.

"Clothes like mine?"

"Oh, no, much grander and refined, like the Prince of Wales wears in the newspapers, with one of them black capes. That's why I noticed him." She caught herself. "Not that you're not well-dressed, I never meant to say that, Mr. Ford—of course not!"

"That's all right, Mrs. Davis," Ford chuckled.

"You're making it all up, Clara," Mabel intervened again. "A glass of Guinness, like you were drinking that night, and you start seeing things. You were telling me how they think that Jack the Ripper might have been a prince, and you're just …"

"I'm not making up nothing, Mabel Norris," Clara retorted. "I know what I saw, as clear as I can see you now."

Ford lost track of the ongoing exchange as he conjured with the notion of a well-dressed stranger half hidden in the shadows. Could she have really seen someone, and, even if she had, could she really have made out his features and his clothes in the shadows of the railway dock? Could it have been …

"… and cold, hard eyes, all a-glittering in the moonlight," Clara's expanded description intruded on him, and Ford's train of thought veered to his imaginary courtroom.

"This alleged man that you saw, Mrs. Davis," the barrister would say. "You have told the court that he was standing in the shadows, and that his eyes were glittering?"

"Yes, sir."

"Can you tell us how that happened?"

"What do you mean, sir?"

"Well, Mrs. Davis, you have testified—under oath, I would remind you—that he was in the shadows, and his eyes were glittering." Here the barrister would whip off his glasses. "If the man was out of the moonlight in the shadows, and yet his eyes were, nonetheless, glittering in the moonlight, did his eyes detach themselves from his face and float forward into the brightness of the moon?" Stab. "I put it to you, Mrs. Davis, that your recollection owes a great deal to the inebriating effects of the beverages brewed by Guinness & Company." Stab, stab.

"The inebry-what, sir?"

"No further questions, Mrs. Davis."

And thus, Ford thought ruefully, Clara's remarkably clear description of the hidden man would be rendered ridiculous—but not to Ford, because shiny dark hair, grand clothes, and cold, hard eyes, all added up exactly and precisely to one Jeremy—such a *lovely* name—Poole, Esq., of Pollock, Pollock & Poole. In which case, he thought with sudden savagery, I will pin this murder on …

"They say they found a German gun, Mr. Ford," Clara intruded into his thoughts. "Is it true?"

"What, Mrs. Davis? Oh, yes, a German carbine. I understand they were sometimes issued to U-boat crews."

"Well that proves it, then!" she crowed in triumph. "The only way it could have been down there is if a submarine sank near it."

"Well, it's a possible explanation," Ford said.

"Now, don't start again, Clara," Mabel said. "We've had enough tall tales for one night, thank you very much." She seized Clara by the elbow and dragged her homeward. As they receded into the darkness Ford heard Mabel's voice wailing in frustration, "But there *aren't* any German sailors!"

If Poole had really been here, Ford thought, returning to Mabel's earlier description, then he'd have to prove it. Brownlee could get Inspector West to interview Mrs. Poole, although she'd probably give her husband an alibi.

Twelve

"WEll, it's obviously completely awful," Victoria said. "But, on the other hand, I'm rather glad Amy Robsart's a victim and not a murderer, if you can follow that rather macabre line of reasoning. I always envisioned her as a happy person."

"It's very sad," Mrs. Croft said. "She was well-liked up at the hospital, there's no question about it, in marked contrast to the *other one*."

"That may well be true, but let's not jump to conclusions, Betty," Croft said. "I agree that Miss Langley's a strange one, but that doesn't mean she did it."

Ford sat back and lit a cigarette. The next best thing to having dinner alone with Victoria was to be having dinner with her and the Crofts. He wasn't sure how long they'd been married, but he assumed it was twenty years or more. If he and Victoria could be as comfortable together after twenty years as the Crofts seemed to be, then he'd be a contented man.

They were eating dinner in the privacy of their room at the Duke, an enormous privilege awarded them by Charlie, who had insisted they needed to be able to talk undisturbed, on account of the distressing discovery of a second murder victim, and Charlie had been laboring up and down the stairs with laden trays as a consequence. In addition, the entire public bar would not be listening over their shoulders, and nor would George Thompson presume to join them.

"Well, Hercule?" Victoria asked Ford. "Did Josephine Langley kill them both, or not?"

"Hercule?"

"I've decided that calling you Sherlock Holmes is not solving the case fast enough. I'm therefore recasting you as Hercule Poirot, the detective in the novel by the new author Agatha Christie. Perhaps Hercule's performance in the *Mysterious Affair at Styles* may inspire you.

"Oh yes, I read that book," Mrs. Croft said. "It was a bit, I don't know, too complicated, if you know what I mean. I don't know if Mrs. Christie's books will ever be popular."

"Well, she's just published a second one, called *Murder on the Links*. Are you a reader of detective stories, Mr. Croft?"

"It's a bit too much like taking the job home, Mrs. Ford," Croft said. "Besides, if I wanted to pick a really clever detective, I'd pick Mr. Ford over any of them."

"Well, that's very kind of you to say," Ford said, blushing a trifle, knowing Croft was not pandering. "However, I've never said anything profound like, 'When you've eliminated the impossible, the remainder, however improbable, must be true,' or, 'The little things are the most important.'"

"But you did say *cui bono,* sir."

"That was Cicero," Ford said. "The credit belongs to my Latin master at school, who drummed it into me, along with a score of other phrases. I'm not sure what Hercule Poirot would do at this juncture, but I suggest we take it step by step."

"Poirot is not pedestrian," Victoria said. "He leaps forward on the wings of inspiration. Nonetheless, please continue."

"*Merci.* Let's start with what we know. Given Josephine Langley's extraordinary statement—the statement she made this morning, that is to say—we now have no reason to suppose there were any difficulties between his lordship and Amy Robsart. It was, one might say, a model affair."

"Yuck!" Victoria groaned. "Painful paradigms aside, they met on the *Justicia* on Tuesday night, but, unbeknown to them, Josephine Langley was also on board, and surprised them."

"Or so she says, Mrs. Ford," Croft commented.

"Exactly so, Croft," Ford agreed. "The question before us is whether we can believe *anything* that Josephine Langley tells us. We suspected Amy Robsart because Josephine Langley lied to us about the relationship between Pengriffon and Amy. Now we suspect Josephine Langley because she claims she was on the *Justicia* on the night they were murdered. On both occasions she was very convincing, but on at least the first she was lying through her teeth."

"Why would she lie about being on the launch, sir?" Mrs. Croft asked. "Why would she put herself at risk by saying she was there?"

"She was completely out of control when she admitted it, Betty," Victoria said. "It was absolutely awful; I simply can't imagine she'd make up a story that was so damaging—so humiliating. She'd been driven crazy by jealousy, and she just couldn't stop herself."

"Perhaps, but let's stick to what we know," Ford said. "Pengriffon and Miss Robsart were murdered in an identical manner and buried at sea in the same spot. We're assuming that means that both murders occurred at the same time and were committed by the same person, but we don't know that for sure."

"Indeed, sir," Croft said. "We'll wait to see what the doctor says—whether he says she was strangled, and whether he can say she's been dead for four days, since Monday night. If his lordship and she were, well, if they were, as Miss Langley said, were, er ..."

His voice trailed into red-faced silence.

"Please don't feel embarrassed, Mr. Croft," Victoria smiled. "Remember that I'm now a married woman."

"Well, yes, of course, Mrs. Ford, but even so ..." Croft spluttered.

"You know, there's something very odd about this whole situation," Mrs. Croft interrupted him. "If ..."

She was interrupted by a knock on the door. Croft rose to answer it. It was not Charlie with their desserts and coffee, as they had expected, but George Thompson.

"I heard the divers found Amy Robsart," he burst out without preamble. He was flushed and breathing hard, as if he had run a considerable distance. "I heard at the mine and came back immediately."

He made to brush past Croft and enter the room, but seemed to realize at the last moment that Croft was not the sort of man one could brush past without potentially adverse consequences, and so he stood on tiptoe in the corridor, staring over Croft's broad shoulder, bereft of his customary self-importance.

"Good evening, Mr. Thompson," Ford said, suppressing a groan at this interruption and cursing his own civility. "Yes, I'm afraid she's dead."

Croft glanced at Ford, who nodded, and Croft stepped back.

"Did she commit suicide?" Thompson demanded, advancing into the room. "If she killed him, and then herself, it would lay matters to rest."

Ford was uncertain just how she would have managed to strangle herself, climb over the side of the *Justicia* and plunge to her watery grave, return on board and sail the launch back to its customary moorings in the harbor, and subsequently return to her resting place beside his lordship.

"Well, it's a bit early to say, sir," he managed to mumble.

"It's the only logical explanation," Thompson pressed on. "Trethgarret could get back to normal. It's my job to keep everyone calm, and I've the good name of the town to consider. The jobs of honest working men hang in the balance."

"Indeed you do, sir," Ford said. "We'll let you know if we confirm your hypothesis."

Charlie appeared in the doorway with a fresh tray. He cleared away their dinner plates and served them spotted dick and coffee while Thompson hovered uncertainly, apparently searching for some reason to remain.

"That's very kind of you, Charlie," Victoria said with one of her brilliant smiles.

"My pleasure, Mrs. Ford," Charlie beamed. "Is there anything else I can fetch you? Mrs. Croft? Gentlemen? No? Then we'll leave you in peace." He turned to Thompson. "Are you coming, Gee-arge?"

"When I've finished my official civic business," Thompson told him.

"I hate to keep you from your duties, sir," Ford said, seizing the opportunity. "We'll keep you informed as soon as we know anything more."

"I say, you're not trying to cover it all up, are you?" Thompson demanded. "Smooth it over so that the aristocracy isn't embarrassed? Putting their selfish needs ahead of the rights of the workers? There'll be a Labor government soon, and then we'll ..."

"We'd love to invite you to join us, Mr. Thompson," Victoria jumped in. "Unfortunately we have to leave for Penzance very shortly, and I know how busy you are."

"Penzance? Why are you going to …?"

Victoria rose and took his arm, and he found himself moving to the door, powerless to resist.

"It's my opinion, Mr. Thompson, that the villagers are very fortunate to have so diligent, so *competent,* a mayor. I'm sure it must make everyone breathe a little easier, knowing you're in charge. Good night and thank you."

By now Mr. Thompson was in the corridor, with nothing to do but to say good night in return. Victoria smiled once more and closed the door.

"I'm afraid I really don't like that man," she said as she sat down.

"First Lady Canderblank accuses me of being a communist *agent provocateur,*" Ford said. "Now Thompson accuses me of being a pawn of the establishment! Is there no room at either end of the political spectrum for a simple detective trying to solve a murder?"

"Don't pout, Hercule," Victoria said. "It makes you look squinty-eyed and spoils your good looks. Besides, you know perfectly well that politicians have no interest in truth."

"You know, Betty, this spotted dick isn't nearly as good as yours," Croft said, perhaps trying to change the conversation.

"*Nothing* is as good as anything you cook, in my opinion," Victoria told her. "Dr. Anderson is concerned that there's a health crisis in Trethgarret, because so many people are showing up at the hospital for treatment at mealtimes."

"Well, where does all this leave us, sir?" Croft asked, and Ford noted, to his private amusement, that the indifferent quality of the dessert had not prevented him from attacking it with gusto.

"The plot has not necessarily thickened, Croft, but it's definitely grown arms and legs."

* * *

"I'm all agog to know what you discovered in London, Thomas, as are we all," Victoria said. "We still haven't heard all the details. However, and not withstanding our joint and several agogeration, we'll miss our train if we do not leave immediately."

"But I need to discuss tomorrow's agenda with Croft, and ..." Ford began.

"You can tell us in the car, sir, if I may suggest it," Croft interrupted. "We'll all go."

"An excellent suggestion, Mr. Croft," Victoria said. "You can drive us, and I'll sit in the back with Thomas and make indecent advances toward him."

"I won't be able to take notes if I'm driving," Croft frowned.

"It's kind of you to assume my advances will be worth preserving for posterity, but you're right, Mr. Croft; Mrs. Croft should drive."

"What about young Frank?" Croft asked. "Didn't you say he was coming with us?"

"Crocker bought him a bus ticket and sent him to Penzance," Ford said. "He should be waiting at the station. I thought we might need to talk privately in the car."

Five minutes of frenzied activity ensued, after which Ford found himself sitting beside Victoria in the Humber, with his view of the road ahead partially obscured by Mrs. Croft's hat.

"Well, I see what you mean by the case growing arms and legs, sir," Croft said over his shoulder when Ford had finished bringing them up to date. "What a couple of days! The Langley woman, the news from the Bank of England, Miss Robsart's body, and this business with the tin mine! My head's spinning, to tell you the truth."

They breasted the hill that climbed above Trethgarret, and the road to Penzance, silver in the moonlight, stretched out before them across the treeless uplands.

"Well, let's begin by deciding what we'll do tomorrow," Ford said. "I'll see Poole and hear what he has to say about the trust accounts. If it's not all some innocent bookkeeping error, we'll have to add him to our list of suspects. Poole told me he'd never met Pengriffon, and never set foot in Trethgarret, but we may no longer believe him."

"Perhaps someone saw him, even if he denies it," Mrs. Croft said, her eyes on the road ahead and her competent hands resting lightly on the wheel.

"True enough, Betty," Croft said. "What's my list, sir?"

"I'm afraid it's a long one, Croft," Ford said, wondering if there was *anyone* in England who could not drive a motorcar better than he could. "First, see what Dr. Anderson has to say about Amy Robsart's cause of death, and search her clothes. Then go out to see Josephine Langley at the cottage and go over her previous statements with a fine-tooth comb. Concentrate on the launch part of her story and see if she sticks to it."

"Right you are, sir."

"You'd better take Crocker with you—just to be on the safe side. In fact, it's a pity we don't have a woman constable available." He paused for thought. "Come to think of it, after you've dropped us at the railway station tonight, please go to the Penzance police station and ask them to send a woman police officer over to Trethgarret first thing in the morning."

"Right, sir."

"If you have the slightest doubt about the Langley woman, you'd better take her into custody."

"Suspicion of obstruction, sir?"

"Exactly, Croft, although I hate strong-arming people who may just be misguided."

"Well, sir, in her state of mind she might do a runner, or she might be a danger to herself. Mind you, that backroom in Crocker's station isn't much of a cell. If I take her in, I'll get the lady policewoman to escort her to Penzance, or wherever they've got proper facilities."

"Good," Ford said, and lit a cigarette.

"Perhaps we might want to consult Dr. Waggoner, sir?" Croft asked.

"An excellent idea, Croft."

"Who is Dr. Waggoner, if I may ask?" Mrs. Croft asked.

"He's a psychologist we use, Mrs. Croft," Ford answered. "He's very good at telling the difference between sane people with bad motives and people who commit crimes because they can't stop themselves. I'll telephone him tomorrow. Oh, and speaking of Crocker, Croft, tell him to keep his mouth shut about the case. I'm tired of hearing what we're doing and what we're thinking from all and sundry."

"I will, sir, but it's not that easy for him."

"What do you mean, Croft?"

"Well, I was in his position when we first met, sir, just a village copper," Croft said, glancing briefly over his shoulder. "These are his people, sir, and he can't get his job done if they're against him. *We're the foreigners.*"

Ford imagined Crocker's daily existence, working in harmony with people he had known all his life. Suddenly, strange superior beings from Scotland Yard drop from the sky, like beings from another planet. The town would be abuzz with rumors and speculation, and Crocker would be peppered with questions at every turn. If Ford were in similar circumstances, where would his own sympathies lie?

"That's very true, Croft; I should have thought of that. I'm being unfair. Don't say anything."

"I'll mention it quietlike, sir," Croft said. "A word in the ear of the wise. What else should I be doing?"

"Let's see," Ford pondered. "There's still the question of his lordship's car—it has to be *somewhere*. In fact, it's a very annoying loose end. And there's still a chance we'll find somebody who was looking out over the harbor on Monday night and saw someone on the *Justicia*."

"True, sir. Anything else?"

"Well, now we have Thompson to consider as a potential enemy of his lordship, in light of Crutchfield's testimony, as well as Miss Langley," Ford said. "However, I have not the faintest idea what to do about it."

"The foreman at the mine is in the hospital with two broken legs, poor chap," Mrs. Croft volunteered. "I could bring up the subject with him, if you like, sir?"

"Now, Betty, I don't like the idea of ..." Croft began.

"I'll be up at the hospital anyway," she overrode him. "There's nothing for the patients to do but gossip, and there's more and more coming in at mealtimes. I'll just ask about, innocentlike, and keep my ears open, if you like, sir? I could ask about people looking out over the harbor, and Mr. Thompson."

"Yes, that's a very good idea," Ford said. Mrs. Croft had so comforting a presence that people might well confide in her, if only to secure a second helping of her delicious liver and onions, or whatever she was serving for lunch.

"Mrs. Granger should be back on solids tomorrow," Mrs. Croft continued, "and I promised her a nice slice of pheasant to start her off on the road to recovery."

"Pheasant?" Victoria asked.

"Isn't that illegal this time of year?" Croft added. "Aren't they out of season?"

"Well, young Frank, who takes the photos, is Mrs. Granger's nephew, and he said that he was taking a photograph of a pleasant when it fell over dead right in front of him."

Croft snorted.

"Who am I to say if it's true or not, Bob?" Mrs. Croft asked. "Besides, there's no law against giving a convalescent woman a good healthy lunch to build her strength up, is there?"

"I should lock you up along with Miss Langley, Betty," Croft chuckled.

"And then you'd have to cook for yourself, Bob."

"God help me!" Croft exclaimed. "Listen, Betty, I won't charge you with a misdemeanor if you bribe me with a pheasant leg."

Ford fell into a pleasant stupor, half listening to the Croft's friendly barbs, staring down at Victoria's hand in his, with his wedding ring miraculously on her finger, a symbol of hope and joy, her binding commitment to a future with him ...

There were houses about them now, and the car was beginning to descend from the moorlands into Penzance—could they really have traveled thirty miles so swiftly, or had he dozed off? The road became steeper, and a sharp left turn loomed up in the darkness ahead. If Ford had been driving, he'd have applied the brakes and crept tentatively around it; Mrs. Croft, on the other hand, executed a fluent double-clutch and the car throbbed smoothly and powerfully through the curve—*damn!*

For a well-liked and generous man, Ford reflected, Lord Pengriffon had a remarkable number of potential enemies; he had been strolling carefree through a minefield—the dispute over the tin mine, his convoluted relationships with women, perhaps the irresistible lure of his wealth.

They pulled into the forecourt of the railway station. Young Frank, clutching a suitcase and his portfolio, was waiting for them. Ford clambered out of the Humber stiffly, and the cool night air set him yawning. He noted that the back of Frank's hair had a curious zigzag pattern; perhaps the barber's shop hadn't been open and Frank's mother had tackled the problem herself.

"I'm so tired I could fall asleep standing here," he said between yawns. "As it is, I'll have to sit up on the train and try to write something vaguely coherent to give to Brownlee tomorrow morning."

"You'll do no such thing, sir, if you don't mind my saying so," Mrs. Croft said. "You're on your honeymoon, and first things come first."

* * *

"Wow," Victoria said to Ford half an hour later. "Perhaps we should spend the rest of our honeymoon traveling about Europe in railway sleeping compartments. We could go back and forth between Paris and Istanbul on the Orient Express."

"An excellent plan, V; I find its practicality particularly appealing. We'll leave as soon as the case is over."

"We'll be trysting in Trieste, and consorting in Constantinople."

"A delightful train of thought, my darling V."

"Speaking of which, Thomas, and to change trains, as it were, what do you think about the subject that poor Mr. Croft was too embarrassed to mention over dinner?"

"You mean ...?"

"I mean that according to Miss Langley's lurid description of the scene on the launch, his lordship would have been in a position approximating your current position, Thomas. The killer approaches from behind you, and strangles you with your tie. You collapse on me, pinning me down. The killer then reaches past your inert torso and wraps a belt around my neck and strangles me. Is that possible?"

Ford laughed.

"Anything is possible, I suppose, V, but I think it most unlikely—in fact, I think it absurd. I think the whole incident is the product of her overheated and prurient imagination."

"Why so?"

"First of all, his lordship might have been killed in that bizarre manner—it would certainly create the greatest single day in the history of newspaper sales if it were true—but Amy Robsart, if she were where you suggest, would have put up a struggle. Strangulation may seem easy to writers of popular detective fiction stories, but in real life it's a difficult process requiring a great deal of strength and a long time, during which the victim literally fights for his or her life."

"And second of all?"

"The killer buried the bodies at sea, so that they would never be discovered. In those circumstances, I think it most unlikely that the killer came upon them *in flagrante*, murdered them in the unlikely manner you have just described, and then went to the trouble of *dressing* them again. What would have been the point?"

"True. I hadn't thought of that."

"I think they were killed in a far less dramatic fashion, V. I think Dr. Anderson may find some other cause of death in Amy Robsart's case. I couldn't tell, but I suspect she may have been struck on the head by a heavy object, and the belt was added as a macabre afterthought."

"Then, perhaps, none of Josephine Langley's story is true."

"We really know very little about her," Ford said. "I have to wonder if she's entirely sane—that's why we might bring Dr. Waggoner in for a consultation. Her self-incriminating description of going out to the launch may have been a particularly sad and self-destructive way of drawing attention to herself. She may have no bearing on the case whatsoever."

"I can't imagine how anyone could bring themselves to do such a thing—invent such a story, I mean, Thomas."

"Oh, I think I can, I'm afraid, V. If one is lonely and thinks of oneself as unattractive, and one fears one might spend the rest of one's life on one's own, then a sort of self-loathing takes over, a sort of self-fulfilling prophecy, I suppose, an inescapable quicksand of one's own invention." He was back in his sterile flat, tossing and turning in his solitary bed. "I desire, therefore I am undesirable. It's not self-pity; it's self-disgust."

"My God, Thomas," Victoria burst out, "you make it sound as if you're talking about yourself!"

He buried his head in the pillow and murmured in her ear.

"Well, in my case an angel of mercy arrived before I sank completely beneath the surface, thank God. Now I try to see myself as you see me."

"My poor darling! Is that why you took so long to ask me to marry you?"

"I was certain you'd refuse me. On the night when I'd finally screwed up my courage to propose to you, I'd bought a bottle of whiskey in advance, so I could rush home after your rejection and drown my sorrows."

"How could you doubt my wishes? I spend an entire year becoming more and more desperately brazen, and convincing myself you had a coterie of secret lovers, each a paragon of perfect pulcritrudinosity. I seriously considered printing up a sign saying, "I want Thomas," and picketing Scotland Yard."

"I'm beginning to realize that I was profoundly stupid, V," Ford said, lifting his head to gaze at her. "I just couldn't bring myself to imagine that a girl like you could fall for a man like me."

"What rubbish! A girl like me, my darling idiot, is brought up to be completely useless. We are given an education that isn't worth a grain of salt and are excluded from almost every useful occupation, except in menial roles. We are taught to have no ambition, no purpose, other than to ensnare a wealthy husband, preferably with a title. It's the vapid in pursuit of the vainglorious—a shadow world. You, on the other hand, occupy the real world, with a real job with real value, living a real life. I'm the one that isn't good enough for you."

She took his cheeks in both hands and stared into his eyes, and, to his infinite surprise, he saw tears welling in her eyes.

"Thank you, my angel, for bringing me into the real world," she said. "Thank you for setting me free."

Ford found his eyes filling also.

"All I can do is love you, V," he managed to say.

"Then do so, Thomas; please do so."

* * *

Ford stared disconsolately at his notebook, in which he had scribbled two tables. He had stolen from the sleeping compartment when Victoria had finally fallen into an exhausted sleep and had found the deserted restaurant carriage, where he could work without disturbing her.

The sense of well-being she had given him had slowly evaporated before the grim reality of the threadbare report that was all he could offer Brownlee.

MURDER OF LORD PENGRIFFON

Suspect	Motive	Evidence
Amy Robsart	Lover's quarrel *Was she expecting his child???*	(1) Seen on the dock (2) Fingerprints on boat (3) Motive given by Langley (highly suspect)
Josephine Langley	Jealous rage	None
Lady Pengriffon	Jealous rage if AR expectant	None
Poole	Hide financial chicanery	None (We don't even know if there were, in fact, any improprieties)
Thompson	Keep mine open to keep his job Political opinions???	None

MURDER OF AMY ROBSART

Suspect	Motive	Evidence
Josephine Langley	Jealous rage	None
Lady Pengriffon	Jealous rage if AR expectant	None
Poole	Silence her as a witness	None
Thompson	Silence her as a witness	None

It was, he thought, a pretty pathetic summary; perhaps he should take up Brownlee's offer to turn the case over to Inspector West, before his lack of progress compelled Brownlee to remove him from it. He lit a cigarette and stared at the long column of "nones."

The only evidence he had was that Amy Robsart had been on the dock and on the boat that night, because Frank and the ladies had seen her on the dock, and Croft had found her fingerprints on the engine controls. Even if she had killed Pengriffon, then someone else must also have been there to kill her. Only Josephine Langley seemed to have a motive, if she were to be believed. If Amy Robsart's killer was not Miss Langley, then she must have been killed because she was a witness to his lordship's murder. Ergo, one of the other three—or some other unidentified person—had killed at least her and possibly his lordship as well.

Ford sighed and wrote again.

OPEN INVESTIGATIONS

Open items	Comments
Amy Robsart's cause of death	Wait for Anderson's report Was she expectant?
Investigation of trust accounting irregularities	See Poole again
Explanation of Pengriffon's secret code and calculations	Wait for experts
Frank's photograph	A dark and fuzzy hope
Background check on Thompson	Wait and see
Opinion on Langley's sanity	Wait for Waggoner
Search for witnesses	Wait and hope
Location of Pengriffon's Bentley	Wait without hope

That was even worse. There was virtually nothing he could do except to wait. He had been reduced to hoping that his sergeant's wife picked up some gossip among the hospital patients or that Inspector West might prove to be more adept at finding exotic motorcars than exotic women. How *pathetic!*

Was Thompson even a legitimate suspect? One's job was not only one's source of income, it also was the basis of one's sense of self, one's dignity, and one's identity. But, even so, would a man actually *kill* his boss to save his job? The notion that Thompson had killed Pengriffon as a blow against the aristocracy seemed even more far-fetched.

Ford groaned and lit another cigarette from the embers of the first. He had only two hours before the train reached London, and then he would face Brownlee's well-justified wrath at the paucity of evidence he had managed to collect.

Perhaps Thompson had rowed out to the *Justicia* to plead with

Pengriffon to keep the mine open. Perhaps they'd argued, or even scuffled, and in the darkness Thompson had grabbed his lordship's tie and yanked. Pengriffon had gone down like a stone, leaving Thompson staring down in horror at Pengriffon lying crumpled at his feet, the victim of a tragic accident. While Thompson was attempting to collect his wits, Amy Robsart climbed over the stern in search of her lover, saw Pengriffon's lifeless body, and opened her mouth to scream. Thompson, beyond rational thought, lunged out to silence her ...

Yes, it could have happened, Ford supposed. Then again, he could replace Thompson with Josephine Langley, pleading for love instead of employment, and the scene could have played out equally as credibly. Damn!

Lord Pengriffon was a man that it was impossible not to like, Lady Justicia had said, and yet the list of people who seemed to have a reason to hate him was growing by leaps and bounds! Double damn!

"Doing your homework, sir?" boomed a voice over Ford's shoulder, and Ford leapt as if he had been scalded. "Door-to-door encyclopedia salesman, are you, writing up your calls? Aardvark to zoology for two bob a week and a new volume once a quarter? I can always tell a bloke's job—ask anyone."

"Yes, yes I am," Ford managed. "That's very clever of you."

"I'm never wrong, never," the ticket collector chuckled, tapping his nose with a knowing smile. "Well, you'd best turn in, if you ask me. It's only a couple of hours to London."

"Yes, I think I'd better," Ford said, standing and stubbing out his cigarette. "Good night."

"Night, sir," the ticket collector said, and passed on his way, leaving Ford to walk back through the rocking corridors to their compartment.

He passed a third-class compartment in which he could see Frank sprawled across the seats, with his portfolio beneath his head as a makeshift pillow and his mouth slightly open as he slept.

None of it mattered, of course—the case, the improbable suspect list, the mishmash of feeble evidence—if Victoria really did love him. She lay sleeping on the upper bunk, and he rolled onto the lower bunk to keep from disturbing her.

But would she still love him when he was drummed out of Scotland

Yard for incompetence and was forced to eke out a living as a private investigator, climbing trees in the dead of night in order to snap pictures of adulterous wives through suburban bedroom windows?

He groaned and turned out the reading lamp. He wasn't good at climbing trees in broad daylight, let alone at night. He was also completely incapable of snapping a recognizable picture—everything always came out black. He'd probably fail at that profession also.

Lady Canderblank would love it. She'd visit him in hospital, where he'd be recovering from his latest fall from a suburban tree. "Aha, Fudge, I always knew you'd fail!" she'd crow in triumph, "I *knew* you'd let my daughter down."

He'd wither up and die, there and then, and his gravestone would be inscribed, *HERE LIES THOMAS FORD / WHO DIED IN DISGRACE / FOR FAILING TO SOLVE / THE PENGRIFFON CASE.*

A train whistle wailed dolefully from afar, and Ford slipped into a sleep in which dark, fuzzy photographs and his grim, furious mother-in-law punctuated his dreams; and in which Victoria, alas, receded from his view on some other train bound for some other destination, her passing mourned by distant train whistles echoing in the darkness. She was calling out, trying to remind him of something important, but he couldn't hear her above the noise. And here was Mr. McIntire, his school English teacher, an anthology of Tennyson's poetry in his hands, declaiming, *Blow, whistle, blow, set the wild echoes flying / Answer echoes, answer, dying, dying, dying*—but that didn't seem quite right either.

Thirteen

As Ford approached the oak door leading to the chambers of PP&P, it swung open, and Miss Edwards escorted an elderly couple into the hallway. They were both wearing heavy topcoats despite the warm weather, and the gentleman supported himself with a walking cane.

"This is *extremely* unsatisfactory," the lady said to Miss Edwards. "Are you quite, quite sure our appointment is not for today?"

"Your appointment was for yesterday, Thursday, Lady Whitetrellis," Miss Edwards told her as if she had repeated this point several times. "I'm sorry that all the partners are out today. I'm sure Sir David will telephone to you as soon as he returns."

"But I'm certain that *today* is Thursday," Lady Whitetrellis insisted. "You are mistaken. Besides, I don't have any confidence in telephones. One never knows if the voice really belongs to the person."

She spotted Ford and turned to him.

"What day of the week is it today?"

"It's Friday, madam," Ford said.

"Then you have made me miss my appointment with Sir David, young man," she accused Ford. "Further, you've made me miss this evening's dinner with Lord Garterhose."

"I'm afraid ..." Ford began.

"This is all *very* unfortunate," she snapped, and turned to the gentleman. "Come Cedric, stop lollygagging! Bustle, bustle!"

Her husband launched himself into hesitant motion, and she shot a poisonous glance at Ford as she passed.

"And, I might add, it's also very *thoughtless* of you, young man."

Ford grinned at Miss Edwards as Lady Whitetrellis disappeared down the stairs with her husband tottering in her wake, leaving Ford to wonder if Lady Whitetrellis might be related to Lady Canderblank.

"Good morning, Miss Edwards," he said, taking off his hat. "All the partners are out, I gather?"

"Mr. Poole will be back after lunch. There's only me, Mr. Ford." She looked at him archly. "I'm all on my lonesome. You'll have to make the best of it."

"Do keep *up*, Cedric!" the old lady's voice carried up from the floor below.

Ford smiled and followed her into PP&P, and Miss Edwards giggled.

"It's a funny thing, Mr. Ford, but you can always tell who has money and who has *lots* of money."

"How does one tell?"

"Well, the ones with less come often, and ask all kinds of detailed questions, and make a big fuss, and question the fees, and such, while the ones with lots of money come rarely."

"I see," Ford chuckled.

"Take that Lady Canderblank, for example," she said, settling herself behind her desk for a good chat. "She's in and out of here like we're a post office, and not two pennies to rub together."

"Lady Canderblank?" Ford asked, startled. "Is she a client?"

"Sir David can't say 'no' to her, and that's a fact," Miss Edwards said. "He's terrified of her, in my view."

She crossed her legs to full advantage and smoothed her skirt over her knees.

"Did Lord Pengriffon come here often, Miss Edwards?" Ford asked, shying away from both the topic of Lady Canderblank's finances and Miss Edwards's gesture.

"Oh, no, only once or twice in all the time I've been here, Mr. Ford, to see Sir David. Usually it's the other way round, because Sir David travels down to Cornwall to see him. As a matter of fact, he was supposed to go this week. I typed the letter myself. It upset Mr. Poole something awful when I told him, because the old man wouldn't invite him to the meetings. So, anyway, his lordship hasn't been here for two years, I'd say."

"But I understand he was in London quite often."

"Well, to tell you the truth, I don't think he cared about the trust very much; at least that's what Mr. Poole says. It must be nice to have so much money you just don't care."

But he *had* cared, Ford knew. He'd spent hours attempting to reconcile the accounts, as if he was convinced that there should more money than PP&P had sent him. His asterisks and exclamation marks bore testimony to his frustration.

Miss Edwards's voice broke into his thoughts. "Mind you, I saw him out and about town a couple of times, by coincidence."

"You did, Miss Edwards?" Ford asked, trying to concentrate.

"I saw him in a pub once, near Shaftsbury Avenue, and another time he was in a bank."

Ford tried to keep his voice neutral.

"A bank?"

"In the pub he was with a very pretty woman—too young to be his wife, I'd say, and certainly not his daughter, from the way they were carrying on, if you know what I mean. I thought at the time it must have been one of his models. I said to my intended—well, ex-intended, actually, but that's another story—'Frankie,' I said, 'she's no better than she should be,' if you take my meaning."

"Goodness me," Ford said. Maybe it had been Amy Robsart, but he had no intention of offering Miss Edwards a description of Amy Robsart's appearance and physical attributes—God alone knew where such a conversation might lead. In any case, he was much more interested in the encounter in the bank.

"Do you recall which bank it was, Miss Edwards?"

"He certainly had an eye for the female form in all its glory," Miss Edwards continued, intent on her own priorities, leading where Ford had no wish to follow. "I saw one of his paintings once, and it left nothing to the imagination, nothing at all. Not that there's anything wrong with that, in my opinion, if it's in the service of art, and tasteful, like. After all, we are all as God made us."

She straightened her back and smoothed out her skirt again, and her eyes flickered toward his, but Ford was focused on far more prosaic matters.

"You mentioned a bank, Miss Edwards?"

"Well, I know he kept a bank account in Islington," she said, clearly annoyed that he had not been drawn toward more interesting subjects. "I saw him one day when I was visiting my sister what lives there, and we popped into her bank, to put a few bob into her nest egg account for Christmas, so that Father Christmas could give the kids a good treat, and there he was—Lord Pengriffon, I mean, not Santa Claus, of course!"

"Which bank was it, Miss Edwards, do you recall?"

"The Westminster, I think; I'm sure it wasn't Barclays, where I go."

Islington, on the far side of Kings Cross, was the gateway to the gray expanses of Northeast London, and was certainly not the sort of place that Ford would have expected Pengriffon to bank—particularly as he had an account in Coutts, the illustrious and prestigious banking establishment for the nobility and royalty.

"Lord Pengriffon was in a bank in Islington? Are you sure?"

"Cashing a check in the Westminster Bank in Islington High Street, right up the road from the Angel—cross my heart and hope to die!" She made the gesture.

Ford's heart missed a beat; he stared fixedly at Miss Edwards as his thoughts raced in circles, like a mouse on a climbing wheel.

"My friends call me Pattie, by the way." She must have misinterpreted his gaze, Ford realized belatedly, for the speculative gleam had returned in force. "What's your Christian name?"

Ford groped for a response. On the one hand he desperately wanted to get away and think—my *God*, the Westminster Bank in Islington High Street, the *WB* in *IHS!*—while on the other he wanted to keep her talking; and, if he'd had a third hand, he would have wanted to defuse that speculative glance as gently as he could, but not so much that the flow of gossip would be staunched. In the end, he said the first thing that entered into his head.

"My parents baptized me Chief Inspector," he said, and laughed ruefully to make sure she knew it was a joke. "I'm sorry, Miss Edwards, but, alas, I am on duty, whether I like it or not."

She seemed about to press the point, but Ford decided that

discretion was the better part of valor. He put on his hat and turned toward the door. She walked with him, and for a dreadful moment he feared she might bar the door.

"I'll be back later," he said, slipping around her.

"Promise, Chief Inspector?"

He removed his hat with a theatrical flourish and bowed deeply, as if he were one of the three musketeers.

"I promise, Miss Edwards."

"On duty, or off?"

"We'll have to see!"

* * *

Ford stood on the corner of Islington High Street and the Pentonville Road.

The Underground station—indeed the entire area—was named for the Angel staging inn that had once occupied this corner. It was, Ford knew, the official start of the Great North Road, which connects London with Edinburgh, in Scotland, and ever since boyhood he had always felt this corner was therefore imbued with an adventurous, exciting spirit, a sense of long journeys of exploration into uncharted territory, in complete contrast to its sooty reality.

He walked along the High Street until he found a local pub, the Camden Head, across from the Westminster Bank, and ate a pork pie washed down by a half of bitter. The beer tasted like vinegar in his throat—perhaps he was becoming too accustomed to the softer, seductive taste of scrumpy.

WB IHS 372435 was, he was convinced, Account Number 372435 in the Westminster Bank in Islington High Street. Miss Edwards—Pattie—had seen his lordship cashing a check in these unexpected surroundings. Why had he kept a secret account, for God's sake? Ford could not image Pengriffon doing anything illegal or hiding anything of import from his wife. It had to be part of some complicated practical joke. It had to be. Well, whatever it was, it was time to cross the street and find out.

Ford entered the Westminster Bank, presented his card to a doleful cashier, and asked to see the manager. In due course he was conducted into the manager's office, a confection of walnut paneling and engraved frosted glass designed to convey sobriety and security. The manager stood before his pristine desk, nervously fingering Ford's card.

"Good morning, sir, I am a police officer," Ford said.

"My name is Smith, Chief Inspector," the manager said. He had a prominent Adam's apple, and he swallowed before continuing. "What can I do to help you? I'm sure there are no irregularities in our books. I pride myself on the strict application of accounting standards, and the staff is very thorough—not a penny out of balance, I assure you. The head office auditors were here last week and gave us a clean bill of ..."

"Please don't alarm yourself, sir," Ford interrupted. "It's nothing like that; on the contrary, I'm investigating the death of Lord Pengriffon."

The manager's expression combined relief that his branch was not under investigation with surprise that it was involved in a murder enquiry. These emotions generated two swallows.

"Do you mean the chap who was murdered in Devon? I think I saw something about it in the *Daily Telegraph*."

"It was in Cornwall, sir. Did Lord Pengriffon have an account in this bank?"

"No, certainly not," the manager said. "I'm sure of it."

"Perhaps he wasn't a customer, but I know he cashed a check here on at least one occasion. Perhaps the tellers might know him, sir?"

Smith drew himself up. "I would know him. I pride myself on knowing all our customers."

"I'm sure you do, sir. But I'm also sure your many responsibilities prevent you from seeing everyone who enters the branch. Perhaps the staff might recognize him, if I could speak to them?"

"It's most unlikely, Chief Inspector," Smith said. Ford watched as Smith's Adam's apple debated the pros and cons of helping a police investigation into a notorious murder against the possible disruptions to the smooth operations of the branch and the potential notoriety that such help might engender. Smith's eyes lingered on the telephone; doubtless he was wishing he could ask Head Office for instructions, thus absolving himself of responsibility. Ford cleared his throat to draw the silent quandary to a close, and Smith swallowed once more and plunged in favor of Ford.

"Well, we're happy to help Scotland Yard if we can, of course," he said. "However, I would ask you not to disrupt the business of the bank any more than is necessary—we're very busy."

"I'll be as unobtrusive as possible, sir, and I appreciate your help."

The manager reluctantly led him back into the main banking area. There were no customers, and the staff was chatting idly.

"Er, there's always a great deal to be done, whether there are customers or not," Smith said, swallowing defensively.

"I'm sure there is, sir," Ford said.

He took out the photograph of his lordship he had borrowed from Lady Pengriffon and offered it to the morose cashier, who examined it as if it might have been a counterfeit ten-shilling note, while the rest of the staff gathered and craned over his shoulders.

"Do you recognize this man, by any chance?" Ford asked him.

"No, no, I can't say that I do," the morose cashier said after a long pause.

"Course you do, Albert—that's Mr. Poole," a young lady cashier contradicted him, almost snatching the photograph away.

"Don't be daft, Maisie!" Albert countered. "That's an earl, a dead earl! I saw his picture in the paper."

Albert and Maisie tussled briefly for possession of the photograph, and Ford was struck by the confrontation between his mousy gray hair and her artificial platinum blond coiffure, between her youth and his indeterminate middle age, his bony fingers and her carefully enameled nails, her assertiveness and his obstinacy—but the result was not in doubt, Ford knew, because he was certain that Albert had never won a competition about anything in his life.

"It's Mr. Poole, right enough," Maisie said in triumph, having pried the photograph from Albert's viselike grip. "Look, he's even got his Sherlock Holmes hat, like he always wears."

"*Deerstalker* hat, if you please," Albert said.

"The man in the photograph is Mr. *Poole?*" Ford broke in, his mind reeling for the second time in two hours.

"Now, don't *you* start," Maisie said to Ford.

"Excuse me," a voice said behind them. "I'm sorry to bother you, but I'd like to make a deposit, if it's convenient."

The bank staff started guiltily, and Ford with them. A lady wearing an unseasonably warm tweed coat stood uncertainly behind them.

"Oh, madam, please excuse us!" Smith gulped. "This is unpardonable. Let me help you immediately!"

The group scurried away to its several posts, and Ford, his mind still digesting Maisie's announcement, steered her into the manager's office and closed the door. He invited her to sit down and offered her a cigarette, which she accepted with a giggle and a glance at the frosted door panels—clearly these were liberties the manager never allowed.

"Now, Maisie, would you please tell me all you know about, er, about this man?"

Maisie said that Mr. Poole, as she knew him, came to the bank regularly, usually early in the quarter, and withdrew the full balance of his account in cash. The amounts were substantial, and they had developed the habit of ordering extra £50 notes, that there was normally very little call for, from Head Office, just to be able to accommodate Mr. Poole.

He also collected his statements, which were held for him at the branch, rather than being sent to him by mail. He was a very nice man, she said, always good for a giggle, and there was something about his way to suggest that he would not be averse to a spot of slap and tickle, if it were to be offered; Maisie, however, was already spoken for, although not yet officially engaged, and therefore that sort of thing would not be proper.

"I see," Ford said judiciously, in acknowledgment of both her customer's banking habits and her moral rectitude. "What about deposits?"

"Oh, Mr. Poole is in some sort of art business, paintings and such, and makes deposits to his account in other branches of the bank, wherever he traveling, he said. He just comes here when he needs cash."

The manager returned. Ford saw him open his mouth to chastise Maisie for not only sitting but also smoking in his office, glance at Ford, close his mouth again, and swallow.

"Maisie has been explaining this customer's banking habits," Ford told him—he still could not bring himself to call him "Mr. Poole." "I'll have to ask to see the details of his account."

"Of course, Chief Inspector," the manager said. "I'll look up the account number."

"I believe I have it," Ford said, and took Lord Pengriffon's cipher from his wallet.

"I knew something was wrong," Maisie said. "I said so at the time."

"What do you mean, Maisie?" the manager asked. "Remember our conversations about the need for precision if one is to succeed in banking?"

"Sorry, Mr. Smith. It's just that another chap came in and claimed he was Mr. Poole, and created a right old scene."

"When was this, Maisie?"

"Oh, it was a few weeks ago. He insisted he was Mr. Poole and accused us of refusing to honor one of his checks—a big check. He turned very nasty; Albert had to come over and help me out with him."

"Why wasn't I informed?" Smith demanded.

"You was on holiday, Mr. Smith, and Albert was in charge, remember?"

"Oh, yes."

"Anyway," she continued, "you know it happens every now and again; confidence tricksters come in and try something or other."

"Well, that's true, I suppose," Smith said. "Nevertheless, I should have been informed on my return."

"Oh, sorry, Mr. Smith; naturally I assumed Albert would have told you." Her eyes flickered briefly to Ford's and away again, and Ford knew she had just lied—and therefore, by inference, she had not lied about anything else.

"Can you describe this person, this confidence trickster, Maisie?" Ford asked.

"Oh, I didn't care for him one bit. Expensive suit, but flashy, with his hair all combed down with shiny oil. A bit of a spiv, if you ask me. You can always tell that sort—bedroom eyes and a cold heart. Thrupence made up like a tanner, in my opinion."

Her description of Poole was perfect—a three-penny-piece pretending to be a sixpence—but what on earth had Pengriffon been doing, impersonating Poole? And why had Poole suddenly appeared?

"Could you identify him again, Maisie?"

"Certainly I could," she said with conviction.

"I'll arrange for a policeman to bring in another photograph for you to look at," Ford said. "Perhaps it will be the man who claimed to be Mr. Poole."

"What's his real name, the spiv?"

"If you identify the face in the new photograph, Maisie, his real name is Mr. Poole."

* * *

Ford found a policeman in Islington High Street, identified himself, and asked for directions to the nearest police station. The desk sergeant found him an empty office with a telephone, and in due course Ford was reporting his findings to Brownlee.

"You'll have to repeat that, old chap," Brownlee bawled. "I seem to be failing to grasp what is, no doubt, obvious."

"It's far from obvious, sir; I couldn't grasp it either. Poole was depositing sizable amounts of money in a bank in Islington, and Pengriffon, impersonating him, was routinely emptying out the account."

"Yes, that's what I thought you said."

"Then, approximately six weeks ago, sir, Poole came to the branch and discovered his account was empty."

"But, presumably, he didn't know it was Pengriffon who had robbed him?"

"No, sir. He must have worked that out some other way."

"*Caruthers—tea!*" Brownlee barked into Ford's ear. Then there was silence as they both thought.

"Are you thinking what I'm thinking, Ford?" Brownlee asked. For once his voice was soft.

"I'm thinking that Pengriffon discovered that Poole was stealing from the trust, sir, and decided to steal the money back."

"That's exactly what I'm thinking, old chap," Brownlee's voice sounded, rising to its customary pitch. "And when Poole discovered that Pengriffon had been recovering the stolen money, he decided to kill him."

"Precisely, sir."

There was a longer silence, punctuated by an occasional slurping noise indicating contact between tea cup and lips, and Ford knew that Brownlee was picking at the logic, trying to find a weakness.

"Well, I suppose it's vaguely plausible," Brownlee said eventually, which meant that Brownlee thought it was almost certainly correct, although not yet proven. "Unproven but plausible; at the very least, it adds a little flesh to your otherwise Spartan report, old chap. You'll go back to Lincoln's Inn, I assume?"

"Yes, right away, sir."

"Shall I send West with reinforcements?"

"That might not be a bad idea, sir, if you would. Oh, and ask him to bring a search warrant, just in case."

There were no taxis in sight outside the police station, and Ford was reluctant to return inside to pull rank and demand a police car; he therefore dove into the Angel Underground station and set off for Chancery Lane Underground station via the Northern and Central lines.

What the *hell* was Pengriffon doing? If he thought Poole was robbing him, why the *hell* didn't he simply go to the police? And how the *hell* did Poole discover it was Pengriffon who was robbing him to get the money back? Of all the convoluted, contorted ... Ford stopped short. The connecting passenger tunnels between lines at the Bank station were almost as confusing as Poole's and Pengriffon's financial transactions, and Ford had almost jumped on a tube train bound for Epping, a northeastern suburb in the farthest outer reaches of London's ever-growing tentacles that Ford had no desire to explore.

Emerging from the Chancery Lane station he walked toward Lincoln's Inn Fields as quickly as his leg and a sleepless night would permit, including a mad scramble to avoid an oncoming fire engine clanging its alarm bell imperiously. If he were to continue to be happily married, and he intended to be, and if he intended to arise each morning at seven, as was his custom, then he and Victoria would have to retire each evening no later than eight o'clock, in order to allow for eight hours of sleep and recuperation.

He turned into Lincoln's Inn Fields and stopped short, domestic plans swept from his mind. The roadway in front of PP&P's offices was occupied by two fire engines, two police cars, and an ambulance, together with assorted firemen, policemen, ambulance men, and sundry passersby. Dark columns of sooty smoke billowed from PP&P's windows and climbed ponderously into the sky. A team of firemen was assisting the occupants from the building, while another team was setting ladders against the blackened face of the building and unrolling canvas hoses.

Inspector West emerged from the crowd.

"The law firm's on fire, Mr. Ford," he said, perhaps fearing that Ford had failed to grasp the significance of the smoke and activity.

"So I see, West. Please make sure that no one, *no one*, leaves the area without identifying themselves."

"Well, I ..."

"This may be arson," Ford cut him off with unaccustomed bluntness. "I want a complete list, and statements from everyone inside the building, or anyone else who has useful information, before the end of the day." He glanced around. "Which fireman is in charge?"

The senior fireman informed Ford that the building had been cleared of occupants; there were, thank God, no serious injuries. The upper floors were filled with dense smoke and fumes and were, therefore, inaccessible without breathing apparatus. The seat of the fire was on the second floor, in the offices of PP&P. It was burning fiercely in a filing room—what seemed to have been a filing room, as best they could tell—voraciously consuming paper, but the building might yet be saved. He was interrupted by a *whoosh* of smoke and steam as a fireman climbed the ladder and directed a brass hose nozzle through a window into PP&P.

"It all depends on whether the floors hold," the senior fireman finished. "That's usually the key. If the upper floors give way they'll knock down the lower ones and that will be that, and then these buildings on either side might catch also. I'm evacuating them, to be on the safe side"

He hurried away to direct his men.

Ford could not see Poole, but he noticed Miss Edwards leaning against a tree, with a stalwart young ambulance man in close attendance.

Ford walked over. She had gray smudges on her face and clothing, but otherwise she seemed no worse for wear.

"Miss Edwards, I'm glad you're safe," he said. "What happened?"

"I was sitting at my desk, and all of a sudden I smelled smoke," she said, her voice high with excitement. "I went and looked, and there was smoke coming out of the filing room. So I ran next door to Cornstalks, and they telephoned for help."

"Were you alone?"

"All alone; Mr. Poole had come in and gone out again. I could have been …"

She shuddered dramatically, and found it necessary to put her arm on Ford's shoulder for support.

"Do you know how the fire started? Were you or Mr. Poole smoking in there earlier?"

"Oh, no, of course not! Sir David doesn't permit smoking in the offices, on account of his chest. It must have started all by itself."

"I see," Ford said, deciding not to point out that spontaneous combustion in a filing room was an unlikely event.

"Well, I think you acted very sensibly and bravely, Pattie," he said instead, and Miss Edwards now found it necessary to place both arms about his shoulders.

"Did Mr. Poole say anything while he was there, Pattie, by any chance? Did you mention I'd called to see him?"

"I told him we'd talked about his lordship, and you'd be back later." Her glasses must have been obscured by soot, for she removed them.

"Did you mention telling me about seeing Lord Pengriffon in Islington?" he asked.

"Yes, of course! Was that wrong of me?"

Miss Edwards's infirmity now obliged her to rest her head on Ford's chest.

"What did he say, Pattie?" he asked. Glancing over her shoulder, he saw several of the policemen had noted that the officer in charge of the Pengriffon case was now wrapped in a tight embrace with a possible arson suspect, but he daren't interrupt her flow.

"Well, he didn't really say anything, apart from a couple of words Dad said when he burnt his hand on the gas stove. Mr. Poole just put on his mean face and went to his office. A few minutes later he went out; he didn't say where. And the next thing I know, I'm all alone in a bonfire, with no one to take care of me."

She raised her face and looked up at him.

"I'm sorry if I look a fright," she murmured. "Do you really think I was brave?"

"Very brave, Pattie," Ford managed, watching West grinning from ear to ear across the street. "Was he carrying anything?"

"What?"

"Was Mr. Poole carrying anything when he left?"

"What? No, just his briefcase and his umbrella, as usual."

This recollection must have been an emotional tipping point, for Miss Edwards gripped him tightly and sagged in his arms.

"Hold me tight! I'm all of atremble—I think I'm going to faint!" she gasped into his neck, although whether this condition was caused by her recent ordeal or by Poole's briefcase and umbrella, or by their current proximity, was not entirely clear.

Fourteen

"I am told the fires were burning brightly in Lincoln's Inn Fields in more ways than one, old chap," Brownlee grinned. "I feel obliged to remind you that you are now a married man."

"God, sir," Ford groaned, "gossip certainly travels quickly. The woman was *impossible!* I'll never live it down."

"You have my sympathies, Ford," Brownlee said. "I had a similarly embarrassing occurrence many years ago. I don't know if it's because we personify authority or security or some similar nonsense—perhaps Dr. Waggoner could explain it."

Caruthers arrived with tea.

"This sort of thing can get taken completely out of proportion and out of context," Brownlee said, with uncharacteristic severity. "It could result in an official enquiry, so, as your superior officer I'll have to ask you a question, Ford, just so the record's straight."

"Yes, sir?" Ford asked, struck by a sudden and unpleasant sense of foreboding—surely Brownlee, of all people, would not suspect he'd take advantage of an unbalanced …

"It's this, old chap," Brownlee said. "Is it really true that the firemen had to pry you apart with a crow bar?"

Brownlee attempted to disguise his merriment by taking a gulp of tea, but that served only to produce an explosive combination of spluttering and convulsive giggles that, in its turn, resulted in a broad redistribution of tea across his desk, to the extent that Caruthers was obliged to hurry around the desk and slap Brownlee firmly on the back.

When, after a considerable delay, order was restored, Brownlee returned to business.

"While you have been conducting close examinations of witnesses, old chap, others have been involved in more prosaic tasks. Let's see …"

He searched his littered desk and found a piece of paper.

"There's the question of the old man's credibility as a witness, which you asked me to explore. There's the question of Miss Langley's emotional balance. There's Dr. Waggoner's comments on that chap Thompson's pamphlet. There are that young chap's photographs—I gave them to Morgan in the photographic lab. If anyone can make something of them, Morgan will."

He paused to fill the devil's-head pipe that his mother-in-law had given him.

"There's the question of Pengriffon's purchase of his launch, the *Justicia IV*. There's the continuing search for his motorcar—are you quite sure that's important, old chap?—it could be anywhere in England!"

"I think so, sir," Ford said. "Who took it? Why was it taken? Where was it taken? Why can't we find it?—it's a conspicuous vehicle. We've assumed it was removed to further the impression that Pengriffon and Miss Robsart ran away together, but there might also be another reason."

"Well, I've now contacted the police in every county south of Birmingham. It'll turn up eventually."

"Let's hope it turns up soon, sir."

"True." Brownlee consulted the list. "With regard to the old man, the codger you call 'the Ancient Mariner,' I asked Sir Rupert Effingham, the War Office chap we use for military matters, to search the records. He'll be here shortly."

"Thank you, sir."

"Next, there's the question of Miss Langley. I believe Dr. Waggoner is in the Yard today, and perhaps he's also read that pamphlet. *Caruthers*—oh, sorry, you're still here, Constable—please find Dr. Waggoner and ask him if he can spare us a minute."

"Right, sir," Caruthers said and left, but returned almost immediately. "Sir Rupert Effingham is here, sir."

He stood aside to admit a bullish man with a military bearing, his back as straight as a rod, his immaculate dark suit worn as if it were a uniform, and his shoes shined to brilliant perfection. He marched into Brownlee's office as if he were on parade for the changing of the guard at Buckingham Palace, and Ford wondered for a second if he would present arms with his tightly rolled umbrella.

Brownlee and Ford rose to greet him, and Caruthers offered tea and a chair, but Effingham declined all creature comforts and got straight to the point.

"You asked about the Battle of Balaclava, Superintendent, and the thin red line," he said in clipped, authoritative tones, and Ford imagined Effingham conducted his life by making up military orders for himself, such as, "Objective: brief Scotland Yard on Balaclava. Method: advance to Superintendent Brownlee's office and deliver briefing," and so forth.

Effingham assumed a posture with one foot slightly forward and one hand thrust into his waistcoat pocket, as if he were about to deliver a speech to the House of Commons.

"Early in the battle, a large contingent of Russian cavalry outflanked the British positions in the hills and swept down on the port of Balaclava, which was almost undefended. If they'd succeeded in reaching Balaclava, they'd have destroyed the British supply lines and very possibly have won the Crimean War at a single stroke."

Effingham's face was alive with excitement, as if he were witnessing the events at first hand, and Ford was forced to change his impression of Effingham from a rigid martinet to that of a scholarly and dedicated historian.

"The only defenders of the port were a single Highland regiment, the 93rd Regiment of Foot, now known as the Argyll and Sutherland Highlanders. The Scottish soldiers were drawn up in a line two men deep, rather than the customary four men deep, because there were so many Russians across so broad a front, and so few British. It is said that Sir Colin Campbell, the commander of the 93rd, told his men, 'There is no retreat from here, men. You must die where you stand.'"

Effingham raised his hand to indicate that a dramatic climax was approaching.

"Several hundred mounted Cossacks, the descendants of Genghis

Khan's Mongolian hordes, and among the finest light infantry in the history of warfare, charged down on the 93rd. One can only imagine the thunder of their horses' hooves and the stoic silence in the British line as death rushed upon them. The Argylls waited until the Cossacks were no more than fifty yards away before opening fire with a shattering volley"—Effingham punched his fist into his open hand with a loud smack, almost causing Brownlee to drop his tea cup—"with such effect and intensity that the cavalry was routed. Horses and men went down like ninepins, and those behind them crashed into their fallen comrades and were cut down by volley after volley from the 93rd."

Effingham was staring into space, the scene before the eyes of his imagination.

"Such was the rout that the Scots moved forward to attack, and had to be restrained. A newspaper reporter, who witnessed the event, described the Scottish formation as the 'thin red line,' and that description has gone down in history."

Ford waited in respectful silence. Yes, he thought, he'd read about it in school, but what had any of this has to do with the Ancient Mariner?

Effingham emerged from his reverie.

"What is not commonly known is that there were a few dozen Royal Marines—marched up hastily from the naval ships anchored in the harbor—mustered with the 93rd. When you telephoned me, Superintendent Brownlee, I consulted the records, and there was a Corporal Jebediah Ham amongst their ranks."

"That's very helpful, sir, very helpful indeed," Ford said. "Is there anything else known about Corporal Ham?"

"The Royal Marine rolls state that he was born in 1830, in Trethgarret Haven, Cornwall, enlisted in 1853, was promoted to corporal in 1855, and was invalided out in 1856 following wounds sustained at Sevastopol. He received an honorable discharge and a pension of five pounds a year for life. He was a sharpshooter—a marksman known for his exceptional steadiness and keen eyesight. As a historical footnote, incidentally, his discharge papers are countersigned by Florence Nightingale, no less."

So the Ancient Mariner—the ancient *marine*, to be exact—had told the truth about his war record. He was ... good lord, he was ninety-three years old! He did not suffer from senile dementia, but that didn't make him a good witness—men half his age, a *quarter* of his age, could misinterpret what they saw, particularly at night. On the other hand, he had had exceptional eyesight in his youth. Ford wandered if there was a polite way in which he could test the Ancient Mariner's vision.

"It's very kind of you to help us, Sir Rupert," Ford said. "I have one more favor to ask, if I may. Could you check on the military service records of Lord Pengriffon, and two other chaps, Thompson and Poole? I've made notes of the names and addresses on this sheet of paper. Pengriffon served in the Boer War, and then in the Royal Engineers in the Great War. I don't know if the other two served at all."

Effingham accepted the list, closed his eyes briefly while, Ford imagined, he gave himself fresh orders, such as, "Objective: research three named persons of interest to Scotland Yard. Method: advance to Military Records Office and conduct research," and so forth.

"Oh, and one other imposition, sir. There's a local rumor that a U-boat foundered in those waters. Would the navy have records of such things?"

Effingham was sure they would and offered to act as the Yard's intermediary. Ford watched as "Objective: act as intelligence liaison officer with Admiralty." was added to the list; perhaps he and Crocker were distant relatives. Effingham again declined tea, turned smartly on his heel, and marched out of Brownlee's office.

* * *

No sooner had Effingham left than Sergeant Morgan appeared, with young Frank in tow.

"Ah, Sergeant, any progress?" Brownlee asked, as Caruthers positioned another cup of tea within easy reach.

"I have to say this young man's a natural-born photographer," Morgan said, patting Frank on the shoulder. "We could use him on the force, no question about it, and he can find his way around a darkroom, and all."

"It's the most amazing place," Frank burst out, as if he had seen a glimpse of heaven. "The enlargers ... the projectors ... the copiers ...

books with tables of logarithmic charts … chemicals I've never even heard of!"

"I have to say that the quality of Frank's camera is very fine," Morgan said. "I've read about the Leica, of course, but I've never seen one. We should get them for ourselves, sir; we really should."

"Are they expensive?" Brownlee asked.

"Very, sir."

"Then that settles that, Morgan, I'm afraid," Brownlee said. "You know how tight our budget is."

"Yes, sir, I do," Morgan said, looking at Frank's Leica mournfully.

"On the positive side, Morgan old chap, have you been able to get anything useful from young Frank's picture?" Brownlee asked.

"We projected the negative and then took negatives of it, each therefore becoming a false positive. We then enlarged the new negatives and printed them using a variety of techniques, photographs of photographs, if you will. Trying different levels of reciprocity …"

"Reciprocity, Morgan?"

"Yes sir—the relationship between the sensitivity of the film to light and the duration of the exposure. There's an inverse linear relationship between …"

"Er, I'm sure there is, Morgan," Brownlee said. "Is that something to do with f-stops?

"Oh, no sir, that's not linear," Frank intervened, "That's based on the square root of two. For example …"

Brownlee held up one massive hand.

"I am in awe of your technical expertise, gentlemen. I bow before it. I am prepared to grovel, if necessary. But, with due respect, can you please tell me if you've been able to get anything out of young Frank's photograph?"

"Here, Frank," Morgan grinned, "show Superintendent Brownlee what we've got so far."

Frank held up a large piece of cardboard, onto which four photographs had been pasted, each representing a quarter of the original, now blown up so that the entire montage was over a foot high and almost two feet wide. Frank laid it on top of the tea-stained clutter on Brownlee's desk, and they all craned over it.

Ford felt as if he had been projected back in time to the night of the murder.

Amy Robsart was leaning against her bicycle, just as the ladies had described. The rear couplings and bumpers of the fish train locomotive framed the photograph on the right, and the bulk of his lordship's Bentley loomed to the left. The maker's ornament, a large B sprouting wings on each side, was clearly visible above the radiator grill. Ghost-like streaks of gray ran horizontally across the picture.

The foreground and the sides of the composite, which had been in shadow, were dark and were filled with amorphous gray shapes. Amy Robsart, in contrast, was sharply defined in the moonlight. Her expression was clearly visible, both pensive and excited, as she watched to her left, across the harbor in the direction of the Duke. Her manner suggested, to Ford's overheated imagination, that she was looking forward to her tryst with Pengriffon, but perhaps she was wondering how long the relationship could last.

She must have waited without moving, Ford realized, for else her features would have been smudged by the length of the exposure—yes, her skirt was ethereal, as the night breeze had fluttered it as she stood. Would someone planning a violent murder have stood so calmly?

"What are these gray lines across the photograph?" Brownlee asked.

"That's the motion blur of the two ladies walking through the exposure, sir," Frank replied. "Mrs. Norris and Mrs. Davis. They looked toward the camera, but they couldn't see me in the dark; I didn't say nothing, for fear they'd stop and ruin the exposure."

And so it was the camera tripod that had become Clara's foreigner, it's black photographer's hood the foreigner's dark hair and elegant evening cloak, and Frank's camera lens and viewfinder had become the foreigner's glittering eyes; so much for proof that Poole had been lurking in the shadows.

Ford took a magnifying glass from Morgan and ran it across the photographic montage, which still emitted a slightly acrid chemical smell. He paused and focused on the Bentley. The front of the vehicle was facing the camera. He could make out the outlines of the windscreen and the canvas top, and, perhaps, even the steering wheel—or were his eyes inventing what they expected to see?

"Can you enlarge the motorcar, Sergeant? Can you make it more visible? Could that dark shape behind the steering wheel be a man?"

"Well, I'd have to ... There's not much light ... The low density of particles of light ... I suppose there's no harm in trying, but I'll not promise anything, sir."

"Just do your best, if you would," Ford said.

*   *   *

Sergeant Morgan and Frank were replaced by Dr. Waggoner, a specialist in criminal psychology whom Ford and Brownlee often consulted.

Dr. Waggoner had been born in Zurich, in the German-speaking part of Switzerland, and had changed his name from Wagner to Waggoner to protect himself from England's pervasive hatred of all things German. To make matters even more difficult, Waggoner had studied under Sigmund Freud in Vienna, and he was therefore assumed, in the popular imagination, to believe that all human behavior, regardless of the circumstances, was motivated by repressed sexual fantasies about one's mother, which revealed themselves more fully in lurid dreams.

He was, however, highly regarded at Scotland Yard. He had spent years at Broadmoor, the prison hospital for the criminally insane in the west of England, studying the nature and symptoms of criminality.

"I read Mr. Thompson's pamphlet with great interest," Dr. Waggoner said, when he had settled into his chair and accepted tea. He spoke English without an accent, and yet he still seemed foreign; Ford had often speculated that it was the precision of his grammar that betrayed him. "Mr. Thompson's thesis is that those who work in factories and farms, and who toil in the depths of mines, deserve to enjoy the fruits of their labor, but these benefits are unfairly taken from them by business owners."

He paused to light his pipe.

"It is, of course, a familiar thesis promulgated by many socialist writers, but Mr. Thompson's work is not simply a rehash of Karl Marx's *Das Capital*. I was particularly struck by a passage in the pamphlet in which Mr. Thompson contrasts the fates of two men born less than a mile apart. One is born in a grand mansion and the other in a humble cottage; one inherits wealth, power, and social position, and the other has nothing. One passes his life in luxury, indolence, and self-indulgence, while the other spends his life in grueling labor, working for the rich man. The wealthy man, in short, lives off the sweat of the poor man's brow."

Dr. Waggoner riffled through the manuscript until he found a particular passage, and he read it aloud. "Ah, here it is: 'The laboring classes carry the affluent on their backs; they produce the wealth that the upper classes consume, and yet the laborers are treated with callous disdain and derided as though they were no better than pack animals.'"

He used his pipe stem to point to the pamphlet. "I concluded that Mr. Thompson's political principles are animated not only by conviction, but also by personal experience. The phrases 'callous disdain' and 'derided' are strikingly personal, as if the writer is recalling real events he has experienced. Mr. Thompson is, therefore, in my view, the man born in the humble cottage."

"Well, Doctor," Ford said, nodding, "Lord Pengriffon certainly owed his position in Trethgarret to his inherited wealth, whereas Mr. Thompson had to work to achieve his own position."

"Exactly, Chief Inspector; but, despite all Mr. Thompson's efforts, what is the mayor of a small town in comparison to an earl, or a mine manager in comparison to the mine owner?"

"Lord Pengriffon was considering closing the Old Morehead Mine, whereas Thompson wants to expand it," Ford said. "Could Thompson, the writer of this pamphlet, have been so enraged that he killed Pengriffon?"

Dr. Waggoner puffed on his pipe and pondered.

"On balance, I think not, Chief Inspector. He might, however, have incited others to do so—let me explain why. Part of the pamphlet is devoted to organizing labor and resistance movements. He describes the role of the political leader, whose function is to instruct and persuade others to carry out a mission, rather than to perform the mission himself. The leader is protected from danger, so that he can survive to fight another day."

More puffing signaled additional thought.

"I must say, it has always struck me as ironic that those who fight against a hierarchical society, as Lenin's Bolsheviks are currently doing in Russia, always seek to replace it with a hierarchy of their own, with themselves at the top. They justify their own ambition by claiming they are acting in the interest of others. Such self-delusion ..."

Brownlee stirred, and Waggoner set down his pipe.

"But I digress, gentlemen. In the matter at hand, if George Thompson had a follower or followers under his influence who shared his animosity toward Pengriffon, then, perhaps, one of them might have committed murder, with or without Thompson's explicit orders."

Ford considered. Could Thompson have had that degree of influence over someone in Trethgarret? Surely not—the general attitude about Thompson seemed to be amusement at his officiousness. Could the mine workers have been so desperate, so fearful that Pengriffon would throw them into penury, that they'd actually strangle him—and Amy Robsart, to boot? No, his lordship was too well liked. He was admired for his generosity, and he was planning to start another business so that the displaced workers would not suffer.

However, Ford had far too great a respect for Waggoner to dismiss the suggestion out of hand.

"I'd like you to come down to Trethgarret, Doctor, if you would, and interview Mr. Thompson in person." A thought struck him—a double thought. "I'd also be grateful if you'd interview a Miss Josephine Langley, a witness who troubles me greatly."

"I am, as always, at your disposal," Waggoner bowed. "Does Miss Langley share Thompson's views?"

"Not that I know of, but ..."

Ford's voice trailed away. What, if any, was her relationship to Thompson? He recalled meeting Thompson on the cliff road. He'd said he was on his way to see Lady Pengriffon, but his pony trap had disappeared at the entrance to the lane that led to the cottage. And she'd seemed dismayed when Ford had arrived in Thompson's car, but without Thompson. If there was a ...

"Excuse me, sirs," Caruthers interrupted from the doorway. "Sergeant Croft is on the telephone for Mr. Ford."

A brief search amongst the tea-stained piles of paper on Brownlee's desk revealed the instrument.

"I've just spoken to Dr. Anderson, sir," Croft's voice said. "Amy

Robsart was *not* pregnant, sir—the doctor's certain. In addition, the cause of death was a blow to the head with a blunt instrument. He found bits of concrete embedded in her skull and thinks she was hit by one of those concrete blocks the murderer used as anchors for the bodies. The crabs couldn't eat the skull or the concrete chips."

Ford shuddered at the thought. "What about the belt round her neck? Did Anderson have an opinion about that?"

"An afterthought—window-dressing, so to say. No bruising."

The murderer strangled Pengriffon and then—no, it was more likely the murderer struck at them both with the concrete block as they lay entangled on the deck, and, in the darkness, happened to hit Amy Robsart first. That would account for why she did not fight back while his lordship was being strangled. Then—no, that didn't seem to make sense, either.

"I'm going back to the launch, sir," Croft said, interrupting Ford's train of thought. "I just can't visualize it somehow, if you see what I mean. If they were, well, if the murderer attacked them when they were, well, er, otherwise engaged, as it were … Anyway, sir, I've taken the liberty of asking Penzance to send two detective constables with a forensic bag, sir. If she was hit on the head there must have been blood, and they can also test the concrete fragments to see if they're the same as the blocks, if you follow me."

"Excellent, Croft, I should have thought of that myself." Another thought occurred to him. "Oh, and get them to examine the lantern in the cabin, would you?"

"The lantern? Very well, sir—oh, and before I forget, the lighthouse keeper says his dog growled at nine thirty and again at ten thirty on Sunday night, sir. It does that when ships pass in and out of the harbor, according to the keeper, but he didn't get up to look because it's nothing out of the ordinary, and he had a nasty turn of the stomach flu, if you know what I mean, and wasn't in a position to go and look. Anyway, sir, that timing would be consistent with the *Justicia* going out to the Little Dogs and back again."

Ford's imaginary defense lawyer would make short work of a canine witness, but it was useful information nonetheless.

"Excellent again, Croft. Incidentally, I think we have an explanation for his lordship's weird accounting. It's a bit convoluted—it's *very* convoluted—but I'll telephone you later to try to explain. Oh, and one more thing, Croft, if you would. Could you somehow give the Ancient Mariner an eyesight test without offending him?"

"You mean if he really saw Amy Robsart on her bicycle or someone driving his lordship's car, sir?"

"Exactly."

"I'll see what I can do, sir," Croft said. "Leave it to me."

Ford replaced the telephone receiver, thanking his lucky stars yet again for being blessed with Croft as his assistant, and relayed Croft's information to Brownlee, who adopted his habitual sphinxlike analytic pose.

The office fell silent as Brownlee, Ford, and Waggoner digested Croft's report. Caruthers appeared in the doorway with tea, the prospect of which was sufficient to rouse Brownlee.

"You appear to have three equally plausible—or, more accurately, equally implausible—explanations for this event," Brownlee rumbled. "One is that the two lovers were killed in a fit of jealous rage, by either Josephine Langley or Lady Pengriffon. The second is that Pengriffon was killed as a result of this complex set of financial deceptions, although I freely admit I don't fully comprehend them. In those circumstances I assume that Poole, the trustee, is the most likely suspect, although it might have been one of—or both—Pollocks."

He paused to drink tea and to light his devil-face pipe. If Brownlee were to drill tiny holes in the carved eyes, Ford thought, so that the smoldering tobacco shone through, the effect would be dramatic.

"Third and finally," Brownlee continued, "we have the possibility that Pengriffon was killed either by Thompson or, to Dr. Waggoner's point, by someone acting under his influence."

Ford reflexively reached for a cigarette, but paused in midmotion. Brownlee's office was becoming enveloped in an ever-denser blue haze as Brownlee and Waggoner puffed away like railway locomotives at full speed, and it occurred to Ford that smoking in enclosed spaces might not be healthy.

"If I might offer an observation, Superintendent," Waggoner said, "I would point out that in two of those three cases Amy Robsart was not the intended victim. She was killed because she was a witness."

"That's true, sir," Ford said. "Inversely, one wonders if there are other explanations, in which *she* was the intended victim, and *he* was the innocent bystander."

"Three explanations are inadequate, old chap?" Brownlee asked with a chuckle. "Is this case not sufficiently complex for your taste? Did the well-loved earl not have enough mortal enemies?"

He sipped his tea.

"Of course, old chap, you might consider adding Sir David and his son to the list to be a load of old Pollocks," he said, and erupted again with equally catastrophic results.

* * *

Ford shuffled impatiently on the platform of Euston Station, his thoughts divided between the extraordinary financial machinations conducted by Poole and Pengriffon, and fear that Victoria would miss the train.

What on earth were Pengriffon and Poole up to? What if she were delayed? Could Miss Edwards be Poole's accomplice?—if Poole had been cooking the books, someone must have been typing false reports. He'd asked Inspector West to recover her typewriter from the ruins of PP&P and compare the typeface against the reports sent to Pengriffon. Did she have ambitions to replace the existing Mrs. Poole? If Victoria was late, should he go back to Trethgarret alone or stay in London and catch the first train in the morning? That would waste an entire day, but he didn't want to travel without her.

The case was gathering a momentum he sincerely hoped it deserved. Dr. Waggoner was aboard the train, in order to interview Miss Langley and Thompson. Croft had brought in forensic reinforcements from Penzance. Inspector West had a sizable list of tasks to perform and was armed with a warrant to search Poole's home. Brownlee had announced he'd travel down in the morning, consult with Sir Oliver Boxer, the chief constable of Cornwall, and, as he had put it, add general *gravitas* to the proceedings.

Everyone seemed to think that Ford was about to yell "*Eureka!*" and unmask the murderer. But who? Poole? Thompson? Josephine Langley? Perhaps Brownlee thought—with good reason—that Ford was stuck, and wanted to make an assessment at first hand. Since Amy Robsart wasn't pregnant, he could probably take Lady Pengriffon off the list.

Was he omitting anything? He rehearsed the list of tasks he'd given Inspector West—a thorough search of the wreckage of PP&P as soon as it was cool enough to enter, with particular attention to Miss Edwards's typewriter and any correspondence that had survived, which would have been filed in alphabetical order, so it might be possible to detect if anything had been removed, rather than destroyed; a visit to Poole's home, in Poole's absence, while he was away attending Pengriffon's funeral, to see what, if anything, Mrs. Poole knew of embezzlement; and yet another call to the *Justicia's* boat builder ...

This wasn't like Victoria—unlike the common belief that husbands spend half their lives waiting for their wives, she was always punctual. Had she had an accident? Was she even now—dear God, no!—writhing beneath the wheels of an omnibus? Was ...

"Ah, there you are, darling," Victoria greeted him. "I was afraid you'd be late."

Now as always when she appeared, the rest of the world receded into a vague haze, leaving her alone in vivid focus.

"How goes the case, angelic Thomas? Have you had a good day? I've brought a picnic basket so that we won't have to endure a railway supper—I dashed into Harrods to buy you some pajamas, and decided they'd get very little use, so I didn't, but I popped into the Food Hall to stock up on pork pies and devilled eggs, and I got a bottle of my favorite Portuguese green wine. I hope you like devilled eggs, darling? Do stop shilly-shallying—the train's about to leave. Why are you staring? Do I have a smut on my face?"

"No, no, V—I'm just very happy to see you, that's all."

Fifteen

Ford felt exhausted as he stepped down from the train in Penzance Station. The mystery of the vaulting horse had been revealed, to spectacular effect, in the small hours of the morning. Croft, looking surprisingly fresh for such an early hour—he must have arisen at four in the morning to be here—shouldered his way through the somnolent passengers to greet them.

"Morning, Mrs. Ford; morning, sir," he said, raising his hat to Victoria. "Is Dr. Waggoner on the train as well? Ah, there you are, Doctor; good morning to you."

Croft gathered up their luggage with the effortless efficiency of a mechanized highway shovel and led them to the waiting Humber.

"I can't quite follow all that banking information you discovered, sir," he said as he settled behind the wheel. "I went over it last night with Crocker to keep him up to date, and I couldn't quite explain it all."

"I'm not sure I can either," Ford said. "We'll go over it again with Brownlee later. He's very good with those kinds of puzzles."

"In the meantime, sir, there's the funeral—both funerals—today, but I thought we'd have time to see Miss Langley first, if that's all right with you, sir? And I know you want to see Thompson with Dr. Waggoner also; I don't know if we'll fit it all in before the church."

They breasted the hill that led west to the high country beyond Penzance.

"Mrs. Croft was afraid you wouldn't have time for breakfast, so she packed something in that hamper for you to eat on the way."

Something turned out to be an assortment of ham, egg, tomato, and cucumber sandwiches; freshly picked blackberries and a crock of cream; cold boiled eggs and crisp slices of toast; and a large vacuum flask of tea.

"Perhaps I'd better skip the interview with Miss Langley, sir," Croft said, as Ford started on his third sandwich. "You could take Crocker, if I may suggest it. I've got the forensics chaps from Penzance to organize, and there's still the eyesight test for the old man, however we're going to manage that."

"I'll do that, if you like," Victoria suggested.

"How are you going to do it without upsetting him?" Ford asked.

"Oh, I'll try something very subtle, Thomas, such as explaining that we need to test his eyes, but you're too embarrassed to ask him."

"I see," Ford said.

* * *

Croft brought the Humber smoothly down the steep hill leading into Trethgarret. Whitewashed cottages, bright with window boxes, grew thicker on each side of the road, and Ford caught a glimpse of the harbor sparkling in the morning sun below them. As they approached the railway level crossing at the top of the High Street, Ford saw two figures waving to them.

"Is that Mrs. Croft?" he asked. "And Crocker?"

Croft brought the Humber to a screeching halt and leapt from the car, and the others scrambled to follow him.

"Are you all right, Betty? What's happened? What's the matter?"

"I'm fine, Bob," she assured him. "Don't worry. I've been helping Mr. Crocker."

"What has happened?" Ford asked.

"Thank God you're here, sir!" Crocker said. He was almost dancing in agitation. "I didn't know what to do, so I did what I hoped was right."

"I'm sure you did, Crocker, but what?"

Crocker gathered his breath.

"Jim Parks, the stationmaster, sent down to tell me Josephine Langley was waiting for the morning train, with a suitcase with her, like she was doing a bunk, sir."

"Leaving Trethgarret?"

"Yes, sir. She told him she'd had it with Trethgarret, and good riddance. He thought it was a bit odd, what with her friend Amy Robsart being buried later on this morning, and her not waiting, so he sent his lad down the High Street to tell me. Well, I came up here, quick as I could, and there she was, walking up and down the platform, jerkylike, and I thought, well, I thought, I didn't know if I should let her go, or detain her, but I didn't know what cause to give, beyond it was a bit strange. So I told her you wanted to see her, and she'd have to wait for you, and she said, well, she said something a lady shouldn't properly say, and then all of a sudden the train was coming round the corner in the distance, and there wasn't time to think."

He paused for breath and ran his fingers beneath his collar.

"Well, sir, just then I saw Mrs. Croft on her way to the hospital, thank the lord, so I went over and asked her, and she said to hold her, against her will if necessary, on account of being an eyewitness in a capital offense. But I didn't want to put handcuffs on her and march her down the High Street and make a public spectacle, so Mrs. Croft said to lock her in the station luggage room, sir. It's got bars on the windows and everything."

"She's still in there?" Ford asked. He could see the stationmaster standing awkwardly before the door.

"I hope I said the right thing, sir," Mrs. Croft said. "I tried to think what Bob would have done."

"You did exactly the right thing," Ford told her. "It was quick thinking, if I may say so. And you, too, Crocker. I'm much obliged to both of you."

"Thank the lord," Crocker said, sighing in relief, and removed his helmet to scratch his head.

"You gave me such a turn, Betty," Croft said. "I thought you'd had an accident."

"Stop fussing, you old softy," she said, patting his arm, and again Ford saw that warm affection could indeed survive many years of marriage.

"Since she's here, I might as well see Miss Langley right away," Ford said. "Perhaps you'll come with me, Dr. Waggoner? Croft, you can go on into town and get the Penzance forensics chaps organized, if you would. Thanks again, Mrs. Croft."

"You're welcome, sir, I'm sure. And now I'd better be getting along to the hospital. The poor starving lambs will be needing their breakfasts."

"I'll borrow the car and go and see if Justie Pengriffon needs any help getting ready," Victoria said. "It must be a bit grim for her, especially if my mother is stirring things up. Now, Thomas, don't be late for the funeral."

The group parted on its various missions and Ford approached the station luggage room. The stationmaster, agog with unasked questions, unlocked the door, and Ford entered cautiously. It was not impossible Josephine Langley might attack him. However, he found her sitting rigidly on her suitcase in the center of the dusty room, smoking a cigarette. A litter of ground-out stubs lay at her feet, and Ford felt a stab of sympathy for her; she seemed almost like a caged animal, trapped by circumstances and forces beyond her control.

"Miss Langley, I'm very sorry to have to detain you against your will," he said, as gently as he could. "Unfortunately, I have no choice. This gentleman is Dr. Waggoner, and he is assisting us."

"I've nothing to say to either of you," she said in a taut, barely controlled voice.

"I am not a member of the police force, Miss Langley," Dr. Waggoner told her. His voice retained its usual precision but seemed somehow softer, Ford thought, and it occurred to him that he had never seen Waggoner talk to a witness—or a patient, for that matter. "I am, however, retained by the police in a professional capacity; my field is criminology. I also teach at London University."

"I'm not mad, if that's what you're here for," she said.

"No one is suggesting that you are, Miss Langley," Waggoner said. "However, Chief Inspector Ford has told me that you have given him more than one false statement. In my experience, failure to tell the truth is a fundamental defense mechanism, rather like the instinct to put up one's arm to fend off a blow. In medical terms it's referred to as autonomic—an involuntary reflex one cannot prevent, like breathing.

But, of course, you're a trained nurse and will be familiar with such matters."

She puffed on her cigarette but said nothing.

"Can you tell us why you wanted to leave?" Ford asked. "The funerals are later this morning, and one would have supposed you'd stay."

"I can come back in the future and dance on their graves whenever I want," she said. She looked at Waggoner. "Is it a sign of derangement to be glad of the deaths of your enemies, Doctor?"

"I consider it a sign of sanity, Miss Langley. It is, however, a legitimate question to ask why they were your enemies?"

"It's a long story, and Mr. Ford thinks everything I say is a lie."

"Well, I have plenty of time," Waggoner said. "Besides, I believe all lies are based on truth."

He sat down on a packing case, made himself comfortable, and drew out his pipe. It occurred to Ford to leave Waggoner to it.

"I'll excuse myself, Miss Langley," he said. "Crocker will be outside the door, in case you need him."

Ford slipped out of the door and spoke briefly to Crocker, who turned the key in the lock.

"Keep an ear open, Constable, in case Dr. Waggoner calls for you. When he's finished, you'd better take her down to your lockup. I hope they sent a woman officer from Penzance to take charge of her. I'll borrow a car from Croft's forensics chaps so you don't have to march her down the High Street."

*　*　*

Ford walked toward the level crossing to turn into the High Street, and he was almost bowled over by Thompson coming in the opposite direction. He was panting with the exertion of walking rapidly—or perhaps even trotting in an undignified manner—up the hill.

"There's a rumor you've arrested Josephine Langley," he puffed. "You have no right to do so, no right at all."

"I haven't arrested her, sir, but I have every right to detain her."

"What's she been saying? She's delusional, you know; whatever she's said is all made up. What *has* she said?" He was sufficiently agitated to seize Ford's lapel. "What has she said about me? Whatever it is, it's not true."

"She's said nothing about you, Mr. Thompson."

Ford hoped urgently that Thompson would let go of his lapel; he had no wish to scuffle with the mayor in public, and, in any case, Thompson was considerably larger. In the distance he could see Crutchfield walking his dog along the High Street and looking curiously in their direction. He stepped back, and Thompson dropped his hand, thank God.

Thompson took a deep breath, and seemed to realize he was behaving very strangely.

"I've spoken to Dr. Anderson about his hospital nurses on more than one occasion," he said, taking refuge in his habitual cloak of pomposity. "One was little better than a street girl and is now a proven murderer, and this one's loony. It does the town no good, no good at all, to be besieged by young women of doubtful character. It's upsetting, and it makes us look bad. A Labor government will set higher standards for the medical professions, you mark my words. The working man deserves no less."

He launched into a broader assessment of the virtues of a socialist approach to medicine, but Ford's mind was elsewhere. Why was Thompson so concerned about whatever it was he thought Josephine Langley might say about him? What was their relationship? He recalled again that Thompson's pony trap had disappeared off the cliff road a few days ago—it must have been Tuesday—when Thompson had made a point of saying he was on his way to Pengriffon Hall. And Josephine Langley had been expecting a visitor and was confused when Ford had arrived in Thompson's motorcar.

Thompson had been bitterly opposed to his lordship's plans to close the Old Morehead Hole. Pengriffon had, perhaps, treated him with disdain in his youth. Had he encouraged her fury against Pengriffon? Had she gone out to the launch to mete out justice on Thompson's behalf, as well as her own?

"Are you arresting her, or not?" Thompson's voice broke into his thoughts. "As mayor of Trethgarret, I'm entitled to an answer."

"I regret that you are not, Mr. Thompson," he said, with an

abruptness that surprised them both. "And now I must excuse myself. I have work to do before the funerals begin."

He left Thompson openmouthed—experiencing a guilty pleasure in so doing—and strode down the High Street toward the harbor.

"It was that little trollop Amy Robsart," he heard Thompson call after him.

Ford wondered at the source of Thompson's venom. He seemed almost priggishly offended by her. Perhaps there was no room in a socialist nirvana for cheerful pulchritude, particularly if it supported the Conservative Party. Unlike every other male within fifty miles of Trethgarret, he had not succumbed to her allure.

Or had he, by Jove? "The haves have whatever they want, whenever they want it," Thompson had said when they met on the cliff road. "What's wrong with an honest, hardworking bloke like me getting a slice of the pie?"

Ford had assumed that Thompson's complaint was economic, but could he have been referring to Amy Robsart? Could he have envied his lordship his dalliance with her?

He tried to imagine Thompson attempting to gain her favor. Had he offered to take her driving in his stately Humber, the medallions on his commodious stomach jingling as they roared along the cliff road? Had he parked on the cliff tops, and whispered to her of repairing clogged sewage pipes, or beguiled her with the glories of an egalitarian workers' paradise?

Ford shook his head in irritation at his own imaginings. This case was like a squirming worm, wriggling out from his grasp every time he tried to seize it. And now, to make matters worse, here was Crutchfield, standing foursquare in his path.

"Ah, a very good morning to you, Chief Inspector," came the oily words, and politeness forced Ford to pause.

"Good morning, Mr. Crutchfield," Ford said. He would have raised his hat and passed on, but he noticed that Crutchfield's dog did not share his master's demeanor; it was large, long-fanged, and growling softly in its throat.

"Oh, don't let Cerberus bother you," Crutchfield smiled. "He wouldn't hurt a fly."

Ford was not so sure. Any dog named for the ferocious three-headed guardian of the underworld should not be taken lightly.

"Did I see you in conversation with our worthy mayor, Chief Inspector?" Crutchfield asked. "I thought I saw Constable Crocker up at the station as well. Is anything wrong?"

"No, no, nothing's the matter, I assure you, sir," Ford answered, hoping he'd kept his irritation out of his voice.

"I hope Crocker told you I saw his lordship's vehicle driving past here on the night his lordship died?"

"Er, yes, thank you," Ford said.

"And that it was shortly followed by George Thompson's own motorcar?"

As usual, Ford felt a pressing desire to escape Crutchfield's company.

"Yes, yes he did, sir," he managed.

"And that these events occurred *after* the time that his lordship must have died?"

Ford repressed an urge to suggest that Crutchfield should take over the case, since he had already solved it. He recalled that Crocker had warned him not to believe Crutchfield with regard to Thompson; but, even so, the coincidence of the two cars following each other, combined with the growing list of Thompson's possible motives, could not be ignored.

"Er, I very much appreciate your help, sir," Ford said. He took a tiny step toward freedom, wondering if Cerberus would guard the way. The dog remained stationary—perhaps it would not rip off Ford's leg without an explicit order from its master—and Ford risked a bolder step.

"As I'm sure you'll appreciate, Mr. Crutchfield, there's a great deal to …" With that he estimated Cerberus' lunging range as carefully as he could, skirted it, and bolted down the hill, knowing that Crutchfield would be grinning in his wake.

* * *

Ford shifted his weight on the unyielding church pew in St. Michael's-By-The-Sea, and the Reverend Theobald Asquith launched into the fourteenth interminable minute of his sermon at Lord Pengriffon's funeral. Ford tried to listen, but Asquith's droning voice was numbing Ford's mind just as the pew was numbing his rear quarters, and the vicar's dolorous voice faded in and out of his consciousness.

"His lordship was blessed with many gifts," Asquith was saying, "which he explored with great enthusiasm—perhaps, in some cases, one fears, with too much enthusiasm."

This was the second funeral of the day.

The first, for Amy Robsart, had been cheap and utilitarian, as if it had been arranged by Woolworths. Ford had almost had to intervene to cancel it, for Croft's forensics officers had been examining her only an hour before the ceremony. Just in time they declared themselves finished, so that the undertaker could screw down the lid on her plain coffin and hurry her remains without ceremony to the gravesite.

Asquith must have intended to rush through it on the far side of St. Christopher's churchyard so that Amy's earthly remains would be buried—and, hopefully, forgotten—by the time the far larger and grander congregation gathered inside the church to pay tribute to Lord Pengriffon.

In this manner, her relationship with his lordship, and the coincidence of their deaths, would not detract from the solemnity befitting the passing of an Earl of the Realm—or so Lady Canderblank had probably instructed Asquith.

In fact, Miss Robsart's funeral had been well attended, with the crowd of mourners spilling back to the pathway from the lich-gate to the church porch. She had been generous and popular and a valued member of the hospital staff; the townswomen seemed to have forgiven the effect she had had on their menfolk. The Ancient Mariner, Ford noted, had tottered all the way from the Duke to stand at her graveside. "Gone, but not forgotten," he had announced solemnly when her casket had been lowered into the ground, and the entire gathering murmured in agreement, thereby completely upstaging Asquith's final hurried amen.

Ford and Croft had positioned themselves amongst the crowd gathered at her graveside so they could search each face in the hope of spotting a remorseful or guilty expression, although they knew, of course, that such things happen only in detective fiction.

233

Lady Canderblank's vast Rolls Royce had led a procession of motorcars that arrived at the church just as Amy Robsart's funeral was finishing, and Ford could tell, even from a distance, that she was furious that the grand event she had planned had been preceded by another, more spontaneous, demonstration of grief and affection.

She had rounded up a respectable number of peers and other worthy members of high society, who now sat in the front pews of St. Christopher's in various attitudes of concealed boredom. Behind them sat the townspeople of Trethgarret, together with an assortment of oddly dressed strangers, Carrington from L'Arte Moderne among them, whom Ford took to be members of the artistic community.

The Ancient Mariner was an exception to this social order. He had inched his way to the front of the church and sat down stolidly among the earls and barons.

Now, as the Reverend Asquith commenced his seventeenth mind-numbing minute, one of Hilaire Belloc's rhymes sprang into Ford's mind, "Her funeral sermon (which was long / And followed by a sacred song) / Mentioned her virtues, it is true / But dwelt upon her vices too."

The heroine of Belloc's poem had been killed as the accidental result of her own excesses—her penchant for practical jokes. Had his lordship been killed because of his penchant for complicated practical jokes, by doing unto Poole what Poole had done unto him? Poole was seated in the front pew next to the Ancient Mariner, and Ford had a clear view of the back of his immaculately coiffed head.

Or had his lordship died at Thompson's hand, to prevent the Old Morehead Hole from being abandoned, and Thompson's job lost along with it? Or had Pengriffon been the victim of Josephine's twisted soul, or even—theoretically—of a jealous demon that had lurked deep beneath Lady Justicia's limpid surface?

Now at last the sermon was over, and Asquith gathered himself to deliver the final prayers, like an actor preparing to deliver a Shakespearean soliloquy.

"Man that is born of a woman hath but a short time to live, and is full of misery. He cometh up, and is cut down, like a flower; he fleeth as it were a shadow, and never continueth in one stay … In the midst of life we are in death …"

Thomas Cranmer wrote those words in 1549, Ford thought, and he certainly knew how to deliver bad news unvarnished.

"… Thou knowest, Lord, the secrets of our hearts …"

His lordship and Amy Robsart had been cut down like flowers, in the midst of their lives, almost certainly by someone in the congregation. Ford looked around the solemn faces. Damn it, Lord, he thought, would you please share the secrets of the murderer's heart with me, so that I can do my job and get back to my honeymoon?

"… We therefore commit his body to the ground; earth to earth, ashes to ashes, dust to dust; in sure and certain hope of the Resurrection to eternal life, through our Lord Jesus Christ …"

At last it was over. Victoria went to offer Lady Justicia their condolences, and Ford slipped away through a side door, partly to smoke a cigarette and partly, he admitted to himself, to avoid the possibility of contact with his mother-in-law.

He stared out to sea and experienced, as he described it to himself, the calm before the storm. He felt he had reached the point in the case at which he knew everything he needed to know, and that the answers were all there, if he had but the wit to see them. Poole, covering up his embezzlement, and egged on by disdain for his victim? Thompson, protecting his livelihood and position, his motives reinforced by his political convictions? Langley, driven by her inner demons, embittered by jealousy and rejection? Which one was it?

The bell buoy clanged, and high above his head the church clock struck two o'clock. Brownlee would be arriving soon, and he'd need to have his thoughts marshaled into order. It was silly to waste his time wishing that he had a confession or unimpeachable physical evidence. Suddenly his suspects seemed pathetic—Langley, scarred by unrequited love; Thompson, trapped inside his own pomposity; Poole, ensnared in a labyrinth of falsehood.

The famous quotation from Sherlock Holmes entered his mind, "When you've eliminated the impossible, the remainder, however improbable, must be true." Was it remotely possible that more than one person had gone out to the launch that night, each with the *separate* intention of murdering his lordship? Could he have been the victim of some ghastly coincidence? But if so, who had done the deed?

Davey Garret had seen Thompson walking on the dock, which

Thompson had vehemently denied, and Clara had seen a car like the Humber. Josephine Langley had offered seemingly absurd versions of the truth, but—what was it Waggoner had said?—all lies are based on truth. And Ford was certain the odious Poole would not shrink from murder.

He closed his eyes to clear his mind. What was the key—the one essential characteristic of the case that would point inevitably to the guilty party? And what was lurking in the corners of his mind, his eureka thoughts, as he privately described them to himself, the facts that he had overlooked?

Sixteen

Brownlee settled his ponderous weight at the head of the table in the upstairs room at the Duke, and Waggoner, Croft, Crocker, and Ford gathered around him. Brownlee had brought a large leather portmanteau filled with files and reports, and he distributed these at random before him, thus re-creating the chaos of his desktop in Scotland Yard. Ford wondered if he needed clutter to concentrate his thoughts.

Victoria had asked Charlie to provide an urn of tea, and it sat on a side table with a tiny flame beneath it, spluttering to itself like an irritated Russian samovar. Ford wondered how Brownlee would survive without Constable Caruthers to pour his tea.

"Now, Ford, old chap, let's see if we can put this all together," Brownlee said. "Tell me a tale."

"We have three sets of motives, sir," Ford began. "We'll take them one by one, if we may. In Josephine Langley's case it's jealousy of the love affair between Lord Pengriffon and Amy Robsart, possibly reinforced by sympathy for Thompson, although I am hoping Dr. Waggoner can shed more light on that. She admits to being on the *Justicia* on the night in question, so we don't need evidence to prove it. And, she's certainly strong enough to have strangled his lordship. Thus, she was at the scene with two people she hated. Any observations, Doctor?"

"I doubt she hated either of them, Chief Inspector," Waggoner said, shaking his elegant head slowly. "Permit me to explain. The young lady is indeed consumed by hatred, I fear, but it is inwardly directed; she loathes herself. She did not hate Amy Robsart because Miss Robsart

237

was attractive to men; she hates herself because she isn't. Similarly, she did not hate Lord Pengriffon because he did not return her advances; she hates herself because she was unable to summon up his interest."

"Is she capable of violence, Doctor?" Ford asked.

"The young lady is more than capable of violence, in my opinion, but her anger is inchoate, aimless—if she struck out, she would strike out at random and without apparent purpose, like a frustrated infant." He nodded, as if anticipating Ford's next question. "However, if she were to be persuaded by someone else to channel her furies against a particular target—well, let me put it this way, she might become someone else's weapon."

"I see," Ford said. "When you interviewed her at the railway station this morning, did you speak about George Thompson?"

"We did; it was, in many ways, the most disturbing part of the entire interview. She spoke of him in admiration, and yet she said she found him repugnant. It seems they've spent some time together; after all, he's a bachelor, and she's a spinster, and so it is considered natural for them to have done so."

He had a tiny leather-bound notebook—in which he wrote notes to himself in German, in tiny but perfectly formed lettering, as if it were an elfin book of magical spells—and he referred to it now.

"She told me she had a deeply impoverished upbringing and a drunken, sexually abusive father. The one might explain her sympathies for Thompson's political views, and the other might explain her difficult relationships with men. One might imagine—and this, I would hasten to add, is mere conjecture on my part—that she saw a future as Thompson's wife. His career might flourish, and she might gain social acceptance, even respectability, at his side. Therefore she had several reasons to wish Lord Pengriffon dead—to preserve Thompson's income and social status as the mine manager, to avenge Pengriffon's rejection of her sexual advances, and to strike a blow against the aristocracy."

"That seems to fit, Doctor, but it not quite," Ford said. "It occurred to me a couple of days ago that Thompson might have set his cap at Amy Robsart and been rejected."

"To the contrary, that buttresses my argument, if I may say so," Waggoner said. "If Pengriffon rejected her, and Miss Robsart rejected him, they might have settled on each other as second best; a dismal prospect, to be sure, but a prospect nonetheless."

Poor woman, Ford thought. On the one hand she faced a cramped future as an unloved spinster, and on the other she faced a loveless marriage. What a choice!—barren solitude or perpetual exposure to Thompson's egotistic pomposity. And every day she'd shared a cottage with Amy Robsart, who could twist every man in Trethgarret around her little finger.

"If you elect to make a case against her, Chief Inspector," Waggoner continued, "I believe it will turn on the question of her mental and emotional competence. A court might accept a plea of insanity, because she was unable to distinguish right from wrong. That's certainly an argument that her counsel could chose to advance."

"But, do you think she's sane, Doctor?"

Waggoner paused to light his pipe, and Ford's mind jumped to his imaginary courtroom, with Waggoner in the witness stand.

"My conclusion is that she is sane," Waggoner said with finality. "Her perspective on the world is undoubtedly warped by her experiences, but she's perfectly consistent within that framework, and consistency is nine-tenths of sanity."

"Come, come, Doctor," Ford heard the voice of his imaginary barrister. "She had been driven to the breaking point, and beyond. Is it not true to say that she came face to face with Lord Pengriffon and Amy Robsart in the height of sexual passion—the court will, I trust, forgive me for so crude an allusion, but the point is crucial—and that she snapped?"

"With respect," the imaginary Waggoner answered, "I believe the legal and medical issue is not whether she snapped, as you put it, but whether, having snapped, she still knew her action was wrong. I believe she did know it."

Ford had seen Waggoner in court on several occasions and had watched him project an aura of invincible scientific logic. Sometimes the other side had offered an expert witness of their own to counter his conclusions, but Ford had never seen Waggoner lose the argument.

"Do you still have her in custody?" Brownlee asked, and Ford returned to the present.

"I don't like it, but I do," Ford said. "There's a self-evident risk of flight. We'll hold her for another twenty-four hours, until we've made our minds up."

"I concur," Brownlee nodded, and rose to replenish his teacup. "Who's next on the agenda, old chap?"

"George Thompson," Ford said. "His motives were his fear of losing his job and—although this is a stretch—his political tendencies."

"Politics are the most vicious form of personal combat ever devised by man," Brownlee observed. "Roman gladiators hacking each other into pieces in the arena pale by comparison. However, political animosities are seldom expressed by physical murder, for else the House of Commons would be totally unpopulated. Political adversaries prefer their victims crushed but alive, so that they can gloat over their discomfitures."

There was a knock on the door and Charlie entered.

"Excuse me for interrupting you, gentlemen, but there's a telephone call from the Bristol police for Mr. Croft."

"Bristol, Charlie?" Ford asked. "Don't you mean Penzance?"

"They said Bristol."

"Bristol? I wonder what they want?" Croft asked, and followed Charlie downstairs.

"One wonders whether Thompson is really a suspect, old chap," Brownlee said.

He had returned to the table and lit his pipe, and Ford, sitting between him and Waggoner, found himself at the busy intersection of two expanding clouds of thick blue-gray smoke.

"We have no evidence against him directly," Brownlee cogitated. "He was in the vicinity, but so was half of Trethgarret. Our assumption, I suppose, must be that he persuaded Josephine Langley to do away with his lordship, but it will be very hard to prove he was an accessory to murder before the fact. His defense would argue that the Langley woman killed them for her own reasons, and we couldn't prove otherwise, even if she testified she did it for him."

"That's true, sir," Ford said. "But whether it's Langley alone, or Langley with Thompson, it's still Langley. Even if she confesses, I wonder if we'll really believe her."

"That's also true," Waggoner nodded. "Her self-loathing could drive her to a false confession."

"And, in that case, the real murderer—if Thompson put her up to it—would walk free. However, that's not the only evidence against ..."

Croft reappeared. He was sufficiently excited to interrupt Ford.

"They found the Bentley! It's been in Bristol, parked outside the station, ever since Monday morning, but they mistook the make of it. They searched the car but found nothing of obvious interest. I asked them to test for fingerprints and blood stains."

"Excellent, by Jove!" Brownlee boomed. "His lordship's murderer took the car and drove to Bristol and made his escape by train. Someone should drive immediately to Bristol with photographs of our three suspects, to see if anyone can recognize them."

"Bristol, photographs, finger prints, bloodstains; got it, sir!" Crocker said, and bolted through the door. They could hear his heavy footsteps clattering down the stairs.

"This will let Thompson and Miss Langley off the hook," Croft said. "After all, they were in Trethgarret on Monday, and they had no cause to flee. No, that can't be right; they might have driven the Bentley, and the Humber, to Bristol, to make it look as if the murderer was escaping—no, his lordship and Amy Robsart doing a bunk—and then brought the Humber back."

"True," Brownlee said. "You have a witness who saw the two motorcars in procession. We'll have to find out if Josephine Langley can drive a motorcar."

"Good point, sir," Ford said. "Well, if that summarizes what we know about them, we are left with Poole to consider. In his case ..."

Again Charlie appeared at the door.

"Sorry again, gents, but this time it's an Inspector West on the telephone for Mr. Croft. Oh, and Mrs. Ford said to tell you that she's driving to Bristol, on the grounds that she's the best driver in Trethgarret, she said. And she also said to bring you sandwiches."

"That wife of yours is an angel, Ford," Brownlee said.

* * *

Ford took the opportunity to open the window, glancing automatically at the *Justicia* and the railway dock beyond her.

He wished Victoria wouldn't go driving madly all over southwestern England. He wanted her here, safe and sound and protected—but then she wouldn't be Victoria, he supposed.

He hoped the murderer wasn't Josephine Langley—he knew, from bitter experience, what it was to be unloved. As for Thompson, his greatest sin was probably excessive self-importance. If that was a crime then half the population of England deserved the gallows. It *had* to be Poole—but because he was an embezzler didn't mean he was a killer.

Victoria was a fast driver, certainly, but she wasn't reckless. But what if she encountered a stray farm animal around a sharp corner, or a drunken driver, besotted by scrumpy, zigzagging in the opposite direction? Suppose ...

Croft reappeared.

"Inspector West gave me several updates. There's also a report from the Bank of England, sir, addressed to you, Mr. Brownlee, that he took the liberty of opening in your absence."

"Good," Brownlee boomed.

Croft referred to his notebook. It looked bulky and shabby in comparison to Waggoner's perfect miniature.

"Well, sir, in the same order as Inspector West told me, they've finished searching what's left of PP&P. It seems most of the files were destroyed in the filing room, but the rest of the place wasn't so bad— water damage from the fire hoses. They found a lot of correspondence intact—it seems they kept letters in another room—but nothing for the Pengriffon trust. In fact, the correspondence was in alphabetical order, and Inspector West said there was a file for Pendleton and next to it was a file for Pennington, so it's as if the file for Pengriffon, which would have been between them, was removed."

"By Jove, that's remarkably shrewd of West, to think of a thing like that!" Brownlee said. "I've misjudged him all these years."

"Indeed it is, sir," Ford said, causing Brownlee to look at him sharply.

"They also got Miss Edwards's typewriter," Croft continued. "It's a bit melted, like, but they're certain the statements sent to his lordship were not printed on it. The capital letter 'P' was a bit worn down on account of typing Pollock, Pollock and Poole over and over; that's how they knew. However, they searched Mr. Poole's house, just as you asked, and they found the right typewriter. They brought Mrs. Poole into the local police station, and they're waiting to get your instructions, sir. She's not spoken a word, and she just keeps asking for her husband."

Croft paused to lick his thumb to turn a page.

"Well, it looks as if we've got Poole on the embezzlement, hook, line and sinker, even without his wife's testimony," Brownlee said.

"So it would seem, sir," Ford said.

"No question about it, sir," Croft nodded, and returned to his notes. "Also, he, Inspector West, that is, spoke to the shipyard owner who built the *Justicia,* per Mr. Ford's request—he spoke to the owner at Mr. Ford's request, that is to say. Anyway, it seems that Mr. Poole bought the *Justicia* first, but couldn't pay for her. He …"

"Good lord!" Brownlee erupted. "What gave you the idea, Ford— the astonishing idea—that the vessel that Poole couldn't pay for, and the pinnace that Pengriffon purchased, were one and the same?"

"Well, sir, when I first interviewed Poole he denied ever having seen the *Justicia,* and yet he was able to describe her as an oil-fired fifty-two-foot launch. It seemed an oddly specific description of a vessel he'd never seen."

"Pinnace, I believe you mean, old chap," Brownlee murmured.

Croft cleared his throat.

"Inspector West also confirmed that the shipyard chap hadn't spoken a word to Mr. Poole ever since his check was dishonored. They parted on very bad terms, it seems. Lord Pengriffon apparently contacted the shipyard shortly thereafter and offered to buy the *pinnace,* sir, and got her converted from coal to oil before taking delivery."

Ford glanced at Croft, marveling that Croft was able to keep a straight face.

"What about the Bank of England report, Croft?"

Croft looked at his notes. "It's mostly a formal statement of everything they did and found out, sir, very thick with lots of addenda and such, but it also says there's something unusual about the trust, because there's a lien against it."

"A lien, Croft?" Brownlee asked. "The trust owes money to someone? I didn't know a trust could go into debt."

"Er, Inspector West didn't know, sir. He didn't have time to read the report in detail. He just put it on the next train to be sent down here. Oh, and Sergeant Morgan and young Frank are still trying to develop those photographs, sir, the ones in the dark."

"I admire their tenacity," Brownlee said. "Anything else, Croft?"

"No sir, except that the Ancient Mariner—Jebediah Ham, that is, Mr. Brownlee, that Sir Rupert Effingham checked up on—is downstairs and wants to speak to us when we get a chance."

"I'll go," Ford volunteered, eager to escape the shroud of smoke that now enveloped the entire room.

"Ah, that reminds me," Brownlee said before Ford could stand. "Effingham came to see me this morning just as I was leaving to catch the train. Lord Pengriffon served in the Great War as a brigadier in the Royal Engineers Signals Service; he was responsible for the introduction of wireless communications on the front lines, and made several technical improvements. Evidently he did an excellent job, and got a decoration for it."

"I see, sir—that explains his enthusiasm for the subject. Anything about Thompson or Poole?"

"Indeed there is, old chap," Brownlee said, draining his tea cup. "Thompson served under him as a sergeant of signals. Pengriffon declined to put his name forward for an officer's commission."

He searched through the files spread randomly before him, and finally he selected an old manila envelope covered with his spidery scrawl.

"Ah, yes, here it is. Thompson applied to the War Office Selection Board, but Pengriffon wrote an appraisal to WOSB that said Thompson had failed to grasp the technical aspects of the new wireless signaling machinery, and would, therefore, be unable to command effectively an independent unit of his own."

Thompson must have been furious, Ford thought; his lordship had thwarted his chance for advancement—the chance to be an officer, the chance to be addressed as "sir," the chance to be saluted by his men.

"I believe that Thompson once blew up the fuse box at the church by accident," Ford said. "It would confirm Thompson's lack of electrical expertise."

"So, therefore, we know Pengriffon wasn't simply being vindictive or unfair in his assessment?" Brownlee asked, nodding approvingly.

"Presumptively so, sir."

"Good," Brownlee said, and searched the manila envelope closely. He found his notes upside down on the rear. "Poole also served. He was some sort of legal attaché in the navy and never left the confines of the Admiralty. There's nothing germane to the case in his file."

Ford was not surprised; Poole did not strike him as a man prepared to risk life and limb on the battlefield.

Brownlee stood and stretched.

"*Tempus fugit*, old chap; *le temps vole*, and other such expressions. Do you think you have enough to make any conclusions, Ford, old chap? Langley, Thompson, or Poole, or some combination thereof? I must admit I could be persuaded in any direction."

"Give me a couple of hours to ponder, sir; I feel we're very close," Ford said with more confidence than he felt.

"Then I'll telephone to the chief constable, Boxer, and ask him to drive over tomorrow. Shall I arrange to gather the suspects when he gets here?"

Ford hesitated—would he be ready? Would he be sure? Would he finally be rid of this wretched case and able to return to his honeymoon?

"Yes, sir," he said.

* * *

Ford sat down at the table as he heard Saint Christopher's clock proclaiming it was eleven o'clock. The room was in deep shadow, lit only by a dim table lamp with a green glass shade. Victoria lay sleeping peacefully in the big four-poster. A night breeze stirred the curtains. Brownlee's files were piled in haphazard fashion at one end of the table, reminding Ford of the steep cliffs along the shore.

Following the conference with Brownlee, Ford had taken a long, solitary walk out to the harbor mole, where he had sat in the lee of the lighthouse and watched the fishing boats entering and leaving the harbor.

He had strolled back to the railway dock. In the warehouse young Frank had stood in deep shadow with his camera mounted on its tripod, experimenting with night photography. Here Pengriffon had parked his Bentley for the last time, and Amy Robsart had waited for him. Here Thompson had also parked his Humber, perhaps pausing briefly to admire it gleaming in the moonlight. Here Clara and Mabel had walked home together, for fear of encountering skulking German sailors. And here, a few days before, his lordship had painted his final seascape, as young Frank's camera had captured.

Victoria had returned from Bristol in time for dinner—she must have driven like the wind—with news from the Bristol police. The Bentley had contained no clues, and the steering wheel had been wiped clean of fingerprints. However, a ticket inspector had reported an altercation with a man with a cut on his forehead, on the Monday morning express to London. The Bristol police would show him the photographs of the three suspects when he returned to duty.

In a flash of inspiration, Victoria had asked the police to test the steering wheel for blood residue—it had occurred to her that perhaps the murderer had used his bloody handkerchief to wipe it. Such were her powers of persuasion, they'd promised to telephone with results the following day, even though it was a Saturday night, even though blood-typing took time, and even though their young forensics chap was something of a ladies' man and was probably canoodling in some Bristolian trysting ground.

Croft's forensics chaps from Penzance, meanwhile, had swept the *Justicia* with a fine-tooth comb, and had found traces of type AB blood on the cabin lamp and traces of Amy Robsart's type on the afterdeck. Brownlee had telephoned to Sir Rupert Effingham, at home in the leafy confines of Henley-On-Thames, and Sir Rupert had generously gone all the way into London on a Saturday afternoon to check Sublieutenant Poole's wartime records; Poole, indeed, had the rare AB blood type—as did, infuriatingly, Color Sergeant George Thompson.

Following Ford's walk they'd all sat down to dinner together. The police party was in a cheerful mood, assuming—to Ford's private discomfiture—that he'd lock up the case when he wrote his report. Brownlee conducted a comprehensive investigation of the effects of scrumpy on his ample frame, but he was sufficiently alert to receive a telephone call from Inspector West, to the effect that the New South Wales police had sent a wireless message. The new Earl of Pengriffon was definitely innocent. He'd never left Cootamundra. He was saddened by his uncle's death, but he had no interest in returning to England to claim his heritage. Indeed, it was his intention to give Lady Justicia full control over the proceeds of the trust.

Last but not least, after dinner Victoria had asked the Ancient Mariner to submit to a nocturnal eyesight test. Dr. Anderson and Ford had sat with him at his habitual table while first Mrs. Croft and then Victoria, and then even Mrs. Crocker, just to be on the safe side, had peddled past in the darkness on a borrowed bicycle on the far side of the road, next to the dock. He had identified them correctly, without hesitation.

"How can you be so sure, Mr. Ham?" Dr. Anderson had asked. "Even I was not certain in the darkness, and, without offense, my eyes are much younger."

"Mr. Foo-ard knows how," the old man had said with a wink.

And then the Ancient Mariner had identified the driver of his lordship's car. He'd seen the driver among the congregation at the funeral, and he had no doubt.

So now, at eleven o'clock, Ford sat to compose his report. He filled his fountain pen and glanced at Victoria's huddled, gently sleeping form for inspiration. He sorted through his notes and pulled out young Frank's photograph of his lordship painting the *Justicia*, and he glanced up at the finished work standing on the mantle.

"Was it Langley, Thompson, or Poole?" he asked Pengriffon's face in the photograph.

"I can come back in the future and dance on their graves whenever I want," Josephine Langley had said to him this morning.

"What has she said about me?" Thompson had demanded in extreme agitation at the level crossing. "Whatever it is, it's not true." But all lies are based on truth, as Waggoner had said.

He glanced through the window at the moonlit harbor and thought of the poet Coleridge's lines, "The harbour-bay was clear as glass / So smoothly it was strewn / And on the bay the moonlight lay / And the shadow of the Moon."

Ford shivered; the beauty of the silent scene had been shattered by malevolence, and Lord Pengriffon and Amy Robsart had perished in the shadow of the moon.

He shook himself, turned back to the table, took up his pen, and wrote: "All the evidence in this case points to a clear conclusion." He thought of adding, "When you have eliminated the impossible, the remainder, however improbable, must be true," but decided against it.

He lit a cigarette, squared his shoulders, and continued to write.

Seventeen

Lady Canderblank sat down at the end of the table in Ford's room at the Duke, and the assembled group arranged itself as if to join her for a dinner party over which she was presiding. She seemed excited, Ford thought, perhaps by the prospect of seeing a murderer unveiled, or perhaps by the opportunity to disrupt the proceedings and belittle Ford. He wished heartily that her presence was not necessary, although he knew it was. He sighed, and took comfort in the knowledge that both Brownlee and Victoria were there—the only two people he knew who could even begin to control her.

Lady Pengriffon sat with her customary placidity at Lady Canderblank's right. Ford wondered yet again whether her composure was her defining characteristic or simply a mask. Yesterday she had attended her husband's funeral, and today she was attending a conference with the police at which her husband's murderer would be revealed, and yet from her demeanor one might have thought she had dropped into the Duke for a cup of tea after a pleasant stroll around the harbor.

Sir David Pollock eased his way cautiously into the chair on Lady Canderblank's left. This was the first time Ford had seen Sir David at close range. He was tall and faded, as if he were a sepia photograph of his former self. He must have been an imposing figure in the full vigor of his youth, a giant of a man; but now he was stoop-backed and angular, and he moved warily, as if he feared his skeleton might disassemble itself at any moment. His face had the texture of old parchment, and his voice was a whisper.

"Is this really necessary?" he asked.

"It is, sir," Brownlee boomed down the length of the table, and Sir David swayed away a trifle, as if the force of the sound waves had pushed him sideways.

"It's totally *unnecessary*," Lady Canderblank shot back, and Sir David was pushed back to a vertical position.

Poole sat down next to Sir David, his saturnine face unusually pale and with a slight sheen of perspiration glistening on his forehead. Ford wondered what happened when copious amounts of hair oil were exposed to heat and strong sunlight, and he shuddered at the possibilities. Dr. Anderson sat next to Mr. Poole and glanced at his wristwatch, and Ford knew he was calculating how much time he could spare before his next appointment at the hospital.

George Thompson took the seat next to Lady Pengriffon, ill at ease and fidgeting like a schoolboy. Perhaps, Ford thought, his usual pomposity had been overwhelmed by the close proximity of two peeresses and a knight. Perhaps he might even be planning an impromptu political revolution, or perhaps his conscience was troubling him in the presence of a large contingent of police.

Josephine Langley, stony-faced and preternaturally still, sat next to Thompson and stared rigidly down at the table before her.

Brownlee, Boxer, Ford, and Croft sat in isolation at the far end of the table by the fireplace, separated from the rest by empty chairs. Sir Oliver Boxer proved to be, in spite of his important position as the head of the Cornish police force, so self-effacing that he seemed almost wraithlike, so that one could not be absolutely certain that he was really there at all.

Dr. Waggoner sat behind them and a little to the side, and Ford knew he'd positioned himself to have a clear view of Lady Canderblank's end of the table.

Crocker closed the door, and he and Boxer's driver stood before it. Crocker was fingering the back of his belt nervously, and it occurred to Ford that he was checking to make sure he'd brought his handcuffs.

Trethgarret harbor sparkled through the open window, and the breeze carried the perpetual cries of the gulls and the shouted laughter of children on holiday. The world outside seemed a celebration of life, while the room seemed gloomy and preoccupied with violent death. We'll move back to the cottage tonight, Ford thought; he couldn't possibly go to bed with Victoria in a room which had been occupied by her mother.

Brownlee stood and prepared to speak, but Lady Canderblank beat him to the punch.

"Very well," she announced, "you may begin."

Brownlee managed to do what Ford had never quite accomplished—he not so much ignored her as conveyed the impression that she simply did not exist.

"Ladies and gentlemen," he began, "we have asked you here to review the current condition of our investigations into the deaths of Lord Pengriffon and Miss Amy Robsart, and the events that surround them. Our inquiries have led us to reach conclusions, with which Chief Constable Boxer of the Cornish Constabulary concurs." He glanced toward Boxer, who appeared to nod in agreement.

"Chief Inspector Ford will summarize our findings," Brownlee finished. He sat down and Ford stood up, gratified to see that Victoria had positioned herself directly behind her mother, so that he could address his remarks to her over his mother-in-law's shoulder.

"This case began on Monday, six days ago," Ford began, feeling as if he were launching on a long journey. "The body of Lord Pengriffon was recovered from a trawling net. Medical examinations conducted by Dr. Anderson determined that he had been strangled with his own tie during Sunday night,"—here Ford glanced toward Anderson who nodded in concurrence—"and his lifeless body had been weighed down by a cement block and tossed overboard in the vicinity of the Little Dogs. It was evidently the murderer's intention that his lordship's body would never be discovered, and it was the merest coincidence that his remains were found almost immediately. Miss ..."

"Can you get to the *point?*" Lady Canderblank demanded. "I am reminded of a dreary monolog in a tedious play."

Ford squared his shoulders and continued. "Miss Amy Robsart ..."

"Delivered by an obscure and indifferent actor, to boot," Lady

Canderblank added in a *sotto voce* whisper that would have carried clearly to the upper balconies of a large opera house.

Ford groaned inwardly, and Brownlee stirred as if to intervene, but help came from an unexpected quarter.

"Deborah, please," Lady Pengriffon said in a low but firm tone. "Mr. Ford is explaining the circumstances of my husband's death, and I would like to be able to hear him without interruptions." Perhaps widowhood was leading her to be more assertive.

Ford watched Lady Canderblank's face as she failed to think of a reason why Lady Pengriffon should not have her husband's murder explained to her.

"Well, get on with it, Foil—you heard what Lady Justicia said," was the best his mother-in-law could offer.

"Miss Amy Robsart," Ford started for the third time, "was discovered to be missing. She had an intimate relationship with Lord Pengriffon and was seen on the docks in the vicinity of his launch on the night of his murder. Miss Josephine Langley, with whom Miss Robsart shared a cottage, gave us testimony to the effect that Miss Robsart and Lord Pengriffon had quarreled bitterly on Sunday afternoon, and that Miss Robsart had threatened to kill him; indeed, according to Miss Langley, Miss Robsart had said she intended to strangle him."

The room turned its attention to Miss Langley, who continued to stare silently down at the table. Lady Canderblank offered no comment, and Ford continued.

"Our initial investigation, therefore, led us to believe that it was possible that Lord Pengriffon was murdered by Miss Robsart aboard the *Justicia*, that she had buried his body at sea to cover up her action, and that she had subsequently fled."

Lady Canderblank took a magazine from her handbag and opened it loudly, feigning boredom. "A *very* tedious play," she muttered.

"Miss Langley subsequently, er, clarified her testimony." Ford saw no reason to accuse Josephine Langley of obstruction of justice. Her eyes flickered up to his and away again, but he saw no expression in them. "However, since her new testimony was that she had seen his lordship and Miss Robsart on the *Justicia* on the night in question, and since we found Miss Robsart's fingerprints on the launch's engine controls, we continued to consider her our primary suspect. It was not until three days later, on Thursday, when Miss Robsart's body was recovered by a naval diver from the seabed where Lord Pengriffon had also been tossed overboard, that we knew she was not his killer."

Lady Canderblank looked up from her copy of *Horse and Hound*. "In other words, you mishandled the investigation from the outset, Follet," she said. "This is, I should say, yet another example of your incompetence." She turned to Sir David. "It's not surprising that the criminality rages amongst the lower classes, when Scotland Yard is so inept."

"Let us be charitable, Deborah," Sir David said softly. "I'm sure …"

Lady Canderblank drew herself up. "Charity, in my opinion, is a *highly* overrated virtue."

"I'm sure he was trying to do his best," Sir David tried again.

"Then his best was woefully inadequate," Lady Canderblank shot back. Sir David subsided, evidently unwilling or unable to withstand her.

"*Please*, Deborah," Lady Justicia appealed, and Lady Canderblank returned to her reading with nothing more than a snort.

"In these circumstances we transferred our attention to Miss Langley," Ford continued, and every head in the room—save Lady Canderblank's—swiveled back in her direction, as if they were marionettes pulled by a common string.

Josephine Langley adopted a defensive posture with her arms across her chest, as if to ward off an impending blow. She lifted her wide-set eyes in Ford's direction for a moment, and he saw they were now bright with apprehension—not because, Ford guessed, she feared he would accuse her of murder, but because she was afraid he might turn her into a public laughingstock. Ford felt a stab of sympathy for her. He too would rather be hanged than humiliated.

"Miss Langley was, by her own account, enamored of his lordship,"— here Lady Justicia raised her eyebrows in surprise, Lady Canderblank leant forward to pay close attention, her magazine dropping unnoticed to the floor, and Josephine Langley cringed visibly—"and jealous of Miss Robsart's relationship with him. She also stated that she had rowed herself out to the *Justicia* that night, in the hope of encountering his lordship. Her assertion that she saw his lordship and Miss Robsart together, and simply rowed away, seemed …"

"What *precisely* were they doing?" Lady Canderblank demanded at this delicious whiff of salacious scandal, but Ford, for once, managed to override her.

"Seemed implausible. Since she was the only other person at the scene of the crime, as far as we knew, we found it necessary to treat her as a suspect, since she had motive, means, and opportunity. In these circumstances, although we had not reached a conclusion, we decided that Miss Langley was the person most likely to have killed Lord Pengriffon; and there matters stood on Thursday afternoon."

"First the Robsart person, and now this one," Lady Canderblank said, with a disdainful glance in Miss Langley's direction. "One wonders exactly how many trollops your husband had, Justicia."

Both Lady Pengriffon and Miss Langley flinched, for their own separate reasons.

"I didn't do it," Miss Langley said to the table. Her hands were bunched into tight fists, as if she might be planning violence. "I didn't do it, and there's no evidence that I did."

"Of course you didn't," Thompson said unexpectedly. "Everyone knows that—he's just trying to trap you. It was a suicide pact, most likely; they did each other in. He's got no real evidence against you."

"Are we finished, Forge?" Lady Canderblank demanded. "Have you concluded your dreary dissertation? Can you arrest this, this *personage*, and have done with it?"

"I fear not, Lady Canderblank," Ford said. "Other possible explanations of his lordship's death came to our attention."

* * *

"It came to our attention that the Old Morehead Hole, Trethgarret's largest tin mine, was in severe financial straits, and that his lordship was considering its closure."

"Nonsense," Thompson contradicted. "There's plenty of tin down there, and nothing that can't be solved by investing in new equipment. Besides, that mine's been in operation since Roman times; no Pengriffon worthy of the name would close it."

"Such a closure would, of course, throw the miners out of work, but …"

"Needless cruelty, in my opinion," Thompson interrupted. "A Labor government won't permit the economic exploitation of the working man—never! There'll be laws requiring companies to employ workers even if they claim they're losing money, you mark my words."

"Socialistic claptrap!" Lady Canderblank snapped. "If the working classes spent more time working, and less time feeling sorry for themselves, then England would be a better place."

"If the upper classes …" Thompson began.

"*Enough!*" Brownlee roared, with sufficient force to cause both Lady Canderblank and Thompson to pause, and Ford hastened to fill the momentary silence.

"But his lordship was planning a new venture to provide employment for the displaced workers. His plans were far advanced; he had arranged a business agreement with the General Electric Company, and he had informed Mr. Thompson of his intentions. He had also advised Mr. Thompson that he would be bringing in a radio expert to run the factory, and therefore Mr. Thompson's services as manager would not be needed, although his lordship would find him work of some sort in the new business, if Mr. Thompson wished."

"He did no such thing," Thompson growled.

"I think you're mistaken, Mr. Thompson, if I may say so," Lady Justicia murmured. "Surely you remember that young man Mr. Carstairs, or perhaps it was Carpenter? I recall you telling my husband you'd never take orders from a young upstart still wet behind the ears."

"I recall no such thing," Thompson snapped, his face reddening. "I was in wireless signals in the war. I know as much about radio as any jumped-up whippersnapper."

"There is evidence to suggest his lordship doubted your technical skills, sir."

"Nonsense—besides, that's all of no consequence now. I'm sure the new earl will have no patience with newfangled gadgetry. He'll see reason and keep the Old Hole in operation."

"Mr. Thompson, we have evidence that supports Lady Justicia's version of events," Ford said. "General Electric has also confirmed the plan. In the circumstances it occurred to us that his lordship's disappearance would have delayed all such decisions, and the status quo would have remained in place. The Old Morehead Hole would continue to operate, and you would continue to ..."

Thompson jumped up.

"Are you accusing me of murder?" The medallions on his fob chain tinkled musically; he was shaking either with righteous indignation or with fear.

"Not at this juncture, Mr. Thompson. I haven't finished explaining our investigation. I am, however, pointing out that his lordship's disappearance was very much in your interest."

"That's not a motive—that's just a guess. Besides, his lordship may have owned the Hole, but the workers have worked there all their lives. They have as much right to decide what to do with it as he did."

"Don't be absurd!" Lady Canderblank snapped. "I shudder to think what would happen to England if common laborers were able to ..."

"There's more of us than there are of you," Thompson said, becoming red in the face, and Ford noted that he seemed at least as much put out by Lady Canderblank's comment as by Ford's suggestion that he might be under suspicion for murder. "When there's a Labor government—and they'll be one soon, you mark my words—there'll be ..."

"Over my dead body!"

"If that's what it takes, your ladyship, then that's ..."

"Mr. Thompson," Ford intervened hastily, although the thought of a dead Lady Canderblank was immensely appealing, "I would strongly caution you against making threats in the presence of police officers. Please sit down, and then we can return to the matter at hand."

"Be quiet, George," Miss Langley said, to Ford's surprise, and—to his further surprise—Thompson did so.

"There are three common motives for murder," Ford bore on. "Extreme emotional distress, such as unrequited love, is one. The other common motives are murder to cover up another crime, and for financial gain. Since Lord Pengriffon was a wealthy man, we had also been investigating his financial circumstances from the outset of the case. Our investigations led us to discover a sequence of events that can only be described as bizarre."

The room seemed to catch its collective breath. Ford nodded slightly to Crocker, who advanced toward the table. Ford sensed Brownlee and Croft stirring in their seats behind him, as if readying themselves to spring into action.

"As you know," Ford continued, "the large majority of the Pengriffon assets are contained within the Pengriffon trust, established by his lordship's grandfather."

"What has this to do with this woman's erotic daydreams, or this man's socialistic ambitions?" Lady Canderblank demanded. "Surely you do not intend to drag private financial matters into the public domain, when you already have grounds to arrest either of these two ragamuffins? Of what possible relevance is the trust?"

"It is of relevance, Lady Canderblank, because we discovered that the trustee responsible for the day-to-day administration of the Pengriffon trust, Mr. Poole, had devised a process to embezzle funds from the trust."

It was as if Ford had tossed a hand grenade onto the table.

"*What?*" Lady Pengriffon burst out. "Sir David ..."

"*Embezzle?*" Sir David demanded, struggling to rise to his feet. "What do you ... Poole, is this true?"

"*Balderdash!*" Lady Canderblank roared.

"How ...?" Thompson started.

"*Rubbish! A pack of lies!*" Poole snarled, and now it was his turn to jump to his feet.

"*Sit down!*" Brownlee thundered above the din. "Constable Crocker, restrain Mr. Poole if he cannot control himself."

Crocker, standing directly behind Poole, stretched out a large hand to Poole's shoulder, causing Poole to sit down abruptly.

"This can't be true," Sir David said, finally upright, and unable to respond promptly to Brownlee's demand. "The accounts are in perfect order; not a penny is missing."

"How am I supposed to have stolen this imaginary money?" Poole asked, his outrage swiftly replaced by cold sarcasm.

"It was a simple but very effective scheme," Ford answered. "You stole money from the Pengriffon trust and deposited it in an account in your name at the Westminster Bank branch in Islington. You covered your tracks by falsifying the trust account statements you sent to Lord Pengriffon each quarter."

"Rubbish!" Poole said. "You heard Sir David. He verified the accounts."

"With due respect to Sir David, and to be blunt, your partners were too inattentive or too careless, in their various ways, to spot the embezzlement."

Sir David did not seem offended by Ford's statement—perhaps he understood it to be true.

"Mr. Poole's wife doctored the books and buried the irregularities," Ford finished.

Poole pointed at Lady Canderblank. "She warned me about you, and she was right."

"You're guessing, Foogle," she said. "You can't prove a word of it. I shall make a point of bringing your incompetence to the attention of the Home Secretary. Your career, such as it is, will come to an abrupt end, and those of your superiors will be truncated."

"Madam," Brownlee said, and his frame seemed to radiate the full power of English law enforcement, even when seated. "I *strongly* urge you not to pursue actions you will subsequently regret."

"I refuse to listen to a trumped-up attempt to impugn the character of Sir David's firm. I ..."

"Then I suggest you leave, madam," Brownlee boomed. "If you chose to remain, you will be quiet, or I will tell the constable to escort you from the room."

"Got it, sir," Crocker said.

"How dare you ..."

"Hush, please, Deborah," Sir David interrupted her, summoning up the strength to raise his voice above a whisper. "I'm afraid the superintendent's perfectly within his rights."

Either the effort of standing or the impact of Ford's revelations was too much, because he sank downwards into his chair as if his knees could no longer maintain him in an upright position. Lady Canderblank gave Brownlee a look that would have scorched a lesser being—a rhinoceros or an elephant, for example—but lapsed into silence.

"Lord Pengriffon discovered Mr. Poole's scheme," Ford continued, as if these outbursts had never occurred. "His lordship was far shrewder in business matters than he appeared, and he calculated the precise amounts that Mr. Poole was stealing. He was also a mischievous man, given to secret jokes and *trompes-l'œil*. Rather than take matters to the police, he decided to render justice in his own way—to create, as it were, a financial *trompe-l'œil*."

The room—even Lady Canderblank—was silent.

"Each quarter, therefore, Lord Pengriffon went to the Westminster Bank in Islington, where he posed as Mr. Poole, and withdrew the money Poole had stolen from him that quarter. He redeposited the money into the account of the L'Art Moderne Gallery and used it to pay himself for his paintings. Thus he could account for the money flowing into his own accounts, and he intercepted the statements the Westminster Bank sent to Mr. Poole, hiding the withdrawals."

Brownlee had made a little diagram on the back of an envelope, with boxes connected by arrows.

"So, let me see," he said, referring to it. "If I follow you correctly, the money came out of the trust into Poole's account, then out of Poole's account and into the L'Arte Moderne gallery account, and then out of the L'Arte Moderne account and into Lord Pengriffon's account."

"Exactly, sir."

"Now, the trust-to-Poole arrow was disguised by Mrs. Poole's falsifications; she simply reduced the reported size of the trust's investments in order to reduce the amount of money earned by them. The Poole-to-gallery arrow was hidden from Poole by Pengriffon's falsification of Poole's bank statements and by imagined purchases of Pengriffon's work by customers of the gallery; and the gallery-to-Pengriffon arrow was justified as payments made by the gallery to Lord Pengriffon for his paintings."

"I must confess I am still having trouble grasping this process—this, shall one say, stratagem of deception," Sir David said weakly.

"That's because it's a pack of lies," Poole told him. "You saw the accounts and signed them—you know they're correct."

"Indeed I did," Sir David said, rallying a little, as if he was helpless to resist the most recent statement addressed to him. "You'll have to justify this allegation, Chief Inspector."

"Let us suppose, Sir David, that the assets of the trust consisted of a single block of a thousand shares of General Electric stock, which

259

generated five hundred pounds in dividends. This was correctly entered into the trust reports kept by Miss Edwards at your office, sir, in the reports you saw. Once you had approved the statement, Mr. Poole wrote two checks drawn on the trust, one for four hundred and fifty pounds, and another for fifty pounds. Mr. Poole took the report home, where his wife retyped it to indicate that the trust had only nine hundred shares, generating four hundred and fifty pounds. Mr. Poole sent this second version of the report to Lord Pengriffon, with the check for four hundred and fifty pounds. He took the check for fifty pounds and deposited it in his own account. Am I being clear, Sir David?"

"I ... I think so."

"When you inspected the books, sir, you would have seen Miss Edwards's correct presentation of the assets and a proposed disbursement for the correct amount of five hundred pounds. This process was repeated for all the various shareholdings in the trust, and you would not have noticed, without a close examination, that there were more dividend checks actually written than you had approved. You would simply have looked at what I believe is known, in banking terminology, as the bottom line."

"Yes ... yes, I see that," Sir David said.

"Lord Pengriffon received Mrs. Poole's doctored version, and the dividends paid were mathematically consistent with the doctored version of the assets. He, too, Mr. Poole assumed, would not have examined the accounts in great detail."

"And Lord Pengriffon realized what Mr. Poole was doing?" Sir David asked. "He developed similar sleights of hand to steal the money back without Mr. Poole or anyone else knowing? Is that what you're asserting?"

"Indeed, sir," Ford nodded. "The entire process had a perfect symmetry—each man stole from the other and falsified each other's statements. And justice was done, in a serpentine fashion, since the money finished up where it should have been—in Lord Pengriffon's pocket."

Sir David and Lady Pengriffon nodded in slow comprehension; Poole stared at Ford without expression, and Lady Canderblank stirred once more.

"Fiddle-faddle!" she growled. "You'll have a hard time proving that."

"On the contrary, madam; the relevant documentation has already been reviewed by the Bank of England, and their specialists have confirmed it."

Lady Canderblank opened her mouth to dispute the financial competence of the Bank of England, and closed it again.

"It's so like dear Clarence," Lady Pengriffon said. "He loved ingenious practical jokes."

Ford glanced at Poole, who remained stony-faced. Ford cleared his voice and was about to continue, but Poole intervened.

"Your, er, your *concoction* could only be proven by comparing the accounts sent to Lord Pengriffon with the accounts held by our firm, is that not true? And, since the latter accounts no longer exist, your version of events remains an unproven theory."

Lady Canderblank stood immediately, and strode to the bell rope near the fireplace to summon service.

"Then we're back to these two," she said, with a jerk of her head toward Josephine Langley and Thompson. "I suggest we now take tea, Sir David; your firm has been exonerated."

* * *

"Wait," Lady Pengriffon said. "I still don't know who killed my husband, and what has become of the trust."

"Are we to wait interminably until we die from thirst?" Lady Canderblank asked theatrically.

"With due respect, Lady Canderblank," Brownlee rumbled. "If you were to remain silent it would not only speed up the proceedings but permit you to conserve your strength."

Lady Canderblank stared at him, as if sizing him up, as a prizefighter might size up an opponent as he steps into the ring.

"Oh, very *well*," she said, and returned to her seat. "Get on with it, Fawn, if you must."

Ford got on with it. "The process of theft and countertheft continued until two months ago, when Mr. Poole attempted to use his ill-gotten gains to purchase a private pleasure launch, and wrote a check to pay for it. However, the check he drew on his Westminster Bank account was not honored for lack of funds, because his lordship had already withdrawn them. Mr. Poole went to the bank and discovered Lord Pengriffon's scheme."

Poole did not react; he was staring down at the table, as if in deep thought.

"One can only imagine his fury," Ford continued. "He had suffered the hideous embarrassment of bouncing a check, as it is described in common parlance, and he had been outfoxed by a man he described to me as 'a drunken Cornish idiot.'"

"You can't prove ..." Lady Canderblank began.

Ford continued to speak as if she were not interrupting, until she was obliged to stop so that she could hear what he was saying.

"The extra checks drawn on the trust accounts are recorded in the financial books of Coutt's & Company and the Westminster Bank, as audited by the Bank of England. The true holdings of the trust have been reconstructed from the shareholder records of the companies in which the trust has holdings, and are beyond dispute, whether the original trust documents survived the fire or not. This reconstruction has been compared with the versions sent to Lord Pengriffon, and it has been found that the statements provided to his lordship had been falsified."

Ford stopped for breath—perhaps Lady Canderblank's description of a dreary monolog had been correct after all. He gulped in fresh oxygen and plunged on.

"An expert has examined Miss Edwards's typewriter, which survived the fire at Pollock, Pollock & Poole, and has determined that the statements sent to his lordship were not typed on that machine. My colleague, Inspector West, has interviewed Mrs. Poole, and she may now assist us in our inquiries."

Ford did not let Poole's *sotto voce* growl of, "she'll never testify," derail him.

"Mr. Poole's unsuccessful attempt to buy the launch, and his lordship's subsequent purchase of the same craft, are supported by the sworn statement of the boatyard owner who built the vessel in the town of Poole in Dorsetshire. Mr. Poole's state of mind upon discovering his lordship's ruse is attested by the sworn statements of the staff of the Westminster Bank in Islington."

"Rubbish!" Poole managed, although with less conviction.

Ford stole a glance around the table. Sir David seemed to be leaning away from Poole as if to distance himself from his partner's crime; Ford was convinced that the old man knew that Ford's explanation was exact in every detail.

Lady Canderblank was deep in thought, drumming her fingers on the table, doubtless trying to find a flaw in Ford's argument, while Lady Pengriffon was staring at Poole in horror, grasping at the notion that this man had defrauded her husband, and then, of course, murdered him to silence him. Thompson and Miss Langley were also staring at Poole—although, Ford thought, more in amazement than in horror.

And Poole himself was now staring down at the table with his eyes closed, although whether in shock that his scheme had been unmasked or whether in frantic search of an alibi, Ford could not tell.

"Naturally Mr. Poole couldn't report the matter to the police— naturally he couldn't accuse Lord Pengriffon of stealing money he, Mr. Poole, had stolen from Lord Pengriffon—and so he decided on a rougher sort of justice, and came down here, to Trethgarret, where he discovered that Lord Pengriffon had purchased the very launch that he, Poole, had attempted to buy. One can only imagine how much further that knowledge embittered him. It must have been a final twist of the knife, as it were."

Poole did not respond. Ford was now desperate to get this entire miserable matter over with, so that he and Victoria could run off to the cottage on the cliffs and lock the door and remain there together until eventually, preferably far, far in the future, they were forced to emerge by exhaustion, dehydration, and incipient starvation. He looked at her over her mother's shoulder and saw the same emotions mirrored in Victoria's eyes.

* * *

"We therefore faced the question of whether his lordship was murdered by Miss Langley, in a fit of jealous fury; or by Mr. Thompson, in order to maintain his employment at the tin mine; or by Mr. Poole, to cover up his scheme. And there matters stood until yesterday evening."

"In Miss Langley's case," Ford said, willing himself to continue, "as we considered earlier, she was driven to the breaking point by her unrequited advances toward his lordship and was enraged by his preference for Miss Robsart. Seeing them together on Sunday night propelled her past the breaking point."

"I didn't do it," Miss Langley said once more, still staring down at the table. "I didn't do it, and there's no evidence that I did."

"That's right," Thompson intervened again. "No evidence, no case."

"We interviewed Miss Langley once more yesterday morning. During that meeting she stated that she was sympathetic to Mr. Thompson's plight. She also indicated that she supported his political ambitions and hoped to support him in the future."

"What are you implying?" Thompson demanded. "Are you suggesting I egged her on?"

Ford felt that the session was slipping from his grasp, and his leg was beginning to throb from standing still for too long.

"If we make a case against Miss Langley, her motives are relevant and might, as I previously suggested, include the intention to right a wrong she thought Lord Pengriffon had done you. If that is indeed the case, then the question of whether you incited her to do violence against him is relevant."

"I must admit I'm somewhat confused," Lady Pengriffon said.

"As were we, Lady Pengriffon," Ford said. "However, let us for the moment set aside consideration of Miss Langley and Mr. Thompson, and consider Mr. Poole in isolation. In Mr. Poole's case, we reasoned that he formed a plan, the essence of which was that he would murder both Lord Pengriffon and Amy Robsart, and hide their bodies by burying them at sea. It would be assumed that they had run off together. And thus the evidence of both his crimes—the embezzlement and the murders—would be expunged. Once Lord Pengriffon was dead, doubtless Mr. Poole intended to restart the process of swindling the trust, for only Pengriffon knew that he had done so and how he had done so."

"And so, Mr. Ford, you believe Mr. Poole killed my husband?" Lady Pengriffon asked.

Ford paused a moment, to review the evidence, to steel himself to commit himself, and to take comfort in Victoria's presence.

"I believe he did," Ford answered, and turned to face Poole's inevitable counterattack.

* * *

Poole raised his head and stared down the table at Ford. There was a glint of triumph in his cold eyes.

"It'll never hold up in court. I'll testify that Pengriffon *knew* what I was doing with the trust and did not report it. Indeed, I'll testify that he *instructed* me to make payments in this unconventional manner and that I humored him, knowing him to be eccentric."

Croft, who had sat passively behind Ford throughout the session, reacted even before Ford could open his mouth. "But you tried to buy yourself an expensive boat with the proceeds, sir," Croft said. "That proves you intended to keep the money for your own benefit."

"A foolish oversight," Poole responded immediately, and Ford, with a sinking feeling, reminded himself that Poole was a barrister, an expert in the cut and thrust of courtroom cross-examination, a man used to weaving strands of evidence this way and that. "I have several bank accounts and simply wrote a check in the wrong checkbook."

"His lordship's calculations on your wife's false statements ..." Croft tried again.

"He was simply checking that the amounts he was receiving from my account in Islington were correct." He shook his head and smirked as if in admiration for his brilliant improvisation. "I'm afraid he cooked up the entire scheme to give the impression his paintings were selling better than they really were. I went along with it because he was my client, although I did so against my better judgment."

"But ..."

"I was acting on his written instructions, Sergeant. Unfortunately, of course, those letters went up in smoke in the fire at our chambers."

Poole sat back triumphantly and waited for Ford or Croft to argue.

"I'm sure they did, sir," Ford said, as he watched the case against Poole turn to dust and ashes.

Poole indulged himself in another smirk. "I regret the need to impugn your husband's memory, Lady Justicia, but it's sad to see what lengths a vain artist will go to and what trouble his pathetic scheme has caused." He was sufficiently confident, Ford saw, to lift his hands in a gesture of sorrow. "I had hoped to save the Pengriffon family the embarrassment and public humiliation that would surely follow if his sad scheme was revealed. But if the police continue to pursue their so-called case to the courtroom, then, I fear, it will all come out …"

Ford saw that Sir David, sitting beyond Poole, was engaged in an inner struggle. There was a high probability that Poole had just invented his version of the story; but, on the other hand, Poole's fabrication would let PP&P off the hook, with its reputation intact.

"Well," he started cautiously, "I'm not quite …"

Lady Canderblank overrode him triumphantly. "Your concoction has once again been proven to be false, Frost. Sir David's firm has again been exonerated. May we now retire to take tea, while you retire to lick your wounds?" She gestured toward Miss Langley. "I presume you will arrest this, er, this person. Be so kind as to do so without further delay, and let us bring this dreary charade to a close. Or do you lack evidence against her also?"

There was a knock on the door. Boxer's driver opened it, and Charlie stood at the threshold.

"Someone rang the bell for service?" he asked.

"Is this, er, this establishment capable of offering afternoon tea to its guests?" Lady Canderblank asked him, before anyone, even Brownlee, could react. "If so, please bring us refreshments immediately. Our meeting has been completed."

Ford looked at Poole and saw him staring back, his cold lips smiling smugly and his eyebrows raised quizzically, as if challenging Ford to introduce more evidence, so that Poole could manufacture yet more alibis, and so on, *ad infinitum*.

"And one thing more, Frog," Lady Canderblank added. "I believe you owe Mr. Poole an apology."

"Well, Ford?" Poole demanded.

"Thank you, Charlie," Victoria intervened. "We'll have tea later, if we may. I'll let you know."

Lady Canderblank opened her mouth to protest, but Charlie withdrew. Ford looked round the table, squared his shoulders, took a deep breath, and plunged on as if there had been no interruption.

"On Saturday, yesterday, and again this morning, we received new information. His lordship …"

"Come, Ford, please don't embarrass yourself further," Poole broke in. "You seem to have failed to make a case against these two"—he gestured toward Thompson and Josephine Langley—"so you're trying to incriminate me. The notion that two different people would both try to kill Pengriffon on the same night, for completely unrelated reasons, and unknown to each other, would be laughable if it wasn't so pathetic."

"Typically pathetic," Lady Canderblank said.

Poole leaned back in his chair as if he had not a care in the world.

"Tell me, Ford, why did I supposedly select this particular time to commit this supposed murder? What drove me to action?"

"You found out last week that Sir David was planning to visit the Pengriffons this week, and you could not risk his lordship revealing your embezzlement. You needed to travel at the weekend so that your absence from London required no explanation. I assume you masqueraded as a holidaymaker and followed Pengriffon to assess his habits and to pick a suitable murder site, and then …"

"And why, pray tell me, Chief Inspector, did I not simply waylay him down some country lane and bop him on the head? Why all the elaboration?"

"You needed to dispose of the body so that it would not be found. You needed Pengriffon missing, not dead. If he were thought to be missing, your theft of the trust could recommence."

"Are we back to that slanderous, baseless, and improvable theory? Is that the best you can do?"

"As I was saying, sir, yesterday we received fresh information," Ford said, and he noted that Poole immediately sat forward and paid close attention. "His lordship owned a motorcar made by a new company named Bentley. Very few have been manufactured to date. The car disappeared on the night that he was murdered, and we have been searching for it ever since. In spite of the unusual nature of the car, we were unable to find it."

"Typical," said Lady Canderblank.

"Yesterday, however, the Bentley Three Litre motorcar was discovered near the railway station in Bristol, where it had been abandoned. It had been noted by the local police force several days ago, but it was mistaken for an equally rare car, the Type Ten made by the French Bugatti company, to which it bears a remarkable resemblance. The radiator emblem, a 'B' with wings sprouting from it, was assumed to stand for Bugatti. Yesterday the local police realized their mistake."

"What has all this to do with ..." Lady Canderblank began.

"Suffice it to say that a ticket inspector identified Mr. Poole's photograph as a passenger on the Bristol-to-London express last Monday morning. He remembers you distinctly, Mr. Poole, because you were in a first-class compartment with a third-class ticket and only paid the difference after an altercation. He also described the dressing upon your head. The question becomes, sir, what were you doing driving his lordship's car from here to Bristol on Monday night?"

"I admit nothing of the sort. I was in Bristol on other business."

"Did you attempt to defraud the railway company by purchasing a third-class ticket and traveling first class, Poole?" Sir David asked querulously.

"I ..."

"That is not conduct becoming a gentleman," Sir David said severely, evidently more affronted by this petty misdemeanor than embezzlement on a grand scale, let alone murder.

Poole ignored him and turned to Ford. "Look, let me make this as plain as I can; unless you can put me on the dock or on the launch or in the car, here in Trethgarret, all you've got is a so-called motive and a circumstantial case. You can't prove the embezzlement so you can't prove the motive, and without a plausible motive your circumstantial case falls apart."

"I agree with you, sir," Ford said. "I have one final question for you, Mr. Poole. When we first met, you told me you had never been here to Trethgarret. Is that correct?

"That is correct. This is my first visit and doubtless my last."

"You said, sir, if I recall correctly, 'I have not met the Pengriffons, nor have I visited Pengriffon Hall, nor its environs, nor the Pengriffon's fifty-two-foot oil-fired launch in the harbor.' You do recall that part of our conversation?"

"Of course I remember—it was only on Wednesday. Those were my exact words. I felt I had to be very clear, given your evident difficulty in grasping simple facts."

"Then, sir, perhaps you can explain how you knew that the *Justicia* is oil-fired?"

"What do you mean?" Poole asked, and Ford imagined cogs and wheels rotating in his mind as he sought an explanation. "What has that to do with anything?"

"The launch was powered by coal when you rented it and subsequently attempted to purchase it. Lord Pengriffon converted it to oil before taking possession. So, my question stands, sir. How did you know?"

"I ..."

"The conversion is not visible. One can only tell the fuel source if one has been on the launch."

"Oil, coal—what the hell does it matter?" Poole demanded, and Ford felt a quiver of excitement that he had finally pricked Poole's armor.

"It matters, sir, because, to use your words, it means I can put you on the launch."

"How ..."

"You would have been able to use the wheelhouse controls, even in darkness, because you were familiar with them. But you would not have been able to start the engine without difficulty, since it had been changed. Miss Robsart's fingerprints were found on the engine controls. It therefore follows that you came on board and killed Lord Pengriffon. We believe Amy Robsart followed. You forced her to start the engine and then killed her also. How else could you know about the oil fuel source?"

"The, er, the shipyard chap told me."

"The shipyard chap, as you describe him, has sworn he has not spoken to you since your check was refused. How did you know?"

"Er, Lord Pengriffon mentioned it in one of his letters—the letters that were consumed in the fire."

"You mean the fire that started next to your office immediately after Miss Edwards told you I had gone to the bank in Islington?"

"That's just a coincidence. No jury will convict on such flimsy, circumstantial evidence."

"Miss Edwards keeps a log of all letters received and sent by your office. It survived the fire intact. There is no record of any letter from Lord Pengriffon."

"A clerical error."

"Several clerical errors, involving only Lord Pengriffon's correspondence?"

"She's a very slack worker."

"We'll let a jury be the judge of that," Ford said. "You were also seen in Trethgarret on Sunday night, driving away in Lord Pengriffon's car. The witness identified your features and the wound on your head."

"An eyewitness at night?" Poole scoffed. "It'll never stand up."

"The witness has been subject to a night vision test, which he passed perfectly. Dr. Anderson provided medical supervision of the examination."

Anderson nodded in confirmation.

"You need physical evidence, like fingerprints, and there were no fingerprints on the Bentley's steering wheel."

"Two people saw you, sir."

"So what? At night there'll be reasonable doubt."

"How did you hurt your head?"

"I slipped on something on the bathroom floor at home."

"That's not possible. You were freshly wounded on the train from Bristol. I believe you hit your head on the hanging lantern in the cabin. The eyewitnesses will attest to the fact that your forehead was bruised and bleeding, and you had tied a handkerchief across your forehead to staunch the flow."

"You can believe what you like."

"Your army records indicate that you have type AB blood, and we found traces of type AB blood on the lantern in the cabin."

"Lots of people have AB blood."

"Less that four in a hundred, sir. Lord Pengriffon and Amy Robsart, the other two people known to have used the cabin, did not."

"I recall cracking my head open some months ago when I had

the launch. It must have been a residue from that. Even a forensic laboratory cannot tell the age of coagulated blood." Poole held up his hand. He was panting, as if he and Ford were fencing and had just fought a furious exchange. "Look, Chief Inspector, I must admire your doggedness, however misguided, but your so-called case against me remains unproven. If you take what you have into court, Scotland Yard will be a laughingstock."

"Again I agree with you, sir," Ford said. "Incidentally, Mr. Poole, how do you know there were no fingerprints on the steering wheel of Lord Pengriffon's car?

"I ... you said so five minutes ago."

"No, I did not. How do you know?"

"You can't get a conviction on the *lack* of fingerprints. That would be absurd."

"Very true, sir, but I can get a conviction on your specific *knowledge* of the lack of fingerprints on the steering wheel of his lordship's car." Again Ford could sense the cogs and wheels spinning furiously in Poole's mind. "As you said yourself, I need to be able to place you in the car or on the boat. Very well; I can place you *in* his lordship's car *in* Trethgarret, based on the sworn testimony of an eyewitness. I can place you on a train from Bristol station, outside which his lordship's car was found, based on the sworn testimony of the ticket inspector on the train. And I can place you *in* the car, because you know that the steering wheel had been wiped clean of fingerprints. You know it because you wiped it clean the night you killed Lord Pengriffon and Amy Robsart."

"It's still circumstantial," Poole said, with a dismissive wave of one hand. "You still can't place me at the scene of the crime. Without ..."

"Miss Langley," Ford said abruptly, cutting Poole off and causing her to jump. "You told us that you rowed out to the *Justicia* that night. You told us you saw Lord Pengriffon and Miss Robsart in an intimate embrace. Is that correct?"

"Yes," she whispered, without her usual "I didn't do it."

"Now, Miss Langley, let me ask you to explain the circumstances of your visit to the *Justicia*. Were you going to see his lordship for, er, personal reasons, or did you have other intentions?"

She did not reply.

"Miss Langley, let me tell you what I think. I think you did go out to the *Justicia* that night, but the rest of your accounts have been pure fiction. Now, for the last time, would you please tell me what you did that night?"

She looked round the table as if in search of advice, and finally settled on Thompson.

"Guard your tongue," he said. "He's trying to trick you."

"He has no case," Poole offered. "No case against me or you or anyone else."

"Just another pathetic and infinitely tedious fishing expedition," Lady Canderblank contributed.

Miss Langley looked around the assembled faces once more and stopped at Victoria's.

"The truth, the whole truth, and nothing but the truth," Victoria said. "Come on—I know you can do it."

Josephine Langley stared at her, squared her shoulders, and turned back to Ford.

"I rowed out, because ... well, I rowed out. The engine started just as I got there. I thought I was too late. I grabbed onto the stern just as the launch started to move, so it was dragging me along in the dinghy. I saw his lordship struggling with Amy. She was fighting back. He grabbed a piece of concrete and bashed her head in. She fell down, and I let go of the launch. I ... I couldn't believe it. I suppose I rowed back somehow, and George—Mr. Thompson—gave me a lift in his motorcar."

"Never," Thompson erupted.

"From the dock?" Ford asked. "He was at the dock?"

"No," Thompson roared.

"Yes ... I mean no," she faltered.

"Did you tell him what had happened?"

"Yes ... I mean no ... I mean I can't remember."

"You did not, and you know it, because it never happened," Thompson growled. Croft stood up, and Ford wondered if he thought Thompson might do her bodily harm.

"Never mind Mr. Thompson," Ford said, fearing another diversion. "When you saw them on the launch, what did his lordship look like?" Ford asked.

"What do you mean, 'look like'?"

"Were they *naked?*" Lady Canderblank demanded, but the room ignored her.

"Did he seem his normal self, Miss Langley?" Ford asked.

"His normal self?"

"You saw him attacking Miss Robsart. You saw him deal her a deathblow. Describe what you saw."

She stared at the ceiling as if to refresh her memory.

"He was like the devil incarnate, big and strong. He was shaking Amy like a dog shaking a rat. She was fighting back, slapping and punching and kicking. Then she tried to get away from him, but he was too quick for her. Then he picked up that lump of concrete and …"

"Are you sure it was Lord Pengriffon?"

"Of course—who else could it have been, on his boat?"

"That's what I'm trying to find out, Miss Langley. Miss Robsart was a strong young woman—very strong. His lordship was in his fifties and corpulent. In addition, he was falling-down drunk that night. Could his lordship have shaken her like a rat? Could he have overpowered Miss Robsart if she was fighting for her life with all her might? Could he have picked up in one hand a piece of concrete weighing forty pounds and slammed it into her head?"

"Well, I suppose …"

"Dr. Anderson," Ford demanded, causing that worthy gentleman to start, just as Josephine Langley had started a few moments before, "in your medical opinion, could Lord Pengriffon have lifted a strong young woman from her feet and shaken her like a rat? Or picked up a forty-pound piece of concrete in one hand?"

"I find it highly unlikely, Chief Inspector. He was inebriated, and his strength and coordination would have been diminished."

"Thank you, Doctor," Ford said, and swung back to Josephine Langley. "Close your eyes, Miss Langley. Think back to that night. You've rowed out, you've grabbed onto the stern. Now the launch is pulling you along; you're almost being dragged out of the dinghy. It's night, but it's also full moonlight. Now, what do you see?"

"I see … I see Amy struggling with his lordship."

"Is he taller than her?"

273

"Yes, he's shaking her ... he's lifting her off her feet."

She moved in her chair, sketching the motions of the fight, her eyes closed tightly.

"Can you see his face?"

"No, not clearly."

"Why not?"

"He's got a handkerchief tied round his head like a bandage."

"Thank you, Miss Langley," Ford said.

"A jury will never accept the ranting of a delusional witness," Poole broke in, fingering, for the first time, the wound on his forehead beneath his shining hair. "She'll never stand up to cross-examination."

"A jury will hear expert testimony from my colleague Dr. Waggoner, who is widely regarded as one of England's foremost criminologists. He has judged Miss Langley to be of sound mind. I will not hesitate to place her on the witness stand to describe the murderer, and the handkerchief he wore."

"Without the physical handkerchief you have nothing."

"The steering wheel of the Bentley motorcar was wiped clean of fingerprints, Mr. Poole, as we have already discussed. The Bristol police, however, have found traces of type AB blood upon it. The jury will have to decide if the murderer used the handkerchief to wipe the wheel, and how traces of your unusual blood type were found upon it."

"A jury will ..." Poole began.

"A jury will consider the cumulative body of evidence," Brownlee rumbled, and Ford, suddenly exhausted, sat down abruptly. "The convoluted scheme to defraud his lordship, which our expert witnesses at the Bank of England will prove beyond doubt; the fact that the fraudulent accounts you sent his lordship were typed at your home; the testimony of the bank's staff at your fury when you discovered that his lordship had stolen the money back; your impossible knowledge of the oil-fired engine in his lordship's launch; the steering wheel of his Bentley motorcar; witnesses who can identify you at the scene of the crime and as you made your escape. The jury will consider all the evidence and decide if there can be any reasonable doubt that you murdered Lord Pengriffon."

Poole said nothing, and Ford thought his elegantly tailored shoulders had slumped a little under Brownlee's summation.

Eighteen

"That's it?" Josephine Langley asked into a sudden silence. "It's over? George and I are innocent? This man did it?"

Ford's leg had stopped hurting, and he stood once more. The case had ended, he thought, not with a bang but with a whimper, as Victoria's poet had written. He wished he could feel triumph, but all he could feel was a sort of helpless exhaustion and an urgent desire to run away with Victoria to some warm, distant place, and never return.

"I believe so," he said. "Crocker, please take Mr. Poole into custody and escort him to the police station. Perhaps Mr. Boxer's driver will assist you."

"I promise you you'll regret this day," Poole said. "When I'm acquitted, I'll ruin you, Ford."

"Good!" Lady Canderblank growled from her chair.

"This case will be tried in a court, Ford, and not in your imagination," Poole continued as if she had not spoken. "You still don't seem to grasp that you have no incontrovertible evidence against me. You simply *cannot* place me at the murder scene. Blood types, imaginary handkerchiefs, far-fetched coincidences, unreliable witnesses ..."

The door swung open with a crash, and young Frank burst through it, red-faced and waving a large photograph.

"We got a face!" he said, his voice cracking with excitement. "Sergeant Morgan and I got a face! We kept trying and trying, and it worked! I didn't think we could do it, but Sergeant Morgan is amazing! The Leica is amazing! Then they drove me across London in a police car with the bell clanging, and I caught the train by a whisker! Then

275

they drove me here in another police car! A face in the Bentley! In the shadow! The night his lordship was murdered! The face of a man! Look, look!"

He seemed to realize that he had burst into a meeting of important-looking people without ceremony and stopped abruptly. "I'm sorry, I didn't mean to interrupt," he finished, his voice trailing away.

"The face of what man, Frank?" Ford asked.

"The face of, I didn't recognize him, the face of ..." He looked round the gathering uncertainly, until his eyes reached Poole.

"That man," Frank said.

"And thus I can place you at the murder scene, Mr. Poole," Ford said. "The evidence is, to use your term, incontrovertible."

* * *

"Are we finally dismissed?" Lady Canderblank asked with heavy sarcasm when an ashen-faced Poole had been led away. "May we finally leave?"

"I fear not, Lady Canderblank," Brownlee rumbled, in a voice that brooked no argument. "This case has other consequences beyond Mr. Poole's arrest. First we must speak to Miss Langley and Mr. Thompson in private, and then we must speak to you and Sir David. Dr. Anderson, I thank you for your time and invaluable assistance, and we will detain you no longer. Perhaps, Mrs. Ford, my dear, you'd be kind enough to help Lady Justicia to her motorcar? This must all have been very trying for her."

Ford noted that he hadn't thanked Boxer; perhaps, like Ford, he wasn't quite sure the chief constable was really there.

"This is unconscionable," Lady Canderblank bellowed, but the rest of the assembly were already in motion and ignored her.

Brownlee and Thompson descended the stairs, and Ford, following them with Josephine Langley, wondered whether the staircase could withstand Brownlee's and Thompson's combined weight. He signaled to Croft to remain with Lady Canderblank and Sir David, for fear she had failed to grasp Brownlee's meaning.

*   *   *

Charlie's office was empty, and Brownlee shepherded Thompson and Josephine Langley into it.

"I will be brief," Brownlee said when Ford had followed them and closed the door. Brownlee must have sensed Ford's exhaustion and decided to take the lead.

"We have decided not to pursue the exact intentions that caused you, Miss Langley, to row yourself out to the *Justicia* that night, nor whether you, Mr. Thompson, had any influence over those intentions. However, I must warn you that we will keep the case open, and that we may renew our investigation at some time in the future. Do I make myself clear?"

"Yes," Miss Langley whispered, and Ford made a mental note to ask Dr. Waggoner to keep her under his wing.

"No," Thomson said. "You've arrested the murderer. What more is there?"

"Conspiracy before the fact," Brownlee said. "You had ample motives; you were at the scene; you ..."

"I was never at the ..."

"We have witnesses attesting to your presence on the dock and your motorcar driving away after the murder," Brownlee cut him off. "A jury might believe you persuaded Miss Langley to go out to the *Justicia*. When she returned to say that she had seen a stranger commit the murder, you waited to see what happened. You saw the *Justicia* depart for the Little Dogs and return later. You saw Poole row back to the dock and drive off in his lordship's Bentley. You followed him up the High Street where Mr. Crutchfield saw you. I'm sure that Miss Langley will tell the whole truth if called upon to do so in court."

"Yes," she whispered.

"You can't arrest me for a murder someone else committed!"

"I have not done so."

"The whole idea's absurd! Are you seriously suggesting that I wanted him dead, but the other chap got there first? Why would I choose that night of all nights?"

"You knew his lordship was going to announce his decision to close the mine this week, as Lady Justicia will attest. Like Mr. Poole, you were running out of time."

Thompson stood panting, momentarily at a loss for words, as red in the face as Josephine Langley was white.

"However," Brownlee continued in a softer tone, "Miss Langley has suffered a great deal of distress already, and I see no need for her to endure further anguish by having to give testimony in court. Therefore, we'll simply leave further action pending."

"When there's a Labor government ..." Thompson began.

"Personally I will welcome it," Brownlee said, much to Ford's and Thompson's surprise. "However, I would never welcome a government that attempted to influence an open case at Scotland Yard. Would you?"

"Are you insinuating ..." Thompson started again, but this time it was Josephine Langley who cut him off.

"Shut up, George, and be grateful for small mercies," she said. "Let it go before the superintendent changes his mind."

She thanked Brownlee and turned to Ford.

"Mrs. Ford has been very kind to me," she said. "I've been a fool, and she's saved me. Please thank her for me."

She took Thompson by the arm and led him through the door.

"You'll never get elected to parliament if you've been arrested," she whispered as they left, and Ford thought that they did, perhaps, have a future together.

"Splendid!" Brownlee boomed, and bounded up the stairs like a young buffalo. Ford limped in his wake.

"Ah, Lady Canderblank, Sir David!" Brownlee roared, reentering the room upstairs. "Thank you for waiting. There is one other matter we need to discuss."

"Some fresh foolishness of Fog's?" Lady Canderblank asked. "He's already ruined the reputation of Sir David's firm, and ..."

"That's the precise topic I wished to discuss," Brownlee said. "The Bank of England's investigation of the Pengriffon trust—they're very thorough, I must say—revealed a lien against the trust, in the amount of one hundred thousand pounds. It seems that the trust's assets were pledged as collateral against a line of credit to a third party."

Sir David, his face more like parchment than ever, emitted a groan, but Brownlee continued without a pause.

"This transaction, although approved by Sir David's signature, was contrary to the deeds and covenants of the trust. Ten thousand has already been drawn down. If the loan is repaid immediately, and I must stress the word *immediately*, we will not be forced to turn the matter over to our Fraud Department."

Sir David sagged in his chair. "You'll have to repay the money to Coutts, Deborah," he whispered. "I'll have to cancel the guarantee."

"I shall do no such thing," she spluttered.

Ford knew that this was another matter for which she would never forgive him.

"I fear you must, Lady Canderblank," he said. "We cannot permit the guarantee to stand."

"This is none of your business, Fudge," she snapped. "I refuse to discuss the matter further in your presence."

"Then you leave us little choice, Lady Canderblank," Brownlee said, shaking his head. "We will leave the matter open for three days, until Wednesday. If the loan has not been repaid by then, and the guarantee canceled, we'll have to take official action." He turned for the door. "We'll leave you to work out the details. Good day to you."

"How am I supposed to maintain my station in life without money?" she wailed as Ford followed Brownlee through the door.

* * *

The police party gathered in the bar for celebratory scrumpy before dinner. Ford found himself holding court as the news of Poole's arrest spread like wildfire, and more and more of Trethgarret's population assembled.

"So that's it, in a nutshell," Ford concluded. "This chap Poole was stealing from his lordship, and his lordship stole the money back. Poole killed him to silence him, and Amy Robsart was killed because she saw him do it. He tried to hide the bodies so that he could start embezzling again."

Charlie announced that Lady Pengriffon had telephoned him to say that she would pay for all drinks consumed that evening, and the crowd began to do its utmost to be worthy of the offer, and Ford was glad to sink into the background.

The Ancient Mariner and Croft were in deep conversation about the appetites of Cornish fish. Mrs. Croft was dictating recipes to the local housewives. George Thompson, apparently unabashed by his recent brush with the law, was disputing the economics of tin mining with Joseph Crutchfield. Brownlee stood benignly at the bar enjoying Lady Pengriffon's largesse. Ford noticed Waggoner talking quietly with Josephine Langley, and he took some hope for her future. Young Frank, balancing precariously on a barstool, was attempting to capture the scene. Ford had no doubt he would be successful.

There was one thing left to do. Young Frank had carried a note from Sir Rupert Effingham on his journey back to Trethgarret. Ford sought out Mabel and Clara amongst the crowd.

"I have some information you ladies might find interesting," he told them. "According to Admiralty records, a U-boat was damaged by gunfire off the Lizard in 1918."

"You mean ...?" Clara gasped, her eyes like saucers.

"It was last seen drifting helplessly toward the Little Dogs."

"There are so *too* German sailors!" she crowed in triumph. "I *knew* it!"

"Rubbish, Clara," Mabel countered. "Just because ..."

Mrs. Charlie intervened to say that dinner was ready, and the police party retired upstairs. She had transformed the room into an elegant private dining room. Mrs. Croft, it transpired, had been cooking a gala dinner all afternoon, and they now sat at the table consuming the fruits of her labors.

"This pheasant is *outstanding*, Mrs. Croft," Brownlee boomed, and Croft almost choked.

"So, Thomas, how did you know, for certain?" Victoria asked.

"I think it was the burial at sea," Brownlee answered for him. "Most killers leave the body to be discovered, but this murderer didn't want the murders revealed. He wanted Pengriffon vanished, rather than dead, so that he could continue to embezzle the trust."

"I think it was *cui bono*," Croft offered. "Poole was the one that stood to gain the most. Am I right, sir?"

"Well, yes and no," Ford smiled. "Lord Pengriffon also told us himself, in a manner of speaking."

"What do you mean, darling?" Victoria asked. "Dead men can't speak."

"Indeed they can, V, if one will but pay attention. As soon as his lordship's body had been found, we went to visit Lady Justicia. This painting was hanging in her sitting room, and I was so interested in it that she gave it to us as a wedding gift."

"Yes, and so? That's a painting of the *Justicia*—that's not evidence."

"It appears to be a painting of the *Justicia*, it's true, but his lordship gave the launch a different name. Rather than using the correct name, the *Justicia IV Poole*, he chose to paint *Justice IV Poole*—'justice for Poole.' In his lordship's whimsical manner, it was. We even have that photograph which shows his lordship painting his pun into the picture."

Crocker rose to examine the painting, and he shook his head. "I said to the missus, I said, you be a deep one, begging your pardon, sir."

"That was the vital clue, darling?" Victoria asked. "A painted ship?"

Ford returned her grin. "Upon a painted ocean."

"Got it," Crocker said.

Made in the USA
Lexington, KY
17 March 2012